Praise for the Dales

'Great fun!' – CAROL DRINKWATER

'Chapman delivers on every level in this intriguing murder mystery' – *Lancashire Evening Post*

'A delightful Dales tale to warm the cockles!' – *Peterborough Telegraph*

'A rollicking read' – *Craven Herald*

'For above all else, there is warmth and heart to her novels' – *Yorkshire Times*

'Bags of Yorkshire charm and wit' – *Northern Echo*

'A delightful read' – *Dalesman*

'A classic whodunit set in the spectacular landscape of the Yorkshire Dales, written with affection for the area and its people' – CATH STAINCLIFFE

'Charming . . . full of dry wit and clever plotting . . . will delight and entertain the reader' – *Countryside*

'Nicely told and rather charming, so it should give traditionalists hours of innocent delight' – *Literary Review*

'An engaging twist on the lonely-hearts killer motif . . . should leave readers eager for the sequel' – *Publishers Weekly*

'An engaging cast of characters and a cleverly clued puzzle move Chapman's debut to the top of the English village murder list' – *Kirkus*

Date with Justice

Julia Chapman is the pseudonym of Julia Stagg, who has had five novels, the Fogas Chronicles set in the French Pyrenees, published by Hodder. *Date with Justice* is the ninth in the Dales Detective series, following on from *Date with Evil*.

Also by Julia Chapman

Date with Death
Date with Malice
Date with Mystery
Date with Poison
Date with Danger
Date with Deceit
Date with Betrayal
Date with Evil
Date with Justice

Julia Chapman

DATE WITH JUSTICE

PAN BOOKS

First published 2024 by Pan Books
an imprint of Pan Macmillan
The Smithson, 6 Briset Street, London EC1M 5NR
EU representative: Macmillan Publishers Ireland Ltd, 1st Floor,
The Liffey Trust Centre, 117–126 Sheriff Street Upper,
Dublin 1, D01 YC43
Associated companies throughout the world
www.panmacmillan.com

ISBN 978-1-5290-9543-2

1 3 5 7 9 8 6 4 2

A CIP catalogue record for this book is available from the British Library.

Map artwork by Hemesh Alles

Typeset by Palimpsest Book Production Limited, Falkirk, Stirlingshire
Printed and bound by CPI Group (UK) Ltd, Croydon, CR0 4YY

Visit **www.panmacmillan.com** to read more about all our books
and to buy them. You will also find features, author interviews and
news of any author events, and you can sign up for e-newsletters
so that you're always first to hear about our new releases.

For Dad

for the stories
for the laughter
for the love

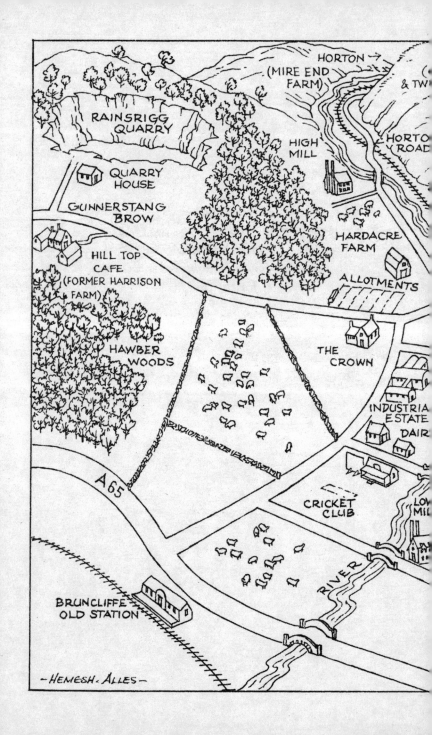

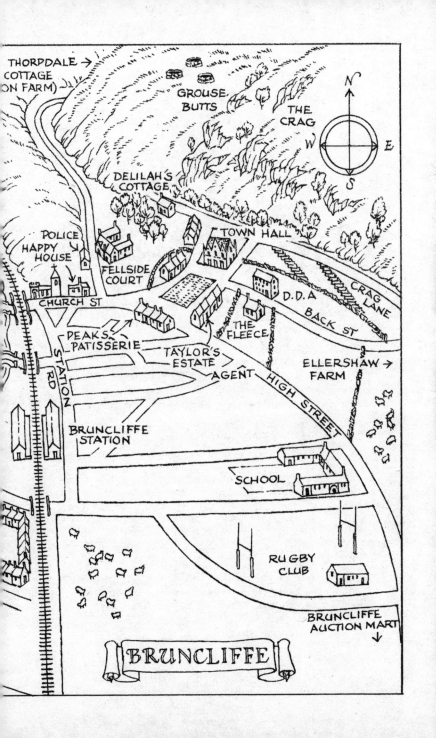

Prologue

A dead weight. This was what they meant. This solid, unaccommodating mass of body, the moving of which dragged at the arms, made the back ache and sent boots slipping on the uneven fellside, threatening to tip the living on top of the deceased.

Another couple of heaves. Closer to the vehicle now. A quick breather, head twisting, checking for witnesses. There were none. Just the bare hillside rising up beneath a darkening sky. And the bird, high overhead, majestic. A peregrine falcon, making a last couple of sorties before settling for the night.

One more effort, rolling the lifeless form into the rear, the vehicle sagging under its sudden load. A slam of metal as the boot closed, shockingly loud in the evening silence. Then the cough of an engine, the rumble of tyres on hard-packed track, and the peace returned.

Overhead, the falcon did a lazy loop, the dying sun catching its wings and turning them into a shimmering brilliance. Down below, the shadows claimed the land, creeping over it, stealing all colours, until even the vivid smear of blood on grass could no longer be seen.

1

Six Hours Earlier . . .

Samson O'Brien was running late. The kind of late that would get him killed.

Delilah checked her watch for the umpteenth time and felt a hand on her arm, solid, offering support and rebuke in equal measures.

'Don't fret it, lass. Happen as he's tied up,' Ida Capstick whispered, leaning over, the feather from her hat tickling Delilah's nose.

'He promised he'd be here.'

'Aye, well, perhaps tha should have thought on that when tha was so persuasive in telling him to bugger off back to London.' The harsh words were tempered by a final pat on her hand. 'Now get a smile on tha face. Tha's at a wedding, not a wake!'

As if at Ida's behest, there was a wheeze of organ pipes and music flooded the cavernous space, lifting the congregation to its feet in a rustle of Sunday-best clothing and a murmur of happy expectation.

A wedding. It was just what Bruncliffe needed after everything that had bedevilled the town over the last year, not least the ongoing fallout from the Rick Procter affair. The unmasking and subsequent arrest of the town's self-made property tycoon a few months earlier was still having repercussions, casting a long shadow over the Dales town as the extent – and impact – of the man's malign influence was realised. Hence the chance to rejoice at the union of two lovely townsfolk had been much welcomed, bringing smiles to the faces of the waiting guests.

Apart from Delilah Metcalfe. She was in no mood for celebrating.

She stood alongside Ida and was twisting to see the bride begin her walk up the aisle when a vibration on her wrist sent a twinge of pain up her left arm. With her bones healed and blistered hands recovered following the fire at Hill Top Cafe, this occasional discomfort was the only physical reminder Delilah carried from those dreadful events back in June. That and yet another new smartwatch.

She glanced at it, the cause of the vibration a notification from her running app. A tracking notification, alerting her that the sender had started an activity . . .

Delilah stared at the blinking dot progressing slowly across a map. Samson wasn't tied up as Ida had suggested. He'd gone for a run – not here in Bruncliffe where he should be, but over two hundred miles away. And the worst of it was, Ida was right. Delilah really only had herself to blame. In giving Samson the freedom to choose how their relationship developed, she'd made a rod for her own lonely back.

That didn't stop her from getting upset about it, however. There'd been so much he'd missed of late because of work. He'd had to skip the Bruncliffe Show and Fell Race a couple of weeks ago, evading the dubious pleasures of judging sheep and busting a gut running up the steep hills out of town. He'd also been a no-show for Delilah's thirtieth birthday, the activities of the criminal gang he'd had under surveillance showing no respect for such personal milestones. All of that, she'd understood. Not been overjoyed by, but had understood. But this time he'd *promised* her he'd be back, no matter what.

Stifling the howl of frustration threatening to explode up into the rafters of the packed church, she forced her furious lips into a smile. But as the bride glided by, radiant and happy, Delilah was planning how and when she was going to kill Samson O'Brien.

Detective Constable Samson O'Brien was running all right. Down a deserted side street, feet slapping tarmac, breath coming in short gasps. Behind him, more feet, all hitting the ground heavily. Big men. If they caught him, he was a goner.

A sting, gone wrong. His cover blown at the last minute, crucial moments before the police raid which would have liberated him. Now he had four angry drug dealers on his tail in the backstreets of East London.

He dived to his left, down a narrow alleyway between two rows of terraced houses, leaping over a couple of up-ended wheelie bins, rotting rubbish strewn across the path.

'This way!' A holler from behind him, he didn't dare look back. Just kept his eyes focused on the strip of daylight between two walls where the end of the alleyway beckoned.

Had the signal reached its target? If not, he would meet his end in this dingy ginnel. A long way from the fells of

Bruncliffe. From the sheep and the stone walls he'd grown to call home all over again. From Delilah—

A stumble, his right foot catching on a brick, sending him sprawling, arms out as he hit the ground. Shouts from the rear, encouraged by his mistake, knowing he was easy prey now. He sprang back up, running, cursing his lapse in concentration. It was what had got him in this position in the first place.

'I'm gonna do for you!' A hand, grabbing his shoulder in a meaty grasp, spinning him round.

He ducked, unzipping his jacket as he spun, shrugging it off. The speed of it surprising his pursuer, leaving him with a handful of clothing as Samson ran on. Three more strides, the exit to the alleyway ahead. This was his last chance. If they weren't there . . .

He burst out of the alley, onto a narrow bit of pavement and straight across the road into the path of an oncoming car. He heard a squeal of brakes and had a quick glimpse of blonde hair behind the wheel before he was flipped over the bonnet, landing on the far side as more cars pulled up, sirens wailing. The slam of car doors, lots of boots on the ground.

'Police! Stop!'

The sounds of pursuit, the shouts of capture. His pursuers had been detained.

Samson O'Brien lay there, breathing hard, staring up past the roofs to the watery sun above and wondering just how many of his nine lives he had left.

'Well, that was a monumental screw up, O'Brien!' Blonde hair spilling down from her ponytail, Jess Green was standing over him. 'What the hell happened?'

No concern for his well-being. No worries that he might be dying after being hit by a car. Which she'd been driving.

He sat up, wincing, pain in his left ribs, his hip and down his leg.

'Sorry, Sarge. Things just went a bit astray.'

She held out a hand, hauling him to his feet, frowning. 'That's one way of putting it. Distracted is how I'd describe it.'

Newly promoted DS Jess Green, now his boss, over-seeing an undercover operation for the National Crime Agency to break up a drugs racket estimated to be bringing in up to three million pounds a month. Drugs which were sent out from the capital across county lines and into the far reaches of the country. To places like Bruncliffe.

And Samson had nearly made a mess of all the team's hard work, because, as DS Green had called it, he'd been distracted. His mind on the wedding he was missing thanks to this unexpected change in plan. His attention on Delilah when it should have been on the deadly men he was dealing with. A slip of the tongue and months of surveillance had been blown. He'd nearly cost the entire operation. Nearly cost his own life.

'I think,' DS Green continued, her voice softening, 'you need a break. Take a few days. A week even. Go home and think things over.'

He found himself nodding. Already thinking of those green hills. The spectacular beauty of the Yorkshire Dales. And the woman he loved.

'Yes, Sarge,' he muttered.

She turned to go, then paused. 'Oh, and Samson, tell Delilah that watch saved your life!'

He grinned, looking down at the Garmin on his wrist, the screen showing an activity in progress. Bought by Delilah so she could track his training in the lead-up to the Bruncliffe Fell Race, he'd reconfigured it so DS Green could follow him too. A quick press of a button as he ran for his life, and she'd been able to see exactly where he was.

'Will do.' He watched his boss walk towards one of the police cars and knew he wouldn't get the chance to thank Delilah. She'd kill him as soon as he walked in the door.

2

'For someone who peddles love for a living, you don't seem to be enjoying the fruits of your labour!'

Perched on a stool with her back resting against the rugby club bar, Delilah was wishing she was somewhere else as she glanced up from the pint she was nursing to see James 'Herriot' Ellison standing next to her. He was gesturing towards the wedding reception in full swing around them with a wry smile on what was a very weary-looking face.

'Crikey!' she exclaimed, momentarily pulled out of her melancholy as she took in his appearance. Even his formal attire, the dark grey suit a far cry from his normal vet's uniform of checked shirt and corduroy trousers tucked into muck-covered boots, couldn't mask the fact that he was shattered. 'You look as forlorn as I do, but on less sleep!'

Herriot managed a grin. 'Thanks, I think. But seriously, I'd have thought you'd have been crowing today, seeing as you should get all the credit for putting those two together.' He nodded towards the bride and groom, Harry Furness and Sarah Mitchell, dancing in the centre of the crowded dance floor, Sarah laughing as Harry clowned around. Herriot was right. The newlyweds had met thanks to

9

Delilah's Dales Dating Agency. She should have been basking in the glory of her romantic achievements. It felt a bit rich to be boasting of her prowess, however, when her own love life was such a mess.

'I'd like to say it was all my doing, but to be honest, I think they were made for each other. Even without my intervention, they'd have found a way to be together. Besides,' she muttered, indicating the empty bar stool next to her, 'I'm hardly the best advertisement for finding love and keeping it!'

'Ah!' Herriot nodded. 'Samson. I'm guessing he's not going to make it today?'

Delilah shook her head. And Herriot sat on the empty stool.

'So what about you?' she asked, focusing on him. The bags under his eyes. The pallor to his sun-weathered skin. All of it compounded by a general air of pain. Like the man was in some kind of personal agony. 'Are you ill?'

He gave a dry laugh. 'No. Just busy. This and that . . . you know.'

She didn't. But she knew a lie when she heard one. She also knew Herriot harboured a shy soul, which didn't need heavy-handed expressions of concern. If he wanted to tell her what was ailing him, he would do so in his own good time.

She lifted her pint, took a long drink, Herriot doing the same.

'God. What on earth is this bloody awful music?' Will Metcalfe had joined them, ordering two pints of Black Sheep as he aired his opinion on the band's current number. 'If this is Bruncliffe's finest, you can keep them!'

Delilah and Herriot both cocked their heads, listening. As did a lot of the guests. Then there was a rumble of laughter, Sarah clapping delightedly as it became clear the band were singing a song about otters.

'It's some folk song from the seventies.' The explanation came from Ash Metcalfe as he flopped his long frame on the stool the other side of his sister. 'Harry knew it meant a lot to Sarah, so he had the band learn it.' He shrugged as he took his pint from his brother. 'I guess ecologists obsessed with otters offer a pretty niche musical selection for a bridegroom trying to impress.'

Delilah smiled. The dance floor was packed now, everyone clapping and singing along while Harry pretended to be an otter. True love truly was daft.

'So what is this?' Will tipped his chin at the three of them, taking in the air of dejection with a grin. 'Crestfallen corner?'

'Bugger off, Will,' muttered Ash, his eyes fixed on the crowd.

'And there was me thinking I was the churlish one in the family. Now take Gareth over there,' said Will, pointing towards a large man slumped on a stool at the far end of the bar, staring morosely into a pint, a springer spaniel curled up at his feet, 'he has every reason to be depressed. Not only has he lost his job, but he was kicked out of his accommodation this morning.'

'He lost his job?' asked Ash.

'Can't be a gamekeeper if you don't have a gun licence,' murmured Herriot. 'It was only a matter of time before he was turned out.'

'Christ, at least I've still got a home.' Having been hired to supply and fit kitchens at the latest Procter Properties development in Skipton, with the company mothballed as the subject of a major criminal investigation, Ash had lost his lucrative contract. He was back to being a self-employed carpenter, struggling to find work, just one of many casualties caused by the reverberations from the Rick Procter affair. But as he said, at least he had a roof over his head.

'Poor bugger.' Delilah looked at the gamekeeper, his face drawn, dark shadows underlining his eyes. Even his thatch of russet hair and bushy beard looked muted, rendering him devoid of his usual vigour. The guilt she carried from events three and a half months ago up at Bruncliffe Manor surfaced, making her feel even more morose. If it hadn't been for her fooling around in disguise, a man's life might not have been lost and Gareth's career might still be intact . . . 'I didn't realise he'd been evicted.'

'The new estate manager at the manor making his mark, no doubt. So, like I said,' continued Will, addressing the three of them, a wide grin on his face, 'compared to Gareth Towler, you lot have no reason for being glum. As best man, I'm officially ordering you to snap out of it. Weddings are supposed to be joyous occasions!'

He turned as he said it, facing towards the room now, towards the guests occupying the small square of floor set aside for dancing. And the grin fell from his face.

'What the hell is he doing here?' he growled.

'Who?' asked Delilah.

'That bloke with Elaine Bullock.'

Delilah searched the crowd, spotted the familiar figure of her friend, the geologist-cum-waitress. In a bright red dress with her thick, dark hair released from its usual plaits, she looked stunning. She was standing next to a tall man

Delilah didn't recognise, engaged in an animated conversation, glasses perched halfway down her nose and her Dr Martens flexed onto tiptoes, positioning her lips close to his cheek so she could make herself heard above the music.

'I don't know,' said Delilah, 'but she looks happy!'

Ash grunted. Sharp focus on the pair of them. He took a long drink from his pint.

'So who is he?' asked Delilah, attention switching to the smartly dressed man. Somewhere in his early forties she guessed, judging by the peppering of grey in his trim beard, he had the studious look of an academic and the lithe build of an athlete. Someone who took care of themselves and looked good for it, the well-cut tweed suit he was wearing carried effortlessly on him.

'A bloody pain in the arse,' grumbled Will, features clouding over.

'His name's Ross Irwin,' said Herriot. 'He's another ecologist. He's got a business over Kendal way but knows Sarah from university, so I heard. Seems like a nice chap the few times I've met him. What's your beef with him, Will?'

'He doesn't know when to mind his own business.' Will had kept his gaze fixed on the man. A gaze so fierce Delilah was surprised flames weren't shooting out the back of the poor bloke's jacket.

'You can say that again,' muttered Ash. 'Looks like a right prat in that bloody get-up, too.'

While Delilah wouldn't have phrased it the same, she had to agree the outfit with its wide navy checks and tan detailing was a bit loud by Bruncliffe standards. But even so, she glanced at Ash in surprise. The youngest of her five older brothers, he'd inherited the amicable nature that came from the Metcalfe side of the family. To hear him being as tetchy as the much more volatile Will was unexpected, even given his current predicament.

She looked back at the man in question. Ross Irwin. His left hand had slipped around Elaine's shoulder, bringing her closer as they tried to converse.

Ash took another long drink, eyes not leaving the two of them. 'That bloke looks like bad news.'

'That's exactly what he is,' murmured Will.

Finally aware of their scrutiny, Irwin glanced over, murmured something to Elaine and began walking towards them, leaving her on the dance floor.

'Herriot, Will,' he said as he approached. 'Good to see you both again. And this must be the delightful Delilah I've heard so much about.'

He extended a hand towards her, his smile warm. Genuine. Delilah grinned.

'Don't know who you've been talking to but I wouldn't say I'm known as that around here. Happy to accept the compliment, though.'

He laughed, a warm, mellow sound. 'Ross Irwin. Lovely to meet you.'

'And this is Ash.' Delilah nodded towards her brother, who was standing now, stretching to his full height, which brought him a head above Irwin. He held out a hand, chin tipped up as he inspected the newcomer. Like a stag displaying its antlers.

'Pleasure,' muttered Ash, gripping the man's hand. Hard.

'Likewise.' Irwin nodded, extricated his hand and turned to Will. 'Any chance we could have a quick word? Somewhere a bit quieter?' He gestured towards the door at the side of the bar and the hallway beyond.

Will looked as though he was about to refuse. Then he slowly placed his pint on the counter and followed Irwin out of the room.

'What's that all about?' Delilah asked.

Ash shook his head, eyes on the two men heading for the corridor. 'Buggered if I know. But judging by the set of Will's shoulders, I'd keep my distance if I was that Irwin fella.'

He had a point. While Will might not be as tall as the ecologist, he more than made up for it in strength, his stocky build backed up by muscle and a hair-trigger temper. Right now he was giving out warning signs most Bruncliffe locals would have recognised. But Irwin wasn't local.

'It's probably something to do with the survey Irwin is doing on the Dinsdale farm,' suggested Herriot, indicating the man talking to Harry Furness, a thinning thatch of blond hair crowning a ruddy face as he held an animated conversation with the livestock auctioneer. Kevin Dinsdale might as well have had 'farmer' tattooed across his forehead.

Ash nodded in comprehension. 'So it's Irwin who's doing the ecological checks for Dinsdale's camping pod idea.'

'That's going ahead then?' asked Delilah. 'Will didn't mention it.'

'Reckon he's still holding out hope that the planning permission won't come through. The ecological survey is probably his last chance of it being turned down.'

'Crikey. No wonder he's grumpy.' Delilah looked out into the hallway at her oldest brother. Having taken on the Metcalfe family farm on the fellside above Bruncliffe, he seemed to have aged exponentially in recent months. And now Kevin Dinsdale had applied to build ten camping pods in a picturesque setting by a beck. Not something Will would normally object to, being realistic when it came to the difficulties of making a living out of sheep farming in the modern world. Diversification was all in the name of the game.

Only trouble was, Dinsdale's proposed diversification was right on the border of Ellershaw Farm, where Will's land butted up against the Dinsdale property. Land historically used to hold ewes in lambing time. Will's concern, and one Delilah shared, was that an increase in the number of tourists would lead to an increase in the number of dogs. And that some of those dogs might not be kept under the best of control when situated in a field next to cavorting lambs.

Sheep worrying was a perennial problem in the Dales, particularly around lambing time. Having the possibility of it becoming an even greater concern wasn't something any farmer would vote for.

Delilah turned her gaze to Kevin Dinsdale, his wife having joined him, chatting away to Sarah and Harry. It was a difficult situation. For generations, Dinsdales and Metcalfes had farmed those hills as neighbours without any discord. And Delilah knew you couldn't get nicer folk than Kevin and Louise, their little girl, Ava, a firm friend of Will's youngest, Izzy. She also knew from the Bruncliffe grapevine that things were hard for them at present. A couple of poor seasons and suddenly they were having to find new income streams, Kevin even turning his hand to wood carving, selling his creations at the local craft market.

It was hard to blame them for wanting to make the most of the stunning setting they lived in.

'I'm sure they'll sort it out one way or another,' said Herriot sanguinely.

'Sort what out?' Lucy Metcalfe, Delilah's widowed sister-in-law who shared the vet's natural inclination to see the good in people, had joined them, Elaine Bullock by her side.

'The possible teething problems over the Dinsdale camping pods,' said Herriot, sitting more upright on his stool, animation coming to his tired face.

Lucy let out a laugh. Looking at the three of them in disbelief. 'Honestly, that's what you're talking about when there's a wedding to celebrate? You farmers and vets – you're all the same. Why talk about love when you could be talking about sheep!'

Elaine let out a belch of laughter, Delilah and Ash grinning. But Herriot . . . he was looking shamefaced.

'You okay?' Delilah leaned over to ask.

Herriot flushed. Nodded. 'Just contemplating getting a round in. Another pint?'

'If you're buying.' She grinned at him.

'Lucy, Elaine, Ash?' he asked, as he gestured the barman over.

'Sparkling water, please, Herriot.' Lucy dangled a set of car keys off her fingers. 'I offered to do chauffeur duty for Will this evening so Alison and the kids can go home early.'

'I'm fine,' said Elaine. 'Ross is getting mine.'

Ash grunted, expression grim for someone being bought a drink. 'Whisky please. A double.'

'Crikey, you're hitting the hard stuff early,' teased Elaine.

'Aye, well not all of us are loved-up,' came the muttered reply.

'Or going on dates.' Lucy gave Elaine a sideways glance.

'You're going on a date?' Delilah asked.

'It's not a bloody date! Honestly. This place.' Elaine shook her head, sending the large silver hoops in her ears dancing, her eyes fierce behind her glasses. 'Ross has asked me to go over to Malham to see the peregrine falcons with him tomorrow. He's interested in the geology of the area and wants me along for my expertise. Okay?'

'Sounds like a date to me,' said Ash.

'How the hell would you know what a date sounds like?' Elaine turned her focus on him, arms on her hips. 'When did you last go on one?'

'Fair point, Ash,' said Lucy, as Delilah and Herriot burst out laughing. Ash drained the last of his pint.

'So,' continued Lucy, turning to Delilah now, 'seeing as it's okay to talk about work at a wedding, any joy on identifying my thief?'

Delilah groaned and slapped her forehead. It had been a week since Lucy raised her concerns about cakes disappearing from her cafe during closing hours, asking the Dales Detective Agency to investigate, and in the intervening time it had clean slipped Delilah's mind.

Bloody Samson. Another curse to be laid at his door.

'Sorry, Lucy. I've just been snowed under. The residents of Fellside Court have tasked me with validating rumours of a new owner and discovering their identity. And we're up to our eyes with insurance claim cases. Not to mention trying to compile several background checks. Nina goes back to school the week after next, so that'll just leave Ida and me and I'm already flat out with the dating agency and putting together a website for Nancy Taylor's new estate agents—'

Lucy leaned over and hugged Delilah, cutting short her monologue which had been getting more agitated by the word. 'Don't worry about it. It's just a few cakes here and there. I know you'll get round to it when you can.'

'Someone's stealing your cakes?' asked Ash.

Elaine nodded. 'It's been going on for about a fortnight. Well, that's when we noticed it at any rate. The odd muffin here and there. A couple of scones . . . Never any of the larger gateaux. I've taken to counting the stock before we close up at night so we can keep track of it.'

'Could it be a member of staff?'

'If it is, they're not using the back door,' said Herriot. 'I mean . . . from what Lucy's said . . . it doesn't appear to be the means of entry . . .'

'Plus, by staff you mean me or Ana,' said Elaine, punching Ash on the arm. 'So take that back.'

He grinned at her. 'I can vouch for Ana being on the side of the angels. But you, you've always had a streak of the devil in you.'

Lucy shook her head. 'I'd trust both of them with my life. So I think we can dispense with that theory straight away.'

It was a theory Delilah hadn't even considered in the scant moments she'd thought about her sister-in-law's case. Ana Stoyanovic was, as Ash had said, an angel, and besides, the former manager of Fellside Court had barely worked at the cafe in the last few weeks, having secured regular hours at a large residential care home in Skipton.

And Elaine would walk through fire for Lucy. So what else could it be?

'Perhaps someone has managed to get a copy of a key somehow,' she suggested. 'Either way, I'll get you a camera set up and see if we can't catch them in the act.'

'Thanks, Delilah. You'll have my undying gratitude—'

Lucy's appreciation was drowned out by a commotion coming from the corridor beyond the bar. A loud voice, raised in anger, loud enough to be heard by most of the room. Loud enough to turn heads, to cause gasps. Because visible in the hallway were two men, one pinning the other up against a wall and looking fit for murder.

3

'Will!' exclaimed Ash, slapping his pint on the counter and running for the doorway.

Delilah followed him, Herriot on her heels, the bride and groom abandoning the dance floor and hurrying in the same direction with a large portion of the guests behind them.

'Will!' Ash shouted again as they all entered the corridor.

But Will Metcalfe was beyond hearing. Face scarlet with temper, he had a deathlike grasp on Ross Irwin's neck, the tall ecologist on tiptoes as he tried to escape the farmer's powerful hold.

'You're scum!' Will was shouting. 'Beyond scum. You don't deserve to be walking this earth. And if I ever see you near my land again—'

'Stop it, Will!' Ash was pulling at his brother's arm to no avail. 'Let him go.'

'Let him go?' Will turned, wild. 'Have you any idea what this bast—?'

'Daddy!' Little Izzy Metcalfe, blessed with the same dark features as her father, had broken free of her mother's grasp and wriggled her way through the adults' legs to stand staring at him in confusion. The fingers of her right hand were playing nervously with the ribbons on her bridesmaid's dress while her other hand, somewhat incongruously, had a fierce grip on a rounders bat.

Will released his hold. Ross Irwin coughed, straightened his tie, smoothed down his jacket and nodded at the crowd of people filling the corridor, before turning and walking away towards the rear exit. A swell of voices rose from the onlookers as he left.

'Show's over, folks!' The commanding tones of Harry Furness swept over the growing hubbub and he stepped forward with a big smile on his face to address his shocked guests, who were struggling to take it all in. Two of them caught Delilah's eye – Kevin Dinsdale watching Will with disquiet, and his wife, Louise, who was standing next to him, rigid with stress, her focus on the departing Irwin. Delilah's heart went out to them, knowing they would be feeling responsible in some way, knowing they would be hating the friction their plans were causing.

'At least now we can call it a proper wedding,' continued Harry, working the crowd with his bonhomie the way he did on auction day, 'as no wedding worth its salt passes without a contretemps of some sort!'

'Is that a posh word for a fight, Harry?' came a call from the back.

'Aye, happen it is. See how being wed can change a fella. Now get thyselves back on that bloody dance floor. I paid good money for that band and I can't abide waste!'

Laughter broke the tension as the gathering dispersed, drifting back into the main room as Harry had suggested. Sarah, Ash and Delilah stayed where they were, while Will bent down and scooped his daughter up into his arms, his wife, Alison, walking over to hug them.

'What the hell, Will?' Harry turned, the smile gone from his face and replaced with concern. He'd known Will Metcalfe all his life and while the farmer's temper was legendary, Harry knew it would have taken something extraordinary for Will to behave so disrespectfully at a friend's wedding. A wedding at which he was the best man. 'What did Irwin say to prompt that?'

Will shook his head. 'Little pitchers have big ears,' he murmured, gesturing at Izzy, who had one arm draped around his neck, her head on his chest and the rounders bat held between them. 'All I'll say is life would be a lot easier if Dinsdale had asked Sarah here to do the survey.'

'A bit more neighbourly, too,' grunted Harry. 'Keeping his business local instead of bringing in outsiders.'

Sarah laid a hand on her husband's arm. 'It's not that simple, love. A lot of people don't want a local connection when having surveys done. It can all get a bit awkward if things are uncovered that hamper progress or add to the development costs.'

'Anyway,' continued Will, kissing the top of his daughter's head, 'I'm going to take this one home – reckon we've both had enough excitement for one day, don't you think, Izzy?'

Izzy nodded. 'Weddings are boring,' she announced solemnly, making the adults laugh.

'I don't mind taking the kids back,' said Alison. 'Charlie's playing with some lads on the rugby pitch but he's ready to go, too.'

But Will was shaking his head. 'I've had my fill of partying. You stay and have a good time, love. Get Lucy or the Dinsdales to drop you back up.'

Alison tipped her head to one side as she passed her husband a set of car keys. 'As long as you're okay to drive?'

'Barely got a sip of my second pint before that bugger soured it,' muttered Will, taking the keys. He glanced down at his daughter, ruffling her hair. 'What say we get Charlie and go play a quick game before bedtime with the present Harry and Sarah bought you?'

The proposal was met with an enthusiastic nod from Izzy.

'Unique bridesmaid's gift, Harry, I'll give you that,' said Ash, grinning as he gestured at the bat in his niece's small hand. 'Not many rounders sets doled out at weddings.'

'Aye, well, I'm not one for gender stereotyping,' said Harry gruffly. 'Same for the lass as for the two pageboys.'

Sarah gave a cheeky smile. 'Nothing to do with the fact it was buy two, get one free?'

The ensuing laughter didn't faze the auctioneer.

'Whatever the reason,' said Will, 'it's grand. Izzy's right attached to it – she's not let go of it since you've given it her. Thanks.'

'Good to hear,' said Harry. 'As for your to-do with Irwin, I'll catch you tomorrow and you can fill me in on what caused it—'

'Tomorrow? I thought you were going on honeymoon?'

Will's question brought the surprised focus of the small gathering onto the groom. Harry shook his head. Cheeks flushing.

'Not just yet. Got a bit of business to sort first.'

'Don't tell me you're staying to conduct the tup sales?' Delilah stared at him, incredulous. As one of the top auctioneers in the county, Harry was always in demand when it came to prestigious sales but surely even he wouldn't put work before his new bride?

'Well, not quite . . . thing is . . .' Harry went a deeper shade of scarlet and looked at his wife in desperation.

'It was my choice to postpone the honeymoon, not Harry's,' offered Sarah, lowering her naturally quiet voice even more than usual. 'It's all a bit hush hush but I'm pitching for my first major project since I set up on my own, so I didn't want to go away right now. It's kind of make or break.'

'I'm sure you'll wow them,' said Delilah.

'I wish I had your confidence. But I'm up against Ross Irwin.'

'Isn't that a good thing? Surely it's better to be bidding against someone you know well? At least you might have an idea of how he'll pitch his tender.'

Sarah shook her head. 'I don't know Irwin at all, really. He's just a passing acquaintance. Plus he's got far more experience than I have.'

'Experience doesn't count for everything,' muttered Will at the mention of the man's name. 'You'll do grand. And now I really must get off before I have a sleeping child on my hands. Apologies for the unscheduled entertainment, Sarah. I'm sure that's not what you expected when you asked me to be best man.'

His words provoked a shy smile from the bride. 'No damage done. And besides, Harry did warn me when we chose you. He said the Metcalfes were a "rum bunch".' She gave her husband a glance full of mischief and Harry started sputtering for a second time.

'I didn't . . . I mean, Will, Ash, Delilah, I wouldn't . . .'

Will grinned. 'No offence taken.' He shook his friend's hand in farewell, and then leaned in to kiss Sarah on the cheek. 'I don't know how he persuaded you to marry him, but I know he got the better part of the bargain.'

Harry placed his arm around his bride, grinning now. 'Too right, Will. So what say the rest of you? How about we get back in and celebrate that this amazing woman agreed to be my wife!'

They all turned to go but as they did so, through the open back door Delilah spotted a flash of red running across the car park. Elaine. Hurrying after Ross Irwin. Delilah watched her catch his arm, gesturing back towards the rugby club as she spoke to him, the ecologist smiling and shaking his head. A little bit more conversation and they both walked over towards a black Toyota Land Cruiser. Ross held the passenger door open for Elaine, provoking a comment which made him laugh. Then he got behind the wheel and they drove away.

'Damn it.' The muttered curse made her turn. Ash was standing behind her, witness to it all. 'I hope she knows what she's doing.' Then he shook his head. Mournful. 'Come on, Dee,' he said, moving towards the noise of the party beyond. 'Let's get bladdered.'

Rucksack slung across his shoulders, Samson stood on the concourse at King's Cross Station as the weekend rush hour milled around him, looking at his watch and making calculations. It would be tight. He'd have to pray that his connections went smoothly. But if the gods were on his side, he'd make it to Skipton in time to catch the last train to Bruncliffe.

He pulled out his phone, the string of progressively irate messages vivid on the screen, Delilah rightly airing her annoyance at his failure to attend Harry's wedding. His failure to let her know he wasn't going to be there. He started composing a response, telling her of his imminent arrival. Then he paused. Thought about how she'd react if he failed a second time to keep a promise.

It had been so difficult living apart, the last eleven weeks being the longest of his life. Work had been flat out, which should have been enough to keep his mind focused. But in the middle of a stakeout, he'd found himself wondering what Delilah was doing. While sitting at a bar working undercover, he'd seen someone with a Weimaraner and found himself laughing about her daft hound, Tolpuddle, and his penchant for drinking beer. And all the time he was hanging out in the seedier side of London, he'd found himself yearning for Bruncliffe.

Yet this was supposed to be what he wanted. What Delilah had given him free rein to try. A chance to get his career back on track with the NCA and put himself in the thick of the action once more, chasing big-time criminals and making a difference.

Only trouble was, making a difference was taking too great a toll on his life, and his relationship with the woman he loved.

They'd tried spending the weekends together a couple of times, but it hadn't gone well. Twice Delilah had come down to London; twice he'd had to leave her in his tiny flat while he was called up for an operation at the last minute. As for the one occasion he'd ventured back to Bruncliffe, he'd been so tired, he'd ended up sleeping most of the time.

Things hadn't been made easier by the way they were with each other during those snatched days together. It was like they were strangers all over again. Awkward. Feeling the need to be on their best behaviour. Which admittedly took more effort for Delilah, he thought with a grin. It had all been so stilted. So forced. None of the natural camaraderie they'd established over the eight months they'd been working together.

Samson was getting tired of having to excuse himself from things, too – the fell race he'd trained for, the sheep judging which he'd been strangely looking forward to, Delilah's thirtieth. So far she'd been great about all of it, saying that she understood. But when he'd seen photos from her birthday party at the rugby club, Delilah being feted by friends and family, he'd found himself thinking that while she might be okay with him not being there, he was feeling left out. As though the best part of life was passing him by.

DS Green had been right. He needed time to re-evaluate. A week to decide whether this existence lived across two worlds was worth continuing with. Or whether he needed to make a final choice, opting for a future with Delilah in Bruncliffe, or one without her, working for the NCA.

The departures board overhead flickered, announcing his train was ready, and Samson began weaving through the Saturday evening crowds, people making way for him when they saw the large bruise blooming on his left cheek from where it had made contact with the road, a constellation of cuts and grazes completing the look. Just as well they couldn't see the mess down his left side, from ribs to knee, the skin already turning numerous shades of purple. Ignoring the wary glances, he walked towards the platform deep in thought, wondering if the next time he was on this concourse, he'd be back in London for good.

4

'I think my aunt is drunk.' Nathan Metcalfe grinned, pointing his phone to video the figure standing barefoot on top of one of the tables, headbanging to 'Mr Brightside'. On the floor below, his Uncle Ash was playing air guitar, looking every bit as inebriated. While Herriot watched on from the sidelines, nodding with drunken approval.

The wedding of Harry Furness and Sarah Mitchell was turning out to be entertaining in so many ways. As a fifteen-year-old lad, Nathan had not been right keen about attending, sitting in church and then enduring adults partying wasn't how he would choose to spend a sunny Saturday in late August. Not when there was farming to be done, or his lurchers to take out. Not to mention the sheepdog pup he was training.

But the news that Nina Hussain was also going to the wedding had seen him donning what passed for formal attire – he'd outgrown his suit and so his mother had had to settle for dark jeans, an ironed shirt and a tie – with eagerness. The fact Nina was sitting here with him now, at a table in the corner of the rugby club watching his family make idiots of themselves, made the day more bearable.

Nina smiled. 'And adults are always warning us teens

about the perils of drink. Delilah's going to regret this in the morning.'

'It's a Sunday. She can just sleep it off.'

Nina shook her head. 'Not tomorrow. Ida's got us in to do what she's calling a deep clean. She reckons it's the only day of the week when we can get it done without someone walking in the door wanting us to take on a case.'

Nathan's grin grew wider. 'Ha! I can't miss that! What time do you start?'

'Nine on the dot. Or beware the wrath of Ida—'

'I heard that, young lady!' Ida Capstick, cleaner, secretary and investigator at the Dales Detective Agency, sat down opposite them, almost unrecognisable in a peacock-blue dress, bolero jacket and a jaunty hat adorned with a huge feather. She had a small glass of port in her hand. 'Happen as cleanliness is a fundamental part of efficient businesses and goodness knows the Dales Detective Agency could do with a bit of efficiency. We've been so busy chasing our tails this past month, everything's been let slide. This'll give us a chance to catch up.'

'Reckon Delilah might not be in the mood for catching anything if she keeps on drinking,' said Nathan, nodding towards his aunt, who had just performed a spectacular leap off the table as the song came to a conclusion, triggering applause and lots of laughter.

Ida tipped her head in acknowledgement, her granite features softening momentarily as she watched Delilah bowing to her audience. 'That lass needs to let off steam. Better like this than like her brother.'

'You mean Will?' Nina asked. 'Do you know why he went for that Mr Irwin?'

'No. But I've got ears. Seems it's something to do with the planning permission out on the Dinsdale farm.'

Nathan nodded. As he lived with his mother in a converted barn just above the Metcalfe farm, he spent a lot of time at Ellershaw helping out and had witnessed at close quarters the darkening mood of his oldest uncle in the previous few weeks. But Will wasn't one for sharing, and beyond sensing it was connected to the proposed camping-pod development, Nathan couldn't offer anything else. Apart from a stark opinion.

'That ecologist does seem like an arse, though.'

Ida's lips pursed, whether in disapproval or holding back a smile, it was hard to tell. 'Never an excuse for violence, lad.'

'And to be fair,' said Nina, 'he ate at our restaurant last night and was super nice. Left a tip and everything – unlike the Dinsdales who were on the next table.' She rolled her eyes in disgust. 'Honestly, folk who don't tip should be forced to waitress on a Friday night and see how hard it is. But that Mr Irwin, he was lovely. He was asking me how my GCSEs went and what I'm going to do next year. Treated me like an adult.'

The smile Nina gave was tinged with something wistful. Enough to send a sting of emotion through Nathan, too complex for him to try to identify. Instead he just lowered his gaze, looking at the glass of coke in front of him and suddenly wishing he was anywhere but here.

'Talking of adults,' said Ida, tapping Nathan's arm, 'there's no need for thee to stay cooped up in here watching them make fools of themselves. Get thyself outside while there's still light in the day and warmth in the sun. And take this one with thee.' She gestured at Nina. 'Tha could do with a bit of help with that project for school.'

Nina looked at Nathan. 'What project?'

'About the Hoffmann kiln. I've got to write a report on it for history.'

The vast lime kiln situated on the fellside above Bruncliffe had seemed like a good candidate to Nathan back in June when asked to choose a monument of historical importance for his summer holiday homework. Basically a huge oval doughnut made of stone and the length of a rugby pitch, the derelict site had been a favourite of his since his dad had taken him up there as a toddler. He'd been first scared and then entranced by the curving network of dark, inter-locking chambers, and it became somewhere he sought solace when his dad was away on duty with the army. He'd walk up there and scramble up the stone side to sit on the grassed-over roof, alone with his thoughts. And his worries. Worries which turned out to be well founded three years ago when his dad never made it back from Afghanistan.

Now though, it seemed like a stupid choice of topic. Unless . . .

'Don't suppose you fancy a walk up there, Nina?' He said it casually, as casually as he could, but his fingers were touching his dad's old Yorkshire Regiment tobacco tin which he carried around in his pocket for luck, and the fizz in his guts had him feeling far from laid-back.

'What, and miss all the fun?' Nina was looking towards the dance floor, where Harry Furness was now wheeling out a karaoke machine to large groans, while defiantly declaring that *his* wedding meant *his* rules. The strains of 'Dancing Queen' began and as Harry started crooning,

Nina stood up, grinning. 'Even a history project has got to be better than this. Come on! Let's escape while we can.'

Nathan was on his feet in an instant. Not so quick that he missed the wink Ida Capstick gave him as he followed Nina out of the rugby club and into the soft evening sunshine.

'You okay to drop by mine so I can change out of this? It's not exactly suitable for hiking up to the kiln.' Nina tugged at the maroon dress that came to just above her knees, her slender legs emerging from beneath to drop into platformed sandals.

Nathan snapped his eyes back up, away from the danger. 'Yeah,' he coughed, 'sure.' Even though he thought she looked stunning. But then, he thought she looked stunning in jeans and a T-shirt.

Stowing that notion in the space he kept in his head for things he didn't want to think about, he fell into step beside her, crossing the rugby club car park and heading towards the town in the distance. Behind them came the faint strains of the bridegroom singing his heart out, making Nina giggle. And Nathan felt the awkwardness dissolve.

This was Nina. His mate. And yes, he knew she was out of his league, sixteen to his fifteen and a full year above him in school. But here she was, one of the most popular girls in the town, whip-smart and gorgeous, walking along beside him on a sunny day.

Life didn't get much better.

The wedding was getting raucous. Too raucous for Ida's tastes.

She'd stayed sitting at the table vacated by the teenagers long enough to finish her port – which took rather less time than normal, her drinking pace urged on by her desire to be away from the racket coming from the karaoke machine – and then she stood to go. As she did, she looked around for Delilah.

Not that the youngest Metcalfe wasn't capable of taking care of herself, but Ida knew how much pressure she'd been under of late. Running three businesses on her own all while pining for a man she'd sent packing. You had to hand it to the lass, she'd managed well these past eleven weeks, keeping her emotions in check while going through torment. And now today, for whatever reason, Samson had failed to come home when he'd promised. It was enough to tip Delilah over the edge, without the added ingredient of a wedding reception and all the alcohol that went with it.

So there was no harm in checking up on her before heading home.

Scanning the melee on the dance floor, Ida spotted the rangy figure of Ash, still dancing, Herriot now slumped on a chair, head on the table in front of him, while on the makeshift stage, Harry was serenading his guests with an off-key version of 'Angels' that was positively diabolical. But no Delilah. Ida let her gaze pass over the gathering and across the many familiar, smiling faces, the only discordant note being Kevin Dinsdale, just coming in from outside with a troubled look, no doubt reflecting on the fracas between Will and the ecologist earlier. Still no sign of Delilah, though. Where was she? And then Ida saw her. At the bar, leaning against the large frame of Gareth Towler, talking to him earnestly, as earnestly as a person who'd been downing shots of whisky for the last hour or so could.

Gareth, for his part, looked remarkably sober, especially considering rumour had it he'd lost his job and his home that very morning. The gamekeeper had an arm under Delilah's, holding her upright, and was enduring her chatter with a good-humoured smile.

Ida gave a satisfied nod. The lass was in safe hands. Not that she needed to worry, as pretty much everyone gathered in the rugby club could be considered safe hands. This was Bruncliffe after all.

Picking up her gloves and removing her hat – the ride home she had organised not exactly one that would respect her fancy attire – she made her way towards the exit, surprised to find the air still warm despite the sun having set. She was similarly surprised to see Sarah Mitchell getting out of a car and hurrying towards the club. No longer in her bridal gown, she was wearing a dress the colour of early heather, its fitted bodice and full skirt embellished with delicate lace embroidery. With her natural tan acquired from years of outdoor work, she looked wonderful.

But despite this, she was frowning as she approached, focus on the ground, thoughts miles away.

'Tha looks as pretty as a picture,' said Ida in pure admiration.

Sarah's head jerked up. 'Oh, Ida. Thanks. I had to go home and change . . . something got spilled . . . and this was all I had that was suitable.' She gave a nervous laugh. 'But now I'm concerned it's a bit over the top . . .'

'Nonsense, lass. It's a bobby-dazzler! Now get on in there and save tha guests from Harry's caterwauling.'

Sarah smiled, a dimple flashing in her cheek, and turned to go. But Ida, ever the cleaner, called after her.

'What got spilled?' she asked.

'Sorry?' Sarah looked confused.

'On tha wedding dress? Happen I might know how to fix it.'

'Oh . . . er . . . red wine.'

Ida nodded. 'Club soda and white wine vinegar. Failing that, soak it for an hour in three-parts hydrogen peroxide and one part washing-up liquid. But don't leave it too long before doing something, mind, or tha'll not shift it for love nor money.'

Sarah raised a hand in thanks and hurried into the rugby club, leaving Ida alone in the car park. She wasn't waiting long before the rumble of a tractor greeted her and a Ferguson TE20 turned onto the club driveway.

'Tha's timed that perfectly, George,' she said as she clambered onto the vintage vehicle.

Her brother merely nodded and pulled away, guiding the tractor towards Thorpdale and, Ida hoped, a bit of peace and quiet.

It was dark.

Or was it? Delilah blinked a couple of times, just to make sure her eyes were actually open. Then giggled. It *was* dark. And in Bruncliffe, with no street lights on the outer margins of the town, that meant proper dark. But Delilah was born and bred in the place. Knew it like the back of her hand.

Which didn't explain why she was standing in one of the many ginnels that weaved between buildings and roads in the town centre, wondering where she was going.

She gave a whisky-scented sigh and looked up. As if that would help, above being nothing but stars and a huge outcrop of rock. Her faculties sludge-slow, it took her a few moments to recognise the Crag, the swell of limestone that loomed over the town. She now knew where she was – the alley behind the office building – but didn't know why, seeing as her cottage was up on the hill at the back of the town. So it wasn't so much she was lost, she mused. It was more that she'd lost her sense of direction.

Which made her think of Samson—

'No!' she slurred into the deserted alleyway. 'Not allowed. No thoughtsss of him!'

So she lurched on, further into the ginnel, a hand on the high wall to her right, fingers trailing across the rough stone as though that would lead her to her true path.

Then she had a moment of clarity. Drunken clarity.

She knew why she was here. She was going to check to see if Sam—

'Nope. Not allowed.'

She recalibrated the thought. She was going to check to see if anyone had arrived at the office building. Someone who might have travelled up from the south and been too late to make the wedding. And be too afraid of her temper to show up until she was calmed down.

She giggled again. At the thought that Sam—

At the thought that anyone could be afraid of her temper.

She stumbled further into the ginnel until she came to a gate she recognised. It was ajar. Saved her getting out her keys.

She went through into the shadow-filled yard, glance automatically going to the empty rectangle of concrete to the left as it had done every day for the last eleven weeks. Under the bright semi-circle of moon, the white space stared back at her. No Royal Enfield. Not that it meant anything, as the motorbike was parked up at Baggy's, the mechanic having offered to store it until such time as its owner came home—

This time the thought was stopped by a stab of alcohol-fuelled self-pity, tears welling up in her already unfocused eyes, the ache of missing him overwhelming her.

'For God'sssake,' she muttered, wiping a hand across her face as she turned towards the back porch. 'Get a grip!'

She reached into her pocket, fingers searching for the office keys, and promptly stumbled over a solid object lying across the doorstep. As she staggered backwards, struggling to stay upright, the large mass got to its feet, looming over her. She opened her mouth to scream but a huge hand was already covering it.

5

The train had been too late. Of course it had.

Just south of Doncaster it had slowed to a crawl before stopping completely, the driver announcing a fault with the signalling system, and Samson had known there and then that his plan was doomed. They'd finally limped into Leeds a full thirty minutes after his scheduled connection and he'd had to endure the painfully slow progress of the subsequent train, which stopped at every station along the way. By the time he'd got to Skipton it had been gone nine o'clock, dusk had given way to night and his options had been limited.

There were no onward trains to Bruncliffe. And no chance of asking someone to come and get him as everyone he knew with access to a car would have been at Harry's wedding and incapable of driving by now. So he'd walked through the park to the Gargrave Road, across the roundabout and onto the A65, where he'd started heading north, thumb stuck out in hope.

It had worked for him once before, back in March, when he'd been returning under an even darker cloud. Just out of the police station, suspected of murder, he'd braved a long walk home over the tops in bitter weather. At least this time it was a mild night, the half-moon as good as a torch as he'd begun walking along the road.

He'd been lucky. A group of four young women in a hatchback, on their way back to a spa hotel in Coniston Cold after a night out in Skipton, had pulled over to offer him a lift only minutes into his journey. They'd done a double take when he'd bent down to the passenger window and they'd seen the state of his face. But he'd turned on his brightest smile and they'd opened the rear door for him to get in. High on being relieved of parental duties for the weekend, they'd kept up a stream of excited conversation, peppering him with questions as they drove onwards. When he'd explained the circumstances of his injuries and the reasons for his determination to get to Bruncliffe that night – no names mentioned – there had been a chorus of ooohs and ahhs, his gesture unanimously described as romantic.

The women had insisted on going a further ten minutes out of their way to drop Samson at Long Preston, wishing him luck before driving off with a lot of waving and blowing of kisses, leaving him to start the trek over the tops with a wide smile on his face and optimism in his heart. If four total strangers could be won over by his endeavours to get home, surely the woman he loved would be too.

Now, over an hour in, he stood on the top of the fell above the town, looking down at the sprinkling of lights nestled below the hills that curved around it. And he was struck with a strong sense of déjà vu. He'd been here before. Heading back in the expectation of a warm welcome. It hadn't turned out that way last time, the news of his suspension breaking before he had a chance to tell Delilah how he felt about her, his name turned toxic thanks to allegations claiming he was connected to drugs.

What if he'd got it wrong this time too? What if her annoyance at yet one more broken promise was the proverbial straw that broke the Metcalfe back? Perhaps he wouldn't get the reception he was hoping for.

Although, seeing as this was Delilah he was dealing with, any expectations on his part would be foolish, for the woman defied them at every turn!

With a wry laugh, Samson started down the narrow track that led into Bruncliffe, his breathing mercifully easier now, for which his aching ribs were thankful. Instead it was his left hip letting him know he'd been hit by a car as he stiffly negotiated the incline. But the pain wasn't enough to prevent him enjoying the sense of being home – the muted bleat of a sheep in the dark; a lonely owl hooting from the copse of trees that marked the start of the Bruncliffe Manor estate. When his route brought him out onto Hillside Lane he picked up the pace, like a horse heading for the stables. Rucksack on his back, a gentle wind in his face, he was at the outskirts of the town and almost at the turn for Back Street when he heard the noise of an engine, coming from behind.

It was upon him in a heartbeat, the vehicle travelling at pace, hurtling out of the dark in a blaze of headlights. Samson had a split second to throw himself against the stone wall to his left, catching only a glimpse of a dark 4x4 as it sped along the narrow road and disappeared around the bend towards town.

He stood there for a moment, hip screaming, his ribs on fire, not appreciating the contact with the wall. Then he glanced at his watch. It was almost midnight. Who the hell would be tearing around at this hour? Lads on a night out? A night that would end in disaster if they kept that up.

Consoling himself that he was almost home, where a comfy bed was waiting, he resumed walking. Five minutes later, he was letting himself into the back porch of the office building. Relieved to have what had felt like the longest day in history almost over, he walked up the stairs, going past Delilah's office and the kitchen on the first floor and on up to the top storey. The bathroom door was open, the landing light spilling into the room to reveal a towel left in a heap on the tiles, toothpaste smeared on the washbasin, and puddles of water pooling in the shower tray.

He grinned, his hopes soaring. Delilah was here! Too drunk and too weary after the wedding reception to go all the way up the hill to her cottage at the top of the town. Definitely drunk because it wasn't like Delilah to be so messy. Ida would have words when she saw that in the morning.

He inched towards the bedroom door and heard the snuffle of a dog. Tolpuddle was here, too!

All at once Samson's trials and tribulations of the past twenty-four hours were as nothing. He was home. Easing the door open slowly, he entered the room, aware of the light filtering around him, not wanting to wake her—

A snore. Loud. Rough. Male.

Samson froze. Stared at the bed. The shadows showing a large shape beneath the covers. Too large for Delilah.

Another snore, broken off this time, as though the sleeper was on the verge of waking.

Samson stepped back out onto the landing, closing the door behind him. Mind racing.

There was someone in his bed. A man. And given that Tolpuddle was in the room and never went anywhere without his mistress then that meant—

It meant, Samson thought, as he headed back down the stairs, that he'd screwed up yet again. It also meant he had nowhere to sleep.

Letting himself back out into the night, he walked across the town with a heart feeling every bit as battered as his body.

Tigger was a bit off her patch. Seduced by the night's late-summer warmth, she'd cut through the ginnels between Plastic Fantastic – the place she nominally called home – and High Street, and had been stealing up towards the market-place, grey-striped body tucked tight in against the shop fronts, when curiosity got the better of her.

A narrow passageway between two walls, down which there was the dark shape of a vehicle. Even from that distance, the scents intrigued her.

Slinking silently towards it, both ears pricked, senses on alert, she walked around, sniffing the tyres, the body-work. Back round to the front and then a light jump, up onto the bonnet. The surprising sensation of warm metal beneath her paws. She would normally have luxuriated in it but her attention was caught by a flashing red light behind the windscreen. Stretching her neck forward, she was cautiously peering at it when there was a crash of sound from inside the building to her right and a flood of light from behind.

Startled, she leaped down as something roared past the end of the passageway.

Heart pattering, she waited for silence to descend once more before deciding it was time to forsake her adventures and flee towards more familiar territory.

The lights cut through the dark, picking out the curve of old stones before the engine was turned off and everything was plunged back into night. The noise of a car door. Then grunts of exertion. It took a bit of shifting. Manoeuvring it out of the boot in the first place. Then dragging it across the grass to its new resting place.

A brief pause. The living shadow looking down at the results of the night's work. Then it turned. Back to the vehicle, the engine loud in the deathly quiet. Soon it was gone and silence returned, settling around the new addition to the ancient landscape where it lay, a cavern of stone arching over it.

It was a fitting tomb for the dead.

6

'Where the hell are my office keys?' Delilah had one hand on her head, holding it together as the pain inside her skull threatened to cleave it in two, and the other was rifling through a jumble of junk in one of her kitchen drawers.

Tolpuddle let out a loud bark, and she shuddered.

'Do you have a mute button?' she muttered, glowering at her hound.

After an evening being fussed over by the residents of Fellside Court retirement complex, the Weimaraner was in much better condition than she was, making her think that opting to spend time in the sober company of Joseph O'Brien would have been a better idea for her too. Tolpuddle barked again, eager to be outside on what was shaping up to be a glorious day – as far as Delilah could tell from peering out of her cottage window through half-closed eyes, the stab of bright sunlight too much for her to endure.

She gave one last look around, nothing on the worktop or the small table in the corner, nor on the hook where her keys normally hung.

'Right. We'll go without. Ida will let me in.'

Clipping on Tolpuddle's lead, she headed for the door

and took a deep breath. She could do this. She could get through the morning with the world's worst hangover.

She put on a pair of sunglasses and stepped out into the sunshine bathing the small terrace beside the cottage. The view was magnificent. Bruncliffe spread out below her, the jumble of roofs a flare of shining slates, the fells rising up a vibrant green, and overhead, a sky gloriously blue and cloud-free.

Normally it was a scene that made her smile. Today it made her clutch her stomach, a wave of nausea threatening.

'That's the last time I drink,' she vowed as she turned towards the road and the route down into town. 'I swear. The very last time.'

With Tolpuddle trotting along beside her, she gingerly made her way along Crag Lane to the steep flight of steps which brought her out in the ginnel at the back of the office building.

At the foot of the steps, she paused, letting the queasiness pass. It had been a good wedding, what she could remember of it, much of the evening a blur of half-recalled images. A snapshot of dancing with Ash, possibly while on a table. Another of leaning against the bar chatting to someone, but she couldn't remember who. And then . . . pretty much just a blank, until she'd woken up on the couch at home, still fully dressed in her wedding finery and with Tolpuddle panting in her face, waiting for her to get up and feed him.

Although, now that she was standing here in the ginnel, the sun streaming down over the Crag towering above her, she had a vague recollection of standing in the same spot the night before. She strained her memory, finding nothing more than the opacity which came with excess alcohol, and the aftertaste of whisky on her tongue. Which was enough to make her gag.

Gathering her reserves, she crossed the alleyway and entered the yard, her tired eyes immediately glancing to the left. Still no Enfield.

She let herself into the rear porch, unclipped Tolpuddle and followed him into the building. The smell of bacon floated down from the kitchen on the first floor. Delilah clutched her stomach and let out a groan. Getting through the day was going to be a challenge.

Tolpuddle had his nose in the air the minute they entered the building and caught two smells. One familiar. One not. The familiar one pulled him towards the stairs at a pace, long legs taking the steps in bounds. Up onto the landing, round the corner and there she was. The woman who made mornings amazing. Calling him towards her.

The smell of bacon flooded his senses as she ruffled his ears. Overpowering the other scent. Making him forget about it. He tucked himself into the far corner of the room, eyes on the frying pan and the woman, knowing to stay out of her way until it was ready.

'Tha survived, then?' Ida Capstick cast a critical eye over Delilah as she slowly walked along the landing and then eased herself down onto one of the chairs at the small table in the kitchen. All the while holding herself steady, like she was doing deportment lessons with a crystal glass balanced on her head. Her face was the colour of old putty and, when she removed her sunglasses, her eyes were no more than pinpricks of pain. 'Mind, I've seen thee looking better.'

Ida turned back to the stove, bacon hissing and spitting. To her left, Tolpuddle was sitting, the epitome of good health, watching the progress of the cooking with interest. Judging by the way Delilah had a hand resting on her stomach, he might be getting double rations.

Tea was what was needed. Ida dropped the spatula into the frying pan with an unintentional clatter of noise, eliciting a whimper from behind her, and picked up the teapot, a brew already stewing. She poured it into a mug, treacle-coloured, and added a good splash of milk. Turning back to the table, she placed it down, along with a strip of paracetamol.

'Get this lot down thee.' It was said with the kindest tone in the Capstick repertoire, Ida having no condemnation for the lass.

Delilah reached for the mug and paused, her focus caught by the set of keys lying on an envelope at the edge of the table. She pulled them towards her and looked at Ida, a question on her face which she was obviously beyond articulating.

'Aye, them's tha office keys all right. Tha must have called in last night. I'm guessing tha's not remembering much of it?'

Whatever response Delilah went to make was drowned out by the slam of the front door in the hallway down below. She grimaced and picked up the tablets Ida had given her as fast feet hurtled up the stairs.

'Sorry I'm late! But guess what – the Taylors' place is up for sale—!' Nina Hussain came to a breathless halt on the landing, staring at Delilah, whose head had dropped into her hands. 'Oh!' A grin split the teenager's face. 'I'm guessing those whisky shots don't seem like such a good idea now?'

'Don't . . .' groaned Delilah. 'Don't mention them.'

Nina winked at Ida. Who turned back to the frying pan, thinking that Delilah's condition wasn't exclusively caused by drinking spirits. Whatever Samson was playing at, he was going to need a good excuse for not turning up yesterday. For not even bothering to get in touch.

'So,' continued Nina, showing no mercy for Delilah's indisposition, 'did you know Mrs Taylor was selling?'

Delilah's response was halfway between a shrug and a shake of her head, culminating in a wince. But Ida knew, even if the lass wasn't suffering, she'd not say owt. She wasn't one for gossip, not even about her former mother-in-law. Although the same couldn't be said for the rest of the town. Given Nina's news that the widow of the recently deceased – and discredited – mayor was selling up and leaving Bruncliffe, there was no prize for guessing what would be the talk of the day.

'Thing is, she's not only selling her house here,' Nina chattered on. 'She was in the restaurant last night and was talking to Dad about things and asked if he knew anyone who might want to buy a villa in Mallorca. Said she had one going cheap. Seems like she's having a complete clear out! Mind you, who could blame her. Have you got any idea where she's going?'

This time Delilah managed an unintelligible sound, part pain, part grunt, and before Nina could start up again, Ida interrupted.

'Did tha get Nathan's project done?' she demanded, shifting the attention off her under-the-weather boss and back onto the teenager.

'Yeah. Kind of.' Nina shrugged, her gaiety of moments before dimming somewhat. 'I'd forgotten we had a large group booked in at the restaurant so I had to get back. I left him at the kiln.' She gave another shrug. 'I presume he got everything he needed.'

Ida flipped the bacon. Reading between the lines. The poor lad – the torch he held for Nina Hussain was as plain as day. Had he made a move, suggesting they take their friendship further, and Nina had had to set him right? There wasn't a bad bone in the lass so she'd have been gentle if that was the case. But the male ego was fragile at any age. At Nathan's age it was at its most brittle.

Another one who'd be nursing hurt this morning, although less self-inflicted.

'Have you heard from Samson?' Nina asked, pulling out the chair opposite Delilah in a screech of legs on floor.

Delilah flinched. Whether at the noise or the question, Ida couldn't tell.

'No. Not yet.'

'Have you had a chance to tell him about this?' Nina tapped the envelope on the table, the logo for Turpin's Solicitors across the top.

Matty Thistlethwaite, taking it upon himself to try to clean up the mess that had been left in the town following the arrest of Rick Procter. The solicitor was keeping everyone abreast of the consequences of Procter's criminal activities, giving advance warning when properties owned by the developer became eligible for auction under the

Proceeds of Crime Act. So far the only business to have gone under the hammer was Fellside Court, the retirement apartments having been identified as a front for money-laundering on a huge scale. The sale had gone through at the start of the month and now the elderly residents were all of a flutter, worrying about what the change of owner-ship might mean. Still cleaning there a couple of times a week despite her increased responsibilities at the Dales Detective Agency, Ida had witnessed first hand how stressed the pensioners were.

And now this. A letter from Matty to inform people that Twistleton Farm, the former O'Brien home which Procter had bought for a song from a drunk Joseph O'Brien, had been deemed by the authorities to have been purchased with the proceeds of criminal activity and, as such, would be coming up for auction in mid-September, a scant four weeks away.

Delilah shook her head, and instantly regretted it, hands going to her face. 'Want to tell him in person,' she managed to mutter, through what sounded like gritted teeth. She was making a monumental effort not to succumb to her hangover.

'Poor Samson,' murmured Nina. 'I can't imagine how this will make him feel.'

Ida could. Having your home taken from you by unscru-pulous means and then having it used to house a diabolical business involving human trafficking and drugs was bad enough, without having it finally auctioned off, probably to some offcumden wanting to have the place as a second home. For who else would be able to afford it with the daft prices for property in the area? Not Samson, that was for sure. The lad would feel like he'd lost the farm all over again. He'd never get over it.

'Bacon's done,' said Ida, beginning to serve it up onto the thick slices of white bread she had buttered and ready.

'Not for me—'

Delilah's refusal was overridden by the slap of two plates on the table, one in front of her.

'Eat it. Tha needs to line tha stomach. There's work to be done and it'll require stamina.'

A whine from the corner, Tolpuddle reminding the room that he hadn't been served. Ida put a couple of rashers on a saucer and bent down to the Weimaraner. 'Good lad,' she murmured, patting his grey head.

'Delicious, Ida, thanks,' Nina was saying, already eating. 'Breakfast of champions—'

The sound of a door opening, followed by movement on the landing above, cut across the teenager, the three women and Tolpuddle all freezing, looking at each other.

'Who's upstairs?' asked Ida.

Delilah blinked, shook her head. 'No one.'

But there evidently was. The soft pad of footsteps coming down the steps.

Eyes all on the landing, they watched, speechless, as a brown spaniel came round the corner and straight into the kitchen. Straight over to the saucer on the floor. To the rasher still lying there. And began eating it.

Tolpuddle looked at the dog. Looked at Ida, a comical expression of martyred disbelief on his face. While the three women stared at each other and the spaniel in puzzlement.

'Isn't that—?' Ida's question went unfinished as heavy footsteps now came down the stairs. Down to the landing.

Revealing a large figure of a man, clad only in a towel wrapped around his waist.

'Can I smell bacon?' Gareth Towler stood in the hallway, russet hair damp, beard bushy, broad chest bare, and grinned at them.

'What on earth—?' Ida was staring at the man and then at Delilah, who was staring at Gareth in horror, like she'd done something dreadful.

'Hello? Anyone home?' Another voice, from downstairs this time. A voice which should have had Delilah leaping from her seat and running towards it – Samson was back!

But the lass was transfixed. Staring at the gamekeeper. And then down at the keys lying on the table. Her alarm now being compounded with what looked like shame.

'Delilah?' Samson was coming up the stairs. Nina giving Ida a look of terror. Ida wanting nothing more than to sweep the huge gamekeeper under the nearest rug. All the while, Delilah just shaking her head, a low moan coming from her.

'You there, Delilah?'

Samson rounded the top of the stairs, and froze. Taking in Gareth and his state of undress. The audience watching from the kitchen. Tolpuddle and the spaniel. Then he looked at Delilah.

'It's not what it looks like,' she said weakly.

'Tea!' said Ida into the ensuing silence, sliding Turpin's letter off the table and into her pocket before turning to the kettle. Although even she, with her perpetual faith in the miraculous properties of a strong brew, knew it would be pushing it for a humble cuppa to sort out this monumental mess.

7

Bruncliffe marketplace was quiet, even for a Sunday. True, it was still early, many of the businesses which surrounded the square late to open on the Sabbath, if at all, but usually there were people around. Today, however, the cobbles were host to nothing more than a couple of pigeons picking at a dropped chip and the sign for Whitaker's newsagent's, swaying in the gentle breeze.

At least the sign was upright, mused Lucy Metcalfe as she surveyed the scene from the interior of Peaks Patisserie. Since Mike Whitaker had purchased it back in the winter it had spent most of its days lying on its back, no match for the winds that howled through the town in the colder months.

She let her eyes drift to the double-fronted building sandwiched between the newsagent's and Kamal Hussain's Rice N Spice, where the jewel in Bruncliffe's crown had once been housed, the success of Taylor's Estate Agents having long been a benchmark for all the businesses in the area to aspire to. Now, the large windows stared opaquely onto the square. Someone had gone to the trouble of smearing Windolene all over the glass to prevent nosy passers-by from seeing in, but other than that, the premises showed no sign of redevelopment since fire had torn through them almost three months ago. Nor were they likely to any time soon, for while enough of Taylor's dealings had been deemed to be legitimate, thus exempting his business from the Proceeds of Crime Act, the building itself was found to have been owned by none other than Procter Properties, placing it under investigation by the authorities.

Yet another thing in the town thrown into a state of stasis thanks to the nefarious Rick Procter.

At the top of the square the bright green sign outside the handsome Georgian house which presided over the marketplace was more evidence of the tornado of destruction the property developer had unleased on Bruncliffe. A 'For Sale' sign. It must have been put up late the night before, as it hadn't been there yesterday. What was remarkable about it was that it didn't bear the Taylor's logo as citizens of the town were used to, but a design of sheep and stone walls, the brand of some company called Dales Homes. No doubt Nancy Taylor's new estate agency Delilah had mentioned. But what was even more remarkable was that the sign had been erected in front of Nancy's own house.

Wife, now widow, of the former mayor. A mayor whose legacy had been tarnished posthumously by his dealings with Procter. Was Nancy fleeing the town? Lucy didn't blame her. The woman had the respect of all but that didn't make it any easier to walk about the place knowing what her husband had been responsible for.

If that were the case, however, why would she have gone to the bother of setting up a business here?

Whatever the reason, Nancy's decision to sell would provide plenty of fuel for the gossipmongers, and for the customers in Peaks Patisserie, if any ever turned up.

A lone figure walked past the cafe window. Seth Thistlethwaite, going for his Sunday papers. He threw a wave at Lucy as he went by, bushy eyebrows raised to see her idling when she was normally flat out with folk wanting a post-church coffee and cake. He wasn't the only one nonplussed by the empty tables. It was like the whole town had a post-wedding hangover.

Luckily, Lucy wasn't one of the afflicted. Unlike most of her family and friends, she'd left the rugby club at a decent hour the night before without having succumbed to an excess of drink. Consequently, she was in fine form despite the lack of clientele, enjoying the sunshine streaming in, the expanse of blue sky over the multiple gables of the town hall, the majesty of the Crag towering over it all. Even the badly parked vehicle on High Street hadn't been enough to spoil her good mood.

Lucy Metcalfe wasn't one to be precious about parking. In a small town like Bruncliffe, it was a gift to find a space at all during the summer months, let alone one close to the cafe. And if she needed to drop anything off, she could always pull up in the ginnel at the side of the building and offload. But on Sundays, it was rare that she had to park far away. Today, however, when she'd arrived at the top of High Street where there were two purpose-built spaces, she'd been confronted by a Toyota Land Cruiser. Slewed in against the kerb with its rear end sticking out, it was straddling the white lines, effectively taking up both gaps and leaving no room for Lucy to slip in behind.

She'd found a space on the side street past the Post Office and walked up from there, so it wasn't really a problem. Just inconsiderate. And Lucy wasn't a fan of inconsiderate people.

Nor was she a fan of thieves.

After a week without incident, she'd opened the kitchen door this morning to shattered glass on the floor, a cake stand having been tipped off the worktop, the chocolate and orange brownies it had been holding all gone. She'd have to have another word with Delilah. Get a camera off her which she could install herself. Because it wasn't the thefts that were upsetting her, a few cakes or savouries here and there not amounting to much in the grand scheme of things. It was the underhandedness of it. The fact that she felt like she was being targeted.

'Morning!' The door swung open and Herriot walked in. Or rather, slouched in.

Eyes ringed with half-moons of fatigue, his hair sticking up in all directions and a day's worth of stubble on his chin, he looked rough.

'Hard night?' she asked with a laugh.

He smiled, stretching his neck to either side with an accompanying crunch of joints. 'Just a bit.'

'Well, that's what you get when you try to keep up with Metcalfes in a drinking contest. Coffee?'

'Please.' He glanced around the cafe as Lucy busied herself with the coffee machine. 'Bit quiet for a Sunday, isn't it?'

'Sure is. Only visitor I've had is the pesky thief.'

Herriot's focus swung sharply back onto her. 'You were raided again last night?'

She nodded. 'A handful of brownies. But this time they smashed one of my display cases.'

'But how . . . I didn't see . . . I mean, do you know how they got in?' Herriot's stumbling words were accompanied by a pained expression. Almost of guilt.

'Not a clue. Same as always.' She smiled, passed the coffee across the counter and squeezed the vet's arm, touched to see him so upset on her behalf. 'Don't worry, it's not the crime of the century or anything. I'll get to the bottom of it eventually.'

'Yes, right . . . it's just . . .' He petered out, wiped a hand over his face and then gave a tired smile. 'Sorry, I'm operating on a low battery.'

Lucy laughed. 'I reckon Harry and Sarah's wedding has left the entire town in that state.'

As she spoke, the door opened again and Joseph O'Brien entered, followed by Arty Robinson, worried expressions on them both.

'Everything all right?' Lucy asked.

Joseph tipped his head in the direction of Back Street at the far end of the square. 'We're just on our way to speak to Delilah. We're desperate to know if she's heard anything about the sale of Fellside Court.'

'The uncertainty is killing me.' The strain on Arty's face bore testimony to his words. 'There are so many rumours flying around the place, folk suggesting the new people are going to slap the rent up. Others saying it's a bunch of venture capitalists and we'll be hung out to dry. I swear I haven't slept since they arrested that blasted Procter!'

'I keep telling him not to be so fatalistic,' said Joseph, patting his friend on the back before placing a set of car keys on the counter. 'Anyway, we noticed these had been left in a 4x4 at the top of High Street.'

'The Toyota that's badly parked?' asked Lucy. She picked up the keys, a distinctive, vivid green resin keyring hanging from them, weird squiggles and blobs set within the polymer.

'The very same. Probably someone coming home from Harry's do last night. Got this far and realised they were a few over the limit so left it where it was.'

'Well, the keyring might narrow down ownership a bit,' said Herriot, leaning forward to have a better look at it. 'Whoever's it is, they're a fan of plants.'

The other three looked none the wiser, so he pointed at the array of what looked like random circles and lines on the fob in Lucy's hand.

'It's the structure of a plant cell. That's the nucleus, the chloroplast, the mitochondria . . .' He paused, blushing as his audience stared at him in awe. 'Sorry, a bit nerdy knowing all that.'

'Not nerdy in the least,' said Lucy, and Herriot's cheeks stained a deeper red. 'I'm impressed. So we're looking for someone who knows more about plants than parking a car. And who was possibly very drunk, seeing as they left their keys in the ignition. But why have you brought them to me?' she enquired of the pensioners.

Joseph shrugged. 'The police station isn't open yet and we figured Sergeant Clayton will be stopping by here on his way in, so it made more sense. Don't want someone joyriding off in the thing just because some idiot made it easy for them.'

'Fair enough. I'll hang on to them.'

The two men turned to go.

'Wait a minute!' said Lucy, reaching for a paper bag. She placed five cherry scones inside and passed the bag to Arty. 'A little pick you up for you and the gang. No charge.'

Arty looked at the bag. Looked at Lucy. And tears sprang to his eyes. 'Sorry,' he muttered, wiping them away. 'Just feeling a bit under the weather of late and . . . well . . . you know, I'm a sucker for a scone.' He made an attempt at a grin but it didn't carry its usual sparkle.

Lucy watched them leave, an air of dejection about Arty in particular as they walked down the steps and started across the cobbles. By contrast, Elaine Bullock came in through the cafe door like a whirlwind, face flushed, plaits flying.

'Sorry I'm late!' she exclaimed. Even though the tardy waitress arriving early would be more of a shock.

'Hardly missing anything,' said Lucy, gesturing at the empty cafe.

'Talking of late,' said Herriot, heading for the door, 'I promised Kevin Dinsdale I'd pop up and have a look at a tup he's having trouble with. Catch you later.'

He waved goodbye and Lucy turned her attention to her friend, noticing as she did a streak of scarlet on Elaine's left earlobe.

'Is that blood?'

Elaine put a hand up, brushed her ear, her fingers coming away smeared in red. 'Damn it. I must have caught my earrings yesterday taking them off. It's nothing.'

'Not the result of a passionate clinch from your date, then?' teased Lucy with a warm smile.

'It wasn't a date!' The tone was sharp. Very sharp.

Lucy's eyes widened. In all the years they'd worked

together, the two friends had never had a cross word. 'Okay. Sorry. I didn't mean to—'

But Elaine was already walking away, towards the kitchen, tying on her apron as she went. The door swung closed behind her and soon Lucy heard the firm thump of a knife hitting a chopping board. Deciding it might be wise to leave her alone to vent her anger on the onions that needed dicing, Lucy put the misplaced car keys in her pocket.

It wasn't just Lucy's friend who wasn't having the best of mornings. Lucy's son Nathan wasn't either. In fact, he was convinced that after the mess he'd made of the evening before, he wasn't going to have the best of lives.

'I'm an idiot,' he muttered to the two lurchers accompanying him on the climb up the fellside. 'A first-class idiot.'

The dogs didn't respond, keeping an easy pace as he marched up the path with furious strides. All the while berating himself.

What on earth had possessed him?

It had been idyllic. Just himself and Nina, sitting on top of the kiln, chatting easily as the sun slid towards the horizon. Then he'd had to go and ruin it by challenging her to walk around the interior of the huge structure in the dusk, with no torch. It was hard to see inside during daylight hours, but once the sun started to set, the light in the curved kiln was minimal.

Of course, Nina had risen to the bait. Happy to walk around in the dark, proving that she wasn't scared. Because she wasn't. Not until Nathan had made a clumsy move on her.

'Idiot!' he cursed again, face burning at the memory.

They'd been halfway along the lozenge-shaped construction, Nathan's heart going like the clappers, his senses heightened by the deep shadows and the proximity to this amazing girl. Then his hand had brushed against hers by accident. It hadn't been planned. Just an innocuous coming together of limbs. But before he knew it, his fingers had tried to link with hers. Of their own volition.

She'd pulled away from him, not saying a word. But had headed for the nearest arch and the fading daylight beyond it. He'd followed, heart still thundering, but in fear now. As though it knew it was about to get smashed to pieces.

Once outside, she'd turned, a small smile on her face. The sympathetic sort. He'd known what was coming.

They were just mates, she'd explained. No need for anything else. She wasn't interested in taking it further. Best not to ruin a really good friendship.

Or words to that effect. Nathan had struggled to hear, what with the blood rushing in his ears, his face a study in scarlet.

She'd leaned forward and pecked him on the cheek. Like an elderly aunt. Then she'd said she had to be going. Her dad needed her at the restaurant. Nathan was left alone at the kiln, his head a mess, his heart hurting, and his history project far from finished.

He'd stayed there until quite late, not in the mood for company. Definitely not in the mood for his mother's questions when he got home, because she'd take one look at him and know something was up. When he'd woken this morning, it was with a sense that the world had ended. Or at the very least, his friendship with Nina had, because he wasn't going to be able to face her ever again.

This agony was only compounded when he'd realised his dad's old tobacco tin was missing. Which was why he was walking back up the fellside towards the location of the Worst Moment of His Life – the Hoffmann kiln.

Ahead, the stone oval came into view. Nathan was pretty sure he knew where the tin would be – just inside the arch where he'd made his fatal mistake. Because when Nina had pulled away from his touch, he'd jerked his errant hand away, trying to undo what was already done. In the process, he must have dislodged the tobacco tin from his pocket.

Loping along slightly in front of him, the lurchers seemed to have the same idea. They suddenly both went still before turning and running towards the very spot where Nathan's heart had been dealt the deadly blow. In a pair of sleek movements, they disappeared inside the kiln. Then they started barking.

Nathan ran after them. Taking a moment to arrive at the archway. Stepping through it, into the gloom, phone in hand with the torch already on—

The scream that came from his throat seemed to echo around the cavern for eternity.

'I can explain,' Delilah said again. Although she knew she couldn't. Not in the least. Because her memory of what had happened to occasion the presence of Gareth Towler in the office building, in a towel, was non-existent – a situation certainly not aided by the pounding in her head. Consequently, she was rendered speechless.

Gareth Towler, on the other hand, was showing no such lack of words. 'Samson!' he declared, stepping forward, hand held out in greeting, wide grin on his face. 'Good to see you home. I was just about to thank Delilah for the best night of my life!'

The crash of the teapot on the worktop indicated that Delilah wasn't the only one sensing things hadn't been improved by the gamekeeper's contribution. Ida was even more granite-faced than usual. And poor Nina, hemmed in by the two men in the doorway, was looking like she wanted to be anywhere but in the kitchen.

'Good to be home,' Samson murmured in reply. 'I think.'

He was watching Delilah. She could feel it. But she kept her gaze on the table, trying to sieve even the slightest fragment of memory from the fog of what had apparently been an eventful evening.

Gareth had obviously slept upstairs. But what about her . . . ? Is that why her office keys had been here? Had she come back with him—?

A stab of horror. A sharp recollection of the ginnel in the dark. Of entering the yard. She *had* come back!

'She damn well saved my life,' Gareth was continuing, so absorbed in his own good humour he was failing to read the room. 'She's the reason I had a warm bed last night.'

'Glad to hear it,' muttered Samson dryly.

Delilah cringed. Half hoping for an opportune return to full lucidity. Half afraid of it at the same time.

'In fact,' the gamekeeper boomed, leaning over to plant a kiss on Delilah's cheek, 'I'd go so far as to say—'

'Tea's brewed!' declared the previously silent Ida, before Gareth could say anything else. 'And I've more bacon on, so get thyself dressed, young man, and tha can have a bite of breakfast.'

Gareth slapped his hands together, the noise raucous in Delilah's tender skull. 'Sounds just the ticket,' he said. 'And then I can tell you all about the difficulty Bounty and I had getting Miss Metcalfe up the hill to her home in the small hours!' His laugh echoed around the kitchen, then he patted Delilah on the head, adding insult to injury, turned and went back up the stairs.

It took a few seconds for Delilah's muddled mind to realise what he'd said.

He'd taken her home. Which meant . . . she hadn't stayed at the office.

'Well,' said Ida into the awkward silence, nodding, as though the gamekeeper's final words had clarified things for her too, 'sit thyself down, lad. Tha looks right shattered.'

'That's putting it mildly.' Samson pulled out the chair opposite Delilah and sat, reaching over to fondle Tolpuddle's ears as he did so. The Weimaraner nuzzled back at his hand but didn't move. He was guarding the empty saucer on the floor, on the off chance that more bacon might be forthcoming. Curled between his two front feet was Bounty, the springer spaniel. 'Seems I'm not the only one adapting to changes around here.'

He turned back to Delilah and she finally looked up, taking in the state of him for the first time. A hideous bruise on his left cheek, a lattice of cuts and grazes on his face, his dark hair falling to his shoulders, all tangled, and his clothes rumpled and dirty. Plus he was leaning to one side, as though in pain. Rough didn't cover it.

'When did you get here?' she asked.

'Last night.' He gave a small smile. 'I was hoping to surprise you. But then it was so late by the time I got into town, I thought I'd crash here instead. Turns out I was the one surprised.'

She flinched. Playing the scenario in her mind. Him

entering the bedroom. Seeing Gareth in his bed. What he must have thought. 'Oh,' she said.

He nodded. 'Oh. Didn't realise you'd sublet my room.'

'Not sure Delilah knows much about it either,' muttered Ida.

Delilah managed a weak grin. 'It's all a bit of a haze, I have to admit.'

'Happen the lad needed somewhere to stay, mind,' continued Ida, addressing them over her shoulder as she cooked. 'Seems Delilah was generous enough to suggest upstairs.' She glared at Samson. 'The lass wasn't to know tha'd be trekking back across the fells at all hours.'

'Fair enough.' Samson nodded.

'So where did you sleep, then?' asked Nina, finally finding her voice.

'At the allotments. I still have a key for Seth's shed from when we investigated those break-ins.' Samson grinned, and Delilah's heart somersaulted. 'He'll be thinking the thieves have been back – I consumed a fair few of his biscuits!'

Nina snorted, Delilah felt her lips twitch and Ida grunted.

'Last thing we need is Seth Thistlethwaite asking us to investigate again. We've more work than manpower as it is,' she muttered as she flipped the bacon.

'You should have come to mine,' Delilah said softly.

Samson looked at her. 'I didn't know if you were home . . .' Then he shrugged. Winced. Grinned again. 'Besides, I wasn't sure what welcome I'd get.'

'A drunk one,' said Ida.

'She was dancing on the tables and all sorts last night,' Nina divulged, laughing now. 'And at one point—'

'What happens at weddings stays at weddings, young

lady!' Ida placed a bacon roll in front of Samson as Gareth came back down the stairs.

'I have to say, Mrs Capstick, that is a smell to tempt a saint!' the gamekeeper declared, entering the kitchen, his huge frame towering over her.

'Hasn't been a Mrs Capstick since my mother!' she snapped, thrusting a plate at him. 'If tha's going to be hanging around here, tha best get used to calling me Ida.'

'I best had, then, seeing as we're going to be working together!' Gareth bit into his sandwich while the others all turned to Delilah.

'Working together?' Ida asked. Hands on hips.

'Erm . . .' Delilah stuttered. Searching the black void of her memory but getting nothing more than brief strobes of recollection – talking to Gareth at the bar, hearing about his predicament, no job, no home . . . 'I think I, erm . . .'

'Aye,' the gamekeeper continued, beaming now. 'Delilah not only offered me free use of the room upstairs until I get back on my feet, but she said I could join the Dales Detective Agency team. So I guess this is our first staff meeting?'

Delilah was saved from further explanation by the ringing of Nina's phone, the teenager turning away to the window to answer it. A low question and then she was turning back. Expression aghast.

'It's Nathan!' she exclaimed. 'He's found a dead body up at the kiln.'

8

There was a split second of silence and then everyone seemed to move at once. Delilah leaped up from her chair, sending it flying and setting both dogs off barking as she ran for the stairs. Gareth wolfed down the remainder of his sandwich and followed her. While Samson eased himself upright, trying to ignore the red-hot pain in his ribs, and hurried after them as fast as his battered body would allow, Tolpuddle and Bounty outpacing him as he limped down the stairs.

'Tell Nathan we're on our way,' he shouted back at Nina, who was still on the phone.

Down in the hall, the front door was wide open, Delilah and Gareth already at the Mini.

The same Mini which Delilah had been given on an extended loan by Nancy Taylor and which was still a lurid orange. But now, instead of flaunting the Taylor's Estate Agents' logo, the letters DDA were emblazoned along the side. Along with two pink love hearts, intertwined.

Samson stared. 'What . . . ?'

'I'll explain later,' muttered Delilah, throwing him the keys. 'You'll have to drive because I'll still be over the limit.'

'And I'm too busted up,' said Samson, throwing them straight back at her, only for Gareth's huge hand to intercept, plucking the keys from the air.

'I'll be chauffeur,' he said. 'I might as well start earning my keep.'

Samson wasn't in the mood to argue. Nor was he in the mood to squeeze in the back, which Delilah must have sensed because she clambered into the rear without demur, the two dogs jumping in on top of her.

'I hope you're not another Bruncliffe wannabe rally driver,' Samson muttered as he got in and reached for the seatbelt.

Gareth shook his head. 'Safe and steady. Never get anywhere fast once you're dead.'

Dead. The word resonated around the car's interior as they drove away, across the market square towards the Horton Road, and the Hoffmann kiln.

'According to his driver's licence, the deceased is one Ross Irwin,' said Sergeant Clayton, reading the name from his notebook. He flipped it shut and stared at the three people standing before him. Considering they were all faring much better than the body residing in the large kiln to his right, none of them were what you would call a good advertisement for being alive.

Samson O'Brien was covered in cuts and bruises and holding himself like a boxer after going the distance; Delilah Metcalfe looked green around the gills, with the distinct air of someone who'd spent too long in the company of good ale; while her nephew, Nathan, was the colour of a ghost. Understandable when the lad had stumbled upon the unsavoury sight that was the aforementioned Mr Irwin.

The sergeant hadn't relished the sight himself. About to enter Peaks Patisserie when his phone went, he'd had to shelve the prospect of some of Lucy's divine strawberry slices, which she only made during the summer, in order to hightail it up here. Given what had been waiting for him, he was rather glad he'd been interrupted before the purchase and not after. He wasn't going to have the stomach for food for a while.

'And that's as much as we know at the moment,' he concluded. 'So if you'll leave us to get on with our job . . .' He gestured towards his constable, Danny Bradley, in the process of securing the scene with the aid of Gareth Towler, the police tape they were rolling out striking a discordant note against the fellside.

Quite what the gamekeeper was doing in the company of the town's private detectives, the sergeant didn't know. Nor did he want to find out. After the last ten months he'd learned nothing good came of getting involved with the Dales Detective Agency.

'You said Ross Irwin?' Delilah turned to her nephew. 'The ecologist guy?'

Nathan nodded. 'I had my torch on and the first thing I saw when I went in there was his face—' The teenager gulped. Eyes wide. 'He had on that stupid tweed suit he was wearing yesterday. So even with . . . with the injuries . . . I recognised him.'

'Not a nice thing to see,' murmured Samson, putting an arm around him.

'You lot know him then?' continued the sergeant. 'He a friend of yours?'

Delilah shook her head. 'He's . . . he *was* an ecologist,

brought in to do the report for the Dinsdale planning permission. I met him for the first time yesterday. At Harry's wedding reception.'

'Well, he won't be celebrating anything again in this life, that's for sure.'

'Was it natural causes?' asked Samson.

The sergeant stared at him. Felt a twinge in his stomach, a common reaction to being around O'Brien and the stress the man induced. 'I'm hoping so. I'm owed a break after all the excitement around here lately. From what I can see, it looks like he slipped and fell, cracked his head and . . .' He let silence fall, casting a look over his shoulder at the nearest of the arches cut into the stone wall. The dark interior beyond seemed to have taken on an even more sinister aspect than normal. 'I've always hated this place,' he muttered. 'Gave me the creeps as a kid. Don't expect this is going to change things.'

'Sarge!' Danny was calling him over to where he was standing next to the crouched form of Towler. 'You'll want to see this!'

Sergeant Clayton groaned. His constable getting excited about something usually only meant one thing. Trouble. He started making his way across the grass, aware that Samson and Delilah were following. Aware that there was no point in suggesting they stay where they were and leave the policing to him.

'What have you got?' he asked as he reached the two men.

'Here. Look!' Danny was pointing at tracks in the long grass at the outer edge of the clearing. They were parallel. About hip width apart. 'Gareth spotted it.'

'Did he now?' muttered the sergeant as he bent down to get a closer look.

'They go all the way out to that patch of concrete.' Gareth Towler was indicating where the two police cars and the Mini were parked, some distance from the kiln.

Sergeant Clayton turned his head towards the cars and then back towards the kiln. The gamekeeper was right. But the tracks stopped where the long grass gave way to the shorter, rougher vegetation which encircled the stone structure.

'Probably nothing,' he said, getting to his feet.

'Don't be so hasty,' said O'Brien. 'These suggest something heavy was dragged across here recently.'

'Very recently,' added Danny. 'In the last couple of days at least. We had rain before that and I'm thinking that would have flattened out any marks like this.'

'Good point.' The gamekeeper nodded. 'I can get Bounty out to see where they go.' He straightened up, gesturing towards the Mini, Delilah's Weimaraner and a brown spaniel both peering out of the rear window, while two lurchers were tethered to the wing mirror.

'Can she track?' asked Danny, excitedly.

'Sure can. She's got an excellent nose. We've been on a lot of courses together for gamekeeping and she was right good at scenting.' He shrugged. 'It's worth a go.'

They were all looking at the sergeant. Who was shaking his head.

'I'm not letting some mutt run loose across a crime scene,' he growled. 'Not when there's no justification for it. The plain-clothes lot will have my guts for garters.'

'But Sarge—'

Sergeant Clayton raised a hand, forestalling his constable's protests. Then he noticed Delilah Metcalfe. She was staring at the parked cars, forehead knotted in a frown.

'How did our dead guy get up here?' she asked. 'Where's his car?'

'Maybe he walked up?' said the sergeant.

'Nathan,' she called out to her nephew, who'd hung back, as though having had his fill of drama. 'What kind of shoes was Mr Irwin wearing when you found him?'

The lad shuddered. Recalling an image he'd rather not have to revisit. 'Brown brogues. The ones he had on at the wedding.' He walked over to the group of adults. 'Why?'

Delilah looked at the sergeant, eyebrow raised. 'Brogues. For walking up a fellside from town?'

The sergeant had to admit it was odd. Especially as the man had been used to being out on the fells or in rough terrain, given his profession. Hardly likely he'd have tried to negotiate the tricky route in his finery.

'Happen he got a lift.' Even as he said it, Sergeant Clayton knew it was a weak argument. One O'Brien was quick to pounce on.

'And whoever was with him just left him here to die when he had his accident?'

The sergeant sighed. Stared at the car park, at the Mini and the two police cars. Knowing Delilah had hit on an anomaly and wishing she hadn't. Wishing with all his heart he could go back to the moment before he entered Peaks Patisserie and not have his mobile ring.

'Get the damn dog,' he grunted to Gareth. 'But keep it on a long lead and stay back behind the perimeter tape. It's a crime scene and I'm not having your size fourteens crushing evidence.'

Minutes later, Gareth was diligently standing on the far side of the police tape while the brown spaniel, with her nose to the ground, confidently walked across the short grass and straight to the archway where Nathan had found the body. Where she started barking.

'There you have it,' said Gareth. 'Whatever made those tracks ended up in there.'

'Christ!' Sergeant Clayton ran a hand over his face. His stomach rumbled loudly.

'What is it?' asked Nathan. 'What does it mean?'

'Seems someone dragged something heavy across here recently,' said Samson. 'Which could suggest that Mr Irwin's death wasn't as natural as we thought.'

'Because a dead man doesn't tend to drag himself to his final resting place,' said Danny.

'Murder?' The boy's voice rose, horror in the tone. 'You think he was murdered?'

The sergeant turned to him. 'What I think, young man, is none of this is cut and dried. We'll have a better grasp of what went on once the forensics lot have had a look around. But in the meantime,' he continued, focusing on Delilah, 'it might help if we could locate this Mr Irwin's car. And find out who was the last person he was seen with. Any ideas?'

'Thing is . . .' she began, shamefaced. 'I don't really have a good recollection of events from yesterday—' She stopped. Gasped. Hand going to her mouth. 'A black Toyota Land Cruiser.'

'That's what Irwin drove?'

She nodded.

'And how,' asked Sergeant Clayton, his guts tightening even further, 'do you know that?'

Delilah was looking at Samson now, face stricken. And Sergeant Clayton knew he'd been right. Nothing was ever straightforward when the Dales Detective Agency was involved.

Joseph and Arty had been out of luck. They'd just turned into Back Street when the orange Mini had come driving towards them, Gareth Towler at the wheel, Samson beside him and what looked like Delilah in the back. Although it was hard to be sure, as there was a lot of Weimaraner and spaniel pressed up against the rear window, blocking the view.

'Bugger!' Arty had muttered as they watched the car go past.

'Samson's home!' exclaimed Joseph.

Arty managed a smile, pleased for his friend, who hadn't complained once over the past few months about the absence of his son, despite having missed him.

'Was I imagining things,' Joseph continued, 'or did he look like he'd been in a fight?'

'Probably Delilah welcoming him back, seeing as he was late for the wedding.' Arty's dry response drew a laugh.

They'd stood there for a few moments, looking down the street, past the gaudy display of colourful buckets and bowls outside Plastic Fantastic to the three-storey building that housed the Dales Detective Agency.

'So, what now?' said Joseph. 'No point going to the office if neither Samson nor Delilah are there.'

'Let's get a coffee while we wait,' Arty had suggested.

And so they'd retraced their steps to Peaks Patisserie, pleased to find that, fresh out of church, Edith Hird and

Clarissa Ralph were already seated at a table near the window, Eric Bradley sitting next to them, the ever-present oxygen cylinder by his side. The two sisters smiled as the men entered, immediately beckoning them over.

'I can highly recommend the raspberry and chocolate tarts,' said Clarissa, beaming.

'And order a fresh pot of tea while you're at it. We've had to endure a rather long sermon and are in need of resuscitation!' Edith added.

Having done as commanded and with the tarts now reduced to nothing more than a few crumbs on Joseph and Arty's plates, the pensioners were discussing the topic which had gripped them most of late.

'How hard can it be to identify an owner of something as big as a retirement complex?' Arty grumbled.

'Very hard, if they choose to hide behind shell companies and the like.' Edith patted his hand. 'I'm sure Delilah has been doing all she can to get to the bottom of it.'

'I don't understand why you're getting so het up about it, Arty,' said Clarissa. 'After all, nothing is going to change. We'll all just keep living as we are. Won't we, Edith?'

Edith caught Arty's eye. Having a more cynical take on life than her younger sister, for whom life had a perpetual rosy tint, Edith Hird knew how things could change, depending on the nature of whoever had bought the premises the pensioners called home.

'Let's hope so,' she said. Her fingers closed briefly around Arty's, and for a moment he felt all his troubles fade away in the pleasure of her touch.

'In the meantime,' said Eric, 'what time is this thing tomorrow?'

'Tomorrow?' Arty looked at his four friends in puzzlement.

'The Silver Solos Afternoon Tea,' chirped Clarissa. 'It starts at three, so I suggest we get there at least half an hour early.'

Arty groaned. He'd completely forgotten. Part of a new initiative Delilah had started through her dating agency, this would be the second speed-dating event aimed at those of more mature years. Which, having been a reluctant participant at the first one, Arty could attest needed to be renamed, as there'd been nothing speedy about the movement of the men around the room as they changed seats between dates.

'Are you going?' he asked.

Clarissa nodded. 'Of course! Most of Fellside Court will be there. Eric's coming as well, and Joseph, too. Aren't you, lads?'

Eric nodded. 'Although I have to confess, I'm only going for the cake!'

The group laughed.

'And you, Joseph?' asked Arty.

The Irishman gave a shy smile. 'Nothing better to do on a Monday afternoon,' he said, 'so I don't see the harm in tagging along.'

Arty could see the harm. In the mood he was in, he wasn't the best company. Certainly not up for making small talk with a bunch of ladies who'd be hoping for a charming afternoon and instead would be faced with a churlish old man beset with worries.

'Well, I for one will not be going,' said Edith, reaching for her teacup. 'Much as I appreciate the effort Delilah has gone to in setting up these events, I'd really rather spend my time in the company of friends.' She took a sip, watching Arty over the rim.

As if she knew. As if she sensed that he was carrying around a burden he really needed help with. A burden he suddenly realised he desperately needed to share with someone. Because the options facing him at the moment were drastic, one in particular even on the wrong side of legal. And it was looking like that was the one he was going to have to take.

'In that case,' he said, with the same measured tone, 'I might stay in and keep you company.'

'Can I get you anything else?' Elaine Bullock was standing at the end of the table, apron strings hanging loose, her plaits coming undone and a general air of distraction about her, even more so than normal. She was looking out of the window as she spoke, frowning.

'That's the third one in a few minutes!' Clarissa was also looking out of the window as a police car sped past across the cobbles, heading towards Church Street. 'Something must be going on.'

'Something big if they've called in support from outside,' said Eric. 'I saw Sergeant Clayton take off that way just as I arrived here.'

'No one's been in and said owt?' Arty asked Elaine.

She shook her head, clearing plates as she spoke. 'Not that I know of. Probably some walker in need of assistance—'

'*What?!* When?' Lucy's shocked tones cut across the cafe, a silence descending as everyone turned to see her on her mobile looking distraught. 'Is he okay?'

She was nodding, then she was looking at Elaine, eyes wide as her hand went to her apron pocket. And she was pulling out the set of keys Arty and Joseph had given her, the unusual green keyring dangling from her fingers.

She lowered the mobile. The call over. 'That ecologist, Ross Irwin,' she said in shocked tones. 'Nathan found him up at the Hoffmann kiln. He's dead!'

A gasp went around the cafe, but Lucy was oblivious.

'They're now looking for his car,' she continued, still staring at her friend. Who in turn was staring at the green keyring in Lucy's hand. The kind of keyring someone into nature would have had.

The plates Elaine had been holding fell in a clatter to the floor.

9

'I didn't kill him.' Elaine Bullock was sitting at the desk in the ground-floor office of the Dales Detective Agency, hands clenched in her lap, eyes massive behind the smudged lenses of her glasses. An untouched mug of tea was in front of her. 'I swear. He was alive when I left him.'

Delilah reached across and took her friend's hand in hers, offering reassurance she didn't necessarily feel. Because things weren't looking good.

'Thing is, Elaine,' said Sergeant Clayton gently, 'we've got a dead man up at the kiln and witnesses who say you were the last person to be seen with him. Being driven off from Harry's wedding in Irwin's Land Cruiser.'

'That doesn't mean I killed him!' she said, her voice rising in pitch with each word.

Each word making Delilah feel even more of a traitor. Because it was her recollection of that flash of red hurrying across the rugby club car park to the Toyota 4x4 which had landed Elaine in this situation. And having accompanied Sergeant Clayton to the interview after he dropped Nathan back into town – the sergeant of the opinion that Delilah's presence might make Elaine more willing to open up about whatever had transpired the evening before – Delilah's initial confidence that her friend couldn't possibly be caught up in Irwin's death was starting to waver.

In fact, she was convinced Elaine was hiding something.

'No one thinks you killed him,' she said. 'We're just trying to get to the bottom of what happened.'

Elaine nodded. 'It's like I told you. We'd agreed to go out to Malham today but after the fracas with Will at the reception, I felt bad for Irwin so I suggested we go right away. We drove out there. Saw a peregrine falcon. And then he drove me home. End of story.'

'And what time did he drop you back in town?' asked the sergeant.

'I couldn't say for sure. About nine?'

'At your place?'

Another nod.

'You didn't invite him in for a coffee or a glass of something?'

'It wasn't a date,' Elaine muttered.

The sergeant raised his hands in appeasement. 'I wasn't implying it was. Just want to check when you saw him last.'

'When he drove off from mine, fit and well.'

'At which point,' said the sergeant, 'someone must have got into Irwin's car, drove him up to the kiln, killed him and then abandoned his 4x4 at the top of the High Street with the keys still in it.' He stared at Elaine.

She stared back at him.

And Delilah knew she was lying.

It had been a while since Samson O'Brien had been present at the processing of a murder scene. Because that's how the death of this Ross Irwin was being treated now.

A murder. With Elaine Bullock possibly mixed up in it all.

He watched as a procession of people filed in and out of the kiln, white-suited, focused, a well-rehearsed team used to dealing with crime of this nature, even if their investigations normally took them to less glorious places.

It all felt so incongruous against the backdrop of the green fells rising from behind a small copse of trees, the grey lines of stone walls intersecting them, and the sun streaming down.

'Not quite the welcome home you were hoping for, I bet,' said Danny Bradley, standing at the cordon, the young constable having been given the unenviable task of guarding the scene.

Samson grunted. It had definitely been an odd home-coming, even before Nathan's gruesome discovery. What with the shock of finding a man in his bed, a night spent trying to sleep on the boards of Seth's shed and then the second shock of walking into the office building to find Gareth Towler sporting nothing more than a towel . . . And before he could really get his head around any of it, here he was, witnessing the start of a murder investigation.

'Is it always this clinical?' Gareth had moved over to where they were standing, Bounty at his heels, the dog looking wary at all the commotion on the other side of the police tape.

'It's supposed to be,' said Samson. 'Takes a bit of getting used to, though. Seeing death as something to be analysed rather than mourned.'

A car door slammed shut in the background and Bounty flinched, cowering against Gareth's leg. He put a large hand down to her head, murmuring to her.

'She still jittery?' asked Danny, bending down to pet the spaniel, too.

Gareth nodded. 'Herriot reckons she won't ever recover. We make a fine pair between us – Bounty no longer any use as a gun dog and me no longer holding the necessary licence to be a gamekeeper.'

The words were accompanied by a lopsided grin, but Samson could see the strain beneath the attempted levity. The man had lost his profession and his home thanks to a shoot which had gone catastrophically wrong, his dog caught up in the middle of it. At least when Samson's world had been turned upside down fifteen years ago, it had been his own choice. He'd left Bruncliffe behind of his own volition.

'What will you do now?' Danny asked, straightening up.

'God knows. Delilah's been good enough to offer me a temporary solution while I try to get things sorted but other than that . . . Gamekeeping is all I've ever known.' Gareth cast a hand at the landscape around them. 'Work long enough in this and it gets under your skin. So now I can't imagine working anywhere else, which narrows the options somewhat.'

'There's always farming,' offered Samson, with a grin.

Gareth laughed. 'No way. Judging by the amount of moaning the farmers around here do, it must be a hellish profession.'

'Careful,' quipped Danny, also grinning. 'Samson might be going back into farming before we know it, what with the sale coming up.'

Samson turned to the young constable, puzzled. 'Sale? What sale—?'

'DC O'Brien! I thought that was you beneath the

bruises!' A tall figure was striding towards them on the official side of the tape, pulling the hood of his white over-suit down as he approached. A tussle of fair hair appeared above a youthful face Samson instantly recognised.

As did Danny. 'Damn it,' he murmured, looking from the man to Samson and back again. 'I don't need any trouble!'

'Why would there be trouble?' asked Gareth, confused.

'Because,' said Samson as he took the hand being offered across the tape, 'this is DC Josh Benson. And the last time he turned up in Bruncliffe, he dragged me away in handcuffs in front of everyone.'

'No hard feelings?' the detective said with a sheepish look.

'None. You were just doing your job. Admittedly with a bit of extra vigour.'

'Not all of which I was comfortable with.' Benson looked down at his feet and then back up at Samson. 'Cooper was out of line. I should have said something at the time.'

'Hindsight is easy. And besides, he thought I was a corrupt copper,' said Samson, with more magnanimity than he felt. The memory of being hauled out of Peaks Patisserie by DS Steve Cooper still burned. 'Is he with you today?'

Benson shook his head. 'He quit – basically he jumped ship before it sank. They found out it was him who leaked the news of your suspension to the press.'

A flash of anger burned through Samson, his fists curling, causing Danny to take a wary step towards the pair. Cooper's actions back in March had resulted in a front-page article in the local paper which had almost wrecked Samson's life. The unfounded allegations implying he was connected to a drugs ring had given plenty of fuel to the folk in Bruncliffe who'd long held suspicions about the O'Brien lad. Even Delilah had thrown him out. Then welcomed him back in when the town turned against him, refusing to just follow the crowd.

The thought of her stubbornness made him smile. Removed the tension.

'I'm guessing you're not missing him much,' he said, hands relaxing, Danny's shoulders dropping in relief.

Benson grinned. 'Not a bit. Especially since I'm now the DS.' Samson laughed while the detective gestured at the vivid colour gracing Samson's cheek. 'I heard you were back on the job. Is that a by-product of a case?'

'Hazards of the trade,' said Samson with a shrug, his ribs immediately reminding him that they were on the injury list too. 'What about you? This is a bit of a step up from wrongly arresting a fellow officer.'

'Sure is!' Benson's grin grew wider before he tipped his chin in the direction of the kiln and fell serious. 'Not sure I'd have chosen this as my first case as sergeant, though.'

'What have you got so far?'

The question sounded innocuous but the newly appointed DS was no fool. He knew he was being probed. He glanced at Danny and then at Gareth, as if weighing them up.

'He discovered the tracks that got you lot involved in the first place,' said Samson, indicating the gamekeeper, 'and contrary to his youthful appearance,' he continued, looking at Danny, his uniform dwarfing his lanky frame, 'I'll put money on Constable Bradley here being your DI in less than a decade.'

Danny blushed. Benson raised an eyebrow. Glanced back at the kiln and then nodded.

'Might be no harm to have some outside input, because

it's all a bit of a puzzle so far. As you suspected, preliminary findings suggest that the deceased didn't die here. Not just the drag marks in the grass and the absence of his car, but the lack of blood at the scene. There's no sign of a struggle either.'

'How did he die?' asked Danny.

'Too early to say for certain but he's taken blows to both sides of his head and the rear, which suggests it was more than just a fall. And the initial estimation is that, however he died, it happened sometime early evening yesterday.'

'While the wedding reception was still going on,' said Gareth, looking at Samson.

'The wedding of this . . . Harry Furness?' Benson was consulting a notebook he'd pulled out of his pocket. He looked at Danny. 'A list of everyone who was there would be a great help, Constable Bradley. Might enable us to rule out potential suspects.'

Danny nodded, making rapid notes of his own.

'And this Elaine Bullock being interviewed by Sergeant Clayton,' continued Benson. 'What do we know about her?'

'She wouldn't have done it.' Samson's words came out with the conviction of having known her all his life.

'Well, at the moment, things aren't looking good for her. As far as we know, she was the last person to see Irwin alive, so you'd think she'd be eager to get her story across. But I've just had a call from the sergeant and he reckons she's not telling the truth.'

Gareth shook his head. 'No way it's Elaine. She's strong-minded and full of character but she's not a killer.'

'Sarge!' Another detective in a forensic suit came hurrying

over, a plastic bag in each hand, an excitement about the woman that Samson recognised. They'd found something. Something which could be pivotal to the case.

Peaks Patisserie was packed. What had been a quiet Sunday morning was now mayhem, every table filled with folk wanting to catch up with what was going on in the heart of their community. And contrary to Lucy's earlier prediction, it wasn't the sale of the Taylor place which was gripping them, the 'For Sale' sign at the top of the square having barely drawn comment. Which wasn't surprising when there was a murder to discuss.

Judging by the volume of chatter in the cafe, the news of the ecologist's death was providing plenty of talking points. And it seemed these animated conversations demanded scones and cakes and quiche and sausages rolls to fuel them, not to mention endless pots of tea. With orders coming in thick and fast, Lucy – unexpectedly a waitress down – had resorted to calling in reinforcements.

'You're a lifesaver, Peggy,' she said, wiping the back of her hand across her brow in a rare lull as she addressed her mother-in-law. 'I'd have been besieged without you.'

Apron wrapped around her waist, sleeves rolled up, Peggy Metcalfe dismissed the thanks with a wave of her hand and a smile. 'I couldn't have left you to deal with this on your own.'

'Still, it's a Sunday . . .' Lucy said guiltily, knowing how much the Metcalfe clan treasured their weekly get-together over a roast dinner up at Ellershaw.

'What use is family if you can't call on them in your hour of need?' demanded Peggy. 'Besides, now I have an excuse for being down among the excitement, without anyone being able to accuse me of prying!'

Excitement was one word for it. The town was abuzz, the once empty marketplace humming with folk conveniently finding the need to pop into the newsagents or go up to the Spar for some essential groceries. All the while, craning their necks to see what was happening at the other end of the square.

For Lucy's premonition had been correct when Delilah called to tell her what Nathan had discovered, and that the search was on for the ecologist's missing vehicle. The plant-cell keyring Joseph and Arty had brought to the cafe earlier that morning belonged to Ross Irwin and it was his Toyota 4x4 which had been left abandoned in Lucy's usual parking space. As a consequence, the High Street had been closed off, an event not having been experienced in Bruncliffe since Clive Knowles' father, Ralph, had managed to lose an entire flock of sheep out of the back of his trailer while on the way to market. There'd been sheep everywhere and a lot of complaining about the state of the town's cobbles once the errant ewes had all been captured.

This time it was all a lot more official. And a lot more serious.

Police tape had been strung across the road from Wilson's outdoor-clothing shop to a lamp post opposite, and a second barrier created with yet more tape running from the corner of Rice N Spice to the Coach and Horses on the other side of High Street. In between the two was the black Toyota, still slewed badly into the kerb, but now the focus of intense scrutiny by a crowd of white-suited police officers.

And as the large windows of Peaks Patisserie offered a

fine view of this part of town, Lucy was doing a roaring trade. Which didn't feel right, considering her friend was embroiled in all the drama.

'Has there been any word from Elaine?' Peggy asked, reading Lucy's thoughts.

Lucy shook her head. 'Not a peep. But at least she's got Delilah in there with her.'

'No one better,' affirmed Peggy, with more than a hint of maternal pride. 'As long as Elaine tells the truth, she'll be fine. Because we all know she's innocent.'

Lucy watched the police working the scene, reluctant to dwell too long on Peggy's assertion. Because there was a small part of her that was very worried. Worried because she'd known her friend was hiding something from the moment she walked in the cafe that morning.

Outside, there was a flurry of movement behind the cordon, several of the officers collecting at the driver's side of the car, the sense of anticipation about them setting off yet more fervid conversation in the cafe.

They'd discovered something. Something important.

Lucy just hoped it was nothing connected to Elaine Bullock.

10

A feather and a tobacco tin. Standing in front of the imposing structure of the Hoffmann kiln, Samson wasn't sure about the first, but he recognised the second.

'That belongs to my godson, Nathan Metcalfe,' he said, indicating the evidence bag in DS Benson's left hand, the Yorkshire Regiment emblem an easy spot. 'He lost it up here yesterday evening and came looking for it this morning. Found a bit more than he bargained for.'

'The teenager who discovered the body? He's your godson?' Benson was frowning, no doubt marvelling at the network of connections that joined the people of Bruncliffe, tying them to each other through the past and into the future. Amused to be considered part of it for once, Samson nodded.

Benson looked at the tin then at Danny. 'What time did the lad say he left here yesterday?'

'Erm . . . about ten p.m.,' said the constable, consulting his notebook. 'He says he was here with a friend for a school history project. They watched the sunset and then the friend left and he stayed on. Until about ten.'

'So he was here alone for a substantial time. Who was the friend?'

'Nina Hussain. Another teenager. She lives in town.'

Samson took the information on board. Wondering whether 'friend' really conveyed what the relationship between the two teens was. Wondering too why Nina would have upped and left Nathan here all alone.

'Interesting.' Benson looked at Samson. 'We found the tin under the body.'

'So you can narrow down the timescale, then. Irwin was brought up here some time after Nathan left.'

'Possibly.' The word was left hanging, along with the doubt it contained.

'You can save your time,' said Samson, sensing that the detective was considering another scenario. One that involved Nathan in a role of more than just unsuspecting bystander. 'The lad didn't have anything to do with this.'

'Sorry, O'Brien, but I'm keeping my options open. Particularly as Nathan is Will Metcalfe's nephew, am I right?' The detective was looking at Danny, who nodded uncomfortably.

'What's Will got to do with this?' asked Samson, feeling like he was on the back foot all of a sudden.

'The fight,' muttered Gareth. 'At the wedding yesterday. Will took exception to something Ross Irwin said. Went for him big style. They had to be pulled apart.'

'Were you there?' Benson asked. The gamekeeper nodded. 'And what about you, O'Brien?'

Samson shook his head. Wishing he had been now, more than ever. Because it sounded like Elaine Bullock wasn't going to be the only one answering awkward questions over the next few days. At least one of the Metcalfes would be, too.

'What about this? Anyone recognise it?'

Benson was holding out the second evidence bag. The feather inside was the length of his hand, finely shaped with a delicate brown hue and shading like the back of a mackerel.

'May I?' Gareth Towler reached for the bag and peered at the contents. 'Peregrine falcon feather,' he said. His tone brooking no queries.

The detective raised an eyebrow and Gareth grinned.

'I'm a gamekeeper,' he explained. 'Or I was until recently. And unlike some in my profession, I took an interest in protecting the wildlife on my patch, so I know my raptors. I can tell you now, that's a peregrine falcon wing feather. Not something you'd find around Bruncliffe.'

'So where would you find one?'

'At Malham Cove, most likely, across the fells.' Gareth gestured past the kiln to the land rising up in the east. 'The peregrines don't tend to stray over this side.'

Benson frowned, turning to the female detective next to him. 'Best give a shout to the Wildlife Crime unit, just to be on the safe side. Don't want to go trampling on their patch if this whole thing turns out to have a connection to those falcons. Maybe Irwin saw something he shouldn't have or stumbled on some kind of raptor crime. We could probably do with their input anyway.'

'Yes, Sarge.' She hurried back across the fellside, mobile already at her ear.

'Where did you find the feather?' asked Samson.

'In Irwin's left hand,' said Benson. 'He must have been holding it when he was killed.'

'Which means . . .' Danny's comment faded into silence.

'Which means it's seeming more likely that Irwin was killed over in Malham, probably while birdwatching as he had a pair of binoculars strung around his neck. And that fits in with what you've said, Constable Bradley, about where he was going the last time he was seen.' Benson looked at Samson. 'This Elaine Bullock has got a lot of questions to answer. Care to come along and sit in while I talk to her?'

'In what capacity? Fellow detective or friend of the suspect?' Samson asked wryly.

Benson shrugged. 'Whichever one helps us get to the bottom of this.'

Curiosity getting the better of him, Samson nodded.

'Great. And when we've questioned Elaine we can find Will Metcalfe and get his side of the story.'

Samson suppressed a groan while Danny and Gareth shot him sympathetic glances. Having only just managed to establish a relationship with the oldest of the Metcalfe siblings, it looked like circumstances were about to ruin it all over again. Because whatever steps had been made to mend fences, being part of an investigation into murder which had Will as its focus was bound to put Samson back to square one.

The downstairs office of the Dales Detective Agency was getting crowded. And Sergeant Clayton's informal questioning of Elaine seemed to have taken on a more official tone.

As Ida and Delilah brought down a couple of the kitchen chairs to accommodate the extra bodies, Ida was muttering about it.

'Wasting good investigating time, they are,' she grumbled.

'That lass couldn't kill a fly, let alone a man the size of Irwin. They've got it all wrong.'

Delilah's instinct was to agree, but as she entered the office and saw Samson's face, cold fingers of fear clutched her chest. Standing over by the window, he was watching Elaine with an expression of intense worry.

'More chairs,' Delilah announced, trying to lighten the mood.

The tall detective thanked her, taking the chairs and placing them beside the desk, where Elaine and Sergeant Clayton were still sitting. Delilah had recognised him the moment he'd appeared in the office doorway. One of the two coppers who'd dragged Samson away in such spectacularly embarrassing fashion, handcuffing him in front of his father, humiliating him in front of his community. While Samson seemed to have forgiven the man, Delilah was made from different stock. It would take some doing for DS Benson to get back in her good books.

'Tea?' Ida offered, to nods all round.

'Not too strong for me, please,' added Benson, with a warm smile.

Ida shot Delilah a look, and Delilah knew she wasn't the only one holding a grudge. Whatever the next hour held, the highlight was going to be watching the detective drinking his brew.

'So,' began Benson, 'Elaine, there have been a few developments—'

'Do I need a lawyer?' Elaine tossed her plaits over her shoulder, looking defiant. But Delilah recognised the small tic in her right cheek and the fingers knotted around each other in her lap. She was nervous.

Sergeant Clayton shook his head. 'No need for that, lass. Just tell us exactly what happened yesterday and we can all get on and find the real killer.'

Elaine looked around the room, Samson still standing by the window, Benson and the sergeant opposite her, Delilah by her side. She glanced at her hands, bit her lip and then stared at Benson. 'You're wasting your time. Nothing untoward happened. Irwin was alive when I last saw him.'

'So you're sticking with what you told the sergeant? That you visited Malham Cove with Irwin, saw a falcon and then he drove you home about nine?'

She nodded. Hesitant. Sensing the trap that was coming.

'In that case, I've just a couple of things to run past you. Firstly, this.' Benson placed a plastic bag on the desk, a flash of light reflecting off the silver hoop inside. Delilah recognised it immediately. One of the earrings Elaine had been wearing at the wedding the day before.

'Is this yours?' the detective asked, manner still gentle.

Elaine's left hand lifted to her ear, as though of its own accord. 'Erm . . . yes, I think so. I lost it yesterday.'

'Can you tell me how you lost it? Because there's blood on the stem and I can't help noticing that your ear has been bleeding.'

There was a silence, Elaine swallowing, her already pale face turning ashen. 'I . . . erm . . . I snagged my hand in it when I was brushing my hair out of my eyes. Up at the Cove.'

Benson nodded. As though she'd answered well. But then he frowned. 'Thing is, Elaine, we didn't find it up at the Cove. We found it in Ross Irwin's car. In the footwell on the driver's side. And the other interesting thing is that whoever drove that car last, it wasn't Irwin. The seat was left too far forward for a man of his size. In fact, I'd go so far as to suggest it was driven by someone about your height.'

'Maybe he moved the seat,' said Elaine, her voice shaking.

'Maybe.' Benson's tone seemed to get even more considerate. 'Problem is, we found this in Irwin's hand up at the kiln.' He put another plastic bag on the desk, this one containing a brown feather. 'It's from a peregrine falcon, but then you probably know that. In fact, I think you saw Ross Irwin pick this up when you were at Malham Cove. Now, the reason this is interesting is that the pathologist reckons Irwin was clutching it when he was killed, which suggests to me that he was killed over in Malham. So you can see why we're having difficulty with accepting your version of events. Because if Irwin was already dead, who drove you home?'

Elaine seemed to shrink in the chair. A low moan of pain coming from her. Delilah put a hand on her arm, the skin cold to the touch.

'Whatever happened, Elaine,' she murmured, 'it's best to tell them now.'

Best to tell them, because even through the fug of her abating hangover Delilah could see the skill with which Benson was wielding his evidence, luring Elaine in by making the main focus of his questions her journey home rather than the murder of Irwin. The man was a first-rate detective and would unearth the truth in the end.

'I . . . I didn't kill him,' whispered Elaine, the defiance gone now, replaced with fear. 'He was alive when I left him.'

'You left him at Malham Cove?' asked Sergeant Clayton.

'Up above it,' she clarified in a quiet voice. 'He parked just below the tarn, intending for us to walk down on the Pennine Way. When I suggested it was a bit of a trek and we'd be best driving down to the village and walking up the road, especially as he didn't have the most suitable of shoes on, he just laughed. Said he'd be fine and that he'd rather a bit of discomfort than have to fight the hordes of day-trippers down in the dale. That it would be more peaceful this way.'

The sergeant nodded, knowing, as did every local in the room, that Malham during tourist season could be a bottleneck of traffic and pedestrians. 'So is that what you did?'

'Yes. We reached the tops above the cove and he took photos. And then we saw the falcon.' She gave a small smile. 'It was magnificent. And Irwin was right, we had it all to ourselves, no one else up there with us.'

'So what happened next? Did you have an argument?'

The question brought a flush of colour back to her cheeks, a spark of temper making her snort. 'That's not what I'd call it. He assaulted me.' She grimaced. 'Or tried to.'

She gestured at the feather, revulsion on her face.

'He found that on the grass and got all excited about it. Then, under the pretence of showing it to me, he made a grab to kiss me. When I protested and tried to push him away, he got rough. His hand was around the back of my neck, pulling me towards him. That's when my earring must have come loose.'

'So what did you do?' asked Benson.

'I kneed him where it hurts,' Elaine snapped. 'Then I shoved him away from me. He lost his footing in his stupid brogues and fell to the ground, hitting his head on a rock. I saw his car keys fall out of his pocket so I snatched them up and ran.'

'What time was this?'

'About ten past eight.' She gave the detective a sardonic look. 'Sorry I can't be more exact but I was running too fast to check.'

'And you drove back in his Toyota, leaving him up there?'

'Yes.' Elaine had her head up now, chin tipped defiantly. 'I left his car on High Street and walked home.'

'Did you leave the keys in the ignition deliberately?'

She nodded. 'I was hoping it might teach him a lesson. Seems like someone else taught him an even harder one.'

Her words fell into a tense silence, finally broken by a long sigh from Sergeant Clayton. He ran a hand over his face.

'Christ, lass, why didn't you come straight to the station and report it?'

'I was angry. At Irwin for behaving in that way. But at myself too, for misjudging him. That's why he'd wanted to stay above the Cove, so he could get me alone. He wasn't interested in my take on the geology of the area.' She shook her head. 'I guess I didn't want everyone knowing I'd been taken for a fool. So I thought taking his car would be punishment enough. Then when I heard the news that he was . . . that someone had . . .' She gulped. 'I didn't think the truth would help my case. After all, I've just given myself a motive, haven't I?'

'That all depends,' said Benson. 'When you ran off, what state was Irwin in?'

Elaine let out a mirthless laugh. 'He'd cut his head but

he was very much alive because he was shouting obscenities after me. But I suppose that's just my word against that of a dead man.'

11

Elaine's testimony left a strained silence in the room and Samson was sure he wasn't the only one relieved to see Ida walk in, a laden tray in her hands.

'Tea,' she announced, placing mugs on the desk along with a plate of biscuits. Then, to DS Benson's visible amazement, she took a seat on the vacant chair the other side of Delilah.

'So,' she said, glaring at the detective, 'has tha figured out this lass isn't capable of murder yet? Or is tha going to handcuff her and take her in anyroads, like tha did with Samson?'

Benson blushed. Reached for his tea to cover his embarrassment, took a swig and started coughing.

'Aye, lad,' continued Ida, 'tha's in the Dales now. Happen we like our tea strong and our motives for arrest even stronger.'

Elaine gave Ida a grateful glance, the geologist noticeably shaken after telling her version of events.

'I appreciate your concern Mrs . . . ?' Benson raised an enquiring eyebrow as he placed the mug back on the desk.

'Ida,' came the sharp reply.

'Ida,' he continued, 'but we have to follow up leads in

every case. Elaine was possibly the last person to see Ross Irwin alive and, as such, she's an important witness.'

'Well, make sure that's what she stays,' muttered Ida, her words aimed at the sergeant this time. 'Tha's known her all her life, Gavin Clayton. Don't let fancy theories twist what tha knows in tha gut!'

Sergeant Clayton scratched his head and leaned back in his chair, so unsettled by Elaine's revelations, he hadn't even reached for a biscuit. 'I'm not doubting the lass when she says what Irwin tried to do,' he said. 'But facts don't lie. And we've got a dead body up at the kiln that wasn't killed there. So we're looking for someone who had motive and opportunity to commit murder and then transport the deceased from one dale to another. Unfortunately, Elaine's timings fit the scenario we're envisaging.'

The sergeant didn't say it out loud, but Samson knew he was also thinking that, as Elaine had predicted, she'd dug her own grave with her testimony. She'd now shown she'd had opportunity and motive in abundance.

But Samson was inclined to side with Ida when it came to Elaine Bullock. He didn't see her as capable of murder. And there was something niggling him about the scene she'd painted for them. Something that didn't tie in with what they already knew.

'What about Irwin's car?' Delilah was asking. 'If Elaine did use it to transport the body, surely there'd be evidence of that in the boot. Bloodstains or the like?'

Elaine shuddered while Benson just nodded.

'We're onto it. And believe me, if there's anything there, the forensic team will find it.' He turned to Elaine. 'Have you got anyone who can corroborate the time you returned home?'

'An alibi?' she asked with a wry smile. 'No. Everyone was still at Harry's wedding getting drunk. I walked home alone. I sat on my couch drinking brandy alone. And I spent the remainder of the evening cursing Irwin and every predatory man like him, all without a single witness.'

Delilah's arm went around her friend. 'I'm so sorry,' she murmured. 'I should have been there. I hate the thought of you having to deal with that on your own.'

'Instead, from what I hear, you were dancing on tables,' said Elaine with an attempt at a smile.

'Aye, and young Nathan has video footage to prove it,' added Ida. She said it to help lighten the atmosphere, which it did. But it also sent a jolt through Samson.

'Nathan!' he exclaimed, pushing himself off the windowsill where he'd been leaning throughout, and advancing towards the desk. 'What time did he say he was up at the kiln?'

Sergeant Clayton studied his notes. 'Nina Hussain was there until around nine and then Nathan lingered on. He thinks it was about ten when he left.'

'That's it!' Samson looked at Benson. 'The tobacco tin. That's Elaine's alibi!'

'Want to fill the rest of us in?' asked Delilah, her gaze switching between Samson and the detective.

'Nathan went back up to the kiln this morning to find his dad's tobacco tin, which he lost last night,' said Samson, Delilah nodding. 'The forensics team found it under Irwin's body.'

'*Under* it?' Her eyes lit up.

Sergeant Clayton wasn't so quick to follow. 'And what does that have to do with anything?'

'Elaine says she got home around nine. Nathan didn't leave the kiln for at least another hour. Which would suggest,' Samson explained, 'that whoever dumped Irwin up there, they did it *after* Nathan left. How else would his tobacco tin have ended up under the body?'

'So I'm in the clear?' asked Elaine, focus on Benson.

But the detective was shaking his head. 'I accept what you're saying, O'Brien, and it's definitely worth considering. That tobacco tin certainly narrows down our timeline somewhat, meaning that the perpetrator didn't visit the kiln until after nine o'clock, but in terms of being in the clear, Elaine, it would really help if you could provide concrete verification of the time you arrived home. And that you stayed there for the rest of the night.'

Elaine's shoulders drooped. 'Right,' she muttered.

'Nine o'clock?' queried Delilah, staring at Benson. 'Why did you say the perpetrator must have arrived at the kiln after nine? Surely it would have been after ten, when Nathan left?'

Benson didn't answer. Just left the gap for Delilah to fill in, which she did with a gasp.

'You're joking?' she exclaimed. 'You can't seriously be thinking that Nathan's involved?'

Ida swivelled round in her chair, mouth open. 'Tha's taken leave of tha senses, lad!' she declared as Benson held up his hands at their protests.

'Nathan Metcalfe is a person of interest,' he said. 'He was up at the kiln on his own at a time when the body could have been placed there. We have to consider all the scenarios in which his tobacco tin ended up where it did.'

'But why?' demanded Delilah. 'What earthly reason would Nathan have for getting involved in the murder of Ross Irwin?'

'To help his uncle, Will,' said Benson, calmly. 'A man who was overheard threatening Ross Irwin on the very day he was killed.'

Delilah's jaw dropped and Samson knew she was feeling the same as him. No matter how they looked at it, this case was going to end up hurting someone they cared about.

They let Elaine go, although DS Benson left no one under the impression that she was out of the woods. Refusing Delilah's offer to walk her home, the geologist, while visibly upset after recounting what had transpired the day before, insisted on going back to work at Peaks Patisserie. The door had only just closed behind her when Sergeant Clayton let out a long sigh.

'If only the lass had reported what happened, she could have avoided all this.'

'Not necessarily,' said Samson. 'After all, Elaine now has a motive for manslaughter, if not murder.'

Benson was staring at the feather in the evidence bag. He looked up at the concerned faces opposite him. 'Is she telling the truth?'

Samson nodded. 'I'd stake my life on it. Elaine's not one for lying. And what she described is exactly what I'd expect from her in that situation. As for why she didn't report it, she probably thought there was no point.' He turned to Sergeant Clayton. 'I mean, honestly, what would you have done if she had?'

'Had a stern word with the bugger,' grunted the sergeant.

Delilah gave a derisive snort. 'And Elaine would have been dragged into it. A classic he-said-she-said scenario, between a young woman just starting out in her university career and an established and respected expert in his field. I'm sure that would have gone through her mind. Not to mention her upcoming field trip to Monument Valley. After saving for years to be able to go, she wouldn't have wanted anything to put that in jeopardy.'

Benson dropped his gaze back down to the feather, not looking convinced. And, to Delilah's mind, beginning to look a bit out of his depth. His first murder enquiry as DS was already proving to be far from straightforward. When his mobile rang, he picked it up like a drowning man thrown a rope.

'Tell me you've got news,' he muttered into the phone. Then he nodded, frowned. Nodded again. 'Notify the search teams over in Malham and send everything from Irwin's car off to the lab anyway. And keep looking.'

He hung up and found himself surrounded by expectant expressions.

'That was my DC,' he said slowly. 'According to initial observations at the scene, the pathologist thinks the weapon used to inflict one of the blows to Irwin is cylindrical in shape. Like a rolling pin.' He grimaced. 'Not exactly a lot to go on but it's all we have for now. And as for Irwin's car, my team have found no traces of blood in the boot nor on the rear seats.'

Delilah let out a relieved sigh. 'So that takes Elaine out of the picture!'

'Not necessarily,' said the detective. 'But she's definitely getting there. We really need a corroboration of her movements before we can rule her out for sure.'

'So if Irwin's car wasn't used, how was his body taken up to the kiln?' asked Ida.

'A different vehicle,' said Sergeant Clayton.

'Which means,' said Samson, 'that the timeline we've devised so far might be wrong.'

Benson nodded. 'My thoughts exactly. We've been presuming that whoever killed Irwin brought him down from Malham in the Toyota, left the body at the kiln and then abandoned the car. But with Elaine's testimony that she was the driver, and the absence of blood in the vehicle, we could be looking at a completely different schedule of events.'

'So if we start with when Elaine claims she left Irwin alive, then we're looking at the murder taking place some-time after ten past eight. And the body being moved up to the kiln after ten—'

'Nine,' corrected Benson, glancing at Delilah as she emitted a noise of protest. 'We have to keep our options open when it comes to Nathan.'

'However we look at it,' grumbled Sergeant Clayton, 'it's a mighty big blank space we have to fill. What we really need to find is the vehicle used to transport Irwin on his final journey.'

'I've requested CCTV footage from businesses in the town centre but it seems there's not much call for surveil-lance cameras in Bruncliffe,' Benson said with a dry smile. 'So I'm not holding out much hope. But perhaps we can go door-to-door along the route from Malham Cove to the kiln? See if anyone noticed or heard anything untoward yesterday evening?'

'Damn!' Samson slapped his forehead. 'I can't believe I forgot about this. Last night a 4x4 went haring past me as I was walking down Hillside Lane!'

'What time?' Benson's question carried the sharpness of excitement.

'Must have been almost midnight? It nearly hit me. I had to dive into the side as it sped past.'

'Plates?'

Samson shook his head. 'Not a chance. I'm not even sure of the make. All I saw was a glare of headlights and then my life flashing before my eyes. Sorry.'

'And this Hillside Lane?' asked Benson. 'It leads to Malham Cove?'

'Aye,' said Sergeant Clayton with a grim look. 'And up to Ellershaw Farm too.'

Benson's head whipped round to the policeman. 'The Metcalfe place?'

The sergeant nodded. And Benson got to his feet.

'Come on. Time we had a talk with Will Metcalfe.'

'But that's ridiculous,' protested Delilah as the two police officers made for the door. 'You've just said yourself that's the way you'd have to come into town from Malham.'

'I'm sorry, Delilah,' said Sergeant Clayton, 'but you know we have to follow up every lead. And Will was front and centre of a dispute with Irwin yesterday. Throw in the fact that Nathan was at the kiln where the body ended up and then Samson's testimony just now . . .' He shrugged, part apology part resignation.

'Well, I'm coming with you,' she said, making to stand.

But Benson shook his head, his tone brooking no argument. 'No. Not you and not Samson either. This is too close to home for the pair of you.'

He pulled open the office door and Nina Hussain stepped

back swiftly in the hallway, the teenager plainly having been eavesdropping rather than mopping the kitchen floor as Ida had left her doing. She watched helplessly as the two policemen left the building. As soon as the door closed, she turned to the others, disquiet on her young face.

'They can't seriously think Nathan was involved?' she said.

'Aye, tha'd think Gavin Clayton would know better,' muttered Ida. 'There's not a chance that lad had owt to do with this.'

Delilah noted with a sense of dread that Ida wasn't so quick to defend Will. She glanced at Samson, who was looking as perturbed as she felt.

'Christ,' he said, running a hand through his hair. 'What a mess. I thought mentioning the 4x4 was a breakthrough that might take the focus away from Will. Instead I've given them even more reason to suspect him.'

'Nowt was ever gained from the wringing of hands, lad!' Ida's voice was sharp. 'It's time we got investigating. And I'd suggest this Irwin fella might be a good place to start.'

Samson took the blunt counsel with a smile. 'Valid points all round, Ida. If we can find out more about Ross Irwin, we might hit on a reason someone wanted him out of the way. So, what do we know about him?'

Delilah shrugged. 'Not a lot. Like I said, I only met him yesterday. He seemed nice enough at the time but after what Elaine said . . .'

'Same here,' said Nina. 'He was in Rice N Spice Friday night and he came across as a genuine bloke. Left a generous tip, at any rate. Now though, I'm not so sure.'

'Happen it might be worth talking to the Dinsdales,' said Ida. 'It was them as brought him over here. They're likely to know more about him than anyone.'

'And Sarah Mitchell,' added Delilah, remembering a conversation with Herriot at the rugby club bar. 'Apparently she knew him from university, so we should talk to her too.'

'How about we break into his hotel room?' Nina's question brought the gaze of all three adults onto her. She grinned. 'I don't mean with a crowbar. My friend works at the Coach and Horses at weekends. She'd be able to get us the key.'

'Would she be willing to risk her job to do it?' Delilah asked gently.

'If she knew it would help exonerate Nathan, then yes, like a shot.'

Delilah turned to Samson and he nodded. 'Worth a try,' he said. 'When they found the falcon feather up at the kiln, Benson mentioned a possible link to wildlife crime. He seems to have conveniently forgotten that line of enquiry, but we might strike lucky and find something to support it – which would take Elaine and Will out of the equation in one fell swoop. And, either way,' he concluded with a look that was pure rogue, 'searching a hotel room is a lot better than sitting here fretting.'

'Right then,' said Ida, getting to her feet. 'While tha's breaking and entering, Nina and I will head over to Peaks Patisserie. Lucy's wanting a couple of spy cameras put in. That dratted thief was in there again last night.'

'What about the deep clean?' asked Nina with a grin.

Ida almost smiled. 'Sometimes there's more important things in life than cleaning, lass.'

12

By early afternoon, the lounge in Fellside Court was thrumming with voices. Such was the excitement, the TV in the background was going largely ignored, even the pensioners' favourite programme, *Flog It*, unable to compete with the news which had broken that morning.

Someone had murdered the young ecologist who was working on the Dinsdale planning permission and dumped the body up at the Hoffmann kiln. And in a twist of fate, Elaine Bullock, known to all the residents as the god-daughter of Fellside Court's Alice Shepherd – who herself had been murdered just eight months past – was being questioned in connection with the crime.

It was enough to keep the residents buzzing for a week. One person, however, was being uncharacteristically quiet.

As the August sunshine streamed in through the wall of windows which overlooked the courtyard of the retirement complex, Arty Robinson was wrapped up in his own selfish thoughts. Because they were selfish, he was aware of that. While the lovely Elaine was being questioned about her involvement in the murder, rather than fretting over how she was getting on, as was the topic among the circle of friends seated around him, all his thoughts were for himself.

How the hell was he going to find out who had bought Fellside Court? With Elaine being dragged into the drama which had beset the town, Arty knew Delilah and Samson would be caught up in it too, eager to prove their friend's innocence. How would they spare the time now to help him with his enquiries?

It was looking more and more likely that he was going to have to go with his Plan B. The nuclear option—

'What do you think, Arty?' Clarissa was sitting forward, looking at him expectantly, awaiting an answer to a question he hadn't heard.

'Sorry? I was miles away.'

'I said, we ought to see if we can help somehow. Offer our services to the Dales Detective Agency, because we all know Elaine didn't do this.'

'What, like another stakeout at the cafe?' asked Eric, his voice filled with optimism, remembering a joyous day filled with endless coffee and cake while they carried out covert surveillance.

Clarissa shook her head. 'Not quite. I was thinking at the scene of the murder. I've been watching—'

'Seriously, Clarissa,' said Edith, 'if you're about to suggest we go up to the Hoffmann kiln and spend a night out on the fells waiting for the murderer to revisit the scene of the crime, just because you saw it on that wretched True Crime channel you're always glued to, you are more demented than I thought.'

'But it's a credible strategy,' her sister protested.

'Not really,' said Eric. 'I have it on good authority that the kiln wasn't even where it happened.'

The group turned to him, stunned by the revelation

but not questioning it for a moment. Because they all knew Eric's 'good authority' was his grandson, Constable Danny Bradley. After a heartbeat of silence, when it became clear that nothing further was going to be volunteered without prompting, Joseph asked what they were all wondering.

'Where was Irwin killed, then?'

'Danny didn't spell it out but he said he was heading over to Malham Cove on a fingertip search. Ergo . . .' Eric let the word hang, taking a deep inhale of his oxygen as though the revelation had exhausted him.

'Malham Cove,' murmured Edith, frowning. 'That's where Elaine went with him.'

'Doesn't look good,' agreed Joseph. 'I hope she has a watertight alibi.'

Clarissa however, was still staring at Eric. 'How long have you known this?' she demanded.

Eric shrugged. 'About half an hour. Danny texted to say he'd not be able to pop in as promised because he was having to work.'

'And you didn't think to tell us this key bit of information which is so pertinent to the case?' Clarissa's indignation had brought red circles to her cheeks and a lawyerly tone to her voice.

'I forgot, your honour,' he grunted, tapping the cylinder by his side. 'I was in my apartment replacing this as I was running low on air, and that kind of took precedence.'

Clarissa's umbrage dissipated when confronted with the reality of Eric's life, where keeping his oxygen supply going was of far more importance than the details of a murder investigation. She patted his hand. 'Well at least we know

now. Although I suspect getting to Malham Cove for a stakeout might prove rather more difficult.'

Edith rolled her eyes at Arty, who managed a grin, only half listening, still consumed by his own concerns. But even he couldn't miss the dramatic appearance in the lounge doorway of a stylish lady, not a hair of her platinum blonde bob out of place as she raised her arms and called for quiet.

'I have news!' she announced once the room fell silent, theatrically clasping her hands in front of her, an expression of consternation on her flawlessly made-up face.

Given that this was Geraldine Mortimer, one of the few residents in Fellside Court that Arty had no time for, he didn't swallow that sorrowful look for a second. Neither did Edith Hird.

'Oh-oh,' she muttered, glancing at Arty, 'she's looking far too smug beneath that masquerade for my liking. She's about to put the knife in someone.'

Arty shared her foreboding. And seeing as there was really only one topic on the agenda which could justify such a melodramatic announcement, he had the awful feeling Geraldine's knife was about to wound Elaine Bullock.

'The police have released the Bullock girl,' she started, proving Arty's intuition wrong and holding up a hand as relieved murmurs could be heard all around the room. 'And . . . have driven up to Ellershaw Farm!'

She didn't need to elaborate. Everyone in the room knew that Ellershaw was the Metcalfe home, and that Will lived there with his family and parents.

'Now, while I don't like to boast,' continued Geraldine, adopting a faux-modest smile, 'as many of you are aware, my son is a criminal barrister so I have a bit of knowledge in this area. So while the police are only referring to Will Metcalfe as "a person of significant interest", I can tell you that translates to him being in deep trouble.'

'It must be about that row he had with the ecologist,' called out a voice.

'That and his fiery temper,' said Geraldine, the smile slipping into malicious delight. 'It seems he might finally have got his comeuppance. I mean, it's hardly surprising. After all, it's a bit of a family trait, that hit-first-ask-questions-later approach.'

The last sentence was aimed directly at Joseph O'Brien and, to Arty's surprise, the Irishman – normally the mildest of folk – shot to his feet, eyes blazing.

'You can keep your conjectures to yourself,' he snapped. 'And as for your malicious slurs about the Metcalfes, you can shove them—'

'Somewhere dark!' said Arty, leaping up to intercept his friend's uncharacteristic outburst and pull him back down to his seat as the room erupted into laughter.

'Sorry,' muttered Joseph, breathing hard. 'But that woman . . .'

Clarissa nodded. 'Would make a saint swear. She's just mean.'

Edith grunted in agreement, although Arty suspected she would have used a harsher adjective than her sister. 'Trouble is,' she said, 'Geraldine might be objectionable but she's got a point. Given what happened at the wedding yesterday, Will has ample motive. Delilah must be out of her mind with worry if the police are focusing on him now.'

A cloud of concern descended on the group, their anxiety

about Elaine now transferred to Will and Delilah. That cloud was darkest over Arty.

'Are you okay?' Edith murmured to him as the others began talking about this latest twist in developments. 'You don't look yourself.'

He shrugged. Embarrassed to be caught out so pre-occupied with his own affairs. 'It's nothing,' he muttered.

She raised an eyebrow. 'Doesn't look like nothing. You've had a face like a wet weekend for over a week now. What's going on?'

'It's just . . . the sale of this place. I really need to know who's buying it but with all this murder enquiry going on, Delilah and Samson are going to be too busy to help.' He gave another shrug, cheeks reddening. 'And I know that's selfish of me, but I can't help it.'

Edith's head tipped to one side, her gaze fixed on him, making him think not for the first time that she must have been an intimidating presence at the helm of Bruncliffe Primary School. 'Arty Robinson,' she said quietly, 'what aren't you telling me? We're all keen to know who the new owners of Fellside Court are, but you seem to be particularly obsessed with it. Why?'

'Because,' he said, gulping, 'I need to know if I can afford to keep living here.'

And he found himself telling her everything. Well, almost everything. He told her about how he was already at the limit of his finances. About how he could just about cover the rent and the service charges, but that any increase in either would see him having to leave. Probably leaving Bruncliffe, too, as it wasn't like the town had much by way of housing in his price bracket.

He didn't mention his Plan B, because he didn't want to witness Edith's horror when she realised the lengths he was willing to go to in order to stay at Fellside Court. Best off she didn't know.

Edith didn't say a word for a few moments. Just continued to stare at him. Then she reached across her armchair and took his hand in hers.

'You daft bugger,' she said. She nodded, a sharp movement of decisiveness. 'If Delilah and Samson are too busy to help us, we'll just have to help ourselves.'

'How do you mean?'

She leaned even further forward, whispering now. 'I mean, this place will be empty tomorrow afternoon when everyone is down at the Silver Solos event and the coast will be clear. Let's break into the manager's office and see what we can discover.'

Arty felt his eyebrows shoot up so high they almost touched his bald crown. Edith Hird, the pillar of Bruncliffe society, was suggesting they do a bit of breaking and entering. But such was his predicament, he wasn't about to talk her out of it.

Danny Bradley was indeed part of a fingertip search. Up on the fells above Malham Cove, he was in the middle of a line of officers slowly working their way across the field where Elaine Bullock claimed to have left Ross Irwin alive. And where it was now suspected the ecologist had met his end. It was a stunning setting. While the wall of limestone that reared up from the landscape to form the cove couldn't be seen from this position, the views were magnificent. Green fields stretching out in front of him, down the fells and into the dale below, where the river had been turned into a ribbon of silver in the afternoon sun. Piecing the patchwork of land together was the grey stitching of dry-stone walls, hemming in the white blots of sheep, and from overhead, adding a sweet soundtrack to the scene, came the song of a lark, the bird a tiny dark shape against the bluest of skies.

Not a bad place to die, mused the young constable. Although murder was a different matter. If murder was what it was.

It wasn't that he doubted the deductions of DS Benson. After all, the deceased had suffered multiple blows to his head, which suggested a simple fall could be ruled out. Plus there was the matter of the body having been moved. But while Danny had been keen for the drama such a high-profile investigation would bring, now that the spotlight was being turned on people he knew – and liked – it was a different matter.

First Elaine Bullock. And now Will Metcalfe, with even the lad Nathan being considered as a possible accessory. Danny's instinct was to rule all of them out immediately, based just on his knowledge of them as decent folk. But if he'd learned anything in the last year, what with all the upheaval which had beset the town, it was that you couldn't pre-judge anyone. Not as a police officer.

So here he was, helping to conduct a search which might lead to someone he liked and respected being accused of murder. It wasn't easy to contemplate. In fact, it made him wonder whether he oughtn't proceed with his original plans to apply for a transfer to the Met. Or to Leeds, where DI Frank Thistlethwaite had promised him a job. He'd put such ideas on the shelf since Samson O'Brien arrived in town, sensing he could learn a lot from a man who'd pretty much done everything in the world of policing. But now . . . At least in London and Leeds he didn't know anyone, so he wouldn't be faced with such a crisis of conscience.

Or with views like this.

He allowed himself a second to take in the glory of the region he was lucky enough to live in, and then lowered his eyes back to the ground. He saw the button first. A small circle of white in the green grass. As he squatted to see it better, he saw the smear of red alongside it.

He raised his hand and shouted, bringing the search line to a halt. And bringing yet more certainty to the theory that Ross Irwin's death had in fact been murder.

Across the fells from Malham Cove, Alison Metcalfe was bringing in the washing at Ellershaw Farm, a task she enjoyed, the sight of the clothes snapping on the line against the most magnificent of backdrops being something she never tired of. It was even more soothing after negotiating a six-year-old's tantrum for most of the afternoon.

When she couldn't find her precious rounders bat, Izzy had thrown a complete wobbly, something which didn't happen often but when it did, it was a spectacular sight. Driven on by tears and wails, Alison had turned the house upside down looking for the blessed thing but to no avail. Thankfully, however, Charlie had shown all the maturity of his eight years and offered to let his little sister play his Lego video game with him and, with the crisis averted, Alison had seized her chance to get the washing in, leaving the pair of them in front of the TV, happily negotiating a virtual world in the form of ninjas.

She stood now, laundry basket at her feet, hands full of half-folded shirt, admiring the view. The sharp green of the fields, so intense at this time of year, and the bloom of purple on the hills, the heather at its peak. The occasional scar of rock where the limestone erupted from the ground, adding a savage edge to what otherwise could have been a saccharine landscape. And those clouds, fluffing up along the horizon, breaking up the monotony of a perfect blue sky.

Nestled in the dale below it all was Bruncliffe, its two mills still standing tall at either end despite being long redundant, the river and the trainline forging twin lines between them, one as direct as a Yorkshireman's opinion, the other meandering blithely along.

Alison had known Will Metcalfe all her life. Had started dating him while they were both still at school. So when he'd asked the inevitable question, some had presumed it was a given – that she would say 'yes' and become his wife. But it hadn't been that simple a decision. Becoming a wife was one thing; becoming a farmer's wife was a different prospect altogether, especially for a lass raised in the town, the daughter of a lorry driver for the local quarry and a nurse, not a drop of farming in their blood. Alison hadn't needed a family connection to agriculture, though, to know how hard the life she'd been offered could be. She'd seen farmers driven to the brink with financial pressures. She knew one or two who'd taken their own lives, shotgun permits and despair being a lethal combination.

So she'd taken her time to agree to joining Will in this partnership at Ellershaw. Because that's what farming was, a partnership of equals forged through early mornings and long days. Of rare time off and even rarer holidays. Plus there was the added complication of her in-laws, Peggy and Ted Metcalfe, living there as well. But she shouldn't have worried. From the moment she'd moved up to the farm, situated above the town with vistas which stretched for miles, Alison had been smitten. Not just with her new husband, but with the land they lived on and the life she'd chosen.

Which made bringing in the washing a joy rather than a chore. Although, she mused as she continued folding the shirt, it wasn't such a joy when the westerly wind blew in with rain and getting the washing out on the line became impossible, the house filled with the smell of drying laundry.

She paused in her folding. Her eyes caught by a trailing thread on the white cotton. She looked closer and saw a button was missing, torn from the fabric with some force, judging by the small rip where it had once been. And just to the right of it, there was a dark, thumbprint-sized mark.

Blood? She licked a finger, gave it a rub. It didn't disappear. She'd have to get the stain remover out or it would be a good shirt lost.

She cursed quietly. That fracas with the ecologist yesterday. She'd witnessed it all, Will driven to temper by the impertinence of the man. They'd been lucky to escape with just a lost button, her husband known for having quick fists when he was riled. Luckily it hadn't got that far in this instance.

'Ali?' Will's voice, calling from the back door as he strode across the yard towards her, mobile in his hand, a frown of concern on his forehead. 'Have you heard?'

'Heard what?' she asked with a smile. 'That it's a glorious day and you're married to a wonderful woman?'

He laughed. Caught her around the waist from behind and planted a kiss on her cheek.

'No,' he said, still holding her, both of them looking out over the dale. 'That ecologist, Ross Irwin.'

'What about him?' She tensed, not wanting the stress the mention of that man induced to ruin a perfect moment.

'He's been murdered.'

The shirt fell from her hands, landing half in and half out of the basket. And in the distance, on the road that snaked down to the town, a vehicle came into sight, its vivid livery marking it out as a police car. Alison Metcalfe felt the day's glory cloud over.

13

'That should do the trick.' Ida stood back and cast a critical eye over the camera positioned on a shelf above the counter in the kitchen of Peaks Patisserie. Sandwiched between a bag of flour and a stack of Menier chocolate bars, it was barely visible. 'It's got a forty-hour battery life but as it's motion-activated that'll last a few nights. Just remember to switch it on before tha leaves at the end of the day.'

'Will do,' said Lucy, staring at the small device with wonder. 'Hopefully it will catch the thief red-handed.'

'But how are they getting in?' asked Nina, looking around the kitchen.

'That's what's been so strange. No sign of a forced entry on any occasion.'

'And the back door?' Ida asked, while simultaneously checking the handle, the door opening to her touch and bringing Tolpuddle expectantly to his feet out in the ginnel at the side of the building. 'Tha locks it every night?'

Lucy nodded. 'Always. We leave it unlocked during the day, propped open sometimes if the heat gets too much in here. But I always check it before I leave.'

Ida stepped outside, wanting to look at the doorframe. And also wanting to look like she knew what she was doing.

Still relatively new to this detective lark, while she was confident her recently acquired combat trousers granted her a more official appearance, she wasn't so confident that her skills backed that up. And today she had young Nina with her, so it was even more important to set a good impression.

She ran a hand over the woodwork around the door. No indication of any forced entry. Nor did the lock show any scuff marks or scratches, evidence of it having been picked – a bit of knowledge Ida had learned the hard way back in May when she'd failed to notice such signs on the porch door of the office building, and had almost paid for it with her life.

She turned, looking at the ginnel where Tolpuddle was also doing a good impression of investigating, snuffling at the ground. She squinted at the dark stains which had caught the Weimaraner's attention.

'Does tha park out here?' she asked Lucy over her shoulder as she crouched down to inspect the blotches, the dog immediately leaning into her with affection.

'Sometimes if I'm dropping something off. But never for long.'

Ida touched one of the stains, brought her finger to her nose. Oil.

'Is it a clue?' Nina had crouched down beside her, excited.

'Could be,' muttered Ida. 'Someone's been parking here for extended periods. And not in the same place each time, either.'

'The thief?'

Ida shrugged, straightening up, noticing that her knees made a lot more noise than Nina's did when the teenager copied her movement. 'Not sure. But I tell thee what lass, let's hedge our bets.' She pulled another small camera out of one of her many pockets and turned back into the kitchen.

It was probably something and nothing. But at least, she thought, as she placed the device on the windowsill, aimed at the exterior, it would make Lucy feel like the Dales Detective Agency was finally taking her case seriously.

It all seemed so polite. Sergeant Clayton and some detective called Benson from out of town, asking if they could have a quick chat. Like calling in at Ellershaw was just a social visit.

Alison Metcalfe had acted surprised, enquiring what they wanted, as if the news Will had relayed only moments before hadn't arrived and turned the day dark. But as the detective explained the reason for their presence – standard procedure, in light of Ross Irwin's murder – she'd regretted playing dumb.

Murder. The sound of it. So stark. So final.

Will had led them into the kitchen, the heart of the Metcalfe home, the three men sitting around the large table at the far end of the room. The view stretching outside. The cluck of hens drifting in through the open window. Standing with her back to the sink, Alison was wishing they were in the more formal lounge instead. For the kitchen was where their memories were made, a place of warmth and joy. Not the setting for something so sombre. So potentially dangerous to the harmony of Ellershaw Farm.

'More tea?' she heard herself offering, unable to stem the customary etiquette Bruncliffe instilled in its inhabitants from an early age.

They'd already had a cup. Cake too, although the detective

hadn't touched his. And even Gavin Clayton had only eaten half. A sign that he was troubled.

They shook their heads.

'Thing is, Will,' DS Benson was saying, 'in the course of our enquiries, your . . . disagreement . . . with Irwin at the wedding reception yesterday has been brought to our attention.'

Will grunted. He was regarding the detective with a steady gaze, head to one side, the same way he looked when he was about to bid on a tup that was stretching their budget. Or when he'd asked her to marry him. She knew from years of living with him that this was apprehension, disguised as contemplation.

'Folk are quick to talk,' he muttered. Then he flicked his hand. 'It were nowt. A couple of cross words combined with a few drinks. A bit of something and nothing.'

Alison steeled her face into neutral while Sergeant Clayton leaned forward across the table.

'Come off it, Will,' he said. 'We've got reports of you having to be pulled off him by your brother. Sounds a bit more than a simple misunderstanding to me. And besides, we both know you're not that quick-tempered, despite what folk think. If you went for Irwin, there'll have been something of substance behind it. What was it?'

Will shook his head. 'Nothing. I'm telling you. He just made some comment about being at a wedding full of hicks and . . . well . . . I saw red.' He shrugged. Stared at the sergeant.

DS Benson nodded. As though he was swallowing Will's line. 'So,' he said, turning to include Alison, sending her pulse thumping, 'what time did you leave the reception?'

The question she'd been dreading. Because they hadn't left it together. She shot a glance at her husband. 'Erm . . . sometime after eleven?' she said, leaving it vague, letting him have an escape route if he needed one.

But the detective had done his homework. 'And you, Will? I hear you didn't hang around after your clash with Irwin. Is that correct?'

'You heard right,' Will said dryly. 'I'd had enough of Harry's crap singing.'

Sergeant Clayton smiled. 'Aye, that'd be a good enough reason to leave. Did you bring the little ones home with you?'

Will nodded and tipped his head towards his wife. 'I'd not drunk much so I drove back up with the kids. Thought it might be nice for Alison to have a bit of fun and stay out late for once.'

'And did you?' Benson was looking at her again, grinning, charm personified.

'What? Have fun or stay out late?' Alison managed, through a throat that was suddenly very dry.

'Both.'

'Yes.' She somehow formed a smile.

'So how did you get home?'

'My neighbours gave me a lift back.'

'The Dinsdales?' Sergeant Clayton asked, taking notes. 'They live on a farm just the other side of the road,' he added for Benson's benefit.

She nodded. 'They dropped me at the end of the track and I walked up.'

'What time would it have been when you got back here, then?' asked Benson.

'Just before midnight.' She flicked a glance at her husband but there was no reaction.

'Were your folks at the reception, too, Will?' continued the sergeant.

'Yes, but they left even earlier than I did. They were still up and about when I got back, before you ask.' It was said calmly but with emphasis. Will making it clear that someone could vouch for his movements.

'And you didn't go out again once you got home? Either of you?' Benson turned from Will to Alison and back again.

They both shook their heads, Alison hoping that her face wasn't giving away the lie.

But their answers seemed to satisfy DS Benson, the detective placing his hands on the table and getting to his feet. 'Okay,' he said. 'Thank you both for your time. We'll get out of your hair now. But if you could let us know if you're planning on going anywhere in the next few days, just in case we need to ask any follow-up questions.'

Will nodded. Alison gripped the worktop behind her. *Follow-up questions.* He'd made it sound routine but she wasn't fooled. There was a ruthlessness beneath the detective's debonair exterior. And besides, Alison knew she had reason to be worried.

She watched Will usher the policemen out, across the yard, past the battered old Land Rover, the detective's head turning towards it. The slightest of movements, but enough to register his interest. To see the bottle-green bodywork shining, where Will had washed it that morning. Inside and out. A rare occurrence.

The fear Alison had been trying to suppress engulfed her. The missing button. The stain on the shirt. The Land

Rover – it hadn't been there when she'd got back the night before. She'd thought nothing of it at the time. A bit drunk, if she was honest. Nor had she questioned the empty bed as she'd climbed between the sheets, glad just to be lying down. But now . . .

Now that she'd heard her husband lying to the police . . .

There was trouble here. Real trouble. The kind that could swoop in and tear her family apart.

The three men were still in the yard, standing in the early evening sunshine, chatting about something. Will looking so relaxed. Through the open window the tang of woodsmoke drifted into the kitchen.

Alison was moving before she could change her mind. Striding now, fear replaced with cold determination, heading towards the rear porch where the laundry basket had been abandoned. She fished out the shirt with the missing button – and that stain, that awful stain – balled it up and shoved it down the back of her trousers, pulling her loose T-shirt over it all.

When she reached the small incinerator round the back of the house, her father-in-law was finishing up, the heap of hedge cuttings he'd been burning almost all gone.

'There's tea freshly brewed and cake ready-cut,' she said. 'Go grab a cup. I'll see to this last lot.'

Ted Metcalfe grinned, bestowing a kiss on her cheek. 'You're an angel, lass.'

She waited for him to disappear around the corner of the farmhouse before she lifted the lid of the incinerator and threw the shirt into the flames. She gave it a few minutes, added the last of the hedge trimmings, and then walked back towards the house.

Will was leaning against the porch, staring into the distance, the police car gone. He turned as she approached, his face crumpling at the sight of her.

'Ali,' he said, voice low. 'Oh God, Ali. I think I've really screwed up.'

'Fifteen minutes, no more!'

Delilah nodded, feeling guilty at the consternation on the pale face of the youngster who'd given them access to Ross Irwin's hotel room. They'd arrived at the Coach and Horses on High Street as instructed – just as the evening food service kicked in – and had taken a seat at the bar, a couple of drinks in front of them as they waited for Nina's friend to give them the nod. It hadn't taken long for her boss to become fully occupied in the crowded dining room, at which point she'd ushered them upstairs, her willingness to be involved in an action which could cost her job visibly diminishing with every step. Delilah had done her best to garner information about Irwin on the way but the strained answers to her questions had revealed nothing other than the fact that he'd checked in five days ago, and had managed to run up a substantial tab.

By the time the lass inserted the key card into the lock, she was a nervous wreck.

'And for goodness sake, don't get caught,' she murmured, standing aside to let them enter. 'But if you do, don't say I let you in!'

'I promise we won't. And thanks!' The door closed on Delilah's gratitude as the teenager's footsteps hurried back along the corridor.

Samson let out a low whistle of appreciation as he took in the room. This wasn't your standard hotel accommodation.

A cleverly designed niche in one corner functioned as a wardrobe, an antique table next to it containing a well-stocked refreshment tray displaying a coffee machine, kettle, supplies of tea and coffee, bottles of sparkling water and lots of tempting snacks, even some Peaks Patisserie delights among them. Hanging on the wall above was a generously sized TV. Between the table and the large window was the entrance to the en-suite bathroom, a glimpse of sumptuous towels, chrome and glass through the doorway suggesting yet more opulence. Then there was a plush two-seater sofa under the window, a desk with USB connections aplenty to its right and, in between the window and the door, the biggest bed Delilah had ever seen.

'Super king,' said Samson with a grin, spotting where her focus had landed.

'Right,' she muttered, suddenly aware that this was the first chance they'd had to be alone since he'd turned up out of the blue that morning. Suddenly aware that it was stiflingly hot and her cheeks were burning. And that Samson was staring at her with the look of a hungry man.

'Work,' she managed to say, tapping her watch. 'We're on the clock.'

'Yes . . .' Samson nodded. Dragged his gaze off her and reached into his pocket. 'Here, put these on.' He was holding out a pair of nitrile gloves. 'We don't want to leave anything for the forensics team.'

'You don't think they've searched in here already?'

He shook his head, casting a look around. 'Not that I can see. It's all a bit too tidy and there's no sign they've dusted for fingerprints.'

He was right. The bed was unmade, as was to be expected, but the clothes were all neatly hung up, Irwin's case stowed at the bottom of the wardrobe, a pile of folders stacked on the desk next to a laptop. Definitely no indication of the police having been through it.

'So how much do ecologists earn?' mused Samson, as he snapped the gloves over his fingers.

Delilah shrugged. 'I wouldn't think it was astronomical. Why?'

'Doesn't this strike you as a bit high-budget for our lad? And it's not like he was here on a one-nighter or, according to our reluctant accomplice, coy about splashing the cash. I hate to stereotype, but I'm not sure this is what I would have expected from someone over here exploring for newts or badgers or whatever it is he was doing.'

Remembering the expensive-looking suit Ross Irwin had been wearing at the wedding, which had triggered caustic comments from her brother, Ash – and which now lay up at the Hoffmann kiln draped around its dead owner – Delilah moved over to the wardrobe and riffled through the clothes hanging there. A mixture of outdoor clothing and more formal attire, there were a few designer labels even she recognised, all of it suggesting quality. Beneath, lined up and polished, were two more pairs of shoes and a pair of hiking boots in a plastic bag. She pulled them out, careful not to knock the mud off the soles onto the floor.

'Le Chameau,' she muttered. 'Cost a fortune. Irwin had money, that's for sure.'

'Worth thinking about,' said Samson. 'Maybe he was involved in something underhand after all.'

'Like wildlife crime?'

'Possibly. Let's see what we can find.'

He turned to the bedside table and started going through it, leaving Delilah to move over to the desk. The laptop was her main concern. She flipped it open and turned it on. All she needed to be able to do was get around the password and—

'Ha! Folk are so daft!' She grinned over her shoulder at Samson, the glow of the computer screen behind her. 'No password.'

'Excellent. Download anything of interest. And if there's a way to cover your tracks—'

She made a sucking noise. Samson laughed.

'I know, I know,' he said, as he crossed to the desk and began flicking through the pile of folders, 'I'm teaching you how to suck eggs!'

But Delilah wasn't listening. She was already dragging files onto the USB stick she'd brought with her. Fieldwork reports, planning permission surveys, protected species licence applications, ecological impact assessments . . . All of it and more, she copied. Aware of time ticking, she focused on the rest of the files, laid out as orderly as the room Irwin had last occupied. Nothing really stood out. Some personal documents. A few blandly titled folders. She had them highlighted and was debating whether or not to copy them across when her smartwatch vibrated.

A text from Nina's friend.

'Shit!' Delilah jumped up, a bolt of panic coursing through her. 'The police. They're downstairs, asking about access to Irwin's room.'

Samson was already moving towards the door. 'Out. Now!'

Delilah went to eject the memory stick but in her haste, copied across the remaining files. 'Come on! Come on!' she cursed, as they began downloading.

'Delilah! We don't have time for this. If we're caught in here . . .' Samson was at the door, holding it partially open.

'Just one more thing,' she muttered, heart rattling. Knowing she couldn't leave before the software on the memory stick had finished doing its special magic and covered any evidence of her incursion.

'Seriously, we need to go!'

'We can't!' she snapped. 'Not until it's complete. Unless you want the police IT experts to know someone was accessing Irwin's laptop long after its owner was dead?'

Finally the red light stopped flashing. Delilah whipped the USB stick out, stuck it in her pocket and hurried towards the exit. Out into the corridor, Samson letting the door close quietly behind them, and then they were hurrying towards the stairs. But drifting up the stairway at the end of the hall was the sound of voices.

'No one's been in there today?' a female voice was asking in an authoritative tone. Benson's DC.

'No. Mr Irwin specifically asked not to be disturbed so not even housekeeping has been in.'

Delilah turned to Samson, fear gripping her. 'We're trapped!'

'Damn it.' Samson glanced back along the corridor, nothing but a window at the far end, looking out over High Street. Their only alternative was the lift, but that was at the same end of the hallway as the stairs, in full view of anyone walking up.

'What are we going to do?' whispered Delilah. The thud of her pulse almost deafening.

'Blend in,' said Samson.

He whipped round, back into Irwin's room, emerging seconds later holding a pile of towels. Grabbing her arm, he strode down the corridor towards the stairs. Towards the danger.

'What are you doing?' hissed Delilah, as he stopped outside a room with the faint sound of a radio playing in the background.

'Trust me,' he murmured, before placing the towels in her arms and knocking sharply on the door.

'Who is it?' came a voice from within.

From the stairs, more conversation, much closer now. And several pairs of footsteps. A posse of police.

'Room Service,' said Samson, voice confident.

The door opened. He stepped forward, ushering Delilah ahead of him, the towels front and centre, forcing the bemused guest back into the room. The man's eyes were wide behind his glasses.

'I didn't order any towels,' he sputtered.

Samson was already letting the door close behind them, the gap no more than a sliver as a group of people could be heard going past.

'You didn't?' he asked, demeanour courteous, assuming his role effortlessly. Even the bruises on his face seeming diminished as he shook his head. 'So sorry, sir. We're training up new staff and, well . . .' He rolled his eyes in Delilah's direction with the exasperation of a beleaguered mentor. 'Quite frankly, it's taking longer than we expected.'

Delilah blushed as the man laughed. At ease now.

'No problem,' he said, giving Delilah a kindly look. 'We all have to start somewhere.'

Delilah clamped her jaw tight, stifling the natural retort, doing her best to look like a hapless trainee.

'Again, my apologies, sir, for disturbing you.' Samson turned to Delilah. 'Let's see if we can find the right room this time.'

With a firm hand in her back he guided her towards the door, the towels still in her arms.

'Check the coast is clear,' he murmured in her ear as he pulled the door open for her.

Towels held high as a shield, she quickly peeked left and right along the corridor, gave a small nod and stepped briskly out. With Samson on her heels, she headed for the stairs. Behind them, through the open door of Irwin's room, they could hear the sounds of a search in progress.

'Christ,' breathed Samson as they turned the corner into the sanctuary of the stairwell and began to descend, 'that was close.'

'Tell me about it,' muttered Delilah, her heart still thumping. The towels still in her arms.

The towels which were partially blocking her view, meaning she didn't see the man coming towards her as she stepped off the final stair into the lobby.

They collided softly, the bundle of Egyptian cotton taking the brunt and spilling onto the floor.

'So sorry—'

'My fault entirely—'

They both froze. And Delilah found herself looking straight into the startled gaze of PC Danny Bradley.

14

'Delilah! Samson!' Danny exclaimed. He looked from one to the other, and then down at the pile of towels at his feet. 'What . . . ?'

'Thefts,' murmured Samson, leaning forward. 'We've been asked to look into some housekeeping irregularities, but it's really hush-hush. The management don't want the staff to know anyone is under suspicion.'

Danny nodded.

Delilah, meanwhile, was gathering up her load. Danny bent to help.

'I'm going to put spy cameras in some of the linens,' she mumbled as they both straightened up, her arms full of towels, eyes not quite catching his and cheeks flushed pink. 'That's why . . . these . . . I'm going to do a test run first.'

'Right. Makes sense.'

'So we'd best get to it. And remember,' said Samson with a wink, as he ushered Delilah ahead of him along the corridor towards the exit, 'you never saw us!'

Danny was left at the foot of the stairs feeling . . . What?

Surprise, certainly, at having literally bumped into them here, the Fleece being their normal watering hole. But Samson had explained the reason for their presence. A very satisfactory reason, thought Danny as he walked up the stairs.

So what was bugging him them? What was it about the meeting he'd just had which was striking him as so peculiar?

He reached the floor above and was almost at his destination when he stopped, inspiration striking him.

Delilah! She hadn't enquired where he was going. He was wearing his uniform, obviously in the Coach and Horses on official business, yet one of the most curious people in Bruncliffe hadn't so much as asked him what he was up to.

Even though she would have known it probably had something to do with the Irwin murder case. A case which seemed to have connections to one of her best friends and her brother.

What could have prompted such uncharacteristic reticence?

Danny's intuition was that Delilah Metcalfe hadn't asked him any questions because she'd been too busy explaining her own presence. Too busy fabricating a reason for being there because the real reason was—

'Oh God,' he groaned as the penny dropped. Samson and Delilah had been doing exactly what he had been sent there to do. Fresh back from the search out at Malham Cove, he'd been instructed to join DS Benson's second in command in going through Ross Irwin's hotel room. Only it seemed the Dales Detective duo had beaten the official investigators to it.

Convinced he was right, and hoping he wasn't, Danny hurried along to the far end of the corridor and knocked lightly on the last door.

'Come in!' The female DC was standing by the wardrobe, looking through an array of the ecologist's clothes, while a second officer was in the bathroom.

'You here to help?' she asked.

Danny nodded, eyes sweeping the room, trying to see if Samson and Delilah had left any signs of their trespassing, something that could get them into deep trouble. Because no one, not even the seemingly affable DS Benson, would take kindly to someone poking around and tampering with possible evidence in a police investigation.

When his gaze rested on a laptop on a desk the other side of the bed, Danny felt the prickle of sweat on his scalp.

'Erm, how about I start by bagging that?' he offered, gesturing towards the computer. 'IT won't want us touching it so I might as well get it to them right now.'

'Sure.' The detective nodded towards a pile of evidence bags on the bed. 'Knock yourself out.'

PC Danny Bradley walked across the room, reached for the laptop and knew his suspicions were justified. The cover was still warm. Someone had been using it very recently. And as Ross Irwin was beyond need of the internet, anyone touching this would have known something was up.

Desperately hoping this was the only slip-up Samson and Delilah had made, he slid the computer into a bag and made his excuses. As he was leaving the pub a couple of minutes later, laptop under his arm to explain any residual heat when he handed it over, he passed the manager having a muttered conversation with a colleague at the entrance. Something about the oddness of guests. The pair of them were looking in bemused surprise at a pile of towels left on a small table just inside the door.

Danny didn't enlighten them.

* * *

The adrenalin buzz resulting from their close brush with the long arm of the law sustained Delilah through the rapid retreat from the Coach and Horses and the return to the office to collect Tolpuddle. It also left her starving after what had turned into a long and fraught day, which had begun with a crippling hangover. So she'd immediately accepted Samson's suggestion that they head to Rice N Spice where, over a table laden with samosas, poppadoms, Mr Hussain's chef's-special thali and an exquisite fish masala, the conversation had been lively. And mostly centred around the case of the dead Ross Irwin.

But when it came time to leave and they wandered out onto the marketplace, Delilah found herself at a loss for words, despite there being so much they needed to say to each other. It was nerves. Which was daft. It wasn't like this was a first date or anything.

'So,' said Samson, pausing as they reached the far side of the square, Crag Hill to the left, Back Street to the right, 'about where I'm going to stay tonight—'

'Aren't you coming back with me?' The question fell from her in a rush of confusion.

He smiled. Took her hand, a glint in his eyes. 'I didn't want to presume. But it's a better offer than sharing with Gareth.'

She nodded, and busied herself with Tolpuddle's lead, which didn't require any attention whatsoever.

'Talking of Gareth,' she began, throat constricting as she finally addressed the subject she'd been avoiding all day. 'I haven't had a chance to clear things up from this morning . . . you know . . . him in that towel . . . I didn't—'

Her explanation came to an abrupt halt as Samson leaned

over and kissed her. The kind of kiss that vaporised all thought.

He broke off, grinning. 'No clearing up needed. Let's just go home.'

They set off up the hill, her stomach full of butterflies and her tongue tied in knots. When they reached the back door of her cottage, the sun was beginning to set, painting the surrounding fells in golden hues and turning the Crag above them into burnished gold.

'That's how this place got its name,' Samson murmured, pulling her into his arms as he gazed up at the outcrop of limestone that dominated the town. 'Folk always think Bruncliffe means "brown cliff". But Mother always claimed that "brun" came from the Old English for burnished. That in fact the town is named after a shining cliff.'

Delilah gave a soft laugh. 'The original settlers must have arrived on a rare sunny day, then. Either that or it was all the rain making it glisten.'

He grinned, bringing his focus onto her, his gaze setting her cheeks ablaze like the sunlit hills. 'Reckon we've got a bit of catching up to do,' he murmured.

Tolpuddle barked, pushing himself between them.

'He's hungry,' Delilah said, the words coming out in a squeak.

'He's not the only one,' said Samson with a look of pure mischief, Delilah's knees definitely wobbly as she opened the door and led them all in through the back porch and into the kitchen.

A kitchen which was normally more than adequate in size for her needs, but now seemed tiny, her heightened awareness of Samson making him appear to fill the space.

She opened the door of the tall cupboard next to the arch through to the lounge and Tolpuddle hurried over, nudging her thigh in anticipation.

Samson laughed. 'He's definitely hungry. Mind if I grab a shower while you feed him? Promise I'll be quick.' He leaned over to kiss her cheek, his hand on the nape of her neck, her senses aflame.

Then he was gone. Up the stairs in long strides, footsteps crossing to the bathroom followed by the sound of rushing water.

Tolpuddle barked again, more impatient this time, and Delilah found she was still standing at the worktop, the pouch of dogfood unopened in her hand.

'Sorry,' she murmured, petting her hound in apology before filling his bowl.

Tea, she decided. Filling the kettle. Keeping herself occupied as the sky darkened outside. When her mobile rang, she was glad of the distraction.

'Dee?' Will, using her childhood name. A sign of something. His voice almost breaking. 'I'm in real trouble. I need your help.'

The call didn't last long, Will not the most loquacious of men in normal times, even less so when stressed. And he was stressed, for Delilah couldn't remember the last time he'd reached out and asked for the help of the little sister he always saw as his responsibility, even now that she was a grown woman with a life of her own.

She hung up, shaken. Will wanted to hire the Dales Detective Agency. He wouldn't say why. Just requested that she head up to Ellershaw House early the next morning so he could explain. But what told her more than anything that he was desperate was the fact he'd asked her to bring Samson too. The man he'd been less than willing to welcome home to Bruncliffe back in October.

She hadn't needed to ask what it was connected to. It had to be the Ross Irwin case. Whatever the police had said when they'd gone up there earlier, Will was proper spooked. Which suggested . . .

Delilah didn't want to think about what that might suggest. She stood at the sink, looking out into the dark in a turmoil of emotions as the silence of the cottage settled around her. It took her a few moments to realise just *how* silent it was.

She turned around. Tolpuddle's bowl empty. No sign of the dog. And from upstairs, the sound of the shower had ceased, replaced by quiet. No footsteps. No noise at all.

Curious, she walked up the stairs. The cottage wasn't large, only one bedroom, so it didn't take long to cross from the landing to the doorway. To see the double bed, a large hump under the covers. A large hump on top of the covers too.

Samson and Tolpuddle, side by side, both fast asleep.

A surge of love flowed through her. Closely followed by the observation that she was probably going to have to sleep on the couch.

15

They drove up to Ellershaw House in the early morning light, the Mini climbing Hillside Lane out of the back of town as the sun crept over the fells to the east with the promise of yet another glorious day. Samson was still none the wiser as to how the car had ended up with love hearts on the side of it, Delilah having been too tense for such a trivial enquiry as they walked down to the office to pick it up. But whatever the cause, the extra decorations hadn't detracted from the Mini's capability, Delilah guiding it up the steep incline towards her family home at a speed which would have blown the engine on her last car. Especially with the added load of Gareth, Tolpuddle and Bounty in the rear.

Hand resting on the dashboard, as was his customary precaution when being chauffeured by Miss Metcalfe, Samson watched the landscape flash by, all hemmed in by the never-ending stone walls. Thanks to the mayhem of the previous twenty-four hours, he hadn't fully acclimatised to being back, the shadow of London's urban sprawl taking longer to shake off each time he returned. He wondered whether it would eventually be the other way round, the uniqueness of Bruncliffe and the dale it rested in becoming something of a novelty as his city life took precedence, like an accent slipping from an émigré as the years wore by.

He wasn't sure how he felt about that. Even after a good night's sleep, it was way too early to be contemplating it.

Delilah had woken him at six thirty, coffee and toast on a tray, Tolpuddle looking on in eager anticipation. As Samson had tucked in to this unexpected breakfast, she'd told him about Will's call the evening before. He'd been aware of the phone ringing as he got out of the shower so he'd lain down, intending just to rest for a few moments while he waited for Delilah to finish, filled with delicious anticipation of what was to come. That was the last thing he remembered, his body having decided that after being smashed into by a car followed by a night roughing it in Seth's allotment shed, it was going to make the most of a bed, in the way for which beds had been originally designed.

So despite the unexpectedly early hour, he'd been bright and alert for what Delilah had to tell him about the distress call from Will begging for their professional expertise. They'd hurried out of the cottage and when they'd reached the Mini, they'd been greeted by Gareth, just arriving back at the office from walking Bounty. Hearing the nature of their mission, he'd offered to accompany them, a firm friend of Will's from school and from years of working the Bruncliffe Manor estate, some of the boundaries of which abutted those of Ellershaw Farm.

From the gamekeeper's sigh of relief as the Mini rounded the final bend and the entrance to the Dinsdales' place appeared on the right, Samson suspected Gareth hadn't factored his new boss's driving into that offer. Delilah eased off the accelerator, but still took the left turn onto Ellershaw's track sharply enough to elicit a few grunts of surprise from her passengers. Up ahead the farmhouse came into view, Will already in the yard, a tight frown of concern on his forehead.

'We brought reinforcements,' said Samson, trying to keep his tone light as they all got out of the car.

'Think I'll bloody need it,' said Will, shaking Samson's hand, then Gareth's, before gathering Delilah into an uncharacteristic hug. He held her tight for a moment, as though garnering strength. Then he stepped back, ran a hand over his face and gestured towards the porch. 'You'd best come in. You're going to want to be sitting down when you hear what I've got to say.'

When Lucy Metcalfe arrived at Peaks Patisserie Monday morning, she wasn't expecting to see anyone. Not given the early hour. Something she was grateful for, seeing as she was still mulling over the disturbing call she'd had from her mother-in-law just as she was leaving home. Peggy had been letting her know that Will was in some kind of trouble in connection to the Irwin murder – the extent of that trouble being evident by the fact he'd asked Samson and Delilah for help. While Peggy was short on details, her concern had been palpable and it had left Lucy in an equal state of unease.

So when she took out her key to open the front door of the cafe and a figure emerged from the ginnel, frightening the life out of her, she almost dropped the four cartons of eggs she was carrying.

'Sorry, lass, didn't mean to startle thee!' Ida grunted as she stepped out onto the pavement.

'Ida! What on earth are you doing here at this time?'

Ida gestured at the bike leaning against the wall. 'Happen I was on my way to the office and thought I'd stop by. See if there's been any sign of tha thief.'

'And?'

'There's fresh oil on the ground, all right,' she said, pointing back down the ginnel.

'Damn it,' muttered Lucy. 'I was hoping they'd just give up and leave me alone.'

'Aye, well, not to worry. Whoever it is, the cameras will have caught them bang to rights.' The solid pat of comfort accompanying Ida's words jolted Lucy's arm and almost knocked the eggs out of her hands afresh.

Despite the threat to her ingredients, Lucy was glad she wasn't alone as she opened the cafe and led the way to the kitchen with trepidation. Expecting more destruction. More evidence of villainy. But when she pushed open the door, she was met with nothing of the sort. Everything was as she'd left it the night before, not a single cake, nor a cake stand, out of place.

While the proprietor felt a sense of relief, her hired detective was displaying obvious disappointment.

'I could have sworn as those oil stains were connected,' Ida was muttering, moving around the kitchen and peering into cupboards, as though in the firm belief that the evidence she was seeking would be found lurking on a neglected shelf.

Lucy shrugged. 'Maybe it's a couple of youngsters, parking up out of sight for a bit of late night romance.' She smiled. 'We've all been there.'

'Huh!' Ida's bark was derisive, whether at the idea of the oil being something other than as she'd postulated or at the idea of her ever having been young and in love, it was hard to tell.

'But at least you'll have the footage from this to give you some kind of answer.' Lucy tapped the camera situated on the windowsill, its lens pointing towards the exterior.

'Aye. I'll get right onto it.' And with an expression even more severe than normal, Ida headed off, out into the sunlit marketplace.

Moments later she was riding her bike across the cobbles towards Back Street, Lucy watching her progress from the cafe window with a smile. Whoever it was who'd taken to parking in the ginnel every night, they were about to get the dubious honour of being the focus of Ida Capstick's attention.

'Whichever way you look at it, I'm in deep trouble.'

'But why didn't you just tell them the truth?' Delilah asked as her brother dropped his head into his hands. From the little Will had said since they'd all sat around the kitchen table, it was clear he wasn't exaggerating when he said he was in trouble. Lying to the police wasn't something that was going to end well.

'I thought it would make things worse,' he muttered.

Delilah glanced at Samson, the gravity of his expression intensifying her own apprehension. Across the table, Alison Metcalfe was gripping a mug of tea with both hands like a lifeline, her eyes red-rimmed, her face taut with concern.

'The only way we're going to get you out of this mess, Will,' said Samson, 'is if you come clean right now. Because at the moment, you're not going to be flavour of the month when DS Benson discovers you've been leading him up the garden path. Let's begin with the argument – what had you pinning Ross Irwin against a wall and uttering death threats in full view of half of Bruncliffe?'

Will looked at his wife, who gave a small nod and took his hand in hers.

'We were being blackmailed,' he said.

Gareth Towler whistled softly, while Delilah gasped.

'By Irwin?' she verified, stunned.

A grim nod from her brother. 'He called me late last week and more or less said that if we didn't pay him, he would make sure his report was in Dinsdale's favour. That the camping pods would be given a green light. Only he didn't put it quite so bluntly. But it was clear he was wanting a payoff.'

'How much?' asked Samson.

'Five grand.'

Another whistle from Gareth. 'What a racket! I'm guessing you said no?'

Will gave the gamekeeper a weak grin. 'I was a bit more robust than that, but yes, it was a clear refusal.'

'And at the wedding? What happened there?' Delilah asked.

'Irwin started up again. Telling me he could make trouble for the farm if I didn't comply. I held my temper but then he said I had no idea how dangerous he could be.' Will shrugged. 'I just lost it. Next thing I knew, Ash was pulling on my arm, Harry was yelling in my ear, and I had a crowd of folk around me. A crowd of folk who are now witnesses to me making threats to a man who was found murdered the next morning. Is it any wonder I lied when the police started asking about it?'

Delilah couldn't argue with Will's logic. Because the revelation about the background to his disagreement with

Ross Irwin provided him with a perfect motive for wanting the ecologist dead. Five thousand such reasons, in fact.

'Okay,' said Samson. 'Trouble is, if you don't tell them the truth, they're going to find out anyway and then it will look even worse. So is there anything else you need to tell us?'

Will grimaced, his wife gripping his hand even tighter.

'I didn't tell them I wasn't home when Ali got back from the wedding,' he said.

'Bloody hell, Will!' Delilah's anxiety burst from her in a blast of Metcalfe temper.

'I know – I lost the plot. But they obviously think I might be involved and I didn't want to give them any more ammunition.'

'So where were you?'

'Up on the fellside off Hillside Lane.' He gestured towards the rear of the farm. 'I changed out of my wedding clobber when I got in and went straight up to check on the sheep and found a dead yow. Poor thing had been savaged by a flaming dog. Right mess, it was. I reckoned the kids had had enough violence for one day so I left it there, came back, had my tea and then got the kids to bed. Once they were asleep, I went back out to collect it. Took me a while to find it in the dark and so it was quite late by the time I got home. Gone midnight.'

'What kind of time frame are we talking?' asked Delilah.

Will frowned. 'Must have been about half seven when I first went out. I got back about nine. Then I let the kids stay up a bit, seeing as it was the weekend and all, so I reckon it was ten thirty when I went out again. I got home after Ali, so it must have been midnight or thereabouts.'

Delilah smothered a groan. It was the worst of answers, giving Will ample time to both kill Irwin and then move his body.

'Can anyone corroborate this?' Samson's question brought an ominous quiet to the table. 'Ali? Did you see him come back at least?'

'No.' Alison's voice was barely a whisper. 'I noticed the Land Rover was gone. But I was a bit drunk. I fell asleep as soon as my head hit the pillow.'

'So now I have motive and opportunity,' muttered Will.

'And that's not all,' continued Alison. 'Will isn't the only one who might have done something stupid.' She glanced at the table and then cleared her throat. A vivid flush rose up her pallid cheeks. 'I thought . . . you know, with the missing Land Rover, and the fact he wasn't at home and then he lied to the police . . . and then there was the shirt and the fact he cleaned the Land Rover . . . I just thought, perhaps . . .'

She petered out with a stricken look towards her husband.

'It's okay, love.' Will took her hand to his lips and kissed it. 'It's okay.'

'You thought Will might have killed Irwin?' Samson asked gently.

Alison nodded. Crying now. A hand to her mouth.

'And this shirt?'

'The one I wore to the wedding,' said Will. 'Ali was bringing it in from the washing line when she noticed a missing button, and a stain. A red stain. Next minute the police are here asking questions. What was she supposed to think?'

'This stain?' asked Delilah.

'Sheep's blood. When I came back the second time I went upstairs to have a shower, and saw I'd left the shirt on the bathroom floor. I picked it up to put it in the wash basket.' He shrugged. 'I must have still had blood on my hands.'

'So where is it now, this shirt?'

Alison shook her head, tears on her cheeks. 'I burned it. As soon as the police left yesterday.'

'I keep telling her it's no big deal,' murmured Will, his arm around his wife's shoulders. 'It's not, is it?'

His question was aimed at Samson, who managed a small smile.

'I'm sure we'll be able to work around it,' he said.

Delilah suspected he was putting on an optimistic front for Alison's sake. For if there had been sheep's blood on the shirt, it could have been vital evidence in determining Will's innocence, providing credence to his version of events. Now they were left with nothing but a farmer without an alibi who had a valid reason for wanting to commit murder. Not to mention the burning of possible evidence.

It didn't look good.

'Tell me a bit more about the ecological report,' Samson was saying. 'How would you feel if it did come back in Dinsdale's favour?'

'It wouldn't be a problem in itself,' said Alison. 'We're not out to stop Kevin and Louise from developing that land. We just want it to be developed properly. Within the regulations.'

'And with respect for the newts living down there,' added Will.

'You've got newts on your land?' asked Gareth.

Will nodded. 'Great crested newts at that. In the pond down by the beck. I told Ross Irwin the first time I met him. Wanted to make sure he took that into consideration, what with them being a protected species and all that. But he didn't seem to be that bothered.'

'Because he was too busy planning how to scam us,' muttered Alison.

'Could great crested newts have proved a problem for Dinsdale's planning?' asked Delilah.

Gareth was nodding. 'Like Will said, they're a protected species. At the very least, any development would have to take pains to make sure their habitat wasn't disturbed. It can be a costly business.'

'You think that could be worth investigating?' Will was looking at Samson. 'Not that I'm comfortable saying this, but the prospect of an expensive hold-up gives Kevin a hefty motive for removing Irwin.'

'Let's not get ahead of ourselves,' said Samson. 'We will of course look into Dinsdale. But first of all, we need to get you in the clear, and that starts with you telling all of this to the police—'

The back door flew open, Nathan hurrying into the kitchen, out of breath.

'Three cop cars, Uncle Will!' he exclaimed. 'Just turned in the drive.'

Will nodded. Resigned. 'Best get the kettle on. This could take a while.'

16

Nathan was right. A trio of police cars pulled into the yard, parking in parallel with the Land Rover. The ultra-clean Land Rover.

While DS Benson's expression was unreadable as he got out of the car, Samson could tell from the strained look of Sergeant Clayton that this wasn't going to be merely a routine follow-up. For a start, they'd brought Danny with them, and an immaculately uniformed female sergeant Samson didn't recognise. Almost as tall as Danny, there was an energy about her, the pixie cut of raven-dark hair only emphasising the strong features and the sharp gaze which was snapping around the farmyard.

She let that gaze pause for a brief second on the Land Rover, gleaming in the sunshine. Noting how odd it was to see a vehicle devoid of muck on a working farm. Then she glanced at Benson, who gave the smallest of nods.

'Morning all.' Sergeant Clayton was leading the group towards the porch. 'I see we have a welcoming committee,' he remarked dryly, taking in the three members of the Dales Detective team and Nathan standing alongside Will and Alison. 'Can I introduce Sergeant Dani Grewal, our wildlife crime lead?'

The female officer gave a decisive nod in their direction, no handshake offered as her distinctive amber gaze brushed across each one of them before coming to rest on Samson. Taking in the injuries to his face.

'DC O'Brien?' she asked.

'Guilty as charged,' he grinned, a little unnerved by the intensity of those eyes. He doubted they missed much, which was good considering Sergeant Grewal's investigative skills offered the best hope of deflecting attention away from Will.

She turned back to Delilah. 'So you must be Delilah Metcalfe. I've heard about your role in the Rick Procter case.' She gave an approving tip of her head. 'It's a pleasure to meet you.'

'Oh, thanks,' muttered Delilah, flustered by being singled out for praise. 'But it was very much a team effort.'

Sergeant Grewal showed no interest in being introduced to the others, stepping back behind DS Benson but keeping her scrutiny on them all.

'I'm guessing you're here with more questions?' said Will, about to show everyone into the kitchen.

Detective Benson nodded. 'Yes, but I wonder if we could have a quick look in the Land Rover first?'

'What for?' demanded Alison, before Will could speak.

The detective turned to her, missing the flicker of unease which crossed Will's face. Judging by the narrowing of Sergeant Grewal's eyes, however, Samson suspected it hadn't gone unnoticed in all quarters.

'We're simply trying to rule things out at the moment,' said Benson.

Alison looked at Will and he gave a reluctant nod. 'Sure,' he said.

The group of police officers turned around and walked back towards the 4x4.

'Nice and clean,' commented Sergeant Clayton as they reached it.

'Aye,' said Will. 'I try to keep it proper. Not easy when it's a workhorse.'

'Mind if we have a look in the rear?' Benson asked, pulling on a pair of blue gloves as he gestured for Will to open it.

Will paused for a second, transfixed by the detective's gloves, as though the significance of what was happening had finally dawned. Then he did as requested, pulling open the rear door, the inside empty apart from a tarpaulin pushed over to one side. Samson saw it straight away – the stain in the middle of the floor, still there despite Will's cleaning.

'What's that?' asked Benson.

The energy seemed to leak from Will. His head dropped and he shrugged. 'It's sheep blood. But you're not going to believe that.'

'When did it get there?'

'Saturday night.'

Benson stared at Will. 'What time on Saturday night?'

'Sometime between eleven and midnight. I had to go pick up a dead sheep which had been worried by a dog.'

Sergeant Clayton inhaled sharply. 'So you're telling us you weren't at home that night like you said yesterday?'

'I lied. I knew it wouldn't look good, so I lied.'

'Christ, Will!' The sergeant gave him a weary look. 'Lying never helps anyone.'

'It certainly isn't helping in this instance,' said DS Benson gravely. 'You didn't take a trailer up with you? Isn't that unusual?'

Will frowned at the detective. Not appreciating being told how to do his job by a layman. 'It was late and the kids were in bed,' he said tersely. 'I didn't want to disturb them getting the trailer out so I just went up in this. I put the tarp down in the back but it must have a tear in it.'

Benson gave a small nod. If he was convinced by the explanation, his face wasn't showing it. Then he leaned into the rear of the Land Rover and gently lifted the edge of the tarpaulin. He jerked backwards like he'd touched a live wire.

'Constable Bradley, an evidence bag please.'

As Danny scurried to get one from the car, Benson turned slightly to look at Will, both eyebrows raised. Behind him, a brown wooden handle could be seen protruding from under the tarp. It was smeared with dark stains.

'Izzy's rounders bat!' exclaimed Alison. 'How did that get there?'

'The very question I was about to ask,' said DS Benson dryly. 'I was also going to enquire how it came to be covered in what appears to be blood.'

Will was shaking his head. Looking like a man in quicksand, whose every movement was just making him sink further. 'Izzy must have left it in there. And then with the sheep it got covered somehow . . . I don't know . . .'

An uncomfortable silence followed while Danny retrieved the bat, the poor lad avoiding eye contact as he carried it back to the police car, torn between duty and loyalty to someone he'd known all his life. Samson was feeling a similar pull of emotions. It was what Bruncliffe did to you, brought you in so close that perspective became hard.

But what was the perspective needed here? Surely Will was innocent and this was all some horrible coincidence?

Or was Izzy's rounders bat the murder weapon Benson and his team had been looking for? It certainly fit the brief description the pathologist had given from her initial inspection of the body . . .

Knowing Delilah would kill him for even holding those thoughts, Samson focused back on DS Benson.

'Let's see if you know anything about this, then,' he was asking, holding out another evidence bag he'd produced from his pocket, this one much smaller. Inside was a button, white thread dangling from it. 'Do you recognise it?'

Alison's hand slapped over her mouth, all the reply Benson needed.

'It's from my shirt,' said Will, voice strained. 'The one I was wearing at the wedding.'

'Any idea why we found it above Malham Cove? At the spot where Irwin was murdered?'

Will blanched. 'I haven't got the foggiest. It must have come off in the rugby club when I was . . . during the disagreement with Irwin. Got trapped on his bloody waistcoat or something . . .'

'I'd like to see the shirt, if I may?'

'I threw it out—'

'*I* threw it out,' Alison corrected her husband. 'I burned it. It had sheep's blood on it so it were of no use.'

Benson was looking from one to the other in disbelief, while Sergeant Clayton was staring at the floor, clearly hating every minute of what was unfolding.

'Right,' said Benson, staring hard at Will now. 'Let me get this straight. The shirt you had on has been destroyed. You've cleaned your Land Rover which has somehow acquired a suspect stain. There is a rounders bat in the back also covered in what could be blood. And you lied about your whereabouts on the night in question. All this after you were seen having a violent confrontation with a man who is now dead.' He grimaced. 'I'm afraid we're going to have to get a team out to do some tests on this vehicle and, in the meantime, I think we'd best continue this conversation on a more formal footing down at the station.'

'Are you arresting me?' asked Will, in a voice brittle with tension.

Sergeant Clayton put a hand on his shoulder. 'Come on, Will, lad, let's not make this harder than it has to be.' He pointed towards the doorway behind them, where two small figures had appeared. 'Not in front of the kids.'

Will turned to see Charlie and Izzy, both watching him with faces more worried than their years merited. He pulled them into a hug, kissed Alison and, with a resigned nod, began walking towards the police cars while his wife led the children back inside. Nathan wasn't so willing to accept the situation, however, the teenager stepping forward to block Sergeant Clayton's path. Afraid his godson was about to do something reckless, Samson caught hold of his arm but, in a surprising display of maturity, Nathan simply levelled an accusing finger at the sergeant.

'You're making a big mistake and you know it,' he said. 'Uncle Will couldn't kill anyone.'

'Aye, well, if you're right, there's nowt to worry about.' Sergeant Clayton gave a curt nod and headed for his car, where Will was waiting.

'Bloody idiots, the lot of them,' muttered Nathan,

defaulting to adolescent angst as he cast a glower at the remaining officers.

'They're only doing their jobs, Nathan, love,' murmured Delilah. But her stricken look suggested she shared his distress. She turned to Benson. 'What about a lawyer? Do we need to organise one for Will?'

'We're just bringing him in for questioning for now,' said Benson, making it sound routine.

Samson suspected that just how routine it turned out to be would all depend on what the tests revealed about the damning stain in the back of the 4x4. And on little Izzy's rounders bat.

'Sergeant Grewal?' Benson continued, as Danny started rolling out police tape, beginning to rope off the Land Rover and secure the evidence. 'Are you driving back with us?'

The policewoman shook her head. 'I'll make my own way down. I want a look around up here first.'

Benson nodded, got in the car, and Sergeant Clayton drove off, Will a small figure in the rear. Sergeant Grewal turned to the shocked onlookers still standing by the back porch.

'I'm interested in seeing the land that was the focus of this report Ross Irwin was drawing up,' she said, addressing Alison Metcalfe, who'd re-emerged from the house in time to see her husband being driven away, tears fresh on her cheeks. 'Including where your property juts up to it. Can you show me?'

Gareth Towler stepped forward, touching Alison's shoulder as he did. 'I can do it, Ali.'

'Thanks, Gareth,' she murmured.

'And you are?' The sergeant's tone was more than a little brusque as she addressed the large man now standing in front of her.

'Gareth Towler. Until recently, I was a gamekeeper on Bruncliffe estate across the road, so I know this place like the back of my hand.'

'A gamekeeper?' The word dropped from Sergeant Grewal's mouth like it was poisoned, a look of distaste on her face.

'Aye. At your service.' Gareth gave a mocking bow.

The policewoman simply gestured for him to lead the way. He whistled for Bounty, the springer spaniel sprinting across the yard to him, and they walked off.

'What now?' murmured Delilah.

'Now,' said Alison, pulling herself upright and drying her eyes, 'I formally hire you both to investigate what happened to this Irwin fella, because I know damn well Will didn't kill him. But after the mess we've made, it might be hard proving that—' She hesitated, looking at Samson with fresh concern. 'That's if you've got the time, seeing as you're back in your proper job. I mean, I wouldn't want to impose . . .'

Sensing it was more the legality of the situation which could be an issue with his bosses down in London, Samson simply nodded, prepared to take the risk. 'I've got the time. I'm on leave for a week and I can take more holiday if needed.'

Alison let out a shaky sigh. 'Thank you. Thank you so much.'

'It's the least I can do,' he said, made awkward by her gratitude. 'I couldn't leave family in the lurch.'

Family. The word caught him by surprise. Delilah too – he saw her eyes widen, the flash of a smile, and then she was drawing her sister-in-law into a hug.

'We'll do everything we can to clear him, Ali, I promise,' she said. She looked at Samson. 'What say we start with the Dinsdales? At the very least, they had a connection to Irwin so might be able to shed light on someone who wanted him dead.'

'Agreed,' said Samson. 'And if we're really lucky, they might even have seen Will go out in the Land Rover looking for the sheep. If we can find someone who saw him head up Hillside Lane rather than down into town, it could go some way to proving he couldn't have moved the body to the kiln.'

'Won't the tests on the Land Rover do that?' asked Nathan.

'They'll only prove Will had a dead sheep in there. And even that will take a few days. The sooner we can cast serious doubt on Benson's theory, the better.'

'So what can I do to help?' The question contained a pent-up frustration Samson remembered well from his own teenage years.

Delilah pointed at the mountain bike Nathan had abandoned on the ground in his haste to warn Will about the approaching trouble. 'Ride down and tell your mum about this in person. It's not something I want her hearing over the phone. Or over the counter. So ride fast before that blasted Mrs Pettiford gets wind of it!'

Nathan was already running for his bike.

* * *

For once, Mrs Pettiford, bank clerk and the driving force behind Bruncliffe's rumour mill, was in the dark when it came to the goings-on in her town. Having spent all of Sunday over at the coast in Filey – her sister had kindly invited her to stop a night at the luxury apartment she'd rented for the week with her husband – her mind had been on other things as she'd returned that morning.

Dropped off in Leeds by her brother-in-law on his way to work, she'd been preoccupied about the future of Lady, her sister's cocker spaniel. For Mrs Pettiford suspected that had been the real reason for the impromptu invitation from her sibling to spend a day by the seaside. The dog had been driving her sister mad and, under the guise of the animal's welfare, she'd beseeched Mrs Pettiford to take it home with her.

'You know the pair of you love spending time together,' her sister had declared, as she poured a large measure of wine into Mrs Pettiford's glass over their evening meal.

The subject of the discussion had been watching anxiously from her bed in the corner of the room, looking unusually subdued. A state Mrs Pettiford was inclined to think had been brought on by frequent reprimands.

For the spaniel could be a bit yappy. But, looking around the pristine apartment, with its cream leather sofas and delicate fabrics, all overlooking the most amazing expanse of sea, it was hard to say that this was the right environment for a dog. Certainly not one with the personality of Lady.

Ruffling the dog's ears on the train back to Bruncliffe, Mrs Pettiford had come to a decision. She would ask her sister if she could adopt the cocker spaniel. After all, with the number of weekends away and spontaneous trips abroad Lady's owners were taking, the poor pooch was spending most of the time at Mrs Pettiford's anyway. And it was true, they had built up a rapport, despite their relationship getting off to the most rocky of starts thanks to that dreadful poisoning incident back in March.

Perhaps that was what had brought them together, Mrs Pettiford was now musing as she walked down towards the marketplace to begin her day's work. Friendship in the face of adversity.

Whatever it was, Mrs Pettiford was convinced it was time for Lady to have a better life. And she could provide it.

It was with these thoughts paramount that she entered Peaks Patisserie for her customary cappuccino to go. But while her head might have been filled with other matters, her finely tuned antennae for all things Bruncliffe were still working. The minute she saw Elaine Bullock looking so grave behind the counter, those antennae started quivering.

'I just need a witness,' Elaine was saying to Lucy. 'Then I'd be pretty much in the clear.'

'A witness for what?' asked Mrs Pettiford, as Lucy broke off the conversation to start making her cappuccino, the bank clerk such a regular she didn't even have to order it.

Elaine Bullock stared at her. Not in the insolent way the young woman usually did, normally accompanied by some cutting remark. No, she was just staring in shock. Similarly, Lucy Metcalfe was standing at the coffee machine, Mrs Pettiford's reusable cup in her hand, and her mouth open as she gazed at her customer in disbelief.

'You haven't heard?' Lucy finally said.

Mrs Pettiford felt an uncomfortable heat steal over her. She looked from cafe owner to waitress and then back again. 'Has something happened?'

Now Elaine let out a hoot of laughter. 'Ha! I get pulled in and questioned for murder and for once, the town's gossip knows nothing about it!'

'*Murder?*' Mrs Pettiford found it hard to keep her voice within its normal alto range.

Lucy nodded. 'A guy named Ross Irwin—'

'The ecologist?'

'The same. He was found dead yesterday morning up at the kiln.'

Mrs Pettiford felt the world tip and sway. Perhaps the most newsworthy event ever to have hit the town – which took some doing after the past twelve months – and she'd missed it.

'Oh my,' she breathed. Thinking about the day ahead. The hours at the counter in the bank when her customers would be looking to her for the latest updates and she would have nothing to say.

'You genuinely didn't know?' Elaine peering at her through those glasses which always looked like they could do with a good clean. 'Where have you been? Mars?'

'Filey,' said Mrs Pettiford, too stunned by developments to offer anything but a perfunctory reply. Too stunned to deploy any of her usual gossip-harvesting methods on the women, neither of whom were known for dispensing tittle-tattle glibly anyway.

She reached for her coffee, dreading the thought of going to work, where a bleak day of being in woeful ignorance beckoned.

'Would you like to know more?' Elaine Bullock was leaning across the counter, regarding her with an intense stare through those smeared lenses, as though she could perceive the painful feeling of redundancy occupying Mrs Pettiford at that moment.

'Why, only if . . . I mean . . . yes?'

Elaine tipped her head to one side, ignoring the warning glance from Lucy Metcalfe, which Mrs Pettiford couldn't help but see.

'Well, basically,' said the waitress, 'this Ross Irwin has been found dead. He was killed sometime Saturday evening and I'm a suspect because I was probably one of the last people to see him alive.' She shrugged. 'That's the guts of it. So, like I was saying when you came in, I just need a witness because at the moment the police aren't inclined to take my word for it when I insist that I was back home about nine that evening—'

'But of course you were!' Mrs Pettiford declared.

Elaine broke off, eyes wide. 'Sorry?'

'You were at home by nine. I saw you. You were walking up Church Road as I was coming back from visiting my cousin. I remember thinking . . .' She paused. Reflecting on the critical nature of her thoughts on Saturday evening as she'd seen the young woman striding home – how she'd disapproved of the bright red dress and those mannish boots; how she'd been consumed by an envy she couldn't explain . . . 'Anyway, I saw you walk up to your front door and go inside. And I know it was just gone nine because I heard the church clock chiming.'

A loud whoop of sound exploded from behind the

counter and before Mrs Pettiford could brace herself, there was a blur of movement and she was being fiercely held in an embrace of perfume and laughter.

For Elaine Bullock, while hugging her, was laughing wildly.

'You genius!' she was declaring. 'You absolute star!'

Mrs Pettiford couldn't say anything in response. She was too busy trying to remember when she'd last been held with such affection by another human being.

Elaine finally stepped back, tears in her eyes. 'Seriously, you're a lifesaver,' she said, as Lucy clapped her hands behind the counter. 'The police are going to have to take this into consideration. You might have cleared my name.'

'Well, that's . . .'

Mrs Pettiford ran out of words at the precise moment that the cafe door flung wide open and young Nathan Metcalfe came barrelling in.

'Mum!' he declared. 'Uncle Will's been taken in for questioning over the murder of that Irwin bloke—!' He froze. Seeing Mrs Pettiford there. 'Shit!'

But he needn't have worried. Mrs Pettiford picked up her coffee, nodded at the women behind the counter – their elation having evaporated in the shock of the lad's news – and turned to leave. Lucy and Elaine were going to need a bit of space to digest these developments, she found herself thinking as she left the cafe. And while she would spend the rest of the day no further informed than the clients she dealt with over her bank counter, any disappointment she might have felt would be negated by the memory of that incredible hug.

* * *

Across the marketplace and down the narrow tarmac of Back Street, inside the downstairs office of the Dales Detective Agency, Ida Capstick was immersed in technology.

Having been a rudimentary mobile user before, capable of texting and messaging but using only a fraction of her smartphone's potential, since her life had been transformed as part of the agency's team she'd had a steep learning curve. Overseeing WhatsApp groups, being in sole command of communications during the attempt on Samson's life and now, being trusted to install and monitor devices necessary to the trade of investigating.

Delilah had walked her through each process in turn as need had arisen and, despite her early misgivings, Ida was now proud of her technical prowess. She was never going to get a job in Silicon Valley but at least she knew how to access the app which was linked to the small cameras she'd installed at Peaks Patisserie.

Which was what she was currently doing, sitting at Samson's desk, a laptop in front of her.

Logging onto the website, she scrolled through the contents and clicked on the two latest files. The interior of Peaks Patisserie's kitchen opened onto one half of her screen, the exterior and the ginnel on the other, the date and time in the bottom right-hand corner of both confirming it was last night's footage. Hunched over the computer, she ran the films at a speed fast enough to get through twelve hours of surveillance quickly without missing anything.

It was monotonous work. After the initial shot of Lucy walking away from the inside camera once she'd set it in motion, the door which led to the ginnel closed. Lucy walked past outside and then Ida was left staring at frame after frame of nothingness. One eye on the clock in the corner, she let the images roll. Reached for her tea and took a sip. Reached for a biscuit and ate it. Drank some more tea and peered even closer as the on-screen hours slipped into night and the picture darkened.

She was on her third Hobnob and musing whether there was such a condition as Detective's Backside when she saw something. Slapping her mug on the desk, she ran the footage back a fraction and then started it again.

There! What was that?

A movement outside, something going past the window, an indistinct blur against the night. But then the darkness was split apart, white light crashing onto the screen, blinding her.

Headlights?

She was right. Seconds later the lights cut out and darkness returned, only this time there was a definite vehicle-shaped addition to the shadows. She'd caught them. Whoever it was. This was surely the thief who'd been plaguing Lucy Metcalfe. But identifying the driver or the car was going to be impossible, the light too restricted in the gloom of the ginnel.

Ida reached for her mug, letting the film roll at normal speed now. Reached for a fourth biscuit to counter her disappointment at the quality of the footage. Let herself have the luxury of dunking it. And then it happened, just as she was raising the soaked Hobnob to her lips.

A light, from inside the vehicle. Enough to illuminate the occupant. Singular. No amorous couple seeking a private space as Lucy had suspected but just a sole person sitting behind the steering wheel.

Totally visible. Totally identifiable.

'What on earth . . . ?'

Staring at the screen in shock, Ida forgot about her pre-dunked biscuit. Until it fell into her tea.

17

The Dinsdale farm seemed deserted. Having left an anxious Alison Metcalfe standing outside Ellershaw House, Samson and Delilah had driven back to the road, cutting across it to pick up the track which led to the neighbouring farmyard. But as they got out into the late morning sunshine, it was eerily quiet.

Samson had been there once before, back in early spring when there'd been daffodils dancing in the grass in front of the old farmhouse and an air of optimism about the place. Admittedly, he'd been focused on a case of sheep rustling at the time, so hadn't really paid much more than superficial attention to the background. Now, however, under a more critical eye, while the surroundings were still neat and tidy, there was a creeping sense of neglect. Paint peeling from windows, a couple of holes gaping in the corrugated roof of one of the barns set back behind the house, a tractor inside surrounded by bits of engine, in the midst of being given a DIY repair.

Either this revised appraisal of the Dinsdale farm was simply a result of the unforgiving spotlight being cast by the sun overhead, or these were signs of recent financial constraint. Samson was inclined towards the latter, well acquainted with such symptoms from his own farming experience.

'Hello?' Delilah called out. She was greeted by a responding shout and the sound of footsteps as Kevin Dinsdale came around the corner from the back of the house, drying one hand on his overalls, the other holding a car-headlight bulb. If the intervening four months had aged the property, they had also aged the owner. The fresh smile which had greeted Delilah back in spring had been replaced with a frown of concern and the look of a man constantly expecting bad news.

'Delilah, Samson,' the farmer nodded, popping the bulb in a pocket and holding out his hand to each in turn.

Samson hid his surprise as he accepted the man's greeting, which had been noticeably withheld last time round. It seemed those same four months had done a lot to change the O'Brien reputation, too.

'What can I do for you?' Dinsdale asked.

'It's about Will,' said Delilah. 'The police have just taken him in for questioning over the murder of Ross Irwin.'

Dinsdale's eyes widened. 'You're kidding me?'

'Wish I was. We just want to have a chat about what happened at the wedding and . . . you know . . . the planning permission.'

There was a pause, as if he was going to refuse, then Dinsdale shrugged and gestured towards the house. 'Sure. Come in and have a brew. I can't tell you much about the wedding, mind,' he added with a rueful smile. 'I wasn't in a fit state to remember my own movements on Saturday evening, let alone those of anyone else!'

They followed him through the side porch and down a

narrow hallway which led into the kitchen extension. If the exterior of the house had shown signs of trouble, the interior suggested more of the same. A couple of damp patches marred the ceiling where the roof abutted the main building, water no doubt seeping in along the valley, and underfoot, a couple of the slate slabs rocked as Samson walked over them. Even the kettle Dinsdale was filling had a handle held together with duct tape. And as for the long table which dominated the space, one end held a stack of beautifully carved birdboxes, all in various stages of completion, while the rest was covered in paperwork, much of it carrying the logos of local agricultural stores or oil suppliers. Samson recognised bills when he saw them. Amidst it all was a laptop, the screensaver beaming out a photo of Kevin and his wife at the Malham Show in happier times, arms around each other, a grinning gap-toothed toddler in front of them, chubby hands holding a trophy and a red rosette. Next to them was a handsome Swaledale tup.

'Best in show,' said Kevin with a wistful air as he closed the laptop, before stretching a broad arm the width of the wooden surface and clearing the clutter, laptop and all, to one end. 'Make yourselves comfortable.'

He turned back to make the tea as Delilah took a seat at the table. Samson wandered over to the end wall, where an assortment of wire figurines were arrayed along the sill beneath a large picture window. Birds, of all sorts and sizes. Robins, wrens, kingfishers, goldfinches, even a curlew, exquisitely depicted, plus many more Samson couldn't identify. They advanced from either end of the ledge towards the middle, where there was a blank space, two circles of clean sill left within the dusty surface, as though a couple of glasses had been resting there a long while and had only recently been removed. But it was what was on the other side of the window that really caught his focus. Out across a small patio area, the dale dropped towards Bruncliffe in a magnificent cascading carpet of green fields stretching into the distance before the fells on the far side rose up to curve around them. He felt a sharp pang of longing for Twistleton Farm.

'Lovely view,' he said, turning back to the room and away from the landscape which was doing strange things to his heart.

Kevin laughed. 'Aye, it's grand all right, on a day like this. Try it when there's a storm blowing and it's lashing down. Nothing so desolate as the sound of rain on glass.'

A noise from the hallway made all of them turn and Louise Dinsdale entered the room.

'Oh, sorry, I didn't hear you come in,' she said, flustered by the unexpected guests. She ran a hand through her hair, smoothed out her crumpled T-shirt and managed a smile. But it didn't hide the weariness. She cast a vague hand at the cluttered table. 'I was trying to get the accounts done while Ava's at my folks for the morning, but I got distracted.'

Kevin grunted. 'Easily done, love. Not like we're living in a bed of roses at the moment.'

'Have you managed to find any work?' asked Delilah, as Samson wandered over to sit next to her.

Louise shook her head and, seeing Samson's querying look, pulled a face. 'I'm yet another statistic in the Rick Procter saga,' she said, with a lightness he suspected came at a cost. 'Two of my main clients went under when Procter

Properties was closed down and at the moment, there's not a lot of call for bookkeepers in the Bruncliffe area.'

'You'll find something, Lou,' said Kevin, dropping a kiss on her head as he placed the teapot down between them. 'A woman of your skills won't be long out of work.'

Louise nodded. Without conviction.

'So what's this about Will, then?' Kevin took a seat next to his wife and leaned strong forearms on the table. 'You're not telling me the police really think he killed Irwin?'

The question was aimed at Delilah but it was Louise who reacted.

'They suspect Will?' Her eyes were huge, shock bringing life to her tired features.

'Apparently so,' said Delilah. 'Which is kind of why we're here. It seems my stupid brother doesn't have anyone who can corroborate his whereabouts for crucial times on Saturday night. We were just wondering if you could help.'

Kevin shrugged, turned to his wife. 'We didn't see Will once he left the reception after he went for Irwin, did we, love?'

Louise shook her head.

'What time did you get back here?' asked Samson.

'No point asking me,' said Kevin with a bashful look. 'I was out of it.'

'Just before midnight,' said Louise. 'We dropped Alison off at the end of their lane and came straight here.'

'So I don't suppose you saw Will coming back down Hillside Lane in the Land Rover at all?' Delilah's question held more hope than expectation.

'What was he doing up there at that time?' asked Kevin, while Louise was shaking her head.

'Collecting a dead sheep off the fell. Only trouble is, he can't prove it. And the police seem to think that means he must have been moving Irwin's body from Malham Cove to the Hoffmann kiln instead.'

'Jesus!' Kevin ran a hand over his ruddy face. 'What a bloody mess. I'm beginning to wish I'd never brought Irwin over here in the first place. It's done nothing but bring bad luck and soured our relations with your brother.'

Louise looked down, running a finger over the rim of her cup.

'Talking of Irwin,' said Samson, 'what was he like to deal with?'

Kevin took a swig of his tea. When he spoke, there was a heartiness to his voice which was at odds with his previous demeanour. 'He were all right. A bit condescending, like, as some folk can be when they've letters after their names and they think farmers are nowt but tractor drivers. But nothing worse than that.' He nodded towards his wife. 'Isn't that right, Lou?'

She gave a simple nod in return. Cleared her throat. And then picked up her own tea.

'You don't know of anyone around here who might have had a grudge against him?'

Samson's question was met with a wry look. 'Apart from that ruckus with Will, you mean?' Kevin shook his head. 'As far as I can tell, the man kept himself to himself and just got on with his work.'

'What about the report he was compiling?' Delilah asked. 'Did Irwin let you know which way he was leaning?'

The farmer's response was to reach over into the mess of paperwork and extract a sheaf of pages from the bottom of the pile. 'Here,' he said, holding it out. 'He dropped this by the morning of the wedding. It's an advance copy of what he was about to submit.'

Delilah took the report, Samson looking over her shoulder as she flicked through the pages, each one watermarked with the word 'DRAFT'. She got to the final page and looked up at Kevin.

'Approved? He was giving you the OK?'

He nodded. 'The police have seen that. First thing they asked when they called in to chat to me. Guess they wanted to know if I had a reason to kill Irwin. That's evidence I didn't.'

'And evidence that Will did,' muttered Delilah.

'Sorry.' Kevin shook his head. 'Like I said, I never wished this to cause trouble for Will and his family, but we really didn't have a choice. The way things are here, we're in desperate need of an added revenue stream. Thanks to this report, we're one step closer to getting the planning approved and making that happen.' Then he grimaced. 'No disrespect to the dead or anything, but I'm hoping Irwin's demise doesn't hold it up any.'

Walking on the fells beneath a benign sun, Gareth Towler should have been in his element, a man of the outdoors such as he was. Instead he was scratching his head. Literally and metaphorically. The literal bit was a slight tic he had when he was nervous, and he was presently in that heightened state, thanks to Sergeant Dani Grewal.

While Gareth would never profess to have worked with the public much, a lot of his former profession of gamekeeping seeing his time spent alone on the land, he'd had a fair amount of dealings with folk while running the shooting parties for Bruncliffe Manor. And he liked to think he was an affable kind of bloke. He'd had to be really, to put up with some of the wealthy types who'd turned up for shoots with attitudes straight out of the Victorian era. Certainly he'd never had a problem getting on with people, as far as he knew.

Today, however, was proving to be the exception.

He just couldn't seem to put a foot right with his companion. Which is why he was scratching his head, in both senses.

He'd tried making small talk on the walk down towards the land Sergeant Grewal had asked to inspect. She'd had none of it, cutting him off with brusque answers or simply ignoring him completely. And when she did have recourse to speak, it was with a tone which left him in no doubt as to her opinion of him. Despite the fact they'd only just met.

But if Gareth was having a problem with her, Bounty wasn't. With no livestock in the fields they were walking through, he'd left the springer spaniel off the lead and as she trotted along, she showed no signs of her recently acquired nervousness, as happy at the police officer's side as she was at Gareth's. At one point, she even brought a small branch back to the sergeant. Who'd willingly thrown it, and then lavished affection on the dog when she returned.

So Gareth had accepted he was the source of the sergeant's hostility and taken the hint, falling silent until they reached the point where the Metcalfe property butted up against the Dinsdale farm.

'This is it,' he said, halting at a gate in a drystone wall which separated Will's land from the site of the proposed camping-pod development.

It was easy to see why Kevin Dinsdale had chosen the location. The field had a gentle gradient, running down towards a sizeable beck which cut across the bottom of both fields, glinting in the sunshine and heedless of the man-made boundary which divided the two farms. A boundary which had been forced to deviate from customary straight lines as it snaked around a sizeable pond on Will's side of the wall, just uphill of the beck. Between the two bodies of water, a small copse of ash, alder and oak provided shelter from any westerly wind, adding a darker green to the palette.

And as ever, in the distance, the far fells rose in purple-heathered magnificence. With the addition of birdsong and the joyous burble of water tumbling over stones, it was a veritable paradise.

'Wow.' The word seemed to be pulled from the sergeant against her will, the frown which had marred her forehead since they'd set out disappearing as she took in the sight. There was even a hint of a smile.

'It's pretty special,' said Gareth. 'Not sure I'd want to mar it with camping pods, mind.'

'Not our place to judge,' came the reply. The frown back in place. She turned and left the gate, heading down to the beck.

'What are we looking for, exactly?' Gareth asked as he caught up with the surprisingly long stride of his companion.

'*We* aren't looking for anything.'

They'd reached the water's edge, Sergeant Grewal crouching down and inspecting the bank, brushing aside foliage to see the soil underneath.

'Too dry for tracks,' said Gareth, helpfully.

She glared up at him. 'But not for droppings.'

He sighed. 'Look, I realise you don't want me here but I could be of use. I know this land probably as well as Will or Kevin. So if you just let me know what you're hoping to find, you'd get finished a lot faster and then never have to see me again.'

She stared at the water for a few seconds, then stood up. 'I'm looking for evidence of something that would have made your friend kill that ecologist. So forgive me if I don't take you up on your offer.'

'What makes you so sure that's what happened? Or has the law dispensed with innocent until proven guilty?'

She snorted, an eyebrow raised in arched disdain. 'We've got a dead ecologist who was in the process of doing an ecological impact survey as part of a planning permission application. And that survey incorporated land belonging to two different farmers, one of whom seemed to have a real problem with our murder victim. I'd say that's a good place to start.'

'How about the peregrine falcon connection?' Gareth found himself protesting. 'That feather found in Irwin's hand? Aren't you going to follow that up?'

'I already have.' The sergeant looked like she was going to offer nothing more. Then she shrugged. 'There's no evidence that Irwin was either involved in, or came across, anything to do with wrongdoing over in Malham in terms of the peregrine falcons.' She gestured at the fells around them. 'If there is any link between his death and wildlife crime, this is where I'll find it.'

The blunt assessment wasn't what Gareth had been hoping to hear, yet another avenue of escape for his friend closed off. He watched Sergeant Grewal return her attention to the side of the beck.

'So you're looking for what, exactly?' he asked. 'A protected species? Like badgers? I can tell you for nowt that there are no badgers round here.'

The eyebrow arched again. 'You think I'd take the word of a gamekeeper?'

Gareth bit his tongue, a rare surge of annoyance rising at the injustice of how she was behaving. At how she was judging him. He was tempted to walk away and leave her to it. But the memory of Will being driven off to the police station made him take a deep breath and try again.

'What about if I told you there were great crested newts on this land?'

For the first time since he'd clapped eyes on her, the antagonism on Sergeant Grewal's face was replaced with eager interest.

'Really? Up here?'

Gareth nodded, gesturing towards the pond beyond the copse. 'Over there, Will reckons.'

She was already moving towards the body of water, talking over her shoulder as she walked up the field, Gareth following her. 'Mr Metcalfe told you about the newts?'

'He did indeed. Which begs the question, why would he have had reason to kill the ecologist? Surely the presence of a protected species on Will's property, right against the border of the area under review, made it less likely that the camping pods would get the go-ahead? He didn't need to resort to murder.'

The sergeant shrugged. 'I'm not here to theorise. I'm just here to make sure that this murder isn't part of a wildlife crime. As in, Irwin stumbled on something that was going on in terms of wildlife persecution and got silenced. Permanently.'

They'd reached the edge of the pond, reeds clumped at one end, the water still and silent in the sunshine. Sergeant Grewal peered down into it. Then she turned, looking at Gareth with a stare made even more intense by those amber eyes.

'When did Mr Metcalfe tell you about the apparent presence of great crested newts here?'

'This morning.'

'When he knew he was already under suspicion for the killing of Ross Irwin?'

Gareth shrugged. 'What's your point?'

'It's a bit convenient.' She gestured at the pond. 'Great crested newts aren't exactly easy to find. Even less so at this time of year when they've left the water. So we really only have his word that there is a species here which could have scuppered Mr Dinsdale's planning without Mr Metcalfe having to take matters into his own hands. It could well be a perfectly timed alibi, of sorts.'

As a large man, Gareth had long learned to hold his temper, aware that he could be intimidating even when in the best of moods. But he could feel his frustration building.

'For goodness sake,' he grunted, 'do you always see the worst in people or are you just making a special effort on my account?'

There was a flare of something in those startling eyes. Like he'd hit a nerve. Then she shrugged. 'Comes with the job. But I'll notify DS Benson. He'll get an ecologist up here to do a survey, see what they find. Like I said, though, while I'm no expert on newts, I do know that most surveys are done using DNA taken from breeding ponds in the spring, so the chances of corroborating Mr Metcalfe's claim at this time of year are slim. To be brutally honest, Mr Towler—'

'Gareth.'

She dipped her head sideways, a wry twist to her lips the only acknowledgement that she'd heard his attempt at informality. 'To be brutally honest, Mr Towler, if your friend is resting his case on the great crested newt, he's going to need a miracle—' She broke off, her gaze moving beyond him, over his shoulder. 'What's up with Bounty?'

Noting that his springer spaniel merited first name terms with the sergeant, Gareth turned to look. At the edge of the copse, Bounty was sitting upright, one paw raised, a quizzical look on her face as she let out a muted whine.

'What's up, girl?' He was already moving towards her, Sergeant Grewal by his side. They reached the spaniel about the same time. But it was the sergeant who spotted it first.

'Look!' she whispered, putting a hand on his arm, holding him back. She pointed.

There, on a small rock right in front of Bounty, was a newt. Not just any newt. Almost black in colour, there was a tell-tale streak of orange visible along the edge of its belly.

'A great crested newt,' murmured Gareth.

Sergeant Grewal had her phone out, taking photos, while Gareth kept his eye on Bounty. Not wanting to move in case he disturbed the newt but wary of how his dog might behave, given that the last few months had left her in a nervous state. But he needn't have worried. The spaniel was simply watching the amphibian, head to one side, her low whine constant.

Until the sergeant dropped her mobile. It fell from

her hands and hit a rock, the loud crack affecting both amphibian and dog. The newt disappeared in a brief flash of that vivid orange, and Bounty went into meltdown.

Jumping back, the spaniel hunkered down as small as she could make herself, her whine now shrill with anxiety, brown eyes wild as tremors rippled through her slim body.

'It's okay, girl, it's okay.' Gareth hurried over to his dog, laying a large hand on her head, stroking her and then picking her up to cradle her against his chest. Underneath his palm he could feel the panicked thuds of her heart. 'It's okay,' he murmured into her fur.

The sergeant was looking distraught. 'I'm so sorry. That was so clumsy of me. Is she okay?'

'She will be. She's not good with sudden noises.'

'I thought she was a gun dog? I mean, I just presumed with you being a gamekeeper . . .'

Gareth laughed softly. 'Former gamekeeper. There was an . . . incident. I lost my gun licence and my job, while Bounty lost her enthusiasm for the chase and nearly lost her sanity. But she's getting there.'

A dawning comprehension came across the sergeant's face, her gaze flicking from dog to man and back again.

'It was you two . . . that accident at Bruncliffe Manor back in May where the man died . . .'

Gareth nodded, an ache in his soul as there was every time he thought about it, the loss of life he would forever feel responsible for. 'Aye. That were us.'

He waited for the look of condemnation. But none came. Instead Sergeant Grewal drew closer and slowly held out a hand for Bounty to sniff. Then she stroked her.

'I'm so sorry. I didn't realise.' She looked up at Gareth. 'So what are you going to do for work?'

'I'm sorted for the interim. But long term?' He shook his head. 'Not a clue. But it needs to be outdoors or I'd be the one losing my mind.'

She smiled. 'Same here. I can't imagine spending my life in an office or behind a desk.' Then she nodded at Bounty. 'Maybe she's your future.'

'How do you mean?'

'That newt. She found him and then behaved super calm, not like most dogs, who'd have gone straight into hunt mode. I reckon she'd make an excellent conservation dog. There are places that can train up the right breeds to help detect protected species, like our newt back there.'

'What, so she'd be a newt detective?' He grinned.

Sergeant Grewal laughed this time, a sound of pure pleasure. 'Yes, I suppose you could say that. Seriously though, more and more developments are using them at the planning stage – seems our canine friends are a lot more efficient at carrying out wildlife surveys than us humans. They can cover the ground a lot faster, for a start. I've also been on cases where we've used them to catch poachers. Or to find carcasses during investigations into raptor perse- cution.' She shrugged. 'It's just an idea.'

'And a good one,' he said.

She nodded. 'As for the matter in hand,' she continued, the flash of friendliness vanishing as quickly as the great crested newt, 'I'll let DS Benson know what we found. But I wouldn't go thinking this means Mr Metcalfe is out of the woods.'

'But surely it proves he had no motive for killing Irwin.'

'Possibly.' She looked back at the pond and then at

Gareth. 'However, you've got to ask yourself why Mr Metcalfe never mentioned his exotic wildlife before now, when it proved useful.'

'I don't follow.'

The look she gave him wasn't unkind. But it was steeled with professionalism. 'Perhaps Mr Metcalfe didn't mention it because he didn't know about it until Mr Irwin made the discovery. And on making that discovery, Mr Irwin informed the landowner that he would be filing a full report to the relevant authorities. Which means there would be certain restrictions placed on how Mr Metcalfe farms this area in future.' She stared at the landscape and up at Ellershaw House in the distance. 'I don't know your friend that well, but from the little I've heard, I don't think he'd take too kindly to some outsider telling him what he can or cannot do on his own property. Do you?'

Gareth found he couldn't disagree. He also found himself thinking about what Will had said about being blackmailed. It wasn't something the gamekeeper was going to mention to his companion. But he mulled it over, wondering if she was partly right. Had their discovery today been at the root of the extortion attempt? Had Irwin been threatening to reveal the presence of great crested newts on Will's property, possibly bringing to an end the use of it as a lambing pasture? But even if he had, would that have been enough to make Will kill him?

As he placed Bounty back on the ground and began to follow the sergeant up the land towards the farmhouse, Gareth Towler realised he couldn't answer that question. Not honestly. Not without feeling disloyal to his friend.

* * *

Date with Justice

Back down in Bruncliffe, Herriot was having an uneventful morning. A quick MOT of some tups the other side of Bowland Knotts, making sure they were ready for the forthcoming season, and then back to the clinic to catch up with admin. So when he got a text from the Dales Detective Agency asking for his help with an ongoing investigation, he was glad to get out of the office and head there straight away. Well, almost. He popped into Peaks Patisserie first to get a takeaway coffee, needing his daily fix. Not of caffeine, that being simply a boost for a body which was flagging already, despite it being barely noon.

His daily fix was of Lucy Metcalfe. A woman he would never have the courage to ask out. A woman he wasn't even worthy of.

Every day he went into the cafe, filled with determination to finally put his heart out of its misery. Every day he came out with a coffee and a sense of failure. He'd even gone on the last Dales Dating Agency speed-dating night, knowing Lucy was going. And he'd spent the evening in agony, watching other men chat away to her with an ease he could never replicate.

He was an idiot.

Musing on this fact, he entered the three-storey building on Back Street, coffee in hand, and began making for the stairs on the presumption that Samson and Delilah would be up there.

'In here!' came a voice from the ground-floor office.

He turned in that direction, pushed open the door and saw Ida Capstick behind the desk, a laptop in front of her and a fierce expression on her face. Fierce even beyond her usual.

'Morning, Ida.' His greeting was met with a grunt. 'Samson and Delilah not here?'

'It's not them tha's here to see, lad,' Ida snapped. 'Tha wants to get Baggy to take a look at tha van. Happen it's leaking oil.'

'Sorry?' Herriot was thrown by the unexpected turn of conversation.

'Perhaps tha'd like to explain what tha's been doing,' Ida continued, twisting the laptop round to face him, 'loitering in a ginnel every night? Round the back of Peaks Patisserie, no less.'

Herriot stared at the screen in horror, at the grainy footage of a vehicle parked up by the kitchen door. 'But that's not . . .' His feeble attempt at denial faded into silence as the footage progressed, a light coming on in the vehicle and his own face unmistakably spotlit.

Ida folded her arms across her chest and glared at him. 'I'm all ears,' she said.

Wishing the ground would open up and swallow him, Herriot sank onto a chair and dropped his head into his hands.

18

'Tha's been doing what?' Whatever Ida had been expecting when she'd seen the footage of Herriot in his van outside the cafe in the dead of night, it hadn't been this.

'A stakeout,' mumbled the mortified vet.

Ida stared at him. Watched the crimson of his face turn even darker. 'And why on earth would a man like thee with a demanding full-time job be messing around trying to catch a thief when he should be asleep in his bed?'

Herriot shrugged. The fire on his cheeks showing no sign of fading. 'Thought I'd help out a friend.'

'A *friend*?'

'Lucy. She's a friend. I mean, you know, she's a mate . . . she's . . .' His explanation trailed away, a look of what could only be classed as agony on his face.

Ida didn't purport to have any expertise in matters of the heart but her time working alongside Delilah at the dating agency had given her a certain amount of insight. And one of those insights was that there was nowt as daft as a man when he fell in love.

The man sitting across from her right now had that air of daftness about him.

'How long has it been going on?' she asked.

'What, Lucy—?'

'No! The stakeouts!'

'Not long.'

She fixed him in her gaze again until he gave another sheepish shrug and expanded on his answer.

'A week. Lucy told me what was happening and that Delilah didn't seem to have time to investigate, so I thought I'd give it a go.'

'Tha's been out in that van every night for a *week*?' exclaimed Ida in disbelief.

He nodded and she realised the dark circles around his eyes and his rumpled appearance were possibly more than just the result of emotional torment.

'Tha needs tha head examining, lad!'

He gave an ironic laugh. 'Thing is, it's not my head that's the problem.'

And suddenly Ida felt for him. For the soul-destroying capacity of love when it blindsides you and there's nothing to be done about it.

'Right,' she said, taking refuge in a business she at least had some understanding of. 'These stakeouts, how did tha conduct them?'

Herriot gestured towards the laptop, the frozen image of him still on the screen. 'I waited until after eleven, when it was fully dark and quiet, and then I parked my van so the dashcam was pointing down the ginnel, towards the kitchen door. Lucy seems to think that's where the thief is gaining access. That's what I was doing when you caught me – I was turning the dashcam on.'

'So tha's got footage of every night over the last week?'

'Yes.'

'And tha's watched it all back?' Ida was getting excited now.

'Yes, and there's nothing on it.'

'Not even the last time something was stolen? The night of the wedding?'

Herriot responded by reaching into his pocket for his mobile. He held it out so she could see. 'A whole lot of nothing,' he said, playing the video on fast forward, a succession of frames showing an unchanging ginnel in dark greys zipping past. Apart from—

'Stop!' Ida pointed at the screen as a flash of white blinded the camera, before being replaced by the habitual grey. 'What was that?'

'A car going past. And,' he added with a grin as he scrolled back to the relevant frame, 'a nocturnal visitor.'

He played the footage at normal speed, the image slightly fuzzy, the ginnel turned menacing in the dark. And then the camera was filled with stripes. And striking green eyes.

Tigger, the cat from next door. Staring down the lens with the hauteur of a movie star. She was stretching forward towards the windscreen when the white light of headlights cut through behind, a vehicle moving across the marketplace at speed.

Startled, the cat leaped round to face the possible danger and then disappeared out of view.

'And that was the highlight of my week's work,' said Herriot with a self-deprecating smile. 'So you don't need to worry about me being after your job. Because while I was sitting there in the van, trying to be a hero but failing miserably, someone broke in and stole a load of brownies, smashing a cake stand while they were at it. And I didn't catch them. In fact, I didn't even see the cat as I was asleep within minutes of parking up.'

Ida was only half listening, partly because she'd never feared her position was under threat, as it took a lot more to be a decent detective than folk realised. But also because she was still concentrating on the video feed from Herriot's dashcam.

'Run that bit again,' she said. 'From where the cat jumps up.'

Herriot replayed it and as the screen was illuminated by the car lights, she saw it. A shadow of movement just about discernible over the cat's head. It was coming from behind the window next to Peak Patisserie's kitchen door.

'Reckon as tha might have caught more than tha thinks,' said Ida, pausing the footage and peering at the image before making a proud declaration. 'Happen as this could be our thief.'

Herriot took the mobile from her and squinted at the screen. At the vague shape highlighted behind the window. Then looked up in amazement. 'I can't believe you spotted that! Wow. Good work, Ida.'

Ida tipped her head in acknowledgement, allowing a fraction of her lips to curve. But like the tip of an iceberg, that fraction concealed the huge rush of pleasure his words had triggered.

'Only thing now is,' continued the vet with a stricken look, 'how do we tell Lucy that you've uncovered her thief without revealing what I've been up to?'

Ida was saved from solving this fresh conundrum by the crash of the front door, Nathan and Nina tumbling into the hallway in a frenzy of excitement, Peaks Patisserie bags in their hands.

'Samson's called a staff meeting in five!' exclaimed Nathan, eyes the size of saucers. 'Uncle Will's been formally arrested for the murder of Ross Irwin!'

Word had come as they were making their way down from the Dinsdale farm. A discreet text from Danny, letting them know that while a dog walker on his way up to the kiln around ten o'clock the night of the murder had seen Nathan leaving – thus eliminating the lad from all enquiries – in what could only be seen as a disturbing development, DS Benson had taken the decision to arrest Will and was keeping him in custody. Trying to stave off the surge of alarm the news triggered, Delilah concentrated on her driving while Samson got to work, calling the troops in for a meeting.

The Dales Detective Agency was about to focus all its efforts on clearing Will's name.

Which explained why the kitchen was somewhat crowded as Delilah walked in behind Samson, Tolpuddle by her side. Nathan and Nina were already perched on the windowsill at the end of the room, Ida was at the worktop pouring tea, and Herriot, somewhat inexplicably, was sitting at the table, a half-eaten slice of pork pie in his hand.

At Delilah's surprised look, the vet spoke up.

'I know I'm not officially an employee or anything but I can't stand by and do nothing while Will's being accused of this. So I'm here to help in any way I can.'

'Appreciated,' said Delilah.

'Happen we're going to need a bigger kitchen,' muttered Ida as she distributed mugs.

Delilah's next glance was at the table itself where a variety of sandwiches cut into triangles, some mini salmon-and-dill tarts, a large pork pie, and a chocolate cake cut into slices had been spread out on plates. From the corner, Tolpuddle was eyeing the lot eagerly.

'Mum sent them over,' offered Nathan. 'She thought we wouldn't have time to break off for lunch.'

'Good woman,' murmured Samson, taking a sandwich and devouring it in two bites before reaching for another and passing the Weimaraner a third.

Ida, meanwhile, had placed her own mug on the counter and picked up a marker pen. She positioned herself at the whiteboard on the wall above the table, ready for action.

'Before we begin,' said Delilah, 'a bit of good news. An eyewitness has come forward to corroborate Nathan's version of events Saturday night, so he's in the clear.' She smiled at her nephew, Nina punching him on the arm in jubilation, while he scowled out from beneath the flop of hair across his eyes.

'It won't be the last time that dimwit detective is proven wrong,' he grunted.

'Hear hear,' muttered Ida, evidently still not a fan of DS Benson. 'So how's about we get started on making that happen.'

Delilah looked at Samson. 'Suspects first?'

'Definitely,' he said. 'Let's list them all up there and then add motive and opportunity and whatever else we know about them that applies to the case.'

'Including my brother?'

Samson gave a resigned nod.

'Motive?' asked Ida as she wrote Will's name on the board.

'Blackmail,' said Samson, to an audible gasp from the others. 'Irwin was demanding five grand for an ecology report in Will's favour.'

'And unfortunately,' added Delilah, 'Will had ample opportunity. He has no alibi for the crucial hours of the murder and the relocation of the body. And . . .' she paused, finding it hard to say the words, 'the discovery of what could be bloodstains in his Land Rover, and on the rounders bat they found in it, doesn't exactly help his case.'

'What about Elaine Bullock?' asked Herriot. 'Is she in the clear?'

'Not totally,' said Samson. He nodded for Ida to add the geologist to the board. 'Irwin assaulted her, so that could be seen as provocation. But the police haven't found any sign of blood in the back of Irwin's 4x4 which she admitted to driving down from the cove, so I don't see how she could have moved the body.'

'On her bike?' offered Nina with a dry smile.

'Plus,' added Nathan, 'I just heard that Mrs Pettiford has provided an alibi for her. She saw Elaine getting home at nine Saturday night.'

'So Elaine is looking less and less likely by the day,' said Delilah, relieved for her friend but also perturbed that the same couldn't be said of her brother.

'Anyone else?' asked Ida.

'Kevin Dinsdale,' said Samson. 'We've come straight from the farm and we both agree that there was something not quite right.'

'Like what?' Herriot asked.

Samson shrugged. 'It's just a gut feeling, but there was

something about the chat we had with him which was off and I can't put my finger on it.' He turned to Delilah.

'Yes, it's hard to say exactly,' she agreed. And it was. As soon as they'd got in the Mini to leave, they'd both admitted to feeling uneasy about the atmosphere in the Dinsdale kitchen. 'It's possible we were just picking up the vibes of a farm in financial trouble. But Kevin's opinion of Irwin as a decent bloke contrasts with what we know about Irwin's behaviour towards Elaine and him trying to hold Will to ransom.'

Ida snorted. 'A difference of opinion is hardly a motive, lass.'

'True. And as Kevin already has a copy of Irwin's report, which has given him the thumbs up, then he has even less of a reason for seeing the man dead. If anything, this murder has put the Dinsdales' plans – and their farm – back in jeopardy.'

'And don't forget he's got an alibi, of sorts,' said Samson. 'He claims he was drunk at the wedding, so he could hardly have driven to Malham Cove.'

'I can vouch for him being drunk,' said Herriot. 'I was up there Sunday morning to check on a tup he's having trouble with and he had the mother-and-father of all hangovers. He was so bad he asked me to drive his Shogun out onto the fells and he was almost green by the time we got back.'

'Does tha still want him up here?' asked Ida, gesturing at the board.

Samson nodded. 'Yes. For now. And let's add the wildlife crime angle, too – that peregrine falcon feather is still a potential clue—'

'Not any more!' Gareth Towler was standing in the doorway, one eye on the table. He reached over, took a couple of sandwiches and ate hungrily, making his audience wait, while Bounty trotted across the floor to sit next to Tolpuddle. Sandwiches finished, the gamekeeper took a slice of pork pie and bit into it before continuing.

'Sorry for being late,' he said. 'Worked up an appetite out there on the fells. Anyway, I hate to dash hopes but Sergeant Grewal has ruled out any tie-in between the falcons and Irwin's death. She was quite adamant about it.'

'How can she be so sure?' asked Nathan.

'Believe me, lad, having spent the best part of a morning in her company, while she's not my cup of tea, she knows what she's doing.' Gareth looked at Samson. 'If Sergeant Grewal says there's no connection, I'd take her word for it.'

'Damn,' muttered Delilah, realising how much she'd been banking on that particular avenue of enquiry to provide the answers they needed. Now they were staring at yet another dead end.

'Any others?' Ida was poised with the pen but her question was met with silence.

It was a silence that brought dread. Because looking at the whiteboard, now covered with Ida's neat writing, only one suspect stood out as having both motive and opportunity to kill Ross Irwin. And that was Will Metcalfe. Unless . . .

A nagging thought had been at the back of Delilah's mind since Irwin's body had been discovered and focus immediately turned to Elaine and Will. A conversation at the wedding reception that was one of the few things she could remember with any kind of clarity.

Feeling like the worst kind of friend, Delilah spoke up. 'Sarah Mitchell.'

Every face turned to her. All of them carrying the same expression of incredulity. Apart from Samson, who simply raised an eyebrow, taking her suggestion seriously and making her love him even more.

'What's your reasoning?' he said.

'She's just set up her own ecology consultancy and she acknowledged at the wedding that things are on a knife edge. She even persuaded Harry to postpone their honeymoon because she's in the middle of tendering for a project which could make or break her company. Irwin was her main competitor. With him out of the way . . .'

'You think she could have killed him to save her business?' asked Herriot, disbelief in his voice.

Delilah grimaced. 'Not really. In my heart I don't believe anyone on that board is capable of murder. But someone did away with Ross Irwin and our job is to find that person. So looking at it from a purely clinical perspective, I'd say Sarah had motive.'

'But she was the bride,' said Nina. 'She would have been at the reception all evening. How would she have had the opportunity?'

'She wasn't there all evening.' Attention switched to Ida, who was frowning. 'I met her coming back into the club when I was leaving. It were about nine.' Ida was looking at Samson now. 'She was wearing a different outfit. Said she'd got a stain on her wedding dress and had gone home to sort it.'

'Nine o'clock?' said Samson, turning to Delilah. 'What time did Elaine say she left Irwin up at Malham Cove?'

'About ten past eight.'

'So given it's a twenty-minute drive, Sarah could have driven over, killed him, driven back, changed and come back to the wedding in that time.' He nodded at Ida. 'Let's add her to the board.'

'Jesus,' muttered Gareth as Ida commenced writing. 'This is awful. We're possibly going to end up exposing someone we really like as a cold-blooded killer.'

'Welcome to the world of being an investigator,' said Ida grimly.

Gareth shook his head. 'Maybe we've got it all wrong. What if it was someone random? Someone from Irwin's life in Kendal who we know nothing about.'

Ida was turning towards the board again but before she could add this latest suggestion, Nina piped up.

'Hang on a sec. It can't be. How would someone who wasn't at the wedding have known where he was going to be?'

Samson was in the midst of eating a salmon tart and paused, the food partway to his mouth.

'Brilliant!' he exclaimed. 'Why didn't I think of that? Even Ross Irwin didn't know he was going to be at Malham Cove Saturday evening. Elaine said herself that the decision to drive up there was spontaneous, a rescheduling of the next day's plan in light of what happened with Will.'

'Which means whoever killed Irwin had to have followed them from the rugby club!' said Delilah.

Ida snorted. 'What am I supposed to write up here, then? The name of every bugger at the wedding?'

'Christ,' muttered Samson. 'It is a lot of suspects.'

'Perhaps we can narrow it down a bit,' said Delilah,

thinking about something Elaine had said. 'Is it true you videoed me dancing on the tables, Nathan?'

Her nephew nodded, looking wary as though expecting a reprimand.

'How many other people do you think took videos that night?'

He shrugged. 'Loads. Why?'

Delilah turned to Samson. 'That's how we reduce our suspect list. We've already got a rough timeline for the murder. Whoever committed it had to have left the club fairly soon after Elaine and Irwin, so that's about six thirty. The murder had to have happened either before eight, if Elaine is the culprit, which we all agree is probably the least likely scenario out of those we've outlined. Or, it happened after she left Irwin. So sometime after ten past eight. Then, the killer stayed at large, possibly up at the cove, waiting to move the body to the kiln when things would be quiet.'

'Or,' added Samson, 'they left the body up there and returned to the reception. And then for some reason, panic maybe, went back to move it.'

'All of which couldn't have happened before ten because, as we now have a witness to verify, Nathan was up at the kiln until then.'

Nathan nodded, giving Nina a sideways glance. She reached over and squeezed his arm.

'So we've got someone either absent from the reception from six thirty who doesn't return,' continued Delilah, 'or someone who left and came back and then left again later in the night. In which case, that second departure happened at some point between ten and eleven. If we believe that the 4x4 which went haring past you, Samson, was the killer en route to the kiln, then it would be closer to the latter.'

'So we use the wedding videos to spot anyone with that pattern of movement.' Samson was nodding.

'Exactly,' said Delilah. 'We can ask around for any footage taken during the reception and sift through it to see who was missing during those crucial hours. It might throw up someone we would never have thought of.'

'Nathan and I can take that on,' volunteered Nina, before turning to Nathan. 'If you're okay with that?'

The lad's responding nod couldn't have been more eager.

'Great,' said Samson. 'We already know Elaine and Will fit the timeline Delilah's outlined, so pay particular attention to Kevin Dinsdale and Sarah, and anyone else who catches your eye. See if you can get a precise idea of how long they were absent from the reception. And remember, not a word of this leaves this room. Bad enough we're having to investigate people we care about without them getting to hear about it.'

'What about me?' asked Herriot. 'What can I do?'

'The land Irwin was supposed to be surveying,' said Samson. 'It would help if we knew more about it. Especially as Will seems to think there are newts up there—'

'He's right about that,' said Gareth, around a mouthful of cake. 'Witnessed it for myself with that Sergeant Grewal. A great crested newt, sitting on a rock, bold as you like.'

'Course he's right.' Nathan's voice was filled with teenage indignation. 'Why would Uncle Will lie about something like that?'

He looked from Samson to Delilah, who dropped her gaze to the floor. The case was far too complicated and far too close to home to be able to offer a straightforward answer to her nephew.

'Anyways up,' continued Gareth, wiping crumbs from his beard, 'it adds another dimension to the whole thing. Them newts are a protected species so having them there could have turned Dinsdale's project into a nightmare. And definitely would have added to the cost—'

'Not when he has a green light already.' Samson was shaking his head.

Gareth looked around the room, puzzled. 'You know that for sure?'

Delilah nodded. 'We saw a copy of Irwin's report. It was favourable.'

'But how can that be possible if there's a protected species up there?'

'Maybe because they're not within the boundary of the planning permission?' suggested Herriot.

'Perhaps that's something you could look into for us?' asked Samson, the vet nodding. 'Meanwhile, good work, Gareth. I presume Sergeant Grewal will be reporting these findings back to Benson?'

Gareth gave a dry laugh. 'Aye, though I'm not sure what good that'll do. She seems keen to pin the blame on Will, even viewing this development as another nail in his coffin. And like I said just now, while she's not the easiest person in the world to rub along with and she made no effort to hide her disdain for me as a former gamekeeper, she's sharp. What if the pretext for Irwin's threat at the wedding reception was the newts? You know, claiming he was going to tell the authorities and make life difficult for Will?'

'You're suggesting my brother might have killed someone over some bloody amphibians?' Delilah couldn't keep the exasperation out of her voice.

But Gareth didn't take offence. He simply shrugged. 'I'm thinking we need to know more about exactly what Irwin said to Will. Oh, and by the way, I didn't say anything about what was going on between them to the sergeant. Figured that was up to Will to tell DS Benson when they interview him.'

'You did right,' said Samson. 'So, in terms of this latest development, we have to accept it gives Dinsdale a motive, but possibly Will, too. In which case, it's even more imperative that we know everything we can about where Irwin was conducting the survey.' He turned to Herriot. 'Seeing as we can't ask Sarah for her expert opinion, perhaps you and Gareth could come up with a report for us of some sort. Maybe even sound out another ecologist?'

'Consider it done,' said Herriot, Gareth snapping out a smart salute before taking another piece of cake.

'Meanwhile, I'll get cracking on Irwin's laptop files,' said Delilah. 'See what I can uncover from those.'

Samson nodded. 'And I'll look into his background. Judging by how he's behaved in the short time he's been in town, I wouldn't be surprised if he has previous. Perhaps someone he crossed in the past finally got even.'

'And me?' asked Ida. 'What does tha want me to do?'

Delilah grinned. 'Everything else. I've had at least three messages from Arty Robinson about the Fellside Court sale, so if you could try digging around to find out who the new owner is, that would be great. And then there's a slew of insurance claims which need writing up plus there's still a couple of background checks outstanding. Not to mention Lucy's mysterious thief—'

'That's sorted,' said Ida.

'Sorry?'

'The thief.' Ida pulled her laptop towards her and opened it up, clicking on a video and turning the screen to Delilah. 'Caught red-handed.'

Everyone apart from Herriot crowded around the computer, peering at the blurred image. Delilah stared along with them, stunned. Spotlit by the headlights of a passing car, just about visible behind the glass of the Peaks Patisserie window was the grey outline of a small animal, a square of food at its mouth.

'A squirrel?' exclaimed Samson.

Ida nodded, more than a hint of pride in the gesture. 'Holding a brownie.'

'Wow, Ida! That's sterling detective work. But how did you get this footage? This was taken from out in the ginnel.'

'And it was on Saturday,' added Delilah, pointing at the date in the bottom right corner. 'You only fitted the cameras yesterday.'

Ida folded her arms across her chest. 'A good detective doesn't reveal their sources,' she said.

'You mean you had help?' persisted Delilah, curious about how the video had been obtained.

'I mean, tha can keep asking till tha's blue in the face and the answer'll be the same.'

'About time I was going,' said Herriot, standing abruptly as though he'd just remembered an appointment.

Delilah opened her mouth to quiz Ida further but a brusque comment cut her short.

'Happen Herriot's not the only one needing to get along.' Ida was tapping her watch, eyebrow raised. 'Isn't tha supposed to be at the Coach and Horses?'

'Damn! Silver Solos!' Delilah jumped up, all curiosity about Ida's investigations forgotten in the shocking realisation that she had an afternoon tea to organise. 'Samson, can you mind Tolpuddle for me?'

Without waiting for a reply, she grabbed a couple of sandwiches and ran from the room, in too much of a hurry to spot the wink Ida cast at Herriot as he followed her out of the kitchen.

Across the cobbled marketplace and up the steep incline of Fell Lane, in the sunlit reception of Fellside Court, Arty Robinson was afraid he was asking rather too much of his fragile heart. Because as he tried to pick the lock of the manager's office, that ailing organ was beating at a rate it couldn't possibly be expected to sustain.

He took a deep breath. Tried to regain his calm, telling himself he'd done this loads of times before. He dried his damp fingers on his trousers and wiped a bead of sweat from his forehead, the perspiration having little to do with the warmth of his surroundings. Then he began working the picks once more.

Success. The lock clicked, he eased inside and closed the door.

At which point it promptly opened again, sending his heart into further palpitations.

'Bloody hell, Edith!' he muttered as the tall figure of the former headmistress, stick and all, snuck around the door, closing it behind her.

'Language, Arty,' she whispered with a smile. Eyes sparkling. An animation to her features that suggested her heart was in much better condition than his.

'I thought you were supposed to be keeping watch?' he hissed.

For that had been the plan. With the vast majority of the residents having left the building half an hour before, heading in an excited gaggle for the Coach and Horses and the Silver Solos dating event, Arty had collected the tools of a trade he'd dabbled in during his misspent youth, and headed for the manager's office in the glass-fronted reception area. Edith, meanwhile, had positioned herself in one of the club chairs situated to the side of the entrance, a book in her hand being her alibi as she kept watch.

Yet here she was, standing inside the office with him. And given what he was about to do, he'd rather not have had her company. Because the last thing Arty wanted was Edith Hird thinking badly of him.

She shrugged. Smiled again. 'I got bored. Besides, there's no one here. It's like the *Mary Celeste* out there.'

He didn't protest that she couldn't possibly have got bored in the handful of minutes since he'd left her. Instead he just pointed at the desk, which was covered in several piles of paper, an indication that Edith's comparison to the *Mary Celeste* wasn't far off the mark, the retirement complex certainly having felt like a captain-less ship since the Procter investigation had scuttled everything.

'Start there,' he said. 'Go through that lot and see what you can find.'

'What are we looking for, exactly?'

'Anything which could be connected to the sale.'

He waited a few beats of his unreliable heart before moving, letting her get engrossed in her search, her back to him. Then he crossed the room to the small bookcase on the opposite wall and pressed a hand flat to its side. At his touch, the entire structure hinged away to reveal a safe built in behind it.

Kneeling down, he took out his picks and set to work.

'I've got two questions, Arty Robinson, and I'm not sure I want to know the answer to either.' Edith's voice froze him to the spot. He glanced over his shoulder and she was staring at him, expression unreadable. 'How did you know that was there and where did you get the skills to open it?'

Arty tapped the side of his nose. 'Like you said, best you don't know.'

The look she gave him was even more penetrating than normal, then she just nodded.

He turned back to the metal door. Needing a double-bit key to open it, the safe was far from easy to break into. But thankfully Rick Procter had gone old-school, opting for a traditional lock rather than a numerical pad. Small mercies, thought Arty, as he gently teased the pick inside the mechanism. From behind came the tap of a cane, Edith moving closer, until she was at his shoulder. Perversely, her presence made him feel calmer. Despite the fact that they now had no lookout positioned outside. And that she now knew more about him than he would have liked. Would she make the connection? To what had happened back in June?

He forced himself to dismiss the thought and concentrated on his picks. A few minutes later he had the satisfaction of the safe door opening.

'Well,' whispered Edith, leaning over his kneeling form to see into the space he'd accessed. 'Anything in there?'

'Not a sausage!' muttered Arty despondently.

He'd been hoping the safe would yield the answers he sought. Instead, two bare metal shelves lay before him.

'Ah well.' Edith patted his shoulder. 'At least we tried.'

Arty twisted round on his knees to look up at her. She was smiling now, the excitement of their illicit behaviour radiating out from her. It had been worth it just for this moment, the pair of them, caught up in something thrilling.

He was about to say something to her. Something about how he felt. But a noise from the other side of the office door made him pause. A key. Being inserted into the lock.

'Someone's coming in!' hissed Edith, excitement morphing into horror at the sound.

Even as she said it, the handle was turning, the door was opening, and Arty knew they'd been caught.

19

Ida Capstick had left the Dales Detective agency hot on Delilah's heels and ridden straight over to start her new case, having an idea of where was the best place to commence it. Which is why she was standing in the doorway of the manager's office in Fellside Court, taking in the scene. Arty Robinson kneeling on the floor, Edith Hird standing over him, a hand on his shoulder. It looked like a marriage proposal. Apart from the incongruity of the safe yawning open behind them.

Ida stared at them. Stared at the bookcase and the hidden safe. And quietly closed the office door behind her.

'Tha's got some explaining to do.' She addressed her statement to Arty, because this escapade had his name written all over it.

'I'm trying to find out who the new owner is,' he blurted out.

'We thought we might come across some answers in here,' added Edith, looking the most contrite Ida had ever seen her.

But Ida was still transfixed by the open safe. She'd known it was there. She'd been working long enough in the building to know a lot about the place and had discovered the real purpose of the bookcase the first time she'd dusted it, her dusting style having a certain Capstick vigour, sufficient to trigger the mechanism. But the safe itself, she hadn't touched.

She'd heard about it, though. The whole of Bruncliffe had. For when Rick Procter had been trying to flee the country back in June, he'd made an unsuccessful attempt to access it. Little surprise, then, that the police had raided Fellside Court the following day as part of their endeavours to uncover the property developer's illegal assets. But on opening the safe, they'd been perplexed to find it contained nothing more than a fake passport and a ledger. Even more perplexing, the ledger had held detailed accounts of Procter's income from money laundering, suggesting there should have been upwards of two hundred grand in there.

There'd been nothing but dust.

The mystery of the missing cash had yet to be solved. Unless . . .

'Happen we're all singing from the same hymn book,' Ida finally said, moving her gaze onto the two unlikely cat burglars. 'Has tha looked at that lot on the desk?'

Edith shook her head. 'I started but then got distracted.'

'Hmph.' Ida crossed the floor, reached for the first pile of correspondence and began rifling through it. 'Bingo,' she murmured, pulling out a cream envelope. She held it up, tapping the Turpin's logo across the top. 'Seems tha safe-cracking skills were uncalled for,' she said to Arty.

He was on his feet in a shot, hustling over to see what she'd found.

She slid a finger under the seal and ripped the envelope open, eliciting a gasp from Edith.

'Aren't you supposed to be more discreet? Steam it open or something? Otherwise they'll know we've been snooping!'

Ida grunted. 'And who exactly is going to care? The staff are as angsty as thee to know who's taking this place over.' She pulled out a letter, the paper of a quality she'd expect from the exacting solicitor, young Matty Thistlethwaite, and read it with a frown, Arty and Edith reading over her shoulder.

'Damn it,' cursed Arty. 'It's just formal notification of completion. It doesn't name the purchaser and doesn't help us at all.'

'Although it does up the ante, somewhat,' said Edith quietly. She pointed at the date halfway down the page. 'The sale will be finalised on Wednesday. Given that today is almost over, we've only got tomorrow before everything is done and dusted.'

Arty groaned. 'There's no way we can identify the new owner before then. I might as well just accept what's coming and get packing.'

'Don't be so rash,' said Ida, laying the letter on the desk and taking a photo with her phone. 'There's still options.'

'Really?' Arty was looking at her with a glimmer of optimism.

'Aye. But at a price.' Ida turned to the safe and then back to him. And he nodded, understanding what the cost would be without her having to say a word.

Silver Solos went like a dream, despite the last-minute preparation. By the time Delilah had rushed home, changed, and hurried back down to the Coach and Horses, a few early arrivals had already been ordering drinks at the bar. Thankfully, the staff had started getting everything ready without her and when she entered the upstairs function room, Delilah was greeted with the wonderful sight of five large circular tables, linen tablecloths a brilliant white, cutlery sparkling, and delicate Wedgwood cups and saucers at every setting. Interspersed on each table were three-tiered cake stands, complete with a variety of finger sandwiches, savoury muffins, scones, mini eclairs, elaborately decorated fondant squares and mini Victoria sponge cakes.

The pub's catering team had excelled and even with her stomach already full from the feast Lucy had provided at the office, Delilah had been drooling at the sight.

Two hours later, as she walked back to the office to pick up Tolpuddle, she was congratulating herself on a successful event. Her decision to opt for larger tables had been wise. For the first Silver Solos dating evening back in June she'd stuck with the traditional speed-dating format, but had quickly come to the realisation that there was nothing speedy about a room full of senior citizens. Not simply because of mobility problems, of which there were a few, but more that these older clients were reluctant to move when the regulation three minutes were up, going so far as to blatantly ignore the bell. By the end of the evening, there had been large groups clustered around a few tables, chairs having been dragged over with them, and animated discussions taking place.

So this time she'd gone with the flow and given them what they wanted. And it had worked brilliantly. Eight people at each table, they'd had twenty minutes to chat away. Then, when the bell had rung, the men had got up and moved to another table. But this time she'd limited the changeovers, only ringing the bell twice. Judging by the feedback she'd already had from the many participants who'd remained in the pub after the event was finished, she'd hit on a winning formula. And, she mused, scrolling through the dating requests already coming in, so had Joseph O'Brien.

'Like father like son,' she muttered as she stared at the full house of date requests the Irishman had secured. Some even from women whose table he hadn't had a chance to sit at today.

She shoved her mobile back in her pocket, a grin on her face, and realised just how much she'd benefitted from the Silver Solos. For if she was being honest, it had been the last thing she'd wanted to do – to spend time helping folk be entertained when she had a much more pressing matter to deal with, her brother's plight at the forefront of her mind. But the love of life so evident in the group she'd just spent the afternoon with had been like a tonic for her, and as she'd watched on, amidst the laughter and the lively conversations, she'd found herself contemplating what it would be like to grow old with Samson.

Walking across the cobbles of the marketplace with the sun beginning to slide towards the horizon, those idle dreams seemed a bit premature. Particularly as she'd barely had a chance to talk to him properly since his return the day before. They'd seemed to spend every waking minute caught up in the trauma of Ross Irwin's murder, and now Will's arrest. And as for the sleeping hours, they hadn't even spent them together, Samson curled up with Tolpuddle while Delilah made the most of the couch.

Which meant she didn't even know what the next month would entail in terms of their relationship, let alone their twilight years. She didn't even know how long Samson was back for. Or why. As for the sale of Twistleton Farm, she'd yet to broach the subject with him, which she really needed to do – at least give him the chance to digest the news in private before someone blurted it out.

It was a task she wasn't relishing.

Promising herself she'd make time to talk to him that evening, she approached the office building and let herself in the front door. She was met by a Weimaraner bounding down the stairs, ears flopping and expression ecstatic. And Samson coming out of his office looking grim, mobile in his hand.

'Delilah! Great timing. I think I've found our killer.'

Sensing this wasn't going to be something to cheer about, even if it did mean proving her brother's innocence, she found herself wishing she was back enjoying the good-natured fun of the Silver Solos.

Ida didn't know where to look. At Edith Hird's face, which had a strange mixture of shock and resignation on it. Or at the old-fashioned faux-leather suitcase lying open on the floor next to Arty's bed, more cash than she'd ever seen in her life bundled inside.

Two hundred thousand pounds. Of Rick Procter's money.

'So it *was* you who took it.' Edith was the first to speak. Looking from the suitcase to Arty and then back again, as though each banknote held a magnet which pulled her attention.

Arty nodded.

'Tha knew?' Ida glanced at Edith.

'I had a hunch. It was mentioned the day Delilah came out of hospital that the police suspected Procter's money had gone missing from the office safe, and I just sensed it in my gut. But I didn't know how. Not until today.' She turned to Arty, his cheeks pink, and not just from the exertion of pulling the case out from under his bed. There was a hint of shame to his appearance.

'It's not what it looks like,' he muttered. 'Well, it is, but it isn't. It's a contingency fund. After Procter was arrested, that evening in the lounge bloody Geraldine Mortimer started banging on about the Proceeds of Crime Act, and how Procter would have everything taken off him by the state . . .' He shook his head. 'None of the other residents seemed to make the connection. You know, between Procter and this place. But I did. And I panicked.' He gestured at the money and shrugged.

'But how did you know the cash was in the safe in the first place?'

'Tha worked it out,' said Ida, nodding at Arty in approval. 'When Procter tried to come back here, tha sensed he was after something. And there weren't much worth risking his life for other than money.'

Arty nodded. 'The police hadn't been near the place at that point so I waited until dark and broke into the office.'

'But what on earth were you planning on doing with it?' asked Edith, gently. 'It's not like you can stick it in your bank and then use it to cover any increases in costs here.'

'I didn't really think it through. Like I said, I panicked. I thought it would at least give me a Plan B.'

'Aye, that'd work. I hear tha doesn't have to worry much about rent in a prison cell,' muttered Ida. 'Did tha not learn owt from all Procter's shenanigans? That money would need proper laundering before tha could use a penny of it.'

'So what do I do with it?' asked Arty. 'Should I just pop it back in the safe? And then make preparations to leave? Because there's no way I can afford even the slightest of rent increase when the new folk take over.'

Ida was thinking. Fast. Her mind leaping ahead, making connections.

'Let's not be too hasty,' she said. 'It's doing no harm where it is for now. But I want thee to promise me, Arty Robinson, that tha'll not do anything rash before I've had a proper chance to find out what's going on with the takeover.'

He gave a dejected sigh. 'Not like I have a choice. Seeing as I don't have a Plan B any more.'

'I've got a Plan B,' said Edith. 'If the new owners do raise the rent, you can move in with me.'

It was stated as simply as if she was offering a cup of tea.

Both Ida and Arty swivelled round to face her.

'Are you serious?' asked Arty. 'What about Clarissa?'

Edith shrugged. 'She's been talking about needing space. She can take your place. She'll be over the moon. And she's as rich as Croesus, so any increase in rent or service charges won't faze her.'

Ida had no idea who Croesus was, but wasn't about to ask, sensing that this was a conversation Arty and Edith were best having in private, especially as the retired bookie was struggling to speak, such was his shock.

'Right, well, that's between the pair of thee to sort,' she

said, before gesturing at the old suit and shirts on the floor which Arty had used to cover the money. 'So get that lot back in the case and push it under tha bed again for now. And I promise thee, I'll have answers one way or another by the end of the week.'

Edith nodded. Arty was still staring at Edith. So Ida took her leave. As she walked down the stairs she was thinking ahead. Thinking about that cash. And knowing how important it was that she solved this case and uncovered who the new owner of Fellside Court was. Not just for Arty's sake.

Only problem was, all she had to go on was the Notification of Sale letter. Somehow she was going to have to make that suffice.

'Sarah Mitchell.' Samson was standing in the kitchen, leaning against the worktop while Delilah had opted for a seat at the table, tired after overseeing a long afternoon of senior citizen romance. 'She's gone from outside chance to viable suspect.'

'What makes you say that?'

He gestured at the whiteboard. 'I did some digging into Ross Irwin's background, starting with his time in academia. I rang the university over in Leeds where he worked before setting up his own business, claiming to be a journalist doing a feature on Irwin and looking for some input from them about his time there. The lady I spoke to in HR wasn't keen to give anything more than the basics – how long he'd been there, which department etc. When I pushed her about his reasons for leaving, she clammed up. A sure sign there was more to it.'

'And was there?'

Samson nodded. 'I'd say so. I spent the rest of the afternoon online, looking up newspaper reports from the time, accessing Facebook pages and the like.' He grinned at her. 'You'd be proud at how easily I negotiate my way around social media now. Anyway, I came across this.' He held out his phone, displaying a screenshot of a page from the *Yorkshire Post*, dated five years ago.

She scanned the articles and at the very bottom, no more than a couple of paragraphs in total, was a small piece which featured Irwin's name on the first line. Delilah let out a low whistle.

'He was accused of sexual assault by one of his students?'

'Yes, but the charges were dropped.' Samson indicated the date. 'A week later, he leaves the university "by mutual consent".'

Delilah looked up at him. 'You think they gave him no choice?'

'That's what it seems like. Strikes me that this might not have been the first complaint raised against Irwin, so the university washed their hands of him. Otherwise, you'd think he would have gone to another academic position. But instead, he leaves town, moves to Kendal and sets up his own business.'

'It's a bit tenuous, though, isn't it? Basing an assumption of Irwin being a serial abuser just on this one vague article.'

'Maybe. But there's this to back it up.' He scrolled across the screen to bring up a Facebook post. 'Kendal Chat,' he said with a wry look. 'I had to wade through a lot of guff about noisy dogs and paranoid posts about suspicious-looking men in white vans, but then I found this. Someone posted news about our man being killed and a couple of the responses were telling. This one pasted a link to the article on Irwin's dismissal.'

'Wow!' Delilah nodded, reading the comment he was pointing at. '"No smoke without a fire!" Not your usual sympathy-laden reaction to someone being murdered.'

'And this,' continued Samson. 'From someone called Leeds Lass: "Irwin got what he deserved."'

'Crikey! So maybe we are onto something here. But how does it tie in with Sarah?'

Samson tapped the screen again, another article appearing, this one including a photo of two people, a man presenting a plaque to a young woman who appeared to be in her early twenties. The woman's blonde hair was falling over her face, a shy smile peeking through, cheeks dimpling. It was Sarah Mitchell, and she was standing next to Ross Irwin.

'Taken ten years ago, in her last year at college. Sarah won the university's ecology prize. She was presented with the award by her tutor—'

'Ross Irwin,' muttered Delilah. 'He was her tutor? And yet she described him as a "passing acquaintance" at the wedding.'

'Now why would she have said that?' Samson raised an eyebrow.

Delilah couldn't think of a legitimate reason. Not one that didn't make her feel awful. Because she was still struggling to see the timid ecologist and Harry's new bride as a murderer.

'So you're thinking this could make the motive we already have for her even stronger?' she asked.

Samson shrugged. 'It's all conjecture, but what if Irwin tried the same thing with Sarah that he did with Elaine? What if we're right that he could be a serial abuser? Or worse?'

'And so she threw us off the scent by claiming she didn't know him? It's possible. So what next? We should go and talk to her I suppose?'

'It's a bit late,' said Samson, checking his watch. 'But we could go now. Then grab something to eat afterwards?'

At which point Delilah's stomach rumbled and Tolpuddle let out a small whine. Samson laughed.

'Okay,' he said. 'Food first. Sarah Mitchell can wait until the morning.'

They'd both been too tired to face eating out, so a quick visit to the Spar on the way back to the cottage had armed Samson with the ingredients necessary to make a delicious stir fry. As the sun sank onto the horizon, Delilah was finishing off the last of the chilli prawns and Samson was leaning back in his chair at the small kitchen table, Tolpuddle's head on his lap, a comfortable silence enveloping them.

As if by unspoken agreement, there was no talk of the future. Of what Samson's plans were and where they would take him. Or even of the dire consequences of the case they were working. Nor did Delilah risk souring the mood by revealing the news about Twistleton Farm. Instead they talked of the past. Of Delilah's lost brother, Ryan, and the magical times the three of them had spent in childhood. And then, with dark claiming the town beyond the window, they moved upstairs, content to spend some precious hours together before the world intruded once more.

Date with Justice

Beyond the walls of the cottage up on Crag Lane, things were less tranquil. For a start, there was a murderer on the loose. Because that's what the locals felt, not many of them believing for one minute that Will Metcalfe was capable of the things he was being accused of. Which meant someone else had killed the ecologist and was still at large.

Back doors were locked. The pubs were quieter and emptied earlier. And a subdued air settled over the town as night descended. Up at Ellershaw Farm, Alison Metcalfe had put the children to bed, fobbing off their queries about the absence of their father with tender lies before returning to the kitchen table. There she sat, as the hours passed, unable to sleep, staring out at the black shadows of the fells under the crescent moon while worry gnawed at her.

Also incapable of sleep was Ida Capstick, although being of a practical nature, she'd at least made the effort of getting into bed. Sitting up, her back supported by her pillow, she was watching the moon move across the sky over Thorpdale while her mind refused to settle.

That promise she'd made Arty Robinson. It had been rash to say the least. But also necessary. Because if Ida could crack this particular problem and allay Arty's fears about his future in Fellside Court, she might, in the process, settle an even larger dilemma. But there were a lot of coulds and mights to be surmounted before that was possible. Especially if she was to proceed with the plan which had come to her in a blinding flash of inspiration as she fried up liver and onions for her brother's tea. In fact, she'd been so caught up in her flight of fancy, she'd stopped concentrating on the cooking and George had to step in to rescue the onions from burning.

Now, from the comfort of her bed, she was working through the pros and cons of this scheme of hers. It was risky. It definitely skirted on the edge of legality. But if she pulled it off, the rewards would be immense . . .

As Ida mulled over her quandary in Croft Cottage, she might have been somewhat put out to know that back in Bruncliffe the subject of her ruminations was also awake, and was banking on her failure. In his one-bedroomed apartment, Arty was staring out of his lounge window at the courtyard below, where the moon-silvered cherry trees stood sentry. The surrounding windows offered nothing but the blank reflections of curtained glass, none of his neighbours the type to keep late hours. Neither was Arty normally, but there was so much adrenalin firing around his system, he knew it was pointless trying to sleep.

It was that extraordinary offer from Edith. Had she meant it? Did she really mean he could move in with her? Because if she did – and knowing her well, Arty couldn't imagine her making such a proposal flippantly – his world had been tipped on its head. For now, after weeks of fretting himself stupid and doing something incredibly reckless in an attempt to protect his current life, he found himself in the strange position of praying that whoever was taking over Fellside Court was going to do exactly what he'd been fearing. That they would hike the rent and the service charges so high, Edith would have no choice but to hold firm on her generous suggestion and allow Arty to move in with her. Having had this slice of heaven dangled in front of him, Arty Robinson was finding he could contemplate nothing else.

While the residents of Bruncliffe marked the night's passing in their various ways, across the fells to the east, over the lonely spot above Malham Cove where Ross Irwin had lost his life and on beyond, all the way to the green edges of Harrogate, in the custody suite of the police station, a sergeant was watching the occupant of Cell Two courtesy of the camera mounted in the cell's ceiling. The man wasn't cut from the same cloth as their usual guests. He had the ruddy air of a farmer for a start. And he'd been unfailingly polite throughout the booking-in process and the subsequent searches. Not the sort you'd take for a murderer.

But the custody sergeant had been around the block, and knew better than to judge books by covers. He was also a firm believer that a guilty conscience will out. Right now, watching the man writhe and wriggle in a tortured sleep, the sergeant couldn't help thinking that the conscience of the suspect in Cell Two was far from clear.

20

On Tuesday morning, the world Samson and Delilah had been able to hold at bay during the night-time hours came crashing back around them with force. And most of that force was liquid. What had been a wonderful tail end of summer had turned into autumn overnight, the temperatures plunged into single figures, the wind whipping down the dale, and the low clouds as dark as the wet slates beneath, issuing a torrent of rain onto the town.

'The Horton Road is closed,' said Delilah, shouting slightly to be heard above the din of raindrops drumming the roof of the Mini. 'And there's flooding on the A65. We'll be lucky to get through.'

'Welcome to sunny Yorkshire,' Samson muttered under his breath, surveying the sodden landscape as they drove out of town towards Bruncliffe auction mart. He hadn't exactly been looking forward to the morning's rendezvous with Sarah Mitchell, given the nature of the questions they would be asking her; the dramatic weather was only adding to his apprehension. Fellsides which had been a vibrant green the day before were now riven with white streaks of streams as the water found new ways to cascade down the hills. In the fields, soggy sheep were sheltering up against stone walls, large puddles having formed in any dip or hollow. And the road was the wrong side of treacherous, the Mini's tyres aquaplaning occasionally as dry tarmac became hard to find.

But Samson didn't need the evidence beyond the windscreen to tell him how appalling the conditions were. The fact that they were travelling at a moderate speed was evidence enough. Face a study in concentration, Delilah was negotiating the Mini along what was more river than road with care and confidence, every corner taken with respect, not a hint of the headlong style she normally favoured.

'Almost there,' she said, flicking him a glance, mistaking his silence for concern at her driving.

'So what gives with the Mini?' he asked. 'I'm presuming Nancy Taylor let you keep it, judging by the rebranding?'

She nodded. 'She didn't want it back. I don't really blame her after everything. So she said I could have it for nothing.'

'And the pink hearts?'

The question brought a rueful grimace to Delilah's face. 'I took it to Baggy to get the logo changed. I should have known better. He mistakenly thought the DDA was for the dating agency and let his creative side have free rein.'

Samson laughed at the idea of the lanky mechanic going to the lengths of adding love hearts to the design.

'You can laugh. It's not you driving around in it!' muttered Delilah.

From the rear seat came a bark; Tolpuddle, spotting a bedraggled pheasant on a wall as they eased around yet another bend. Ahead was the grey arch of a railway bridge, the road dipping as it dropped beneath it. The road which had suddenly disappeared into a deep pool.

'Blimey!' Delilah slowed to a crawl, eyes fixed on the water lapping against the sides of the bridge. 'This bit is always the worst but I don't think I've ever seen it this bad!'

She inched the Mini forward, even Samson tense now as the little car nosed into the flood.

'Easy does it,' he muttered, hand on the dashboard.

She shot him a fiery glance before focusing back on the road, the Mini almost at the deepest part as they moved fully under the bridge, the sound of the rain momentarily replaced by the slosh of the backwash they were creating hitting against the stone supports.

'Come on, girl,' she murmured. 'Come on.'

Tolpuddle shifted in the rear, thrusting his grey head forward between the seats, waves of anxiety coming off him. Equally anxious, Samson put a hand back to fondle his ears but kept his eyes glued to the expanse of water in front of the bonnet, the headlights refracting eerily off it.

'Almost there,' muttered Delilah.

A few seconds more, wheels pushing through the flood, and then they emerged from under the arch, the rain thundering down on the Mini's roof once again. With audible sighs of relief from all three of its occupants, the car was finally onto drier tarmac.

'Christ,' said Samson, letting go of his tight grasp of the dashboard and turning to Delilah as she lightly tapped the brakes to test them. 'Brilliant driving, partner!'

She grinned and patted the steering wheel. 'She's a star.'

'She sure is. Love hearts and all!'

Delilah broke into laughter, making Samson's soul sing, and he was contemplating persuading her to pull over so he could show her how happy he was in more detail when his mobile rang.

'Danny?' he said, voice raised to combat the sound of the rain. 'What's going on?'

A barrage of language came from the phone as the agitated constable tried to say everything in one go.

'Easy, take a deep breath and start again,' Samson counselled.

Delilah glanced at him, brow furrowed, sensing there was trouble coming, so he switched the mobile to speaker.

'Will's going to be charged,' Danny blurted out into the tense silence of the car.

'What? When?' Delilah's shocked reply took her attention from her driving as the Mini hit a patch of water, the wheels skidding, snapping her focus back onto the road.

'Within the next thirty-six hours,' came the blunt response. 'DS Benson got a custody extension and he's adamant Will is our man.'

'But that's mad . . . I mean, there's no way . . .'

Samson shook his head. 'See it from Benson's angle. Will has already lied repeatedly. Destroyed key evidence. Add to that his strong motive and that he has no alibi, not to mention the stains in the Land Rover, the rounders bat and the button they found at Malham Cove – a button Will freely admitted was his – and you're looking at a suspect mired in guilt.'

'Folk have been convicted with less,' agreed Danny. 'DS Benson has a corpse and, as Samson said, plenty to go on.'

'What makes you so sure he's going to take it to the next level?' asked Samson.

There was a pause, as if Danny was steeling himself to break more bad news. 'The pathologist,' he finally said. 'While she hasn't submitted her full report yet, she's given DS Benson an indication that the rounders bat could be a match for one of the wounds on Irwin's face.'

It was like the air had been sucked out of the car, Delilah's grip on the steering wheel so tight that her knuckles were stark white, while Samson felt the need to open the window, despite the storm raging outside.

'Jesus, Will,' murmured Delilah. 'What kind of mess have you landed yourself in?'

'A deep one,' said Danny. 'So if you two want to help him out, then you need to get going. And for God's sake, come up with something concrete, because sometime within the next day and a half, Will is going to be charged with murder—'

The phone went silent, Danny cut off in mid-sentence as the car moved out of range. But they'd got the gist.

'I can't believe this is happening,' whispered Delilah, face drained of colour. 'They can't make it stick, can they? Even if they charge him?'

Samson gave a half-shrug, knowing there was no way to sugar-coat the truth. 'As Danny said, folk have been convicted on less, and not always fairly.'

'So we've only got thirty-six hours to prove Will's innocent?'

'Yes.'

Delilah nodded. Then put her foot down, the little car surging forward. Samson didn't say a word. Because he understood the urgency, perhaps even better than she did. For he knew from personal experience how a murder charge could change a man's life and leave a stain that no amount of good living could ever remove.

In the distance, the sprawling structure of the auction mart came into view. What they were about to do wasn't going to be easy. But if Will Metcalfe was going to come out of this as an innocent man, Sarah Mitchell was going to have to answer some very frank questions. Even if Samson didn't like asking them.

Back in Bruncliffe, standing in the open doorway of the office building, Ida Capstick didn't like what she was about to do either. It was sneaky for starters. And then there was the weather.

Pouring down didn't do it justice. The amount of rain falling from the skies was torrential, way more than could be held off with an umbrella. That's if you were capable of hanging onto such a thing in the wind which was howling down Back Street.

Practical as always, Ida had opted for a waterproof and was thankful she didn't have far to go. One last check of her watch. Nine o'clock on the dot.

Pulling the hood of her jacket tighter, she stepped out into the rain, closed the door behind her and began walking up the street. In one hand she carried a red bucket. In the other, a mop. A Vileda 1-2, recently purchased from Barry at Plastic Fantastic. She knew the versatility of such a utensil, having seen one in action several times. And while she wasn't expecting to have to wield it in self-defence on her latest mission, it added to her cover.

For she was undercover, not that anyone would have noticed, dressed as she was in her cleaning clothes, a checked pinny on under her waterproof. Walking in quick strides, she headed up the street towards the marketplace and was instantly rewarded by the sight of a suited figure dashing from a doorway and off across the cobbled square, his back towards her.

Timing was everything.

Heart beating fast, she headed for her target. The same doorway the figure had come out of. This was going to be the tricky bit. The part which would require all of the skills she'd acquired in the last three months working at the Dales Detective Agency.

Of course, standing at the range in Croft Cottage the night before, surrounded by the flavoursome aroma of frying liver, all this had seemed a lot easier. Now, walking towards the building on the corner of Back Street, it all seemed a bit daft. And she still wasn't convinced about the legality. But short of any other ideas, Ida was determined to see it through.

Reaching the entrance, she stepped into a small foyer, took off her jacket, shook the worst of the wet off it and smoothed down her pinny. With firm steps, she headed for the stairs. One floor up, and she was outside a glass door. Beyond it was the reception area, a young man at a desk, busy on the phone.

Perfect.

Without even breaking stride, she pushed open the door, nodded at him and headed straight for the small cupboard to his left, praying things had stayed the same since she last worked there twenty years ago – before being sacked by that crook Turpin for telling him exactly what she thought of him. Fired up by indignation two decades old, she marched purposefully across the room.

'Can I put you on hold a moment . . .' she heard the lad say, the phone being placed down, and then he was looking at her, rising from his seat to halt her progress. 'Excuse me? Can I help you?'

'Just here for cleaning,' she said, continuing apace, opening the cupboard, feeling a surge of relief at seeing a bright green hoover inside. Cordless. She held back her disdain. Wheeling out the vacuum, she headed for the office behind the desk.

'But . . . I'm sorry . . . I didn't know . . .'

Not giving the young man a chance to process whatever thought was forming, Ida stopped, turned, and went on the attack.

'Happen I'm right pressed for time, lad, so don't be keeping me gassing. I'm normally in and out of here long afore tha's even thinking of getting out of bed of a morning. But the flooding on the back road's had me all out of synch. So I'll just get on with it if tha doesn't mind.'

She could see him taking it all in. The bucket. The mop. The vacuum. The pinny. She was Ida Capstick. The town's cleaner. Why would he have reason to doubt the veracity of what she was saying? Even if he'd never seen her there before? Because whoever saw the cleaners in an office?

'Right . . . okay . . . I'll just call and check—'

'Tha'll do no such thing!' she snapped. 'Disturbing a hard-working man on his break! Get back to tha phone call and let me do my job.'

He swallowed. Sat down, and picked up the phone. Ida walked on, reached the office and turned back, interrupting his resumed conversation.

'And if tha's inclined to make a brew, I'll have one. Strong, mind.'

She closed the door on his nodding. Leaned against it and wondered if the rush of blood causing her pulse to throb was potentially lethal.

Then she set to work. The desk first. A large glass creation which was on the high end of the Capstick scale of tidiness, a pile of paper neatly stacked, a couple of files on the side and a computer. Switching on the vacuum and leaving it idling, she began sifting through the folders, one eye constantly on the time because she didn't have long. If the other part of her plan was going as it should, she had maybe ten minutes, fifteen tops. If it wasn't, she was already in trouble. And might even end up being arrested.

She was trying not to think about that as she flipped open the final folder. Straight away she knew she'd struck gold.

A copy of the same letter she'd seen in the manager's office in Fellside Court. The notification of completion for the sale of the retirement complex.

'Bingo,' she muttered.

She spread the rest of the papers out on the desk, skimming them quickly. And there it was. A letter to a client, informing them of the successful purchase of Fellside Court, Bruncliffe. The client was Phoenix Enterprises.

It meant nothing to Ida. But she took photos of every page in the folder, knowing that if she was caught now, there would be trouble.

A look at her watch. Fifteen minutes already gone. Placing the papers back exactly as they had been, she hurried towards the window. There he was. Striding across the cobbles. Head down into the rain. Heart thundering, she turned back to the desk, flicked a duster over the phone, which was needing a thorough clean, resisted the urge to spray air freshener, switched off the vacuum – glad not to have the added burden of winding up a cord – picked up her bucket and opened the door.

'Tha'll have to do with a lick and a promise,' she declared, striding into the reception area just as the young lad was walking towards the office, mug in hand.

'Thanks,' he said. All smiles now. 'You've earned your tea.'

Ida put the vacuum away before casting a look at his offering. Milky, with the heavy scent of leaves left to sit. It was a perfect brew.

'Thanks,' she said. More contrite now. For the lad knew how to make a cuppa. 'But happen as I've no time.'

She walked through the glass door and into the hallway, waiting until she was out of sight before picking up her pace and fair scuttling down the stairs.

By the time Matty Thistlethwaite turned the corner onto Back Street, Ida was already halfway down it, the red bucket and the mop marking her out as a cleaner, on her way to her next job. The solicitor thought nothing of it. Not least because he was still mulling over the urgency with which Arty Robinson had beset him in Peaks Patisserie, demanding to know about wills and inheritance law with an insistence which had seen the solicitor feel obliged to offer some counsel, despite his usual routine being thrown out because of it. His regular nine o'clock visit to Peaks for a takeaway coffee had become an unexpected fifteen-minute break. Not that he minded. Arty was a good soul and deserved help.

Still thinking on this, Matty entered the reception to Turpin's, his assistant on the phone nodding in his direction. Matty didn't notice that there were two mugs of tea on the man's desk. Nor, when he sat down in his own office, did he notice that his phone was looking markedly less dusty than when he'd left.

'I'm taking it this isn't a social visit?'

Harry Furness's tone was dry as he took a seat in one of the armchairs at the far end of his office on the first floor of the auction mart. Samson, Delilah and Sarah were already sitting around the small table, a tray of coffees resting on it.

Delilah spread her hands in apology. 'Sorry, but no.'

'Is it about Will?' Harry asked. 'I heard he'd been arrested.'

'Yes. We're trying to clear his name and some things have come up we think you could help us with.'

'Anything!' said Harry, Sarah nodding in agreement. 'Anything at all.'

Delilah gave Samson a nervous glance and he found himself wondering how much of his friend's magnanimity would remain after they'd asked their awkward questions of his new bride.

When they'd contacted Sarah to set up the meeting the day before, the ecologist had explained that she would be spending the day at the auction mart, working from Harry's office while he was down in the auction ring, overseeing several sales. But with the weather turning out the way it had, the morning's sales had been cancelled, buyers and sellers all struggling to reach the mart due to flooded roads.

And so here they were in an eerily quiet mart, about to interview Sarah, with her husband on hand.

It wasn't ideal. Samson was aware just how carefully they were going to have to tread if friendships were going to come out of this intact. And just how ruthless he would need to be if Will was to have his name cleared.

'Perhaps we can start with how you know Ross Irwin,' Samson said, addressing his question to Sarah.

'"Know" is putting it strongly. He was a lecturer on my course at university but I'm not sure I spoke more than three words to him during the three years I was there.' She smiled, something of a rare sight given her nervous nature, and Samson felt awful for what he was about to do.

'And since?'

'He's – he was – a professional acquaintance. A competitor even.'

Samson nodded, allowing a pause, creating space for Delilah to chip in as she normally did. But his partner had her head down taking notes, showing no inclination to contribute. She was leaving this one to him.

'Right,' he said, reaching for a coffee, trying to keep things nonchalant. 'So how come he was at the wedding?'

Sarah shrugged. 'I don't know. I didn't invite him, that's for sure.'

'You didn't?' Harry looked at her, an eyebrow raised. 'The cheeky muppet! I don't mean to speak ill of the dead or owt, but all that commotion with Will could have been avoided if Irwin hadn't gatecrashed the reception.'

'And perhaps Will wouldn't now be the prime suspect in his murder,' said Samson.

Sarah looked fraught. 'I'm so sorry. If I'd known what

was going to happen I'd have asked Ross to leave. But at the time I figured he wasn't doing anyone any harm and what with us both competing for the same tender, I didn't want it to look like I was being petty.'

'What kind of person would you say he was?' Delilah had lifted her head and was watching Sarah carefully, Harry frowning, as though sensing there was something more here than innocent questions about Irwin's conduct at the wedding.

'I don't know . . . like I said, I've had very little to do with him. Perhaps a bit arrogant?' Sarah looked from Samson to Delilah, as though seeking approbation. 'And he certainly had a reputation as a bit of a Lothario. I mean, it was well known at university that the pretty women in his tutor group got more of his attention.'

'Were you in his tutor group?'

Sarah shook her head. 'I applied for one of the modules he was running but I didn't get on it.' She gave a lopsided smile. 'I don't think my face fit, in more ways than one.'

Samson reached into his pocket and pulled out his phone, knowing this was the point of no return. But if they were to exonerate Will . . .

'So how do you explain this?' he asked, holding out the mobile, the photo from ten years before of Irwin presenting the plaque to Sarah on the screen. 'It says here he was your tutor.'

21

The laugh that emerged from the woman opposite wasn't the reaction Samson had been expecting, as Sarah studied the decade-old photograph of herself and Irwin.

'Oh, that. The only time Ross Irwin showed any interest in me or my studies.' She looked up with a self-effacing smile, cheeks dimpling. 'My real tutor was extremely shy, even more so than me. It's probably why we got on so well. He didn't want his photo in the paper and so Ross seized his chance for a bit of free publicity. The journalist mustn't have realised a swap had taken place, or wasn't bothered to make the distinction.'

'So Irwin never made a move on you at all?' Delilah asked.

Sarah frowned. 'A move? No. Never.'

'He wasn't predatory in any way—?'

'Look here,' Harry spoke up, shrewd gaze fixed on the Dales Detective duo, a bite to his tone. 'What's with the third degree? Whether Sarah knew this bloke or not, what's that got to do with him being murdered?'

'It's just . . . we wondered . . .' Delilah floundered, face flushed as she stumbled into the barriers of friendship.

'We've got reason to believe Irwin had previous when it

came to what he did to Elaine,' stated Samson, 'that he assaulted other women. In fact we're pretty sure it was such an incident which saw him leave his university position. And so we just wanted to know if that had been Sarah's experience of him, too.'

While his wife was looking shocked at this revelation about Irwin, Harry was looking cross, a snort of disbelief breaking from him.

'You mean you wanted to know if Sarah might have a motive for killing him, more like!' he declared. The embarrassed silence which met his statement brought red streaks of anger to his cheeks. 'Seriously? You came here to see if my lass had owt to do with his murder? The bloody cheek of it! If you two hadn't saved my bacon not long back, I'd be sending you out of here with the print of my boots on your backsides.'

'Hush, Harry,' Sarah said, stroking his arm. 'They're just doing their job. You'd be the same if I was the one in a police cell.'

'But it's bloody ridiculous!' he fumed. 'You'd think they'd have learned from the last time they went round casting aspersions, thinking you were capable of killing folk. Not to mention that you weren't exactly out of sight during the reception.' He turned his anger back on his two visitors. 'I mean, how was she supposed to have done it? Driven over to Malham in her bridal gown, killed Irwin and then driven back to party the night away? Is that what you really think?'

'Actually, there is a bit of a discrepancy when it comes to the reception,' Samson persevered, Delilah hanging her head beside him. 'We have it on good authority that Sarah left the rugby club for a while and returned in a different outfit—'

Harry jumped up out of his chair, knocking one of the mugs over on the table, coffee spilling in all directions. 'That's enough!' he shouted. 'I won't stand by and have you malign my wife like that. You can leave, now!'

But Sarah was tugging on his arm, pulling him back down into his chair, smiling apologetically at Samson and making him feel like the worst person in the world.

'They're right, love,' she murmured to her husband. 'I did leave the reception for a bit.'

'Aye, but only long enough to change,' muttered Harry. 'Can't have been more than twenty minutes, tops!'

'It was a bit longer than that.' Sarah tipped her head to one side, her gaze steadfast as she regarded Samson. 'I'm guessing you want the details?'

'If you don't mind,' he said.

'I left the club about seven thirty or so. Someone had spilled some wine on my dress – it was an accident and I didn't want to make a fuss, so I nipped home to put on a different outfit. My grandmother wasn't well enough to come to the reception so while I had a bit of peace and quiet, I took the opportunity to call her on Zoom. I got back to the reception around nine, which Ida Capstick can vouch for.'

'You were gone an hour and a half and I didn't even notice.' Harry now looked shamefaced.

Sarah laughed. 'You were too busy with the karaoke machine.'

'And your grandmother . . . ?' Samson asked.

'Can corroborate it. She records all of our calls so she

can watch them back, so if it's an alibi you're after, I've got one. I'll send you a copy.'

Samson nodded. 'That would be great. And I'm sorry. Genuinely. But we had to ask these questions.'

'I understand,' said Sarah, giving her husband an affectionate look, 'even if Harry doesn't. But is that true, what you said? Was Ross Irwin really made to leave the university because of his behaviour?'

'It seems that way,' Delilah said. 'Officially he left of his own accord but, reading between the lines, I'd say he was given the push. An undergraduate had accused him of molesting her and although the charges were dropped in the end, he resigned not long after.'

Sarah was shaking her head. 'I couldn't believe it when I heard what happened to Elaine. I genuinely had no idea he was capable of such behaviour.'

'But surely,' said Harry, 'if this Irwin was such a serial abuser, the university would have other records of complaints against him?'

'Not necessarily,' said Delilah with a weary sigh. 'Given he was in such a powerful position, the man who could dictate how an academic career began or continued, some women might not have dared complain. Even Elaine wasn't going to go to the police after what happened at Malham Cove, and she's not exactly afraid of confrontation. But she said she didn't want the hassle, and felt ashamed she'd fallen for his smooth patter.'

Harry's expression turned fierce. 'Christ. Sounds like he was a right piece of work. But do you really think this could be at the root of his murder?'

'We're not sure. To be honest, we're up against time and

we're clutching at straws, pursuing any line of enquiry we can. Even one that causes our friends distress . . .' Delilah gave an awkward smile. 'What we do believe, however, is that whoever killed Irwin was at the wedding, so that narrows down our pool of suspects a bit. But we could really do with a break or we're never going to find a way to get Will out of this mess.'

Harry grunted. 'Aye, well, much as I'm not keen on you casting your net in Sarah's direction, I can vouch that you're right about one thing – there's no way Will murdered that bloke. So if there's anything we can help with, just ask.'

'There is something,' said Delilah, turning to Sarah with a sheepish look. 'After what we've just put you through, it feels a bit cheeky asking, but we could do with another expert opinion on the land earmarked for the planning application.'

'An ecological impact assessment?' Sarah's voice held surprise. 'Don't you have the one Ross Irwin completed?'

Delilah gave a non-committal shake of her head. 'We'd just like to make sure nothing's been missed.'

'Of course. I can certainly give you my initial impressions. Just let me know when suits.'

'How are you fixed this afternoon? Gareth Towler and Herriot are heading up to Ellershaw about three thirty – that's if this wretched rain lets up.'

Sarah nodded. 'Tell them I'll meet them there.'

'Thanks.'

Sensing this wasn't the time for lingering now their questions had been asked and answered, Samson got to his feet.

'We really appreciate your time,' he said as the others stood too. 'And I can only apologise if we've offended you. But the questions had to be asked.'

He held a hand out to Sarah, who shook it without hesitation. Her husband, however, looked to be in two minds about accepting the gesture.

'I don't know how you do it,' Harry said gruffly, finally shaking Samson's hand. 'Going through life with so little trust, even of the folk you call friends.'

Samson kept his expression neutral, accepting the criticism despite the pain the words caused. 'It's just part of the job,' he said.

'Aye, well, perhaps it's time you found another job.' A twinkle returned to the auctioneer's eyes as he indicated the hues of purple and blue on Samson's left cheek. 'I hear farming is a lot less riven with suspicion. Less likely to leave you walking around looking like a failed boxer, too.'

'Farming? Why would I—?'

'Thanks again,' interrupted Delilah, her hand in the small of Samson's back, urging him towards the door before he could finish his reply.

'You know where I am when it comes time to buy livestock!' Harry called after them, laughing now. 'Not that I can promise mates' rates!'

Samson made to turn, to ask him what he meant, but Delilah wasn't having any of it, pushing him ahead of her, hustling him down the stairs and out into the pouring rain, where the Mini and Tolpuddle were waiting for them.

'God,' she exclaimed as she started the car and drove off, 'that was one of the worst experiences of my life! Poor Sarah!'

Drying the rain from his face with his sleeve, Samson grunted his agreement. 'A complete nightmare. Don't think I've ever felt quite so sordid interviewing a suspect.'

'On the bright side,' continued Delilah, 'at least we know Sarah is innocent. But on the other hand . . .'

She fell silent – whether because the wet road conditions demanded her full attention, or she couldn't bear to complete the thought, Samson couldn't tell. But he let the silence linger. Because they both knew that if Sarah wasn't the murderer they were seeking, their chances of acquitting Will had just got even slimmer.

Ida was vexed and concerned in equal measure. When she'd returned from her reconnaissance trip to Matty Thistlethwaite's, she'd been on a high. Thrilled that her plan had gone off without a hitch, she'd found it hard to settle to the next bit of the task, too geared up for sitting in front of a computer. But the desire to get to the bottom of the puzzle she was so close to solving had seen her take her place at the desk in the downstairs office, armed with a brew and a couple of celebratory biscuits.

An hour later and the biscuits were still on the plate, the mug of tea had the congealed look of a hot beverage gone cold, and Ida's euphoria had dissolved into pessimism.

Phoenix Enterprises was refusing to yield its secrets.

Ida had been confident that she'd find the owner of the entity which was buying Fellside Court with a simple check on Companies House. But it hadn't turned out to be that straightforward. While Phoenix Enterprises was registered on the government website and everything seemed above board, the identity of the person or people behind it wasn't clear.

Instead of the name and address of the individual in charge, there was yet another company listed.

Phoenix Abroad.

She'd suspected what it meant the minute she'd seen it but had felt obliged to do the relevant searches. So she'd trawled through the internet, trying to discover more about Phoenix Abroad, but had come to a dead end.

Ida stared at the screen, letting herself accept what she knew was true. Thanks to Rick Procter, after the past few months there weren't many folk in Bruncliffe who didn't know what a shell company was. Who didn't know how they could be used to hide ownership, to create smoke-screens. To do malicious deeds.

And from everything Ida could see, it looked more than likely that Phoenix Enterprises was owned by such a company.

She got up from the chair and crossed to the window, the rain still hammering down outside, the road slick with puddles. It matched her mood.

A shell company. Buying the homes of Arty and Joseph and all the others. How could that possibly be a good thing for the community? Why would the future owner have gone to such lengths to conceal themselves unless they were planning something wicked?

Ida didn't have the answers. But she did know that when she passed on this news to the pensioners, it was going to break their hearts. Because Bruncliffe had seen the damage shell companies could do.

Samson and Delilah returned to an office building as down-beat and depressed as the weather outside. On the ground floor, Ida was hunched over a computer, barely grunting as they entered, even Tolpuddle getting nothing more than a cursory pat as he bounded over to greet her. Heading up the stairs was no better, the atmosphere in Delilah's office heavy with despair as Nina and Nathan sat on the couch, laptops open, video footage from the wedding reception scrolling past, the scenes of folk having fun in complete contrast to the bored expressions on the teenagers' faces.

'Learned anything?' asked Delilah.

'Only that if I ever get married, I'm not having a bloody wedding reception,' muttered Nina.

Nathan groaned in agreement, stretched his long limbs and shut his laptop. 'I'm not sure I can take any more. I swear adults shouldn't be allowed anywhere near alcohol.'

'I totally concur,' said Samson with a grin. 'But as for the case, nothing of interest?'

'Not a sausage,' said Nina. 'But we've barely scratched the surface of the videos we've been sent. It's going to take for ever.'

'Well, you can discount Sarah Mitchell from your search.'

The teenagers both looked up in surprise.

'How come?' asked Nina.

'She's got an alibi. She's sent us a copy of a Zoom call she had with her grandmother while she was absent from the reception.'

'Have you seen it? Is it real? You can fake a lot these days . . .' Nathan's question contained desperate hope.

Delilah shook her head. 'It's real. And she wasn't faking her surprise at hearing Irwin had history when it came to accusations of sexual abuse. She's no longer a suspect.'

'Bugger,' muttered Nathan. And instantly looked chastened. 'Sorry. I didn't mean I want her to be . . . I mean, I wasn't wishing . . .'

Nina put a hand on his arm. 'We all know what you

meant. And we all feel the same.' She looked at Samson and Delilah. 'So how does this affect the investigation?'

'It means we keep digging,' said Delilah. She took a deep breath, as though debating what to say next, then she gave a nod and continued. 'And I hate to tell you both this but there's even more pressure now. We've heard that Will's custody has been extended and the police are preparing to charge him with murder.'

Nina just blinked while Nathan's mouth dropped open. 'But that's ridiculous!' he spluttered.

'Sorry, son,' said Samson, knowing the lad revered his Uncle Will and would be feeling the frustration of the situation as much as any of them. 'But according to Danny, the rounders bat is looking like a good match for one of Irwin's wounds, so they think they're onto something.' He put a hand up to forestall the objection Nathan was forming. 'There's no point wasting energy getting cross about what's happening – it's standard procedure. Instead, let's use that energy to make sure we crack this case before they bring charges.'

Nathan looked like he was about to protest but then gave a reluctant nod. 'You want us to stick with the video watching, then?'

'I'm afraid so,' said Delilah, the teenagers already reverting their attention onto their laptops. 'Meanwhile, I'll start on Irwin's computer files, and Samson—'

'I'll do my best Ida impression and get the kettle on,' he said with a grin, trying to lift the mood.

He was rewarded with smiles and crossed the landing to the kitchen, Tolpuddle accompanying him in the hope of food.

'I'll never replace Ida, will I, boy?' he murmured,

stroking the dog's head before reaching for the tin of Dog-gestives.

With Tolpuddle happily crunching on his treat, Samson filled the kettle and was about to throw the teabags in the teapot when he paused. Heat the teapot. Do it how Ida would do it. Do it right.

Laughing at himself, he poured in some hot water, swilled it round and tipped it out. He even included an extra teabag to get the required Capstick strength. And when the boiling water had been added, he reached for the tea cosy at the far end of the worktop. A handmade knit-job, dark green with a redundant pompom on the top, it was a creation he'd never used before. He didn't see the point, as he repeatedly told Ida when she scolded him for his omission. But today, he was doing it right. So he pulled the cosy towards him.

It crinkled. An odd sound for something made of wool.

Intrigued, he looked inside and saw a folded envelope, the Turpin's logo coming visible as he pulled it out. He opened the flap and extracted a single sheet of paper. And straight away he understood all the questions and quips about farming and buying livestock which had been aimed in his direction since his return to town.

Twistleton Farm was coming up for auction.

Pain, sharp, like a shard of glass through his heart. A sense of loss for something he couldn't even begin to contemplate getting back. A life he'd left behind with the arrogance of youth, thinking it would always be there.

How wrong he'd been.

He stared at the letter, at the sale date. Christ! Of all days, it had to be that bloody one. The type blurred, hot tears threatening.

'How's that brew coming on, Imitation Ida?' Delilah, shouting from across the landing, the others laughing.

'Nearly there,' he replied, hurriedly folding the letter back inside the cosy and placing it at the end of the worktop where he'd found it.

He understood why they'd hidden it from him. And he appreciated their concern. But it didn't lessen the agony of knowing his family farm was going under the hammer.

22

The afternoon crawled by. Nathan and Nina lasted another hour sifting through video footage before Delilah shooed them out to go and have a prolonged break, Nathan having to be forcibly led from the room by Nina, such was his concern for his uncle. Meanwhile, Samson had been trying to help Delilah go through the data they'd copied from Ross Irwin's laptop, but that help turned out to be more of a hindrance, given her partner's basic computer literacy. Not to mention he was unusually subdued, which she put down to the fact that their morning had resulted in a dead end for the investigation. So with the rain having finally stopped, Delilah had shooed Samson out too, tasking him with taking Tolpuddle for a long run on the fells.

Which left just two people in the office building; Delilah on the first floor pulling apart Irwin's files and Ida on the ground floor working on the ownership of Fellside Court. From the gruff answer Delilah received when she'd enquired how things were going on that front, it seemed like none of the Dales Detective team were having a particularly brilliant day.

Stretching away from the screen she'd been hunched over, Delilah rubbed her back and looked at her watch.

Three o'clock already! While she felt the hours were passing slowly, her lack of progress making things drag, in fact they were speeding by. Especially for Will, the time he had left before becoming a man formally accused of murder being frittered away by an investigation which seemed to be going nowhere.

Unfortunately, her search through the contents of Irwin's computer was proving no more productive than any of their other avenues of enquiry. So far she'd unearthed several files of work-related reports dating back five years, all seemingly above board; a folder of personal photographs, which she'd skipped through, learning nothing other than the fact that Irwin had a penchant for taking selfies; and several drafts of academic papers, the contents of which she couldn't begin to claim to understand.

Nothing out of the ordinary. Nothing which screamed of motive for someone seeking to murder the ecologist. Unless they had a problem with his narcissistic tendencies?

Delilah browsed through some of the photos again, many showing a much younger Irwin, often with his arm draped around an even more youthful woman. Judging by the fact a couple of the women were wearing hoodies branded with the university logo, they were from his days as a lecturer. In one, he was standing with a large group of people, all students by the looks of it, binoculars around the necks of many. Some kind of group outing. A bird-watching society maybe?

Not sure she was gaining any meaningful insight from the photographs, and conscious she was wasting precious time, she switched her attention to the final two folders on the screen, imaginatively labelled 'New Folder' and

'New Folder (2)'. Both were small in size, less than a meg each, which is why she hadn't intended to copy them in the first place, the rapid departure from Irwin's hotel room having seen her transfer them in error. She clicked on New Folder, the largest of the pair. Inside was a single spread-sheet titled 'Species Count'. Delilah opened it up and found herself staring at rows and rows of gobbledygook.

Numbers and letters made up the majority of the entries, no symbols to indicate what they might refer to, no column or row headings to assist in deciphering what exactly she was looking at. The only sense of a rational mind was that no column featuring digits contained letters, and vice versa, and the final column contained either a tick, a cross, or a question mark, obviously to signify success, failure or uncertainty.

According to the heading it was a record of Irwin's surveys, some kind of environmental tally of the species he'd encountered, but after puzzling over it for a few minutes, Delilah had to concede she lacked the expertise to decode it. Deciding it was something Sarah might be able to help them with, she turned to New Folder (2).

Two word documents were contained inside: 'KD1' and 'KD2'. But at least this time when Delilah opened up the first one, she knew what she was looking at.

The report on the land Kevin Dinsdale was hoping to develop. She skimmed through it, recognising it as the original of the draft Kevin had shown them the day before. Leaving it open on the screen, she clicked on KD2.

A second copy of the Dinsdale report.

Why would Irwin have kept two copies on file? She was about to close it when she spotted something on the final page. Her breath caught in her throat, that familiar pulse of excitement which came with a breakthrough on an investigation gripping her. She went back to KD1. Pulled it up so the pair of them were parallel on the screen and began going through them line by line.

From below came the sound of Samson, shouting hello. His heavy post-run steps on the stairs, accompanied by the much more energetic patter of Tolpuddle.

'That hound of yours almost ran me into the ground,' Samson was saying, laughing in exhaustion as he reached the landing. 'Next time, I vote you go for the run and I stay sitting on my backside in front of a computer—'

He broke off, sensing her tension.

'What is it?' he asked.

'Come and see.'

He was by her side in a couple of long strides, leaning over her, looking at the two documents, eyes flicking from one to the other. 'Dinsdale's report, in duplicate. What about it?'

She scrolled down and pointed at the bottom of the screen. At the final summations. And Samson swore.

'One is a pass and the other a fail?' Eyebrows raised, he turned to her. 'Irwin had two reports ready, with different verdicts?'

Delilah nodded. 'Which seems a bit out of the ordinary, don't you think?'

'Just a bit. Makes you wonder whether the pass came with strings attached.'

'You mean another hustle on the side, like his attempt to blackmail Will?'

Samson shrugged. 'Who's to say Irwin didn't charge

Dinsdale for the pleasure of getting the result he wanted? Trouble is, how do we prove it? It's not the kind of thing Irwin would have left hanging around in plain sight.'

'Unless . . .' Delilah was back at the spreadsheet, the complicated entries of digits and letters still making no sense. Apart from the penultimate line:

1008 KD EcIA 10 ?

'KD,' Delilah muttered, looking at the second column. 'Kevin Dinsdale.'

Samson let out a murmur of agreement. 'And EcIA?' he asked, pointing at the third column.

'Ecological Impact Assessment?'

'Sounds plausible. What about the numbers?'

Delilah let her eyes drift to the row below:

1808 WM PSL 5 X

The letters WM were directly underneath the KD. And suddenly it was like she'd broken the code.

'This lot could be a date.' She pointed at the first four numbers of the final row. 'Will said Irwin approached him late last week. So this could be the eighteenth of August, that would fit the timescale. Then the letters are Will's initials and . . . PSL . . .' She faltered.

Samson indicated the row above. 'Whatever kind of report Irwin was proposing? That's what it was for Dinsdale.'

It came to her in a flash, a memory of Irwin's other files. 'Protected Species Licence!' she said.

'So Gareth could have been right,' murmured Samson, nodding. 'The newts were what Irwin was hitting up Will for at the wedding.'

'Seems so. But this is the interesting bit.' Delilah put a finger on the final number and looked up at Samson, a half-smile on her lips.

He shook his head. 'I don't get it.'

'Five grand?'

Samson's eyes grew large. 'Of course! Five grand!' he exclaimed. 'The amount Will said he was being pressured to pay. You've cracked it! Which means . . . this is a record of all the cash Irwin was pulling in on the side . . .'

They both stared at the screen. At the numbers in the full length of the column.

'That's a lot of money,' murmured Delilah.

'Kind of explains all the fancy clothes and the extravagant hotel room. Irwin was living a lifestyle fuelled by corruption. Pay him enough and he'd deliver what you wanted, with the odd bit of blackmail thrown in for good measure.'

'Makes you wonder if that's why Dinsdale chose him. Maybe he knew Irwin's expertise was for sale?'

'And was willing to pay through the nose for it.' Samson pointed at the penultimate line of the spreadsheet once more, moving his finger to the second last column. 'If we're right, Irwin was asking ten thousand pounds for that report—' He went still. His finger now resting on the question mark ending the entry for Kevin Dinsdale. 'What do you think that means?'

Delilah ran her eyes up the table, taking in the majority of ticks, only a handful of crosses and question marks among them. 'I'd say they indicate payment or not. And perhaps payment pending?'

'So this means Irwin hadn't been paid?'

'Looks that way.'

Samson whirled away from the desk, energy pulsing from him. 'Which could mean Kevin had a reason to want him dead after all. He knew the report had been compiled in his favour so he no longer needed an ecologist, especially not one he was having to pay over the odds for.'

'Is this our motive?' Delilah asked, feeling the excitement.

'Maybe. We just need to prove Dinsdale had the opportunity—'

He broke off as the front door slammed shut, accompanied by raised voices, Tolpuddle lifting his head from his bed and barking in excited response.

'Samson, Delilah! We think we've found something!' Nina was hurtling up the stairs towards them, Nathan close behind her, laptop in his hand, with Ida following at a slower pace and Constable Danny Bradley bringing up the rear.

'Kevin Dinsdale,' blurted out Nathan as the teenagers charged into Delilah's office and placed the laptop on her desk. 'He went missing from the reception!'

'We went over to the cafe for a break, like you told us to,' Nina was explaining as Nathan leaned over the laptop, cuing up a video while Samson, Delilah, Danny and Ida crowded round, 'but we thought we might as well keep looking through the footage from the reception. And look what we found!'

She gestured at the screen where, amidst the festivities of the wedding reception, in the background Kevin Dinsdale could be seen entering the rugby club, a worried frown on his face.

Samson checked the time at the bottom of the video. Nine o'clock.

'Okay,' he said calmly, keeping a lid on the buzz he could feel thrumming through him. The buzz of a case being broken open. 'So we can say he came back into the reception, but have you got him leaving?'

Nathan grinned. His fingers flashed over the keys. And there it was – the farmer heading out of the club with a glance over his shoulder.

'We've combed every inch of material we have from the period between these two clips and he's not on any of it.' Nathan's eyes were dancing with excitement. 'It's proof, isn't it? He could be the killer? That's why we brought Danny with us – the police need to see this, don't they?'

Danny Bradley held up a Peaks Patisserie takeaway cup. 'I've got a bit of time left on my break. Said I'd take a look. And I wanted a word anyway.'

Delilah was looking at Samson, no doubt thinking about what they'd just discovered. Was this the evidence which would exonerate Will?

'Let's not jump to any conclusions,' Samson said, still tempering his own burgeoning hope. 'What you've found is brilliant and definitely suggests Dinsdale could have killed Irwin. But he's back at the reception by nine. If we're going to take this to DS Benson, we need footage of Dinsdale disappearing again to show he had the opportunity to return to Malham and move Irwin's body.'

Danny murmured in agreement, while Nina hung her

head and the air seemed to go out of Nathan. He slouched away from the desk and sank onto the couch.

'Bugger it!' he muttered. 'I thought we'd cracked it.'

'You're partway there,' said Delilah. 'And we've uncovered a fair bit about Kevin Dinsdale which makes me think you're on the right track.'

'Like what?' asked Danny.

Delilah hesitated, aware of where they'd found the information. Aware of how they'd come by it, and how many rules they'd broken doing it. But Danny just rolled his eyes.

'I wasn't born yesterday! If it's to do with the contents you copied from Irwin's laptop during your illicit search of his room the other day, then spit it out.'

'How did you know we'd done that?' Delilah's voice had gone up an octave.

Danny simply raised an eyebrow. 'Let's just say that you were too concerned with explaining why you were at the Coach and Horses when I bumped into you. It made me suspicious. That and the fact Irwin's laptop was still warm when I got to his room.'

'Oh! Damn! Did anyone else notice?'

'I didn't give them a chance. I had it in an evidence bag and off to the lab before they could.'

Samson laughed and slapped him on the back. 'You'll go far!' he said.

'Aye,' said the young constable, frowning. 'As long as I don't get caught.'

'We appreciate it, Danny. We really do,' said Samson. 'And yes, what we've uncovered comes from that very laptop so we'll have to be careful how we reveal it to Benson. But suffice to say we've got reasons to suspect Irwin was making money on the side by giving customers the results they wanted, for a fee.'

'And Dinsdale partook of that service?'

'Looks like it. There were two ecological survey reports compiled for his land, one a pass and one a fail. And what appears to be a record of the amount Irwin was demanding for the more favourable outcome. If we're right, it was ten grand. More importantly, we don't think the bill had been paid before Irwin was killed.'

Ida sucked air through her teeth. 'Sounds like a motive if tha asks me. There's plenty of folk will do dreadful deeds for less.'

'But it means nothing if you can't show Kevin Dinsdale had the opportunity,' insisted Danny. 'We need concrete evidence that he left the club a second time to go back over to Malham to move the body. Without that, we've got less on him than DS Benson has on Will.'

'We're on it,' said Nina, taking the laptop and crossing to sit next to Nathan on the sofa. 'We'll keep going through the footage and see if we can find something.'

'And maybe put a shout out to folk who weren't even at the reception,' said Delilah. 'There might be video out there of something unrelated – some kids larking around on the playing fields, someone filming his dog while out walking – completely unconnected footage which just might have captured Dinsdale going past at a crucial time.'

'Will do,' said Nathan.

'Meanwhile,' Samson said, turning back to Danny, 'you said you needed a word? Have there been developments?'

Danny hesitated. A bloom of colour stealing up over his collar. 'Thing is, I've gone out on a limb for you a few times over this and, well . . . I came over to say I can't do it any more. Benson is keeping an eye on me and . . . I just . . .'

Delilah put a hand on his arm. 'We understand, Danny. And we're grateful for all your help so far.'

The constable nodded. Looking uncomfortable. Then he shrugged, a grin breaking through the awkwardness. 'But seeing as I'm here, I might as well give you one last update . . . Yes, there have been a few developments, but none of them are really earth shattering. First, the lab has sent through a preliminary post-mortem report, which I managed to sneak a look at. Irwin had three notable contusions – one on the left side of his face, one on his right, and one on the rear of his skull. While the pathologist said she's still working on it and will send through her final analysis tomorrow, she seems to think it was the blow to the back of Irwin's head which proved lethal.'

'The killer struck him from behind?' asked Samson.

'Not necessarily. Given the blood on the scene above Malham Cove, it's likely Irwin fell a second time after Elaine left him, struck his head on a rock, and that's what killed him.'

'So one of those bruises can be attributed to where he fell after his fracas with Elaine—'

'The one on his left cheek.'

'Another from a possible second fall. And the remaining one on his right side . . . ?'

'So far, it's still looking like the rounders bat.' Danny shot a look at Delilah. 'But if it does turn out that Irwin died from the impact of hitting his head on a rock, then we could be looking at manslaughter instead of murder, depending on what led up to it. So at least . . . I mean if Will . . . you know, it wouldn't be as bad . . .'

Delilah gave a dry laugh. 'You mean my brother could be falsely accused of a lesser crime as it stands? I'm not sure that gives me much hope.'

'Sorry, I did say it wasn't much.' Danny was looking awkward once more, his face crimson, giving Samson a sense that perhaps, following the pathologist's comments about the nature of Irwin's wounds, the constable's belief in Will's innocence wasn't as robust as before.

'There is one other thing,' Danny continued, holding out his mobile to show a photo of two black circles of what looked to be plastic, connected by a small bridge. 'Binocular lens caps. They were found tucked up inside Irwin's clothing. DS Benson reckons they came off Irwin's binoculars in some kind of a tussle between him and his killer and that when the killer moved the body, the lens caps got caught up in the deceased's clothing.' He shrugged. 'I don't see how it changes anything, but I guess every little helps.'

'Thanks,' said Samson. 'And like Delilah said, we're really grateful.'

'I know. I just wish—'

Whatever Danny's wish was, it was cut short by a loud groan from Nathan.

'Dinsdale can't have done it,' he muttered dejectedly. 'Look!'

He turned his laptop around so they could all see the frozen image caught on it: Kevin Dinsdale being helped out of the rugby club, one of his arms slung around his wife's shoulders, the other across Sarah's. Even in the paused footage, it was clear he was drunk. Very drunk. Definitely beyond the capability of driving.

'What time was that?' asked Samson.

'About half past eleven.'

'Perhaps he'd already moved the body?' Delilah suggested. But Samson could tell from her resigned look that she was grasping at straws.

'Maybe,' he said. 'But that would mean he returned from killing Irwin at nine and then, at some point before this footage, went back to Malham, got the body and drove to the kiln. And still managed to get to the club in time to get absolutely hammered.'

'It's possible.'

'Yes. Although it would rule out the 4x4 which almost hit me as being the killer's vehicle. That was nearer midnight, so Dinsdale couldn't have been the driver.'

'Unless he was faking it?' Nina's comment drew all heads in her direction. 'What proof do we have that he was actually drunk? A bit of video footage and Herriot's testimony that he was hungover the following morning. But no blood tests or anything.'

Danny was nodding. 'True enough.'

'In which case, even more urgency for us to go through every inch of the video footage we have,' said Samson. 'We need to find evidence of Dinsdale slipping out of the reception or everything is simply speculation.'

'Sounds like it's time I got the kettle on,' said Ida, heading for the kitchen. 'And this time,' she added with a parting glare at Samson, 'it'll be a proper brew. None of that lighthouse tea like tha made earlier!'

She stomped across the landing, leaving Samson to turn to Delilah. 'Lighthouse tea?'

Delilah grinned. 'Blinking near water.'

The others started laughing and Samson was grateful for

the distraction. Because he could sense that this case was taking them down one cul-de-sac after another and, with time ticking by, they were no closer to clearing Will's name. Or finding the real killer. The murder weapon, their best chance of distancing Delilah's brother from the scene, was also remaining elusive. In fact, everything seemed to be stacked against them.

He glanced again at the stilled image of a drunken Kevin Dinsdale on Nathan's laptop.

Was it possible they were being fooled by a consummate dissembler? And if so, was Dinsdale the perpetrator? Or, Samson wondered, feeling disloyal even as the thought formulated, was the hoax being carried out by someone closer to home?

A tussle that turned into a deadly fall. An unintentional killing.

That's what Danny seemed to have been suggesting might have taken place. And Samson knew someone with a temper fiery enough to have triggered such a scenario. Could Will be leading them a merry dance?

Maybe it was time to set local allegiances aside and give Will's testimony a second look. Because if there was one thing Samson had learned from his years as a police officer, it was that when the evidence all pointed one way, there was usually a reason for it.

And in this case, it was all pointing at Will Metcalfe.

When Ida brought through the tea minutes later, Samson drank it without complaint. Hoping it would remove the bitter taste of betrayal from his mouth.

23

By late afternoon, the howling winds and driving rain which had ravaged the dale all morning had given way to apologetic sunshine and an appeasing breeze. Standing by the gate which separated Ellershaw Farm from the Dinsdale property, Gareth Towler was appreciating the view. The same view he'd spent time admiring only the day before and yet it looked so different. So much more intense. The green of the sloping fields was positively flamboyant, the grass wearing its glittering water droplets like rhinestones, while the newly swollen beck had dropped its song from soprano to a sonorous baritone as it rumbled over rocks. And further up the fellside, carrying over it all, was the trilling of a lark, as though in joyful salute to the abrupt cessation of the inclement weather.

It was one of the things Gareth loved about the place where he'd been lucky enough to be born and raised. No two days were the same, the scenery changing in relation to the seasons and even to the elements.

But while his surroundings were sufficient to soothe the soul, the reason which had brought him there was far from serene. A dead man, and a friend about to be charged with murder.

Gareth turned from the vista and back towards the group gathered around the edges of the pond on Will Metcalfe's land. Herriot was looking concerned, Sarah Mitchell was crouched by the water, frowning, Bounty was nose-down investigating some rocks and Sergeant Grewal . . .

Standing to one side, watching Sarah with that characteristic sharp expression, the wildlife officer was hard to gauge. She'd called Gareth that morning to say she wanted another look at the site where they'd seen the great crested newt and asked him to smooth the way with Alison Metcalfe. So he'd invited her along to join them while Sarah conducted an unofficial second survey at Delilah's request. But if he'd expected their interaction of the day before to take the chill off his relationship with Sergeant Grewal, he was mistaken – she'd been just as brusque with him in their few exchanges so far. Although Bounty was getting the benefit of extra affection, a couple of dog treats having already been offered and accepted between the two of them.

If the sergeant was still proving to be a closed book, however, Sarah Mitchell was like a woman transformed. To be fair, Gareth didn't know her that well, the ecologist having only arrived in the area in the last couple of years, but in what little he had seen of her, she'd come across as painfully shy. To the point of barely speaking at times. Today, in her element, she was confident, professional and undeniably passionate about her job.

They'd set out from the Metcalfe farmhouse, walking down towards the beck, intending to enter Dinsdale's field where the camping pods would be situated so Sarah could have a proper look around. But before they'd even reached the gate at the edge of Will's land, she'd been striding towards the pond and had spent the intervening time inspecting it, gently lifting foliage at the edges, taking photos and making notes, all the while carrying out a muttered conversation with herself.

She stood back up, now, hands on her hips, something obviously perturbing her. 'You're sure Kevin Dinsdale was going to be given the all clear by Ross Irwin?' she asked, addressing her question to the sergeant.

'That's what DS Benson said. Apparently, Irwin provided Dinsdale with an advance copy of the report to set his mind at rest.'

'Hmmm.' Sarah looked back at the pond, shaking her head, and then at the gate and the land beyond. 'And that field was definitely the one earmarked for the camping pods?'

Sergeant Grewal nodded. 'I've seen the planning documents. There's no doubt. Why? Is there a problem?'

'This pond is the problem. I just don't understand how it could have been missed.'

'Maybe Irwin didn't see it,' offered Herriot with a shrug, gesturing behind at the stone wall which ran along the boundary of the two farms. 'It would be easy to overlook if you were on that side.'

Sarah snorted. 'Ross Irwin was a respected ecologist. And any ecologist worth their salt would have come through the gate and inspected this side as well, regardless of who owns the land. It's not as if newts, or any creatures for that matter, take any notice of manmade constructs like borders.'

'What makes you think he overlooked it?' asked Gareth.

'Because if he'd seen it, there's no way he would have endorsed Dinsdale's project.'

The statement had Sergeant Grewal watching Sarah even more keenly, while Gareth felt his own pulse pick up.

'Sorry, but I'm not following,' said Herriot. 'I thought newts of any sort are notoriously difficult to find in the wild.'

'They are,' agreed Sarah.

'In which case, if Gareth and the sergeant hadn't stumbled across one yesterday and given us a heads up, are you telling me you would have known this was a newt habitation just by looking at it? And that Irwin should have known too?'

'Yes and no.' Sarah smiled. 'Basically, the initial phase of any ecological impact assessment is merely to ascertain the *potential* problems which could be incurred on a site. So you don't arrive looking for newts which, as you said, are really hard to find. You arrive looking for the *possibility* of them.' She gestured at the body of water in front of her, the still surface reflecting the light-blue sky and puffs of cloud above. 'This is a prime example of a possible newt breeding pool. A generous size with a sloped basin, plenty of underwater plants like watercress and forget-me-not to provide places for egg laying, and not too much shade. Not to mention good terrestrial habitat nearby,' she continued, lifting her hand to point at the small copse down towards the beck. 'That's a perfect spot for refuge and foraging opportunities.'

'Okay, so how should all that have had an impact on Irwin's report?' asked Sergeant Grewal.

'Like I said, Irwin was only carrying out the initial phase of the survey. When he saw this and recognised it as a potential habitat, he should then have notified the relevant bodies – Dinsdale, the national park and the planning authority – via his report that a full newt survey would be needed. And *that's* when the presence of newts would have been established.'

'How much would that cost?' asked Gareth.

'It's not that straightforward,' said Sarah with an apologetic shrug. 'If you mean in terms of direct outlay, anything up to three grand for a full survey, which involves multiple visits to the site to detect the newts. But the other costs can be more complex. For example, we're in late August. If Irwin had done his job and sounded the alert, Kevin Dinsdale would have had to wait until spring for the survey to be started, as they can only be carried out when the newts have migrated back to the pond, so between mid-March and mid-June. Which means you're looking at a delay to your project and any expenses that might incur. Not to mention ongoing costs if that survey does detect newts . . .' She raised her hands. 'There's no denying it can be an expensive business.'

'But surely this is far enough away from the proposed camping area to not prove a problem? I mean, it's not like newts are big buggers or owt.'

Sarah laughed. 'True, but our amphibian friends have a habitation zone extending quite a way, so any suitable pond within five hundred metres of a planned development should trigger a survey requirement.'

Gareth looked from the pond to the field behind the gate. Well within the parameters Sarah had described, yet Irwin hadn't seen fit to call in a full survey. Which begged the question—

'Can you think of any reasons Irwin might have over-looked it?' Sergeant Grewal had taken the words out of

Gareth's mouth, the query delivered with a smile which didn't disguise the sharpness of the content.

Sarah shook her head, a flush coming to her cheeks. 'None that are legitimate.'

The simplicity of the reply only highlighted what hadn't been said.

'Interesting,' said the sergeant, letting her gaze shift to Gareth. An eyebrow arched. 'But before we go leaping to conclusions, let's not forget whose land this pond is on. While I agree that the presence of great crested newts could have had a negative impact on Mr Dinsdale's plans, they would have had an impact on Mr Metcalfe's long-term use of this field too.'

Gareth let out a laugh. 'Seriously? We've just had an expert in her field pass judgement on Irwin's professionalism, with the possibility of corruption not being out of the question, and you still want to pin the blame on Will? Much as I'm loath to point the finger, surely Kevin Dinsdale deserves a bit more of a look at after this?'

Sergeant Grewal tipped her head in acknowledgement, a lock of dark hair shielding her face momentarily. When she looked back up, she bore the expression of someone calculating their options.

'I suppose I've got the benefit of insider information,' she said, glancing around at the three of them, 'so what I'm about to say doesn't go any further. DS Benson has had some initial feedback from the pathologist and I'm sorry but it's not looking good for your friend. The rounders bat found in the back of Mr Metcalfe's vehicle is a potential match for the murder weapon.'

There was a stunned silence, then Herriot groaned,

shaking his head, turning away from the pond, while Sarah just went pale. But it was Gareth the sergeant was watching, waiting for a rebuttal.

He didn't have one. He had no air in his lungs for a start, the news like a punch to the solar plexus, knocking every bit of wind out of him.

'I have to stress, this is awaiting verification from a full post-mortem,' the sergeant added gently, as though realising the impact of her pronouncement, 'so it's not final yet.'

Yet. Such a small word for carrying such weighty hopes. Hopes which Gareth had been clinging to resolutely but now found himself doubting the validity of.

Could Will Metcalfe, someone he'd known since primary school, be capable of murder? Four days ago, Gareth would have laughed at the suggestion. Now? That fight at the wedding. The way Will had lied. None of it was helped by the fact that the words of Sergeant Grewal from the day before had wormed their way into Gareth's head.

Was the presence of a rare species on his land something Will had known about before this mess all unfolded? Or was the sergeant right? Had Irwin spotted the potential and threatened Will with revealing it to the authorities? And had that threat spiralled into a confrontation far more deadly than an exchange of punches in the rugby club?

Gareth ran a hand over his face, feeling the strain of the case, seeing that strain reflected in the expressions of Sarah and Herriot. Because this was a case which couldn't be resolved without someone they knew and liked being outed as a killer, Sarah herself having already been considered a suspect. Now it seemed to have boiled down to a stark choice – if it wasn't Will, then it was Kevin Dinsdale, another person Gareth had known all his life. Another one he'd have vouched for only a week ago.

'Now you know why I work wildlife crime,' said Sergeant Grewal with a dry smile. 'There are rarely any mitigating circumstances for the atrocities I deal with and while it means I get to see humanity at its worst, I never have conflicting views about the perpetrators.'

Gareth grunted in response. Aware she was trying to lighten the atmosphere. But what Sergeant Grewal wasn't taking into account was the impact of crimes like this in a place such as Bruncliffe. It wasn't simply the victim and their killer who would be caught up in the fallout. It was the entire community. Delilah. Her brothers. Her parents. Not to mention Alison and the children. As he looked up the hill towards Ellershaw House, he was aware he was already bracing himself for the worst.

It was early evening when Gareth and Herriot returned to the building on Back Street. Up on the first floor, the Dales Detective team were on the verge of calling it a day – Nina and Nathan were packing up their laptops, Ida was giving the kitchen one last wipe down, while Samson and Delilah were discussing the evening's plans. With Bounty scurrying ahead to make herself at home next to Tolpuddle in his basket, the vet and the gamekeeper walked up the stairs and into Delilah's office, an air of deflation about them. A weariness Samson recognised as endemic to this particular investigation, which seemed to offer no outcome without heartache.

'Tha looks like folk who were buying a tup and got sold a wether,' muttered Ida as she crossed the landing to follow Gareth into the room, clearly picking up the same vibes.

Delilah looked up from her computer. 'If it's bad news,' she said on a sigh that hurt Samson's heart, 'I don't think I want to hear it.'

Herriot looked at Gareth, who just slumped against the doorframe and began speaking.

'Sarah confirmed that Irwin's report shouldn't have given Kevin the green light—'

'But that's great!' exclaimed Nathan.

Delilah was nodding. Smiling for the first time in hours. 'Surely that proves Irwin was as dodgy as we think he was and Kevin was paying him for the result he needed.'

'Sorry, to get your hopes up, but . . . there's a "but",' continued Gareth with a grimace. 'I take it you've heard about the rounders bat?' At the despondent nods, he continued. 'Well, based on that, Sergeant Grewal is convinced DS Benson will still be looking to charge Will, despite there being the possibility that the survey was some-what shady, if not downright corrupt.'

'What?' Delilah was on her feet, hands on her hips. 'But that's mad! Sarah is every bit as much an expert as Irwin was. Doesn't her opinion count for anything?'

Gareth shrugged. 'I think the police are looking at it from both angles. If Kevin was desperate enough to bribe Irwin, maybe Will was desperate enough to kill in order to stop the news of those newts becoming public know-ledge. And you have to admit, it's a valid point.'

Delilah stared at him, taken aback. Then she looked at Herriot, whose eyes dropped to the floor. When she whipped round to Samson, he met her gaze, despite knowing she would read his own doubts on his face.

'Oh my God,' she whispered, turning back round the

room. 'You lot think Will might have done this. You really believe he could be capable of killing someone.'

'It's the rounders bat, Dee,' Samson said gently. 'It's a likely match for the injuries Irwin sustained and it was found in Will's Land Rover. There's no refuting that.'

'But there is,' protested Nathan, moving across the room to stand beside his aunt. 'Danny said himself that the pathologist hasn't confirmed the murder weapon yet. And I just know Uncle Will wouldn't have done this. He couldn't have done this!'

The last sentence was more plea than affirmation and Samson knew the fresh pain this would inflict on the lad if his hopes for his uncle were dashed. Another loss, a man who'd been a substitute father for the last three years taken from him. It would tear him apart.

'Fair point, Nathan,' Samson said, 'but without a suitable alternative for the weapon which was used to kill Irwin, the police have every right to be looking hard at Will. It's what I would be doing if I were running the case.'

'It's what you're doing now,' snapped Delilah, her tone sharp enough to lift the heads of the two dogs in the basket.

'Perhaps,' said Ida, taking a step into the room, 'we ought to leave it there for now and come back at this in the morning when we've all had a bit of sleep. There's no good ever come from frayed tempers.'

'And maybe we can start looking for that other weapon then, too,' muttered Nathan, glaring at Samson as he picked up his laptop and left the room.

With an embarrassed nod at the remaining adults, Nina hurried after him.

'Right, I'm off for a shower,' said Gareth, making for

the stairs, Bounty immediately abandoning the dog basket to follow him. Pausing in the doorway, he turned to Delilah. 'Is there anything else I can do this evening to help?'

She took a deep breath, and nodded. 'We've put a call out for any video footage taken on Saturday around the time of the reception, so five o'clock onwards. It doesn't have to be wedding related. Anything which was filmed around town at that time. If you could spread the word, that would be great.'

'Will do,' said Gareth. 'And for what it's worth, I don't want it to be Will either.'

'I know,' said Delilah softly. As the gamekeeper made for the stairs, she turned to Ida. 'Any chance you could contact that mysterious source of yours and have them look through the video they took outside Peaks on Saturday night? Just to check?'

'Consider it done,' said Ida. She glanced at Herriot and he rose from the couch, cheeks flushed.

'I'll see you tomorrow,' he said. 'And like Gareth, if there's anything I can do, just call.'

'Thanks,' said Delilah, managing a smile.

'Happen it's time I was off too,' said Ida, turning to go. At the top of the stairs, she looked back over her shoulder at the pair of them, as though she was about to say something. But then she simply nodded, brow furrowed with worry, and followed the vet down into the hallway. The porch door opened and closed and only then, with no one else there, did Delilah speak.

'Ali's asked me to spend the night at Ellershaw,' she said as she logged off her computer and grabbed her hoodie from the back of the chair. Her eyes making contact with anything but Samson's face. 'She's in a right state. So I'm heading straight there. Can you take Tolpuddle for the evening?'

'Sure, but can we talk before you go—?'

'Sorry, but she's asked me to be there for the kids' bedtime and I'm already going to be late.'

The words were measured, the tone polite. Then, without waiting for any further dialogue, Delilah rubbed Tolpuddle's head and hurried down the stairs. The back door slammed shut in her wake.

'Christ, Tolpuddle,' muttered Samson as the hound crossed the room, looking as bemused at the hasty exit as Samson felt, 'I could have handled that better.'

Tolpuddle let his head drop onto Samson's lap, whether in agreement or rebuttal, it was hard to tell. But one thing was for sure, if this was their first argument as a couple – which Samson suspected it was given the nature of Delilah's departure – then they'd sure chosen a hefty topic. The debate on a man's innocence or guilt. A man who happened to be a brother to one of them and a friend to the other. As a seasoned police officer, Samson couldn't pretend that all would work out fine and that Will couldn't possibly be guilty. Just as he understood Delilah's fierce loyalty to her family and her disappointment that Samson didn't share that view.

Somehow, he doubted a bunch of flowers from the Spar was going to solve this one.

24

In the cottage on Crag Lane, Samson didn't get much sleep. Tolpuddle, on the other hand, slept like a log, sprawled out on the other side of the bed. The side Delilah should have been occupying, her absence the reason Samson had lain awake into the early hours, trying to work out how to best sort things between them. Because this disagreement was more than just a lovers' tiff. It had the potential to rip apart the fragile fabric of their relationship, already stretched thin by distance and an unsettled future. So it needed sorting. Or at least talking through.

With the sun already up and casting its light across the town, he rose at six, with a vague idea of how to make the first move. Even though he knew it would be painful. After a quick muesli bar for breakfast, he was out the door, Tolpuddle at his heels, the pair of them standing below the outcrop of limestone which towered over them.

'Be kind to me,' Samson muttered at the Weimaraner. Then he started running.

Pain didn't come close. Within metres of the house, the track went uphill, sharply, and Samson's body began to complain. His bruised ribs hurt with every breath, his left hip screamed in agony and his legs, fatigued from the run the day before, ached, making him wonder about the wisdom of what he was doing. But then wisdom was of little use when dealing with Delilah Metcalfe.

Round the edge of the Crag, up the fellside, the land continued to climb relentlessly, and his muscles continued to burn. In stark contrast, Tolpuddle was trotting ahead with ease, waiting for him occasionally before running on again. At the point where Samson felt his calves were about to combust, they emerged onto the tops and began to follow a sheep trod as it wound across the rough grass and rocks, Samson breathing easier, his legs moving more fluidly.

It was glorious. The inclement weather of the day before banished by a balmy sky, the sun bathing the fells and turning the heather into a riot of magenta. And there, in the distance, running ahead of them, was the small figure Samson had been banking on seeing. The reason he was putting himself through this torture.

Even without recognising her running kit, he'd have known it was Delilah, moving with that distinctive grace and effortlessness which had seen her win so many fell races in her teens. But any hopes he'd had of running up behind her in some kind of romantic surprise were scuppered by his companion. The minute Tolpuddle saw her, he was off, racing across the land at a speed Samson could only dream of.

Samson set off after him. Saw Delilah turn as Tolpuddle let out a delighted bark. Saw her pause. Let her dog catch her. And then she started running again. Away from Samson. Faster than before.

He dug deeper. Calling up every ounce of effort, making his legs work harder, forcing his lungs to cope with the snatched breathing as he ran flat out. He was gaining ground. But he was burning every match in the box. Another thirty seconds of sprinting and he was by her side. Close enough to speak. But not able to make it coherent.

'De–li–lah,' he panted. 'Pl–ea–se–st–op!'

The last word came out on a high-pitched wheeze but she kept on running. He collapsed to a halt. Spent. Doubled over as he sucked in oxygen, black spots before his eyes. The first he knew of her presence was the pair of shoes and four paws which appeared below his downcast face.

'Drink?' A water bottle was being held out.

He slowly straightened up, feeling the blood rush from his head, the impact of that massive effort. 'Thanks,' he managed.

He took the bottle, noticed the twitch of a smile pulling at her lips. He drank. Let his breathing settle. Then handed her back the bottle.

'Are you laughing at me?' he asked, smiling.

'Maybe.' She looked at him now, letting the grin show. 'I'm guessing this meeting isn't an accident?'

He shook his head. 'I knew you'd be up here. It's where you always came when you were upset.'

She dipped her head, turned away from him, lip caught between her teeth. So he went with his instincts. He stepped forward and pulled her into his arms.

They stood there for a few moments, her head tucked under his chin, letting the silence wash over them. When the coarse call of a grouse broke across it, Delilah gently eased away and looked up at him.

'We need to talk,' said Samson.

She nodded. 'I know. And I get it, I do. I understand why you're not convinced about Will's innocence. But I think there's someone you need to hear from first. If you're capable of running any further, that is?'

The last was said with that familiar mischievous glint in her eyes. Samson grinned.

'You lead, I'll follow.' He set off after her and Tolpuddle, aware that he was so smitten with Delilah Metcalfe, he would follow her to the end of the earth.

Delilah showed him no mercy on the run down to Ellershaw Farm. By the time they reached the house, Samson's legs were beginning to cramp and his lungs felt like a permanent fire had been lit within them. His two companions, however, looked as fresh as daisies as they entered the kitchen, where Alison Metcalfe had tea and breakfast waiting for them despite the relatively early hour – a full English, Samson's plate piled high with sausage, egg, bacon, beans and thick rounds of black pudding, several slices of buttered bread by the side.

Samson didn't need to be asked twice, a ravenous hunger coming over him as his tired legs happily collapsed him onto a chair next to Delilah at the kitchen table. They both started eating, and Alison started talking.

'Dee said I should tell you more about what happened with that Irwin bloke,' she began, nothing but a mug of tea in front of her, the strain on her face suggesting her own appetite wasn't up to much. 'I don't see as how it makes any difference – blackmail is blackmail – but if it helps to convince you that Will can't have killed him, then I'm happy to give it a go. Because right now I'm at my wits' end with worry.'

'It's not that I think—' Samson started to protest, but Alison just smiled wearily.

'I'm not judging you, Samson. You're a copper, after all – and it's not like you've seen the best of Will since you've been home. So I can't blame you for viewing all this with an offcumden's eye, or for accepting what seems to be irrefutable evidence.'

Offcumden . . . outsider. That was how he was still perceived in Bruncliffe. Samson concentrated on cutting into the black pudding, trying not to let the sting of Alison's words show as she continued speaking.

'Anyway, Irwin arrived in town last week and called by to ask permission to access our land so he could carry out the ecological impact assessment for the Dinsdales. Nice as pie he was, sitting right where you are now, drinking coffee and eating my homemade brack. Complimenting me on my lovely home . . .' She shook her head. 'We never suspected a thing. And when Will told him about the newts down in the Beck Field, he thanked him for the heads up. Next time we saw him, he was down the hill, looking around, making notes. We just left him to it, not wanting to intrude or anything.

'Then a few days later, Will gets a call on his mobile from an unrecognised number. It's Irwin. And that's when he started putting the screws on. He wasn't daft enough to come straight out with a demand for money, so he told Will that his report was inconclusive, at present.' Alison gave a tight smile. 'With emphasis on the "at present". But that with a bit of cooperation from us, it could be something we would approve of.'

'"Cooperation"? That's the term he used?' asked Samson.

Alison nodded. 'Will didn't get what he was saying at first, not being used to sharks like that. So he said he didn't

understand and that's when Irwin just said the amount –
"five thousand" – in isolation, nothing else, but there was
no mistaking what it was. I heard Will start spluttering on
the phone and realised something was up. Then I heard
him tell Irwin what he could do with his suggestion in
language that left no room for doubt. When he ended the
call, Will was so mad it took a good five minutes before
he could tell me what had happened!'

'I don't suppose you have a recording of the call . . . ?'
Samson's desperate question got a raised eyebrow in
response.

'No. It's not customary round here to tape calls. And
Irwin wasn't daft. He didn't email, nothing in writing, and
the second time he called—'

'He called again?'

'Yep. Bold as brass. But from a different number, as Will
had blocked the last one. So like I said, he wasn't daft, that
dead ecologist.'

'What did he want this time?'

'To change the terms of his offer,' said Alison with a
harsh laugh. 'I guess he knew he was flogging a dead horse
when it came to us paying to stop the Dinsdales' planning,
so instead, he tried to frighten us. He told Will that unless
he coughed up, the planning would not only go ahead but
Irwin would also notify the authorities about the great
crested newts down in the Beck Field. He made it clear
what that would mean – greater scrutiny of the land and
how we use it, the listing of the site on an ecological register,
restrictions of all sorts in the future . . .' Alison tailed off
and just raised her hands.

'And the amount for his silence?'

'The same. Five thousand. Will shouted at him, told him not to contact us again and . . . well . . . he threatened him.'

Samson looked at Delilah, puzzled as to how she thought Alison's story could help Will's case when all it did was paint a bleaker picture of a man desperate enough to commit murder. Delilah just shrugged.

'Yeah, it looks bad,' she said. 'But if Will was really guilty, surely he'd have kept all of this a secret. Instead, he's told the police.'

'Is that true? Benson knows all of this?' Samson turned to Alison, who nodded, both women now watching him with hopeful expressions.

He scratched his head and wondered, not for the first time, why all the cases in Bruncliffe had to be so complicated. Give him a straightforward drugs bust any day of the week, or a sting operation on a gang of money launderers. He knew where he was with those. Instead he was trying to prove his girlfriend's famously hot-headed brother was innocent of a crime he'd had every opportunity and motive to commit, with the odds firmly stacked against him. Samson had a fleeting image of the rounders bat in the back of the Land Rover . . .

'Look,' he said gently, 'you have to admit that no matter what Will has or hasn't confessed to the police, there's nothing in this testimony which is going to help his cause. While we've found evidence that Irwin was keeping some kind of record of payments, we can't prove what they were for, and even if we could, it only strengthens the case against Will. Not just the five thousand pounds but the threat Irwin was holding over him of that ecological register, of the land being placed under permanent regulations—'

'Except that's not true!' protested Delilah. 'We know from our investigations that Irwin omitted the newt pond in his report so he could give Dinsdale the OK. So how could he have then notified the authorities about it? Questions would have been asked about why he'd not included it in the survey in the first place and, apart from destroying his own reputation, he'd have lost the ten grand from Dinsdale. He would have been shooting himself in the foot.'

Alison was watching the exchange with surprise. 'You mean it was all lies?' she asked.

Samson nodded. 'I reckon Irwin was relying on Will not knowing much about planning regulations when it comes to ecological concerns. His second demand was a gamble, pure and simple. If Will paid up, he made two lots of money out of the one scam. If he didn't, he still had the payment from Dinsdale. So that final request which prompted the confrontation at the reception was one last chance to wheedle something out of you. What Irwin wasn't banking on was Will's temper.'

'Aye, Will's temper.' Alison smiled. 'And you know what he was angry about? Not the money. Not even the threat to our land and our future with it. Nope, Will was most angry about the fact that Irwin, an expert in ecology, was willing to barter with the future of the great crested newts. Because if Will had been less scrupulous, he'd have paid off Irwin and then gone down and filled in that bloody pond and killed every last one of those critters, and no one would have been any the wiser. But instead, he was fuming about it. That Irwin had so little regard for a species which is under threat and was supposed to be under his protection. And look where it's landed my principled husband! In a police cell about to be charged with murder.' She sighed, a look of affection on her face. 'But then that's typical Metcalfe. Always standing up for the little guy, even when it's a bloody newt!' She shot a stern glance at Samson. 'That don't mean he's daft enough to have killed over it, mind.'

'And even if Will did get into some sort of a tussle with Irwin above Malham Cove which caused a bad accident,' said Delilah, 'he'd have called the emergency services straight away. He wouldn't have left the man there to die, and he damn well wouldn't have moved the body and placed Elaine under suspicion!'

Samson looked at the two women, both of them unshaking in their belief in Will Metcalfe. And he felt a pang of regret for this level of connection, this security of place and person which he'd never had. For the trust which living among folk for a lifetime engendered.

Harry had been right when he'd decried Samson's inability to take things on faith, even from friends. And, Samson realised, Delilah was right to place her confidence in her insight into her brother, gleaned from decades of living alongside him.

'Fair point,' he conceded. 'Will might have had a fight with Irwin but I agree, I can't see him just walking away from it.'

Delilah smiled, while Alison sagged in her chair, as though a weight she'd been carrying alone had finally been taken from her.

'But we still have no concrete evidence to help Will,' she said. 'So what can you do?'

Samson mopped up the last of his beans with a corner of bread, finished his tea and got to his feet. 'We'll go and see DS Benson. First thing, once we're back and showered. Let's lay it all out before him and see if we can't persuade him to hold off on charges for now.'

Delilah jumped up from her chair, disturbing the snoozing Tolpuddle in the corner, and made for the door.

'I'll drop you off at the office to grab a shower there while I head home,' she said. 'We'll be ready faster that way.'

Alison saw the two of them and the Weimaraner as far as the back porch and as they crossed the yard towards the Mini, Delilah threw her arms around Samson's neck and gave him a kiss.

'Thanks,' she said.

'Does this mean I'm forgiven?' he asked with a grin, part of him wishing they had nothing else on the day's agenda other than a return to the cottage.

'For now,' she said, laughing.

He didn't press her for a more definite answer on the drive down to town. He was too busy clinging to the dashboard as she took the corners at breakneck speed.

25

Luckily, the bathroom on the top floor was unoccupied when Samson arrived back at the office building. In fact, the entire place was eerily quiet, only the rumble of snores coming from behind the half-closed door of what had been his bedroom disturbing the peace. Snores of a sleep so deep, Samson was able to creep past the comatose hump of bedcovers that was Gareth Towler and grab a change of clothes from the wardrobe. Bounty lifted her head and accepted a pat as he crept back out, leaving the door ajar as he'd found it.

Samson showered quickly and emerged, feeling fresh if not rejuvenated, onto the landing and into the sharp smell of polish. And frying bacon. Ida was in. He hurried down the stairs to tell her he'd already eaten and came around the bottom newel post to see her standing at the kitchen counter, bacon spitting in a pan to her left as she stared at the tea cosy in her hand.

She turned, hearing him. A look on her face of defiance, chin jutting out.

'Tha's seen it,' she said.

He tried for ignorance. 'Seen what?'

The look turned into a scowl. 'Don't play daft with me, lad. That letter from Turpin's.'

For the life of him, Samson couldn't work out how she knew he'd seen the notification of sale for the old O'Brien farm. But there was no point in trying to deny it any further. Feeling strangely guilty, when he hadn't been the one being deceitful, he nodded.

'Twistleton's up for sale,' he said, the words coming out with an undercurrent of emotion he hadn't expected.

She gave a sharp nod of her head. Pulled the envelope out of the tea cosy and passed it to him. 'The lass thought . . . we *all* thought . . . it was best not to upset thee with it. So . . .' she gestured at the tea cosy and gave a disgruntled tut. 'Happen tha never uses this confounded thing so I thought it were safe in there.'

He looked at the letter, felt a wave of sorrow flood over him. Twistleton Farm hadn't been at the forefront of his mind, but somewhere deep in his heart he'd been harbouring hopes. Of coming home to Bruncliffe. Of being able to buy back the family farm and start a life there. One which always seemed to feature Delilah standing at the door of the house in the morning sun, which was presumptuous of him in so many ways. But now . . .

Those dreams were like the cold ashes in Twistleton's burned-out barn where Rick Procter had left his mark.

He folded the envelope and stuffed it in his back pocket.

'Tha's not going to deal with it like that,' Ida muttered.

Samson gave an exasperated sigh. 'What do you expect me to do about it?' he muttered right back. 'I don't have the funds to buy it so there's no way I can even begin to hope . . .'

'If tha did have the funds? What then?' Ida was watching him closely, the bacon still cooking behind her.

He blinked. Unexpectedly blindsided by the question. London or Bruncliffe? Would having possession of Twistleton Farm make any difference or was his decision about where his future lay purely about the woman who'd captivated his heart?

'I'd stay,' he said, barely conscious of the words leaving his mouth. Of the truth he hadn't known lay inside him.

She continued staring at him with her severe regard for a couple of beats and then she gestured at the tea cosy. 'Tha's not asked how I knew.'

'About me finding the letter?' Samson shrugged. 'How did you know?'

'Tha put it back inside the cosy the wrong way round!' There was triumph in her look now, her lips fighting a smile, and he burst out laughing.

'I've trained you well, Ida,' he said. 'First class detective work.'

'Talking of which,' she continued, her chin jutting back up in preparation for an argument, 'tha needs to have more faith in the lass so far as the Irwin case is concerned. Tha's always talking about gut instinct. Well, I can tell thee for nowt that when it comes to this town and the folk around here, there's no gut as good as Delilah's. If she's telling thee that Will Metcalfe is innocent, tha'd do well to take heed.'

'I agree.'

It was Ida's turn to blink. Samson grinned.

'We talked it through this morning over breakfast at Ellershaw—'

'Breakfast? Tha's already eaten? Both of thee?' Ida shot a look at the frying pan and back to Samson, making him feel the same sense of misplaced guilt he'd had earlier.

'Sorry, I was going to tell you but . . .' He petered out in the face of her disgruntlement as she turned to the bacon and began flipping it, the metal spatula clanging more than normal on the pan. He was saved from further apologies by the arrival of Delilah, her voice carrying up the stairs in the company of someone else.

'No problem,' Delilah was saying as she rounded the corner onto the landing, the well-dressed form of Nancy Taylor right behind her. 'I'll get it for you now.'

Delilah disappeared into her office and Nancy wandered over towards the kitchen, the smile on her face not enough to disguise the lines of worry the past few months of trauma had etched upon her.

'Welcome back, Samson,' she said, offering her hand. 'Lovely to have you home. For good this time?'

He gave a non-committal shake of his head. 'Working on it. And I hear you're starting afresh yourself,' he continued, moving the subject rapidly on as Ida clattered about in the background, the unusual noise levels reflecting her umbrage. 'How's the new business going?'

'Too early to tell,' said Nancy candidly. 'But both Stuart and Julie are on board, so at least there'll be someone in the office who knows something about selling houses!'

Samson nodded at the mention of the two young employees of what had been Taylor's Estate Agents, approving of Nancy's decision to hire them. They'd pretty much kept the business going after Bernard Taylor's death and had shown themselves to be completely trustworthy in the process.

'To be honest,' continued Nancy, 'I'm just hoping I can put something back into this town and build something fresh out of all the damage Bernard did . . .' At the mention of her husband, she paused. Shook herself and gave a rueful grin. 'A bit like a phoenix rising from the ashes—'

There was a crash from the far end of the kitchen and a startled yelp.

'What on earth was that?' Gareth Towler had appeared at the bottom of the stairs, Bounty cowering on the last step, eyes wild, while Delilah had rushed out of her office.

'Everything all right?' she asked.

Samson couldn't answer. He was too busy staring at the shards of pottery on the floor by the sink. At the tea leaves scattered over them. And at Ida Capstick, who was looking at Nancy Taylor like she'd seen a ghost.

'Whoops!' said Nancy into the stunned silence. 'Looks like you've broken a teapot, Ida! How many years of bad luck is that?'

'Got to be at least the same as a mirror,' Gareth laughed, gathering Bounty up into his arms to calm her, while Delilah was crossing the landing.

'You're not cut or anything, Ida?' she asked.

Ida, who wasn't making any move to clean up the mess. Who was standing stock still, looking more surprised than anything. As though the act of breaking a teapot was something new to her.

'Ida?' Delilah put a hand on her arm and Ida's gaze snapped round. A flush rising on her sharp cheekbones. 'You okay?'

'Yes, lass. I'm fine.' Her glance darted back to Nancy and then onto Samson, a strange look on her face. 'More than fine.'

Samson bent down and began gathering up the shards. 'You're going to be keeping the teapot makers in business at this rate,' he quipped from the floor, trying to make light of it. Taking that rare blush for embarrassment. 'How many is it now?'

Ida let out a humph. Then looked over at Gareth and the dog in his arms. 'Sorry about the noise,' she said, nodding towards the spaniel. 'Happen a bit of bacon wouldn't go amiss for the shock.'

'That'd be grand,' said Gareth, moving towards the table. 'Have to say I'm suffering a bit of shock myself.' He winked at Ida.

And Ida gave a sound somewhere between a laugh and a snort. She picked up the spatula and began serving the bacon with an air of . . . gaiety? Samson shook his head. It couldn't be gaiety. Ida Capstick didn't do gaiety. But yet, as Delilah left Samson to finish clearing up while she showed Nancy out, there was what was unmistakably a tuneless hum of contentment coming from Ida as she went about her work.

At nine o'clock on the dot, when Constable Danny Bradley unlocked the station doors, there was no mistaking his surprise at seeing two people already waiting on the doorstep.

'Morning!' He looked from Samson to Delilah with unconcealed curiosity.

'Is DS Benson in?' asked Delilah.

'He is. The sarge too,' laughed Danny, gesturing at the bulging Peaks Patisserie bag she was carrying.

He led them through to the office at the rear of the station, where DS Benson was sitting at what was normally Danny's desk. The man seemed to have aged a decade in four days, the stress of manning a murder enquiry having taken its toll. His eyes were red-rimmed and raw with sleep deprivation, the skin beneath them puffy and grey. And there was a weary air to him as he lifted his head at their arrival.

'Christ, O'Brien,' he muttered. 'Whatever you're here for, it had better be important because I'm not in the mood for time-wasting.'

Sergeant Clayton was less abrupt, his own focus more on the bag Delilah had in her hand.

'Whatever it is, it'll no doubt go better over a brew. Get the kettle on, Danny lad,' he instructed his constable, as he drew up a couple of chairs for their visitors.

Delilah laid the bag on his desk, knowing her bribery was blatant, but unrepentant. Pecan tarts still warm from the oven, baked at short notice by Lucy, who was equally sick with worry and only too happy to help out. Will's future was at stake and if securing a bit of police attention meant dangling some pastries below the sergeant's nose, both women were fine with that. Judging by the way he was opening the bag and inhaling deeply, a wide smile on his face, it was fine by Sergeant Clayton too.

'What is it?' asked Benson before they'd even had a chance to sit, showing none of his colleague's tolerance for their presence.

'We want to go over the case against Will Metcalfe with you,' said Samson. 'We think you might be jumping to conclusions.'

Benson let his head drop into his hands, a low groan issuing from him. When he looked up, he addressed Samson. 'Listen, while I acknowledge your experience and have appreciated your input so far, I've got every faith in the decisions we're making. Notwithstanding that forensics have yet to fully confirm it, we're pretty certain we have the murder weapon. We're sure we have motive and opportunity. And we're very confident we have our man. So I fail to see what you can tell me which would sway that.'

'Bribery,' said Samson.

Delilah shot him a glance, heart thumping. She hadn't expected him to go in so hard. And she had no idea how he was going to explain away their knowledge of what he was about to reveal. But Samson seemed unperturbed.

'You already know Will has claimed he was being blackmailed,' he continued. 'We've uncovered evidence to support that claim. It also shows that Irwin was bribing other people and taking backhanders in order to smooth planning permission applications and bring about favourable results.'

Benson stared at him. Interested now. 'And how have you come across this evidence?'

There was a crash of cups over in the corner where Danny was making tea, Sergeant Clayton raising an eyebrow.

'Bit fingers and thumbs over there, Constable. Everything okay?'

Danny nodded, face scarlet. And Delilah knew he was as worried as she was about what Samson was going to say next. How he was going to spin the truth and keep them all out of trouble.

'I found it on Irwin's laptop.' Samson's blunt statement made Benson jerk upright while there was another crash of crockery from the corner.

Delilah dropped her gaze to the floor, knowing her poker face was one of the worst in Bruncliffe. But it was too late.

Sergeant Clayton's focus had shifted away from his unusually clumsy constable and onto her. It rested there as DS Benson found his voice.

'Irwin's laptop? How the hell did you get access to that? And bear in mind that what you're about to say might land you in some very hot water.'

Samson nodded. Unfazed. 'I broke into his hotel room and copied everything on it onto a flash drive.'

For a second there was silence, then Sergeant Clayton let out a long breath, cheeks puffed out, while Benson pushed back in his chair, eyes wide, his face mottling.

'You're bloody joking me?'

'No. And before you get mad, listen to what I have to say.'

Judging by the purple tinge rising up Benson's neck and face, Delilah thought Samson was a bit late on the advice front. Benson was already furious. He shot to his feet, leaning on the desk with both hands, head thrust forward.

'You are in so much shit, O'Brien! I'm going to have you thrown out the force! Again! And I'll have you up on every charge in the book – breaking and entering, tampering with evidence, perverting the course of justice—'

'Now then, DS Benson,' came a calm voice, Sergeant Clayton laying a hand on the detective's arm. 'Let's not go making rash decisions. How's about we listen to the man and then take an objective view on what we do next. Happens I've had a fair bit of experience with this pair in recent times and, while it pains me to say it, they've yet to be wrong.' He turned to Danny in the corner and gave a dry smile. 'Wouldn't you agree, Constable?'

There was so much content in the comment. The way

Sergeant Clayton was looking at Danny and then at Delilah. He was under no illusions as to who had broken into the hotel room and taken the data from Irwin's computer, or that his own underling had had full knowledge of the fact.

Danny gave a meek nod. 'That's right, Sarge.'

'So let's get that brew sorted,' continued the sergeant, 'and Samson can tell us what he discovered over a cuppa and cake, and *then* we can decide whether to lock the bugger up or not.'

DS Benson opened his mouth. Closed it again. And then sagged back onto his chair with a weary flick of his hand. 'Fine. Let's hear what you have to say.'

Delilah felt the breath she hadn't even known she was holding leave her lungs in a long sigh of relief.

Over on Back Street, a few doors down from the Dales Detective office, Ash Metcalfe was hard at work in what had been the old antique shop, and was feeling grateful for it. Grateful to his sister, too. For he knew full well that Delilah had put in a good word for him in order to secure this contract.

A complete strip-out and refit of the shop premises, with further work commissioned to update the two-bedroomed flat above. A new bathroom. A new kitchen. It would keep him busy for a while at least, and keep the wolf from his door. It would also keep his mind off the fact that his oldest brother was perilously close to being charged with murder.

Ash had spent the evening before up at Ellershaw with his fraught parents and sister-in-law, while Delilah outlined all the Dales Detective Agency was doing to try to find the real culprit. The real culprit, because Ash knew Will wasn't capable of killing someone.

Didn't he?

He had a split second of memory, Will holding Irwin up against the wall of the rugby club, features contorted in fury.

Ashamed at his disloyalty, Ash forced his attention back onto his work. He put the last lick of gloss on the skirting which ran under the front window and got up off his knees, just in time to see his boss approaching. The door opened and in she walked.

'Wow, Ash, you're working wonders!' Nancy Taylor strode into the room, placed her hands on her hips and smiled.

'I wouldn't go that far,' said Ash, not sure how much praise he deserved, considering that the design of the place had been all Nancy's doing.

In what would be the reception area of her new business, there was a 'soft' area to the right by the window, three club chairs in moss-coloured fabric arranged around a coffee table balanced on the back of a ceramic sheep. On the other side, three desks and several office chairs, still in their wrapping, stood waiting to be put in place. Behind them the wall had been painted a gentle shade of green, like the fells in May. But it was the wall opposite which made the biggest impact.

Spanning the length of the room and reaching from floor to ceiling was a map of Bruncliffe and the surrounding area, an OS map with hill-shading showing the topography of the fells and dales. It was stunning. And while Ash had muttered words his mother would have admonished him for as he struggled to paste it onto the wall, he had to admit the effort had been worth it.

All in all, the office of Dales Homes was sophisticated, inviting and totally in keeping with its environment. If Nancy had wanted to distance her business from the clinical – and, as it turned out, corrupt – premises her husband had lorded over for so long, she couldn't have done it better.

'Just happy to be a part of this,' he added with his customary candour. 'I'll be starting work upstairs from tomorrow, if that's okay?'

Nancy nodded. 'It'll be nice to have things sorted up there. I've had a couple of positive viewings on the house already so I might need to be moving in soon. No pressure,' she added with a light laugh.

He grinned. 'I'll have to take on help at this rate.'

She laughed again, then placed a hand on his arm, face turning serious. 'Delilah updated me on the situation with Will. How are your parents coping? And Alison and the kids?'

Ash shrugged. 'Not so good. The stress of it all is tearing them apart. But Delilah is confident she and Samson can unearth something to help Will's cause.'

'No one better for it,' said Nancy. 'They'll prove this is all some dreadful mistake, you'll see.'

Wishing he shared her confidence, Ash merely nodded.

'Right, well, I'll let you get on.' With a final nod of approval at his work, Nancy headed for the door which led to the small office kitchen and the stairs to the flat above.

Ash turned back to the window, and was treated to the bizarre sight of Ida Capstick skulking across the road. That was the only word for how she was moving, a furtiveness to her as she came closer, a tan seventies suitcase in her hand, like the one Grandad Metcalfe had kept his sheepdog-trials trophies in. With a couple of glances over each shoulder, she made a dart for the shop door and in a flurry of movement and fake leather, was inside and in front of Ash.

'I've got an appointment to see Nancy,' she said, glaring at him, as though she expected him to query her presence in some way.

'Sure,' he said. He pointed towards the back of the room, the stairs visible through the open door. 'She's just gone up to the flat. You off on your travels?' He accompanied the question with a nod towards her case and a grin.

The latter froze on his face as she regarded him through narrowed eyes.

'None of tha business, young Metcalfe,' she snapped. Then stalked past him and off up the stairs.

If you'd asked Ash Metcalfe later that day how long Ida Capstick spent talking to Nancy Taylor, he'd have struggled to tell you, so engrossed was he in applying the final coat of gloss to the architrave. But what he did notice when she eventually came down the stairs and gave one of her distinctive sharp nods as she passed him, was that Ida was travelling a lot lighter, the suitcase nowhere to be seen. And it looked like – and here he had to pause as he reflected on it, because it seemed so improbable – but it looked like she'd been smiling. Like she'd just hastily rearranged her features into their more recognisable scowl but had failed to erase the trace of uplift lingering about her lips.

It was an observation which could have been endorsed by Barry Dawson, owner of Plastic Fantastic further up the street. For when he saw Ida walking by some minutes later, he noted that, as she gave him a cordial tip of her head before she disappeared through the door of Turpin's solicitors, there was an unusual air about her. Something feline. Like a cat who'd not only got the cream, but had found a reliable source of more to come in future.

26

Compared to the hectic start to the day for the Dales Detective team, things had commenced quietly at Fellside Court. For Arty Robinson it had been yet another night of troubled sleep, followed by an early rise, the knot of anxiety in his stomach forcing him from his bed in search of sustenance. Thinking food would ease the biliousness, he'd prepared a bowl of cereal, but only managed a few spoonfuls and had still been sitting there looking at it gone nine o'clock when he'd had an unexpected visitor. Which had only added to his stress.

Now he was in the cafe with his friends for the post-armchair-aerobics coffee and cake which he normally looked forward to with relish, all those stretches and bends building up an appetite. But today he was toying with the slice of chocolate gateau in front of him, pretending to be listening to the chatter around the table. In reality, he had only one thing on his mind.

What was he going to do if Ida Capstick was successful in her mission to unmask the new owner of Fellside Court? Because given that was who his early morning visitor had been, and given the reason for her call, Arty could only surmise that she was close to completing the task she'd been set.

He'd spent the past forty-eight hours terrified that she'd come back with good news which would shatter everything. News which would remove any obstacle to him staying in his one-bedroomed flat overlooking the cherry trees in the courtyard, and simultaneously remove the need for Edith's offer to be formally extended.

Moving in with her – it was all he'd been able to think about since she'd blindsided him with the suggestion. Had she meant it? Not that it mattered if Ida unearthed positive news about the future of the building. In one fell swoop the possibility of a different outcome, one which had been placed in front of him like the sweetest of temptations, could be snatched from him before he'd even had a chance to truly savour it.

If there was no financial reason for Arty to move flat, there would be no reason for Edith to uphold her proposal of cohabitation.

'What do you think, Arty?' Clarissa was asking.

Arty didn't have a clue what the question was. 'Sorry,' he said, grin forced. 'Miles away. What did you say?'

'I said, we should do something to celebrate if Ida finds out that all is well. A party of some sort.'

'Agreed,' said Eric. 'We need something to liven this place up. Been like a bloody morgue for the last few months.'

'Certainly,' said Arty, trying to make his voice hearty, when the last thing he wanted to be doing was celebrating. 'Definitely need to do something—'

A symphony of phones pinged, trilled and, in Eric's case, chirped around the table and heads bent, handbags and pockets were reached for and into, five mobiles being produced.

'It's the WhatsApp group,' said Joseph.

'From Ida!' said Edith.

While Clarissa – who was far more adept with modern technology than her sister or friends and had opened and read the message in the time the rest had taken to wake up their screens – let out a shriek. 'Fellside Court is safe!'

She was on her feet, clapping her hands, calling for quiet as she announced the news to the rest of the residents in the cafe, and as a cacophony of cheers and hoots broke out, Arty stared at the phone in his hand. With a typically Capstick level of terseness, Ida had notified them of the developments.

> *New owner Fellside Court promises no increase to fees or rent.*

So she'd done it. Ida had found the owner and secured the information which only a week ago Arty would have given his eye teeth for. The threat which had been hanging over him since Rick Procter's arrest was finally gone and there would be no need for him to move.

'An afternoon cocktail party!' Clarissa was saying. 'Tom Collins, Piña Colada, Harvey Wallbanger, Tequila Sunrise . . . we can even throw in a few mocktails! Let's do it today! No point putting it off, not at our age!'

'I'm in,' said Eric. 'Just don't go asking me for Sex on the Beach.'

Edith let out a snort of laughter, Joseph grinning while Clarissa was already on the move, talking to the next group of pensioners, getting them on board.

'Isn't it grand news!' Joseph had turned to Arty, joy and relief emanating from him. 'We're safe where we are! That's worthy of a drink or two.'

And in that instant, Arty felt like the worst of friends. For there was Joseph, in the same boat as he was, juggling his meagre pension to be able to stay in Fellside Court and having suffered a similar amount of angst when it came to the uncertain future. Unexpectedly granted a reprieve, he was wanting to raise a toast – non-alcoholic of course – to mark the occasion, yet Arty was struggling to raise a smile.

'It's the best of news,' managed Arty, hoping he sounded more convincing than he felt.

He turned his head and saw Edith watching him with that inscrutable regard, her thoughts impossible to read, and he felt a fresh pang of regret at what could have been. Whatever festivities Clarissa had planned for the afternoon, Arty was going to find it hard to join in wholeheartedly.

Constable Danny Bradley was holding on to his temper. It was a rare thing for the mild-mannered lad to lose his cool, but the infuriating stubbornness of DS Benson was testing his patience to the maximum.

After over an hour of hearing Samson and Delilah put forward their theories on the Ross Irwin case, the detective had outright dismissed each and every argument. Even the spreadsheet retrieved from Irwin's laptop hadn't been enough to sway things, Benson claiming that while it proved the ecologist had been on the shady side, it also gave Will even more of a motive for killing him. And as for Kevin Dinsdale, the fact that he'd already secured a green light on the ecological impact assessment – albeit through illicit means – had made DS Benson declare he could see no reason for the farmer to murder the man who'd helped him get what he wanted. Samson's suggestion that Irwin's records cast doubt onto whether he'd actually received payment from Dinsdale prior to his death – thus creating motive – fell on deaf ears.

Finally, Delilah's attestation as to her brother's character and that he was incapable of leaving a man to die out on the fells, had been met with a shrug, Benson pointing out that the law dealt in concrete evidence. Concrete evidence like a rounders bat covered in blood. At which point, Sergeant Clayton, perhaps spotting the clenching of those infamous Metcalfe fists, had stepped in and declared that it might be best to leave it there for the day.

Danny was the kind of person to give everyone the benefit of the doubt, so he'd tried making allowances for the detective, especially considering he'd been put in a foul mood by the revelation that Samson had broken into Irwin's hotel room and taken a copy of vital evidence – a revelation which had had Danny sweating profusely inside his uniform, aware that his own behaviour relating to that incident was a dismissible offence. But even so, Benson's refusal to give Samson and Delilah's arguments reasonable consideration was exasperating the young constable.

As was Sergeant Clayton's offhand manner about it all. Having seen Samson and Delilah off the premises, he'd returned to the office and completely taken the detective's side. And when DS Benson had said he was heading over to Harrogate to finalise things for charging Will Metcalfe, the sarge had simply nodded. As though Will was just another criminal rather than someone he'd known all his life. Someone he should have known deep down wouldn't – couldn't – have committed this crime in the manner it had been carried out. Because despite his wobble the day before, Danny was back trusting his gut, which told him Will Metcalfe was innocent. No matter the evidence.

He was bitterly disappointed his sergeant didn't share that view.

'Aye, makes sense to get things sorted at your end,' Sergeant Clayton was saying now as DS Benson gathered his things. 'Happen as I'll come over with you.'

Danny looked at his superior, hopeful of getting an invitation to join them. Anything to get out of the station. But the sarge had already anticipated this and was pointing at the stack of folders in front of his own computer.

'Paperwork, Constable Bradley. There's several reports as need filing in that lot. Dig them out and get them sorted, there's a good lad.' With a nod of satisfaction, he followed DS Benson out of the office.

Cursing from behind clenched teeth, Danny threw himself down onto his chair, setting the peace lily on his desk shaking in its pot. He was definitely going to get a transfer. Call DCI Thistlethwaite and get moved to a place where his talents were appreciated and he wasn't simply viewed as a bloody pencil pusher—

'Oi!' came a sharp whisper from the doorway. Sergeant Clayton, glancing quickly over his shoulder before back at Danny, a shrewdness to his gaze which hadn't been there earlier. 'Stop moping like you're in a leaky caravan on a wet weekend in Bridlington and listen up. While I keep Benson out of the way, I want you going through every single shred of evidence in this blasted case – witness statements, forensic reports such as we have so far, the whole bloody lot. I know that sharp eye of yours is better than mine – sharp enough to have known Samson and Delilah had broken into Irwin's room at any rate—'

Danny went to protest his innocence but the sarge held up a spade-like hand.

'Save it, son. I can read you and the Metcalfe lass like a book. So turn that laser-like focus of yours on, and go through everything with a fine-tooth comb. If anyone's going to find something untoward that points in a direction other than Will Metcalfe, it'll be you. But get cracking, mind – we've not got long left before DS Benson goes ahead and makes an idiot of himself by charging the wrong man.' He paused, casting another glance back out into the corridor before lowering his voice even further. 'And while you're at it, if that forensics file found its way to Samson and Delilah, it wouldn't be a bad thing.'

Danny's mouth dropped open, thinking of all the red lines such an action would cross, and the ramifications which would surely follow. The sarge grinned.

'Don't worry, young Danny, if you get caught I'll go down with you. Happen we'd get on fine sharing a cell over in Harrogate.' Retrieving his helmet from the hook on the wall behind his desk, he declared, 'I'll forget my head one day,' the volume and tone suggesting this admission was more for the waiting Benson's benefit than Danny's. Then, with a final wink over his shoulder at his constable, Sergeant Clayton turned to go.

'Sarge,' said Danny, heart thumping at the responsibility he'd been given, 'what's made you so sure DS Benson has got it wrong?'

The sergeant shrugged, a movement which had as much impact on his protruding stomach as it did on his shoulders.

'While I'm not as easily swayed by a pecan tart as Delilah might think, the lass has a point. Will Metcalfe would never have left a man to die in isolation, no matter the consequences. That's a good enough basis for me to set Bruncliffe's finest copper onto the case.'

He left the room, Danny sitting there in silence for a few moments with a wide grin on his face, the extent of the praise he'd just had heaped on him sinking in. That grin swiftly faded as he thought about sharing a prison cell with his sergeant. Before he could lose his courage at the thought of such a prospect, Danny got to work.

Edith was waiting for Arty as he came down the stairs, with him having gone to his apartment under the guise of getting his reading glasses before joining his friends in the lounge, but actually just needing to get away from the mass jollity. She was sitting in the same club chair she'd been supposed to keep watch from while he broke into the manager's office. Only two days ago, yet it seemed like a different world. One in which the horizon had been infinitely brighter.

'Arty Robinson,' she said, in that voice which suffered no arguments, patting the chair next to her. 'Come here a minute.'

Arty slapped on a smile and walked over, sitting as he'd been instructed.

'Did I see Ida leave with the suitcase this morning?' she murmured, leaning across the small table between their chairs.

He nodded. Edith raised an eyebrow and Arty shrugged. 'I don't know what's going on,' he said. 'But I trust her.'

'Implicitly,' agreed Edith. 'Well,' she said, folding her hands on the top of her walking stick and tipping her head to one side, gaze fixed on him. 'it's been quite the day.'

'Hasn't it just.' Arty managed to keep the dejection from his voice.

Or at least, he thought he had. But Edith didn't miss a trick.

'I sense you're not sharing the same level of jubilation as my sister,' she said in an arid tone, lights dancing in her eyes.

He shrugged again. Tried to widen his smile. Didn't quite pull it off. So he opted for honesty.

'Did you mean it?' he asked. 'When you made that offer the other day?'

She didn't play games. Just nodded. 'Of course I did. You were in a potentially difficult situation. I had a solution, so I offered it. That's what you do for friends.'

Arty felt crestfallen all over again. That use of the word 'friends'.

'Well, thanks anyway. Even though your generous suggestion wasn't needed in the end.'

'Hmph.' Edith's focus moved off him and out to the courtyard. 'Would you have missed it?' she asked, gesturing towards the cherry trees and the green beyond them. 'The view from your place?'

'I didn't really give it a thought,' he said. For he hadn't. His thoughts had only been concerned with moving in with her and what that would bring.

'In that case, move in anyway.' She stood as she said it, one hand on her walking stick, the other on her hip, which gave her a bit more trouble these days. She was looking down at him now, an impish smile on her, devilment below the surface.

He knew he was sitting there with his mouth wide open

like a gormless fool, but he could do nothing about it. 'Seriously?' he managed.

'Why not?' She shrugged. 'As Clarissa so aptly put it earlier, no point putting things off at our age.'

He was standing too now. Mouth turning up into a foolish smile. Nodding.

'Let's get this month out of the way and start from September, like the school year.' She smiled back at him. Just as joyous. 'And we'll give it a term. If by December we realise things aren't working, well, we can take it from there.'

'And Clarissa?' he asked. 'She's on board with this?'

Edith laughed. 'You need to ask? It'll give her two lots of housewarming parties to organise!' She held out her hand, firm and businesslike, for him to clasp. 'Deal?'

He placed his hands in hers in return. 'It's a deal,' he said.

With that she nodded. 'Right, well, let's join the others and learn how to make some cocktails. I want to see Eric sipping a Sex on the Beach before the afternoon is out.'

Feeling like he was walking on air, Arty followed her into the lounge, in a mood much more conducive to having fun.

Ida's message, which had brought such elation to the residents of Fellside Court, had been received far and wide, for it had been sent via the WhatsApp group established at a time when Samson's life had been in peril. It was a group which included a good many members of the Bruncliffe community. Hence, as they walked back up Church Street towards the marketplace with Tolpuddle by their side, Samson and Delilah got notice of Ida's achievements.

'Good on her,' said Samson, subdued. 'At least one of the team has had some success.'

Delilah just nodded. Disheartened and despairing. She'd really thought they'd had a chance of swaying DS Benson's opinion, or at least getting him to consider what they'd discovered. But he'd point-blank refused to even contemplate a link between Irwin's extracurricular income stream and his murder, other than as further justification for charging the oldest Metcalfe sibling with murder.

So as they headed back to the office in the glorious sunshine which late August often produces, a black cloud was loitering above them, casting gloom on even this fantastic news from their Dales Detective colleague.

'Your dad will be relieved,' Delilah finally managed.

Samson's nod was as muted as Delilah's had been.

In a silence scarred by defeat, they walked around the corner onto the market square. It was bustling with locals lingering to chat and tourists meandering past shop windows while eating ice creams, all making the most of this last flurry of summer. In normal circumstances, Delilah wouldn't have noticed the odd combination of two people standing in the mouth of the ginnel which ran beside Peaks Patisserie. But it was the furtive nature of their conversation, so out of place against the carefree dallying of everyone else, that caught her eye. Ida Capstick and Mrs Pettiford, having a discussion which was far from trivial, judging by the seriousness of their respective expressions.

'That's odd,' said Delilah, gesturing towards the ginnel. 'I wouldn't have thought those two had much in common.'

Samson glanced over. Shrugged. 'Maybe Ida's asking where you can buy unbreakable teapots.'

Delilah smiled. Half-heartedly.

They crossed the cobbles at a rapid pace, not wanting to get caught in chit-chat with anyone they knew, and then walked past the top of Back Street and on to the ginnel which would take them down the back of the office building. When they entered the yard and shut the gate, Samson turned to Delilah.

'I'm sorry,' was all he said.

She nodded. 'We did our best.'

'And we'll keep on doing it. Somehow we'll prove that Will didn't do this.'

She placed a hand on his cheek. 'Thanks,' she said. 'For believing in me and in Will.'

He gave an ironic grin. 'Don't think I've ever been accused of letting my emotions get the better of me on a case before,' he said, parroting back the words DS Benson had flung at him just before they'd been shepherded out by the sergeant. 'Maybe I'm becoming more of a Bruncliffe local than I thought, like one of those hefted sheep who lose the longing to stray.'

The comment caught her sideways, made her heart thump. Brought a gazillion questions to the tip of her tongue, about the future, his plans, where all that would take them . . . She took a breath, shaped the words and was about to speak when both their mobiles went.

'Clarissa on the WhatsApp group,' said Samson, phone already in hand. 'There's a party at Fellside Court this afternoon at two o'clock, to mark the good news. We're invited.'

It was the last thing Delilah needed. Having to make the effort to be cheerful when all she felt was depressed. From Samson's face she could tell he was the same.

'We should go,' she said.

He nodded. As though he understood that this was the price of living in a small community. Sometimes you had to do things you'd really rather not.

Another ping, from Delilah's mobile, an unknown email address on the screen. But the message within was certainly from a recognised source. Danny Bradley had sent her an attachment.

She clicked on it, stared for a few seconds and then looked up at Samson.

'It's the forensics files. From Danny – with Sergeant Clayton's blessings!'

'Jesus!' Samson looked over her shoulder, shaking his head. 'I thought Danny was done helping us. They could get in so much trouble for this.'

'So we'd best make sure we make it worth the risk,' said Delilah, heading towards the porch, a surge of optimism forging through her. 'Come on, let's have a good look through what Benson has, and see if we can find the chink in the armour we need to destroy his case.'

Samson followed her into the office building, speaking as they reached the stairs. 'Were you about to say something out there? Before Clarissa's message came through?'

Delilah shook her head and continued on up to her office, her courage back in its box, buried deep beneath layers of fear and self-preservation. If she didn't ask, she couldn't get hurt.

27

Delilah wasn't the only one worried about getting hurt. After months – possibly even years if he was truly honest – of dithering, Herriot had decided it was time to pluck up his courage and ask Lucy Metcalfe out on a date. Enough of this creeping around like a lovesick youth. Enough going on Delilah's Speedy Date nights simply to get a few minutes in Lucy's presence only to squander them on meaningless chatter because he didn't have the nerve to address his real intentions. He was a mature individual, a respected professional in the community, surely he had it in him to do this?

Putting himself in such jeopardy hadn't been on his agenda when he'd woken up that morning. He'd been planning on going up to the Dinsdales' to check on the tup which still seemed to be under the weather, but a call from Kevin first thing had seen the visit rescheduled for the following day. Herriot was left with time on his hands, and Cupid, just like the Devil, makes work for hands with nothing to do.

Which is how Bruncliffe's vet had found himself walking into Peaks Patisserie. Ostensibly just for his usual takeaway coffee, but with the real motive making his pulse pound. Trouble was, he hadn't chosen a particularly good time to declare his intentions. While Wednesdays weren't normally the busiest day of the week, the late burst of summer weather had enticed both tourists and locals out into the sunshine, Peaks benefitting as the clock moved past midday and folk started to think about sustenance. So when Herriot entered the crowded cafe and realised Elaine was manning front of house, Lucy no more than a glimpse of hurried movement as the door into the kitchen opened and closed, he decided to stay for lunch.

There were a couple of tables free, so he opted for the one which just happened to be opposite the kitchen door, and perused the menu while his heart did weird things in his chest. He settled on an aubergine parmigiana – a harried Elaine brusquely explaining that it was 'veggie lasagne for posh folk' – and as he sat there waiting, he felt his resolve weaken. What if Lucy said no? Or even worse, laughed at him?

She wouldn't do that, he reasoned with himself. She wasn't that sort of person. But she might pity him. Would that be worse than laughter?

His meal arrived and as he ate his way through it – aware that, even with his tastebuds being in a heightened state of benevolence given the identity of the chef, the food was truly outstanding – he devised a strategy. He'd linger long enough over his lunch to allow the cafe to quieten down. And then, on some pretext which he'd yet to come up with, he'd get a moment alone with Lucy.

All went according to plan. The peak rush passed and the tables began to empty, Elaine looking less hassled as she carried dishes back into the kitchen. But then Herriot realised he was sitting there, his aubergine parmigiana eaten and his plate cleared, with no further excuse for remaining in the cafe. Intent on rectifying the situation, he called Elaine over and ordered dessert – homemade sticky-toffee pudding and ice cream. With fewer people sitting around him as he waited for this impromptu second course, however, Herriot began to feel conspicuous, cursing himself for choosing the table right opposite the kitchen so that every time it swung open, he could see Lucy beyond it.

What if she noticed him sitting there twiddling his thumbs, like a pillock? Would she spot the anxiety coiling in his gut? Would she realise why he was there?

So he did what every person in the modern world does when they want to pretend they're otherwise engaged. He picked up his mobile, and saw the WhatsApp message from Ida about Fellside Court. And another from Clarissa, who was organising a cocktail party in celebration.

Good old Ida. Sorting things for the pensioners and putting minds at rest. She was turning into an excellent detective.

Which reminded him. Ida had been on his case earlier in the morning to have another look at the video he'd taken in the ginnel the night of the wedding, the night he'd captured Lucy's nocturnal visitor on camera. While Herriot was confident there would be nothing on the footage which would help Will Metcalfe's case, he knew better than to disobey a woman who could freeze fire with a look, and besides, reviewing it would lend legitimacy to his attempts to appear busy. So he pulled up the app for the dashboard camera in his van and scrolled down to the relevant date.

He watched it through, the haughty stare of Tigger the

cat down the lens, the bright light of the passing car and then a return to the grey nothing of the empty ginnel. Not a thing which could be used to exonerate Will. Even so, Herriot gave it another watch. Again, he saw nothing out of the ordinary. It was only on the third viewing – which he only initiated because his sticky toffee pudding had yet to arrive – that he spotted something.

There was an inconsistency in the distribution of light across the lens as the vehicle in the distance went past. He started the clip a fourth time, muttering a thanks as Elaine put a bowl down beside him but too engrossed to break off. This time he proceeded frame by frame, peering at the screen, trying to work out what it was about the moment-ary brightness which had caught his attention.

'Something wrong with my sticky toffee pudding, Mr Vet?'

Herriot nearly leaped out of his skin. Lucy Metcalfe was sitting in the seat opposite him, leaning across the table and pushing a strand of hair off her pale face as she nodded at the untouched dessert with a smile which looked like it took a lot of effort.

And suddenly he realised how selfish he'd been. Thinking only about his own interests while Lucy and her family were going through such torment, Will Metcalfe on the verge of being charged with the most serious of crimes. How could it possibly be appropriate to ask her out in the face of what was going on?

'Ah . . . so I . . . erm . . .' he spluttered, and she laughed.

'Just teasing. I can see you're otherwise occupied. But how come you're in here at this time of day? No animals to rescue?'

His brain went into overdrive. Neurons fired, ideas

formed, and in those split seconds, one in particular seemed like pure genius.

'Erm . . . no, I had a bit of spare time and well . . . I thought I'd see if I could find anything on my phone that might be of use for the call-out Delilah made. You know, video footage from the night of the wedding that might help Will?'

Her brave mask slipped and Lucy's face crumpled into concern. 'Yes, what a mess. I can't believe the police are going forward with charging him. We're all beside ourselves with worry. So, have you found anything?'

Before he knew what he was doing, Herriot was turning his mobile towards her, partly because he knew it would pull her even closer towards him but also because he was genuinely puzzled about that blaze of light.

'See what you make of this,' he said, playing the video.

It took Lucy just two viewings to spot the anomaly. 'The car headlights,' she said. 'I think they seem a bit odd. Like there's only one of them working.'

Herriot stared at the image he'd frozen on the screen and then back up at Lucy. 'That's it! That's what it is! I couldn't work out why the whole thing seemed so unbalanced.'

'Do you think it could be important? I mean, where did you film this anyway?'

Only then did Herriot see the huge flaw in his tactics.

'I took it . . . I mean it's not what it looks like . . . I was just . . .'

Lucy had leaned even closer towards him, doing nothing to help his jangling nerves, and was peering intently at the screen.

'That's the ginnel!' she exclaimed, looking towards the wall beyond which was the scene of Herriot's crime. She turned her gaze back onto him, expression curious. 'What were you doing parked up out there after the reception?'

He could feel the heat searing through his body and congregating in his face. He coughed.

'I was on a stakeout.'

Lucy's expression turned to surprise. 'Of what?'

'Here.'

She jerked back, her lips opened and she just said, 'Oh.' Then she tipped her head sideways, gaze resting on him. 'This is the footage which caught the squirrel.'

He nodded.

'You were staking out the cafe trying to catch the thief.'

He nodded again. Felt he should be honest and added, 'I fell asleep. It was Ida who spotted the culprit.'

Lucy turned back to the video and then smiled. 'That's such a lovely thing to have done. Daft, but lovely.'

Herriot could feel a grin forming across his lips. 'I'm glad you think so.' And then a torrent of language issued from him despite his reservations about the appropriateness. 'Perhaps you'd like to show your thanks by coming on a picnic with me tomorrow lunchtime?'

Her day off. He knew her rota almost as well as his own.

She paused, and he started babbling.

'Sorry . . . I shouldn't have . . . not when you're all going through such a tough time . . . just forget—'

'I think,' she said, cutting across his flustered back-tracking, 'it would be a lovely way to take my mind off things. And besides, going on a picnic would be the least I could do for someone crazy enough to spend an entire evening outside—' She halted, seeing the colour creeping back up his face. 'More than one evening?'

'Possibly,' he said.

She was laughing now. Not the kind of laughing he'd feared but a healthy, happy sound that wrapped around him and made him feel invincible. 'Right,' she said, getting to her feet. 'I'd better get back to work but yes, let's have a picnic tomorrow. How about you pick me up at mine around midday?'

Herriot nodded, his senses so overwhelmed he could barely speak.

'And as for that video from your daft stakeout,' Lucy continued, pointing at his mobile, 'perhaps you should run it past Delilah and see if she can make something out of it. It might seem trifling but given how bleak things are looking for Will, I think we need to clutch at each and every straw.'

'Consider it done,' said Herriot.

She gave him a smile, something extra in the way her eyes regarded him, a shared secret between them. He watched her walk back into the kitchen, aware this hadn't been how he'd envisaged things going but over the moon with the result.

He glanced back at his phone and saw the invitation from Clarissa to the cocktail party, due to start at two o'clock. It was already half past and he had some admin to catch up with that afternoon but . . . he didn't think his current mood would lend itself well to paperwork. It wouldn't hurt to pop into Fellside Court and show his face, and he might even catch Delilah there to tell her about the video. Now that Lucy knew all about his nocturnal habits, Herriot no longer had any reason to hide the fact that he was behind the footage Ida had used.

But first he was going to finish his meal. Pulling the

bowl of sticky toffee pudding towards him, he tucked into the dessert, each mouthful made more divine by the knowledge of what tomorrow lunchtime would bring.

Back at the police station, Danny Bradley had done as he'd been instructed by Sergeant Clayton. Heart in mouth and palms sweating, he'd copied the forensics file and emailed it to Delilah, taking the added precaution of using a VPN and a burner email address to at least try to hide his tracks. Then he'd spent time trawling through the material connected to the Irwin murder case. Initially sceptical that anything would be revealed, he'd come across something which was probably irrelevant, but was curious enough to have held his attention for the past few minutes.

On his computer screen were two photographs taken by the forensics team. One was of the pair of binoculars found around Irwin's neck. The other was of a piece of black plastic which closely resembled a pair of swimming goggles without straps, narrow eyelets on either side, one of which had been snapped. The binocular lens caps which had been found in the dead ecologist's clothing.

Nothing untoward there. Except, on the right-hand lens cap the name 'ZEISS' was written in capital letters. Whereas on the bridge of the binoculars was a blue circle with the words 'Viking Optical', along with a small badger icon on the right barrel. Danny had started googling binoculars and soon found himself in a world he knew bugger all about.

Feeling his eyes starting to cross from too long staring at a screen, he leaned back in his chair and stretched, his gaze drawn to the window and the bluest of skies outside it. He needed a break, he told himself.

Along with many others, he too had received Clarissa's message concerning the get-together at Fellside Court. But while he was relieved that his grandfather, Eric, and his friends could stop worrying about losing their homes, he'd dismissed the idea of calling in, as he was too busy. Now, however, he caught himself thinking about it. And about the binoculars, and the expertise which was just a few strides away up the street from the station . . .

Two birds with one stone. The notion made him laugh. Glad to be getting away from his desk, he got to his feet, picked up his helmet, and headed for the door.

When Samson and Delilah arrived at Fellside Court at the appointed hour, their mood was no more upbeat than when they'd received Clarissa's invitation. Having worked through the forensics file Danny had sent to them, they'd discovered nothing which could punch a hole in DS Benson's case against Will. If anything, seeing the evidence piled up in black and white had simply made things bleaker. And so they'd left Tolpuddle with Nathan and Nina – the teenagers refusing to break off from their exhaustive search of the video footage which had come in overnight, determined to keep working to try to prevent Will being charged while time remained – and headed for the retirement complex. But while Samson and Delilah might not have been in a frame of mind for partying, Fellside Court was already in full festive swing.

A string of bunting, the red, white and blue pennants suggesting its original purpose might have been for a royal jubilee of some sort, had been draped across the entrance to the residents' lounge, while just inside was a makeshift bar, bottles of spirits and liqueurs ranged along the surface and an elderly gentleman behind the counter, busy with a cocktail shaker, a queue of customers before him. Around the room itself, occupying clusters of armchairs and small sofas centred around coffee tables, were groups of joyous pensioners.

'Samson! Delilah! Over here!' Joseph O'Brien was beckoning them towards where he was sitting with the usual gang, by the large window which overlooked the courtyard and the cherry trees.

'Congratulations,' Delilah said as they approached the circle, Arty gesturing for them to take the two vacant armchairs. 'You must all be so pleased at the news.'

The wide smiles and vigorous nods which greeted her words made Samson feel guilty that he'd been so reluctant to join in marking something of such import for the people he'd come to cherish as friends. Something which must also have brought his father great relief.

As Clarissa drew Delilah into a conversation about how they'd managed to organise everything so quickly, Joseph leaned over to Samson, who'd sat down in the club chair next to him.

'I can't tell you what a weight off this is,' he murmured, echoing Samson's thoughts. 'I'd been fretting about it ever since we heard. Thinking I might have to leave, because, well, you know . . .'

His father was watching him warily, as he did whenever they broached the topic of his finances and the fact that Rick Procter had paid him well under the odds for the family farm, making capital out of the alcoholic stupor which had been Joseph's permanent state in those days. As a result, Joseph had been left substantially worse off than he should have been.

'I'd have seen you right, Dad,' said Samson. 'Even if it meant us moving in together.'

Joseph gave a soft laugh. Then his smile slipped. 'Have you heard the old place is up for auction?'

Samson nodded, not sure he was ready for this conversation. Out of the corner of his eye, he saw Delilah's attention snap their way, face tinting red at the realisation he knew about the coming sale.

'*Sorry!*' she mouthed at him.

He shook his head, smiling. Letting her know there was no blame. Amazed that she of all people had thought such a secret could be kept here in Bruncliffe.

'17 September,' Joseph was now murmuring beside him. 'That just makes it a bit harder.'

'Just a bit,' muttered Samson.

The understatement was typical of his father. The date was a hammer blow, almost as bad as the news that Twistleton was to be sold. It marked the day their worlds had imploded.

'Ah, sure, maybe it's a good sign,' Joseph continued. 'I should have a go at the lottery, see if I can get lucky and win enough to buy it back. Unless . . . I don't suppose you're in a position . . . ?' His hopeful expression was painful to see.

'Not a chance.' Samson tried to smile, to hide the hurt he was feeling. 'I don't have a lot saved and certainly not near enough to put a bid in.' He shrugged, making out it wasn't a big deal. Not wanting to heap more guilt on his father's frail shoulders.

But the guilt was already weighing heavily. 'I'm so sorry, Samson,' his father began. 'Selling the place like that—'

'Don't be. What's done is done. Besides, let someone else have the joy of living there.'

Joseph nodded. But Samson saw he wasn't buying it. He stood, took his father's arm and drew him out of his chair into a hug, feeling the shoulder blades beneath the wool of the cardigan.

'I'm sorry, too, Dad, for not being around. We've both made mistakes, but we're here now and that's all that's important. And as for the farm, it doesn't matter. It's only bricks and mortar.'

His father clasped him back, surprising strength in his hold as though it had been kept in reserve for fourteen years, just for this very moment. 'Ah, son, it's so good to have you home, wherever that is.'

'Ahem!' came a pointed cough from Arty. 'If you two have quite finished, this is supposed to be a party, not a bloody funeral!'

Samson and his father broke off their embrace to see the group watching them, Clarissa dabbing at her eyes, Delilah's cheeks looking suspiciously wet and Edith nodding in approval, while Arty just looked happy. As though he knew this was something his friend had been longing for.

Eric, meanwhile, was pointing at a black fold of weathered leather lying on Joseph's chair. 'You can tell you're not a Yorkshireman,' he declared. 'If that'd been my wallet, I'd have felt it like an ache in my heart the minute it fell out of my pocket! And if it had been Arty's, we'd be dealing with a moth infestation.'

The pensioners broke into laughter, while Arty stretched across to retrieve Joseph's wallet and hand it back, a piece of paper fluttering to the floor as he did so. Samson bent over to pick it up, noticing the age of it, the edges crinkled, the paper almost worn through.

It was a dry-cleaning receipt for the laundrette in town, from a decade ago.

Samson handed it back with a laugh. 'Seriously, Dad, I'm not sure why you're holding on to this. It's ten years old. Whatever you had cleaned at Bruncliffe Bright Whites, it will be long gone.'

Joseph quickly took the receipt back and stowed it in his wallet, muttering something about having been meaning to throw it out, before resuming his seat.

'Well,' said Clarissa, getting to her feet and raising her cocktail glass high, her voice carrying across the room and bringing it to silence, 'here's to Ida Capstick and the new owner of Fellside Court, whoever they may be. Long may they remain as altruistic as Ida seems to think they are.'

Everyone raised their glasses in unison at Clarissa's toast, a hubbub of joyful noise following in its wake.

'So Ida didn't say who the owner was?' asked Delilah, as Clarissa sat down.

Edith shook her head. 'We just got the message on the WhatsApp group, same as you did. Nothing more than that.'

'Anyone got any ideas?'

There was a ripple of shaking grey and balding heads around the group.

Delilah raised an eyebrow. 'Enigmatic. I wonder how she worked it out.'

'She didn't tell you either?' asked Arty.

'Not yet. But then, we've hardly been around what with Will and everything . . .'

Edith leaned over and placed a hand on Delilah's arm. 'About that,' she said. 'We heard the news that DS Benson is going to charge him with murder. I'm presuming you've exhausted all avenues in trying to change that idiot detective's mind?'

'Pretty much,' said Delilah on a sigh.

Arty shrugged. 'There's still one avenue you could try.'

'What's that?'

'Us lot. Run the evidence past us and see if we can spot anything.'

Delilah looked at Samson, who shrugged. 'What harm could it do?' he said.

And so they started outlining the case, the forensics details they'd received from Danny and what they'd discovered themselves from Irwin's computer, along with the theories they'd already discounted. By the time Samson finished speaking, the pensioners were all sitting forward in their chairs, faces animated, foreheads creased in frowns of concentration.

'That blasted rounders bat,' wheezed Eric, the excitement taking a toll on his breathing. 'That's the stumbling block. Hard to argue with it.'

'The final forensics report isn't in yet,' pointed out Edith. 'Let's not make assumptions or we'll end up in the same cul-de-sac as DS Benson.'

'So what do you suggest?' asked Joseph.

'We need to look at it from a different angle,' continued Edith.

'The binoculars,' said Eric. 'What make were they?'

'What does it matter?' Arty asked, a hint of exasperation in his voice.

'You can tell a lot about a man from his binoculars.' Eric's tone had something of the huff about it. 'Back in the day, when I was a serious twitcher, I knew folk who'd quite happily spend a small fortune on a good pair of bins while baulking at the cost of a bus fare. And as for the state they're kept in . . .' He tapped the oxygen cylinder by his side, face full of regret. 'Of course, that was before all this came along and constrained me to watching birds from the window of my room.'

'And there was me thinking those binoculars on your windowsill were for keeping an eye on me across the court-yard,' joked Arty, winking at his friend.

Eric grunted. 'Wouldn't want to crack a good set of lenses!' He turned to Delilah, who was pulling up the photos Danny had sent through on her mobile. 'So?'

'Viking Optical,' she said, peering at the screen before passing him the phone.

He enlarged the image, nodding as he zoomed in on various parts. 'Not the most expensive out there but not beginner-level cheap either. I'd say he was a mid-level twitcher. More of a hobby than a passion – useful for his work, too, without going overboard on cost. And they've been kept in decent enough nick. No rainguard, mind, but then they're not for everyone as they can get in the way a bit. You know, if you spot a hawfinch or a nightingale and you swing up the bins and the rainguard gets stuck on your jacket. It can be a right bugger.'

'A rainguard?' asked Samson.

Eric nodded. 'A bit of rubber shaped to fit the eyepieces which does what it says on the tin. Stops the rain getting on them.'

'And that would normally be attached to the binocular strap?'

'Yep. So if your binoculars are hanging around mid-chest level, the rainguard would be higher up the strap and just drops down over the eyepieces when they're not in use.'

'And these?' Delilah was holding out her mobile again, the photo of the black plastic discs found in Irwin's clothing now on the screen. 'Would these lens caps have been attached as well?'

Eric cast a scornful eye in her direction. 'They're not lens caps, lass. That's a rainguard, like I've just been telling you about.'

'Oh.' Delilah looked at Samson. Puzzled. 'Danny said they were lens caps.'

'Not sure how a grandson of mine made that mistake. It's a rainguard, I'm telling you straight.'

Samson shrugged. 'I'm not sure it changes anything.'

'Happen it might.' Eric had taken the mobile from Delilah and enlarged the image. He pointed at the writing on the right-hand circle of black plastic. 'It's a Zeiss,' he said. 'Top of the range.'

'And?' demanded Arty.

'And,' came a voice from beyond the circle of chairs, 'the binoculars are made by Viking.' Danny was standing there, grinning at Eric. 'Should have known you'd get there faster than I did, Grandad. I came over to pick your brain on this very topic.'

'Just as well,' grunted his grandfather affectionately, 'seeing as I've taught you all I know and still you know nothing. Imagine confusing a rainguard with a lens cap!'

Danny's grin grew wider as he perched on the arm of Eric's chair and planted a kiss on his cheek. 'Excuse my ignorance.'

'So is it a problem that it's a different make?' asked Delilah, pointing at the photo still in Eric's hand.

Eric shook his head. 'Not necessarily. You can mix and match your kit, although it's rare you'd splash out for a top-notch protector when you've stinted on the bins. More likely to be the other way round. But in this case . . .' he scrolled back to the photo of the binoculars and sucked air through his teeth. 'Yep, it's a problem all right. This rainguard wouldn't fit these binoculars.'

Delilah's eyes widened and Samson felt his heart start to pick up pace. Something itching in the back of his brain. Something staying just out of reach of his grasp.

'You're sure they wouldn't fit?' he made the mistake of asking.

It wasn't just Eric who gave him a look of disdain, the rest of the pensioners taking exception at his querying of their friend's expertise.

'Sure as sh—'

'Sugar,' intercepted Edith, cutting off Eric with a benevolent smile.

'So we've got a mid-level pair of binoculars and a top-end rainguard which wouldn't fit the eyepieces on the Vikings,' murmured Samson. 'Which leaves us where?'

'Perhaps Irwin was using an old rainguard, back from when he used to be flush?' suggested Clarissa. 'Maybe he was just making do.'

'Only thing is,' said Delilah, 'we happen to know Irwin had quite a bit of money thanks to his side hustles, and he wasn't afraid to splash it about. So I don't see him as the type to make do.'

'Whatever his reasoning, it didn't pay off.' Danny took Delilah's phone from his grandfather and focused in on the edge of the rainguard. 'This was broken at some point.' He pointed at the snapped hoop of plastic on the outer side of the right-hand circle. 'Presumably in the tussle which led to Irwin's death.'

Eric nodded. 'Aye, that'll be why they weren't still on the strap.'

'Curiouser and curiouser,' said Clarissa. 'Don't you just love it when we have a mystery to solve!'

'And here comes a man who looks like he might have more to add to it,' said Arty, gesturing towards the doorway of the lounge where Herriot had just appeared. The vet had spotted them in the corner and was indeed advancing like a man on a mission.

'Thought I'd find you two here,' he said, addressing Samson and Delilah as he approached. 'About that video footage you put a shout out for—'

'You've found something?' Delilah was on her feet, excited.

Herriot shrugged. 'Don't get your hopes up too high – it might be nothing but Lucy thought it was worth sharing with you.' He was fishing his mobile out of his back pocket as he spoke. With a couple of swipes of the screen, he held it out for Delilah to see. 'This was taken on the night of the wedding, in the ginnel outside Peaks Patisserie.'

The pensioners and Samson all gathered around Delilah, looking over her shoulder as the footage began to play.

'This is the video Ida had which caught the squirrel that was raiding Peaks,' said Delilah, looking up at Herriot in puzzlement as the first few frames played out. 'How come it's on your phone?'

The vet turned a shade of scarlet a cardinal would have been proud to wear. 'We can discuss that later. Just watch.'

'Ooh, Tigger!' cooed Clarissa.

'I can't see bugger all,' muttered Eric.

'Bloody hell, that light's bright,' grunted Arty.

'It's a car's headlights,' said Joseph.

'Headlight, singular,' said Edith.

And Samson's heart really began to pound, a snapshot of someone placing a car headlight bulb in their pocket coming to mind. 'What time was this?' he asked.

'About midnight,' said Herriot. 'The vehicle in question was going through the marketplace and past the end of the ginnel when it was caught on the camera. That's why I thought it was worth bringing to your attention.'

Delilah was already playing it again, nodding as the light split the screen. 'Edith's right. This car – or whatever it is – only has one light working.' She was looking at Samson now, hope in her eyes.

'You think it could be the murderer?' whispered Clarissa, her mouth a circle of awe.

'Driving past as they moved the body,' agreed Eric.

'Well, if it is,' said Arty, slapping Herriot on the back, 'our lad here has just narrowed down the pool of possible vehicles.'

Samson was nodding. 'It could be. The timings would work. And if that's right, this is indeed a major breakthrough.'

'As long as whoever it was hasn't got his light fixed in the meantime,' said Edith.

She was right again. A splash of cold water on the theory

but not enough to stop Samson's growing belief that he was close. So close. There was something there, something he wasn't quite seeing. Something which would be the means of cracking the case wide open—

He turned to Eric. 'Do you really keep your binoculars on the windowsill?'

Eric squinted at him, wondering at the sudden change of subject. 'Always have. Never saw the point in having them in a box when the birds are outside the window—'

'Birds!' Samson exclaimed, suddenly grasping it. That elusive memory crystal clear now. The meaning of it there right in front of him. Not something he'd seen but something he *hadn't* seen.

A rainguard that didn't fit. A distinctive shape to the wound. It was so obvious . . . The weapon used to kill Irwin had been in front of their noses all this time.

While the rest of the group were looking startled at his outburst, Delilah was watching Samson intently, knowing he was on to something.

'Where to?' she said.

'The car.' Samson turned to Danny. 'Get back to the office and as soon as you have the full forensics report, call me. And Herriot, get a copy of that video to Danny ASAP.'

'Where are you going?' asked Danny as Samson began hurrying from the room, Delilah at his side.

'We're going to make a citizen's arrest!'

28

Delilah had her foot to the floor and for once Samson wasn't complaining. He had a fear that they might be too late. That somehow the evidence he needed to confirm his theory would have been got rid of. As the Mini roared out of Bruncliffe and up the hill, he was on the phone to Nina, desperately trying to find other means of nailing the person he suspected to be Ross Irwin's killer.

'Yep,' he was saying, 'it's Kevin Dinsdale. I'm certain of it. And we've possibly got all we need to prove it. But I want you to go back through everything you have on video, this time just focusing on the car park and any changes there – you're looking for his Mitsubishi Shogun. We need to know if it moved at all during the reception.'

From behind the wheel, Delilah made a noise of approval at his suggestion, shaking her head at the same time, clearly as irked as he was that they hadn't thought of it before – checking for vehicle movement rather than just that of the suspects.

'Thanks, Nina,' he concluded. 'And given the situation, you need to work fast!'

He hung up and almost immediately – as Delilah cornered a blind bend at a speed not normally advisable – his phone rang.

'Danny?' he said, putting him on speaker.

'Got the forensics report in!' The constable's excitement spilled into the car's interior. 'The blood on the rounders bat isn't human!'

'Yes!' exclaimed Delilah. 'Was it sheep's blood?'

'Spot on. And it matches the stains in the back of the Land Rover.'

Delilah let out a whoop.

'But that's not all,' continued Danny. 'They found glass in the wound on the right side of Irwin's head.'

'The wound which they were claiming was from the bat?' asked Samson.

'The same. Which gives DS Benson a bit of a headache – no pun intended – as that's his murder weapon pretty comprehensively ruled out. No glass on a rounder's bat.'

Samson let out a long breath. Feeling the certainty now. Kevin was their killer. 'Anything else?'

'One last thing. The pathologist highlighted an impression in the wound which was made by whatever the perpetrator used to knock Irwin over. She couldn't be sure but she thought it resembled the number seven.'

Delilah looked at Samson, puzzled, but Samson was far from confused. For his instincts in Fellside Court had been right. He knew what the murder weapon was.

He smiled. 'Thanks, Danny.'

As he hung up, Delilah started slowing down, marginally, for the turning. With a squeal of tyres, she turned right into the Dinsdale farmyard.

Kevin Dinsdale met them at the back porch. There was a wariness to him, no doubt sensing the tension fizzing in his visitors.

'Social or business?' he asked, a half-smile on his lips.

'Any chance of a cuppa?' Delilah countered, before Samson could speak. And as Kevin dipped his head and led the way into the kitchen, Samson had to acknowledge yet again that his Dales Detective Agency partner was a maestro when it came to manipulating the social codes of Bruncliffe in order to get what she wanted. A request for a cup of tea was rarely refused. Or queried. And in this case, it gained them the access they needed.

They entered the large kitchen, the table in the same state of disarray as before, if not even worse. Certainly there was more paperwork cluttering the surface.

'Still not got round to sorting the accounts,' Kevin muttered, staring at the bills with resentment. 'Lou's just at her folks dropping off Ava for a few days in the hope that a bit of peace and quiet might give us the time we need to finally get it done.' He gave a rueful smile. 'Six-year-olds and finances don't mix. But then there's not much seems to mix with finances round here these days.'

He rubbed a hand over his weary face and gestured at the chairs while he went towards the kettle. Delilah sat but Samson walked over to the large expanse of glass overlooking the dale. And the windowsill beneath it.

He glanced down. Saw the procession of wire figurines advancing towards the middle from either side. Robins, wrens, kingfishers . . . advancing on the two circles of clean sill within the dust. Only now those circles were occupied by a pair of binoculars, left upright between the birds, ready for action. A pair of binoculars which fitted well within the circles left by their predecessors, a perimeter of clean sill outlining each lens.

'They new?' Samson asked over his shoulder, pointing at the binoculars.

Kevin nodded. Watching Samson keenly.

'What happened to the old set?'

'They got dropped. A long time ago. Thought it was time I replaced them.'

Samson glanced back down at the windowsill. At the dust yet to cover the outer edges of the circles around the new lenses and which gave testament to the lie. Taking his mobile from his pocket, he took a photo.

'What's this all about?' asked Kevin, noticeably jumpy now, any attempt at making tea abandoned.

'Your 4x4,' commented Delilah. 'Danny said he spotted it had a headlight out. He asked us to pop in and tell you.'

'Right.' No denial, just Kevin looking from one to the other. 'You came all the way up here to pass that on?'

Samson looked at Delilah. Who shrugged. Handing the baton back to him. At which point his phone vibrated, a message from Nina on the screen.

You were right! The Shogun was moved!

He felt a shot of relief, and then that familiar pressure of blood pounding in the veins as a case came to a close.

'How about we all sit down,' he said, moving across to the table to pull out a chair.

Kevin sat, leaned forward, thick forearms on the wooden surface. 'Seriously, I don't have time for fun and games. I've got a sick tup out there that needs checking. So I'll ask again, what's going on?'

'We're here about Ross Irwin's death,' said Samson. 'I'm guessing the binoculars you broke were a set of Zeiss?'

Again that twist of the head as Kevin glanced between the Dales Detective duo. 'What's that got to do with Irwin?'

'Everything, seeing as the pathologist has just confirmed that Irwin was struck by something resembling a set of binoculars, most likely a pair of Zeiss binoculars, to be specific. The resulting wound has an indentation which corresponds to a partial letter Z. And there was glass in it. I'm sure it's only a matter of time before DS Benson gets round to matching those glass fragments to the lens of a pair of Zeiss binoculars. Just like the ones you had to throw out and replace in the last week.

'What's more,' he continued, 'we have evidence that your car was moved during the wedding reception, at a time which would correspond with the movements of Irwin's suspected killer. And then there's the slight matter of a vehicle with one headlight being seen driving through the marketplace around the time Irwin's body was taken up to the kiln. No doubt the headlight you'd just finished changing when we called in on Monday.' Samson paused. Shrugged. 'It might not sound like a lot, but once the police get their teeth into it . . . It's game over, I'm afraid.'

Kevin stared at Samson for what felt like a lifetime, Samson bracing himself for pursuit. But it didn't happen. The farmer gave a final nod and then just seemed to implode, his shoulders slumping, his head dropping and a low moan escaping from him.

'We know it was probably an accident,' Delilah was saying, a hand on his arm, this man she'd known all her life, a man her brother had grown up with. 'And we know about the money Irwin was taking for the planning.'

'He was a snake!' spat Kevin, head snapping up, anger blazing. 'An abomination of a human being. He got what he deserved.'

Delilah nodded. 'Yes.'

In the face of her simple acknowledgement, Kevin's anger turned to contrition. 'I'm sorry,' he said. 'I'm sorry about Will. He was never meant to get caught up in this. Everything just went wrong somehow . . .'

'I know.' Delilah had hold of his hand now. Tears in her eyes.

Kevin turned to Samson. 'Call them,' he said. 'The police. I want to be gone before Lou gets home from her mother's.'

But there was no need to make the call. From the distance the sound of sirens was floating up the dale.

29

There were no celebrations to mark the apprehension of Ross Irwin's killer. When Samson and Delilah returned to the Dales Detective office late Wednesday afternoon they found Gareth, Ida, Nathan and Nina gathered there, all as subdued as they were at the conclusion of the case. For while Will had been exonerated and was on his way home from Harrogate, Kevin Dinsdale's arrest had been harrowing to witness.

A good man who made a mistake. That had been Sergeant Clayton's downbeat verdict as he stood next to Samson, watching the farmer getting into the back of the police car. That fatal mistake was going to ruin his life and probably bankrupt the farm he'd been desperately trying to save. The moment she heard what had happened to her neighbour, Alison Metcalfe had come over from Ellershaw and insisted on staying at the farmhouse until Louise returned, so she could break the news in person and not over the phone. Samson and Delilah had left her there, torn between relief at her own husband's acquittal and dismay at her friend's predicament, a feeling shared by many in the town. For Kevin had always been popular, an upstanding man in the community and a generous neighbour and friend. The news which had filtered down the fellside and into the town that day had left Bruncliffe in a state of shock.

On Thursday morning, the low spirits of the town's inhabitants were reflected in the weather, a cold front having come in from the north, bringing with it the first taste of autumn and the winter to follow. Under a leaden sky, Delilah was driving out towards the auction mart, Samson beside her, Tolpuddle in the back. They'd closed the office and given Nathan and Nina a day off and had ordered Ida to take a holiday too. An order which had been greeted with a scowl and a declaration, as she arrived in the kitchen wielding her new mop, that dust and dirt took no time off, so neither would she.

The auction mart was busy, its trade of buying and selling livestock continuing despite one of the regular attendees having been arrested for murder. But there was no denying, as Samson and Delilah walked through the corridor past the heaving cafe, there were a lot of serious expressions and muted conversations as the impact of what had happened the day before hit home.

One of their own, driven by financial pressures into an act of violence which had led to dreadful consequences for all involved. It was a situation most farmers there could empathise with, that perpetual struggle to keep heads above water, the stresses which accompanied the precarious nature of the living they made in an occupation they loved. Stresses which always found a way to the surface like the water in the normally dry Hull Pot, roaring up after a deluge, with potentially catastrophic results.

While there was no condoning what had happened, there was a lot of sympathy for Kevin Dinsdale. And not just among the farming fraternity. Both Danny Bradley and Sergeant Clayton had been ashen-faced earlier that morning as they'd relayed to Samson and Delilah what Kevin had said in his first police interview the evening before. He'd admitted to it all. That he'd followed Irwin from the reception with the intention of just talking to him, seeing if the payment could be renegotiated, or even waived completely. He'd watched Irwin and Elaine from afar through the binoculars, and when Elaine shoved Irwin to the ground, he'd made his move, approaching the ecologist as he got to his feet. But Irwin had turned aggressive at Kevin's proposal, and told the wound-up farmer that far from eschewing the ten grand, the amount he expected had gone up to fifteen thousand.

Kevin had flipped. Swung at his tormentor with the binoculars and sent him sprawling. According to Danny, Kevin had clammed up at that point in the interview and, apart from confirming that it had been his vehicle which had driven past Samson and Herriot on his way back from Malham with the body, had provided only monosyllabic answers from there on. Like he felt the shame of what he'd done and simply wanted justice to be served, swiftly and efficiently.

'Have you ever worked a case like this before?' muttered Delilah as they weaved through the throng of farmers making their way to the auction ring for the imminent sale. 'One that's left such a bad taste in your mouth?'

Samson shook his head. 'One of the joys of being under-cover is that the folk I bring to court don't deserve sympathy. And there's something to be said for running investigations where you don't know anyone personally. Emotions don't get involved.'

Delilah gave a short laugh. 'No chance of that round here.'

Then she paused at the foot of the stairs leading up to the first-floor offices. 'Do you think we did the right thing?'

He placed a hand on her shoulder, seeing the uncertainty in her gaze, the guilt too. 'Will was about to be falsely charged with murder, remember?' he said softly. 'And while I would have preferred a different outcome, everything we did was for the right reasons.'

'I just wish . . . that it had been a stranger. Someone we didn't know who had a grudge against Irwin. That the mysterious 4x4 speeding through the town at night had remained that way . . .'

Samson went to reply and then paused. Head to one side. Feeling an echo of something Delilah had just said. What was it? Something which had jarred in connection to the Irwin case and sent a flicker of unease through him.

'Come on, then,' said Delilah, tapping the bag in her left hand. 'Best we hand this over before I succumb to temptation and eat it.'

Samson wasn't sure their gift would quite make up for the grilling they'd put Sarah Mitchell through earlier in the week. But they'd both agreed that a visit to the woman they'd falsely accused of being a killer – for what, to be fair, was the second time in less than twelve months – was needed, not least to set things right with Harry, too. And, to be honest, they were also here because there was a mound of paperwork waiting for them in the office which neither of them could face right now.

With heavy hearts, they started to climb the stairs, Samson brushing aside whatever it was which had set his senses tingling.

* * *

Danny Bradley was feeling honoured. Give DS Benson his due, there'd been no hubris when it came to him admitting the mistakes made in the Ross Irwin case and he'd been quick to set the gears in motion for the change of direction following Kevin Dinsdale's confession and arrest. He'd also invited Danny and Sergeant Clayton over to Harrogate to witness the interviews, saying it was the least he could do, considering how much they'd contributed to getting the right result.

'Contributed to saving his arse, more like,' the sergeant had muttered good-naturedly as they'd sat in the Harrogate Police Station canteen that morning and eaten cake decidedly inferior to their usual fare. 'See what you'd have to put up with lad, if you put in that transfer request you've been thinking about,' he'd continued, pushing the slice of lemon drizzle cake – which was more mist than drizzle – around his plate and demonstrating yet again that he knew his constable better than he let on.

For Danny, though, the sub-standard cake had been made up for by being able to witness the culmination of his hard work. Although it was painful to watch a friend and neighbour being on the other end of the quest for justice.

Kevin Dinsdale's first interview the evening before had been fairly straightforward, the farmer admitting to his deeds before he was even asked. But towards the end, when DS Benson had started to drill down into the details, the man across the desk from him had become less forthcoming, a gruffness to his answers which hadn't been there before. So much so, the detective had called it a day. Now the interview was about to resume and Danny was sitting in front of a monitor, watching on, Sergeant Clayton by his side.

'So I'd like to pick up from where we left off yesterday,

if you don't mind,' DS Benson was saying, his voice carrying through the speaker.

'Like Dinsdale's got a bloody choice,' muttered Sergeant Clayton.

'You've outlined for us what happened in the lead up to the confrontation with Irwin and that you struck him with your binoculars,' continued the detective. 'So let's start with how you moved his body.'

There was a long pause, Kevin Dinsdale sitting in a chair on the other side of the small table, a duty solicitor by his side. After a night in a cell the farmer should have been looking desolate, but if anything, he was looking determined. As though he was focused only on one thing: getting his misdeeds off his chest.

'I just lugged him into the back of the Shogun,' he said.

'Why? Why not leave him where he was?'

The farmer blinked. Shrugged. 'I didn't really take the time to think it through.'

'And the kiln? Why there?'

'Out of the way, I suppose.'

Benson looked at his notes and then up at the farmer. 'I'd like to run through the timings for the whole evening again, if that's okay?'

Dinsdale gave an exasperated sigh. 'Look, just type up what I've said, bring in a statement and I'll sign the bloody thing. Just quit with all the damn questions!'

The door opened and a constable arrived with a mug of tea, placing it down in front of Dinsdale, the interruption allowing the farmer to regain his equilibrium.

'Sorry,' he muttered across the table. 'Didn't mean to lose my temper. It's just . . . you know . . .'

Benson nodded. 'I realise this is difficult but we really do need to get it all down for the record so the sooner we get to it, the quicker it will be over.'

'Right. Fire away then.'

'Walk me through what happened after you realised Irwin was dead.'

'I drove straight back to the reception—'

'What made you do that?'

'It's not as though I was thinking rationally! I'd just accidently killed a man, for Christ's sake!' Dinsdale reached for the mug of tea, took a long swig and put it down. He ran a hand over his face and gave a resigned shake of his head. 'I went back into the rugby club and pretended to get steaming drunk. Let Lou drive me home. And then when she'd gone to sleep, I crept out and drove back to Malham—'

'Why?' asked Benson. 'Why not leave the body where it was?'

'I dunno. I thought it would help cover my tracks.' He gave a wry laugh, lifting both hands as though he had just explained how to do something mundane, rather than describing the actions of a killer. 'That didn't work out too well.'

Sergeant Clayton shot Danny a glance. 'This has got to be the strangest confession I've ever heard,' he muttered.

Danny nodded, something not sitting right with him. He watched Dinsdale take another drink and had a flash of comprehension, there and gone like a trout in deep water, leaving only ripples of frustration on the surface.

'Right,' said Benson. 'Thanks. That's helped clarify things. So all we need to do now is get the statement typed up and then we'll be onto the next stage of the process.'

He went to stand and Dinsdale reached out towards him.

'How long?' he asked, voice breaking, his composure cracking for the first time. 'The sentence, how long is it likely to be?'

DS Benson shook his head, compassion on his face. 'Not for me to say. But you're looking at manslaughter rather than murder so it will be a lesser term.'

Dinsdale's shoulders slumped, he ran a hand over his face and gave a grim nod. 'Thanks.'

'Christ,' grunted Sergeant Clayton, tearing his gaze away from the monitor and picking up his coffee, 'that was a hard watch. In all my years as a copper, I don't think I've ever felt as sorry for someone on the wrong side of the law.'

Danny nodded, eyes still on the screen. Brain still working furiously for that something just out of reach. And then Dinsdale stretched for his mug of tea again and Danny shot to his feet, making Sergeant Clayton spill coffee everywhere.

'What on God's earth has got into you, lad?' the sergeant grumbled crossly, dabbing at his stained shirt with a tissue. When he looked up and saw the pale features of his constable, staring at the monitor, he fell silent.

'We've made a huge mistake!' Danny exclaimed, eyes glued to the screen. 'Sarge, we've got it all wrong!'

When Samson and Delilah reached Harry's office, the door was open and Sarah Mitchell was sitting behind his desk, working away on her laptop.

'Congratulations are in order, so I hear,' said Delilah as they entered the room.

345

Sarah glanced up, a surprised smile on her face at seeing them approach. 'Did Harry tell you I got the contract?'

Delilah nodded. 'It's great news, in a week where there's been precious little to enjoy.'

The compliment was met with typical self-effacement, and an apologetic grimace. 'To be honest, with Irwin out of the picture, the company we were both pitching to didn't really have anywhere else to go. I think I might have been the best of a bad bunch.'

'Don't sell yourself short,' said Samson, taking a seat opposite her. 'You won fair and square. And here's to many more successes in the future.'

'Thanks.' Sarah's smile grew wider and then morphed into a cheeky grin, a dimple appearing in her cheek. 'If it's Harry you're here to see, however, he's down in the ring fleecing farmers by selling them fleeces. Or are you back to interrogate me again?'

'Actually, it is you we're here to see.' Delilah sat next to Samson and placed the bag on the desk by Sarah's laptop. 'This is a small token by way of apology for giving you such a grilling.'

Sarah shook her head, waving away their mea culpas. 'There's really no need,' she said.

'You might want to see what it is first, before you say that,' suggested Samson with a wink.

There was a rustle of paper and then Sarah let out a sigh of appreciation.

'Oh, he's lovely,' she said, pulling out a box containing an otter, made of chocolate. 'But I don't think I'd ever be able to eat him!'

'I don't think Harry will share your qualms,' said Delilah.

Sarah laughed. Then shook her head again. 'Really though, I didn't take offence. You were only doing your job and from what I hear, you did it better than the police.'

'Can't say we took any satisfaction from it,' said Samson. 'While we cleared Will, seeing Kevin Dinsdale in such trouble is not easy to take.'

'It is all a bit grim. And all because of one man's corruption.' The dimple on Sarah's cheek had disappeared like the sun behind a cloud as her expression became grave. 'Harry's really struggling to take it all in. Him and Kevin were good mates. And as for Louise, I've no idea how she's going to cope. No matter how you look at it, it's a horrible mess.'

'I can't help thinking,' said Delilah, 'that if only Kevin hadn't followed Irwin and Elaine. Or if only he'd left the binoculars in the car. Anything which could have averted this. I mean, saving a farm on the brink of bankruptcy isn't worth losing your life over, for Irwin or for Kevin.'

Sarah nodded. 'I know. Timing is everything.'

'Timing . . .' Samson muttered to himself, staring at the floor. An alertness coming over him Delilah recognised.

'Of course,' continued Sarah, oblivious to the change in her guest's demeanour, 'the irony is, they weren't even Kevin's binoculars.'

Samson's attention snapped up onto Sarah. 'Whose were they?'

'Louise's. Her grandmother bought them for her when she was eighteen. They were her pride and joy.'

'And the birds on the windowsill?'

'Louise's. She's the twitcher in that house. Always was. I remember her getting the first one when she was at uni – the robin, I think it was. She's been collecting them ever since – less so recently as things got a bit harder financially.'

Samson had gone still next to Delilah, a throb of energy coming from him. She glanced at him. 'What is it?'

'I don't know, just . . . a sense of something not being right. I had it when we were walking up here and now again . . .' He shrugged, getting to his feet and pacing over to the window, Sarah's focus flicking between the two of them, as though she too was now picking up on the vibes.

'Was it something I said?' she asked.

'The timing. It doesn't add up.' Samson turned, a deep frown on his forehead. 'You were at uni with Louise?'

'Only for the first year.' There was something in the way Sarah said it. A sadness to the words.

'What happened?' asked Delilah.

Sarah opened her mouth. Closed it. Looked at the pair of them. 'I don't know the full story. I just know something happened. Something bad enough to make her leave.'

'She's never talked about it?'

'Not really. At the time she claimed it was boyfriend trouble but looking back, I think there was more to it. Something which changed her overnight. She went from being outgoing and cheerful, to being a recluse – by the time she left, she barely went out of her rooms. I suppose I should have pressed her a bit more to open up but I was eighteen and not exactly an extrovert myself and, well . . . I didn't. And now it seems too late to be digging up the past.'

'What did Louise study in that year?' asked Samson, a weight to his words.

'Not ecology, if that's what you were thinking,' said Sarah, showing a perspicacity which didn't surprise Delilah.

'She was doing accountancy. I only knew her because we were next door to each other in halls.'

'So she didn't know Ross Irwin?'

A silence greeted the enquiry. As though it had unleashed a dark mass of trouble which was supposed to have been banished. When Sarah spoke, it was in a measured tone.

'I'm not sure why you're asking all this, seeing as Kevin has been arrested and the case is supposedly solved, but I respect how your mind works when it comes to investigations. So all I can say is that to my knowledge, Louise never had any dealings with Ross Irwin and certainly didn't know him as a tutor. And if she did have previous dealings with him, she didn't reveal the fact when he showed up here to carry out the assessment on her land. To all appearances, she'd never met him before.'

Delilah watched the way Samson absorbed the information, seeing that frown deepen, the cogs turning. She turned to Sarah.

'How about apart from her course?' she asked 'Was Louise in any clubs or societies?'

'Just the Birdwatching Society—'

'Oh God!' Delilah had her phone out, scrolling rapidly through the documents from Irwin's computer. 'The photo...'

She found it. That group of students, a much younger Ross Irwin in the middle, most wearing binoculars, all looking happy. She held it out towards Sarah.

The reaction was immediate. A widening of the eyes, an index finger extended, pointing, shaking as it touched the screen on the face of a young woman, university hoodie on, her features partly shielded by the man in front but her smile visible.

'That's her,' said Sarah, hand now going to her mouth. 'That's Louise. I had no idea . . .'

'Christ!' Samson ran a hand through his hair, expression grim. 'How the hell did we miss this? Louise Dinsdale knew Ross Irwin from a decade ago and never said a word about it. Now why would that be?'

'But it doesn't prove anything,' said Delilah, despite the feeling of certainty in the pit of her stomach. 'It could just be a coincidence.'

'Or it could be the key to bloody everything.'

'How sure are you about this, son?' Sergeant Clayton demanded, a restraining arm holding back his constable who was trying to get to the door. 'Because if you're going to march in there claiming a detective sergeant has a case all back-to-front and upside down, then you really need to make sure you're right.'

'I'm certain,' said Danny. Because he was. He could feel it burning in him, the knowledge that Kevin Dinsdale wasn't a killer. That the case wasn't solved.

'And you're basing this on what exactly?'

'The forensics report.'

'The same report which I'm damn sure Benson has read cover to cover?' The sergeant wasn't hesitating to let his scepticism show. 'What makes you so convinced you've seen something he hasn't?'

'Dinsdale drank his tea with his right hand!' Danny said. Desperate now. Wanting to get to the interview room so he could stop what was a travesty of justice.

'Jesus wept,' muttered the sergeant. 'You're going to risk your career over a bloody cuppa?'

'Yes.' Danny stared at him. 'You don't have to come with me.'

'Sod that,' said Sergeant Clayton, a grin forming. 'If you blow this then you'll be stuck in Bruncliffe with me for the rest of your time on the force. So seeing as it's in my best interest that you screw up, I'm coming in to witness it.' Then he winked. 'Besides, you're better off back home with me. As I said earlier, the cake round here is crap.'

And with that he led his constable out into the corridor and towards the interview room.

30

Samson and Delilah arrived back with an urgency which brought everyone in the building hurrying into Delilah's office. Everyone being the entire Dales Detective team, who were all supposed to be on a day off.

'What is it?' demanded Ida, hastening from the kitchen, wet mop in hand. 'Tha's like a couple of scalded cats!'

'The Irwin case,' said Samson, 'we've made a mistake.'

'What kind of mistake?' asked Nathan, his long legs propelling him up the stairs faster than Nina, who lagged a few steps behind.

'We don't believe Kevin Dinsdale is the real killer.'

'Bugger me!' Gareth was coming down from the top floor, Bounty on his heels. 'That's a mistake all right!'

'But we saw his car had been moved on the video and everything,' protested Nina. 'And he admitted to it.'

Samson nodded. 'Yes, and we all fell for it. But things don't add up.'

'Like what?' asked Nathan.

'The way Kevin described Irwin when we went to confront him, for starters. He was mild as milk until it came to Irwin himself and then he exploded. Said Irwin had got what he deserved—'

'Happen he thought he had,' said Ida.

Samson shook his head. 'It's more than that. I didn't think anything of it at the time but today, that phrase – "got what he deserved" – it kept niggling at me. And then Delilah said something about grudges earlier and I realised Kevin had said the same thing about Irwin as some lass said on the Kendal Chat page when Irwin's death was announced. Someone who sounded like she'd met the same predatory Irwin that Elaine had the misfortune to encounter above Malham Cove.'

The others shared confused looks. Apart from Delilah, who was nodding. 'Someone who had real reason to be angry,' she said, 'whereas what did Kevin have to be so angry about when it came to Irwin?'

'Exactly!' said Samson. 'It can't have been the fact that Irwin was corrupt – that's precisely why he hired him in the first place. And then there are the timings. Danny told us that Kevin confessed to driving the 4x4 which went past myself and Herriot on Saturday night. Only problem is, he's also claimed he was on his way back from retrieving Irwin's body in Malham at the time.'

'So? Isn't that what we thought had happened?' asked Ida. 'That the killer left the reception a second time to go and get the body?'

'Indeed. Trouble is, we have footage of Kevin leaving the rugby club with his wife and Ali Metcalfe around half past eleven. Ali reckons she was dropped off on Ellershaw track about twenty minutes later, so –'

'Kevin couldn't have got to Malham and back in time to drive past thee at midnight.' Ida was nodding. 'So one way or another, he's lying.'

'All good and well,' said Gareth, stroking his beard. 'But if that's right, why the heck would Kevin fess up to a crime he didn't commit?'

'Why would anyone?' Samson asked softly.

'For love,' said Nathan.

Samson nodded. 'We think Kevin knows it was his wife, Louise, who killed Ross Irwin.'

There was silence, stunned and disbelieving, until finally Gareth spoke.

'Not Louise,' he said, shaking his head. 'You can't be thinking Louise did away with Irwin? Kevin, I could just about accept, but Louise . . . there's no way. She wouldn't hurt a fly!'

'We wouldn't be saying it lightly,' said Samson. 'Which is why we're here. We need to find proof before we go making accusations.'

'But surely if you've ruled out Kevin because of the timing, then the same applies to Louise?' asked Nathan. 'How could she possibly have got over to Malham and back after she dropped Ali off?'

'Because we've been making an assumption, which any detective worth their salt should know is a sure-fire way to come a cropper. We assumed the murderer was coming from Malham Cove when they drove past me, which meant they'd gone back to get the body. We didn't consider that they might have been coming from a different destination on that road, like the Dinsdale farm. I think Louise simply turned the car around after she dropped Kevin off and then headed straight for the kiln.'

'So if she didn't go back to Malham, what about the body—?' Gareth broke off and went pale as he followed the logical progression of his question.

Samson gave a grim nod. 'Louise had no need to go back to Malham because Irwin was already in the boot.'

'You mean she was cold-blooded enough to return to the reception with him in there?' asked Nathan incredulously, while Nina blanched.

'Yes. Like the rest of us, however, Kevin presumed Irwin's killer made two trips out to Malham. And in doing so, he revealed himself to be innocent.'

'But what's tha reasoning?' muttered Ida, looking sceptical. 'Why would the lass have done such a thing? To save the farm?'

Delilah grimaced. 'We've reason to believe she knew Ross Irwin from years ago—'

'But that can't be true,' said Nina, shaking her head. 'Kevin and Louise were in our restaurant on the Friday evening, the same time Irwin was in there, and she didn't speak to him all night.'

'How did she seem?'

'A bit grumpy, if truth be told. Definitely tense about something. But then I wasn't paying much attention as Irwin . . .' Nina blushed. Shuddered. 'Irwin was being super attentive to me, which I thought was nice at the time. Now that I know what he did to Elaine, it gives me the creeps.'

'Attentive how, exactly?'

'Making compliments, suggesting I go to him for help when it comes to applications for uni, things like that.'

Samson and Delilah shared a glance.

'And Louise could hear all this?' asked Samson.

Nina nodded. 'The Dinsdales were on the next table.'

'Christ. If we're right about what we think happened in the past . . .' Samson was looking at Delilah now.

'Then Louise was hiding the fact she knew Irwin while having to listen to him probably trying the same thing on with a teenager a decade later.'

'Not to mention watching him leave the reception with Elaine the next day.'

'Tha thinks Irwin abused Louise in some way?' murmured Ida, catching on faster than the others, who were looking puzzled by the exchange.

'It's highly possible,' said Samson. 'We've just discovered that she knew him when she was a fresher at university. And that she left after some unspecified incident which Sarah Mitchell seems to think might have been an assault, or worse.'

Silence greeted the statement, all of them putting the dreadful pieces together.

'Oh no,' groaned Ida. 'The poor lass . . .'

Delilah nodded. 'And then Irwin shows up here, demanding money from her husband, and she's catapulted back into the trauma. God knows what she must have been going through. Or how it manifested itself.'

'And we're going to provide evidence to arrest her?' Nina's honest question brought the room to silence.

'It's what we do,' said Samson gently. 'Even when it doesn't seem fair. Because if we don't bring the truth to light, someone else will suffer.'

Nina stared at the floor, biting her lip, then nodded and reached for her laptop. 'Right. So what can we do to help?'

DS Benson didn't know what was going on when the door to the interview room flung open and Sergeant Clayton strode in, brandishing a sheaf of papers, his constable right behind him, face flushed.

Date with Justice

'We need a signature,' the sergeant declared, not even giving the detective time to stop the interview tape as he thrust the papers and a pen on the desk in front of Kevin Dinsdale.

A bemused Kevin Dinsdale, who was looking from Benson to the sergeant and back again, even as he reached for the pen, doing as he was told.

'What the—?' Benson started to rise, but a solid palm was thrust on his shoulder, the sergeant pushing him back down into his seat.

'This won't take a moment, DS Benson, and then we'll be out of your hair,' he said. But his focus wasn't on the detective. It was fixed firmly on the accused man, who was signing his name, in triplicate, in the spaces marked by post-it notes.

'You're right-handed,' Constable Bradley finally spoke, a tremor of excitement in his words.

And DS Benson felt a swell of panic mixed with terror, a sensation he'd felt once before when he realised he'd been complicit in apprehending Samson O'Brien on false charges. A sensation many others in officialdom had experienced when having dealings with the folk of Bruncliffe. For there was something about the question. Something about right-handedness. He had a flashback to the forensic report which he'd had no time to read in depth. But in that brief perusal before the shout went up that a suspect had confessed, there had been something . . .

Unable to call it to mind, DS Benson watched on help-lessly as Kevin Dinsdale nodded.

'Yeah, I am. What of it?'

Sergeant Clayton leaned onto the desk. 'You can stop the act, Kevin. We know it wasn't you.'

'I don't know what you mean—'

'Ross Irwin's killer was left-handed.' Danny Bradley's voice brought silence to the room. Swiftly followed by pandemonium.

The duty solicitor started kicking off, Benson got to his feet and began demanding answers from the Bruncliffe coppers, Sergeant Clayton was arguing back, something about city-based incompetence and rubbish cake, and Danny Bradley was trying to make the peace between the two. All the while, Kevin Dinsdale kept protesting his guilt.

But it was a guilt no one in the room believed in any longer.

Herriot had died and gone to heaven. So what if the weather wasn't exactly picnic-perfect? So what if he had a bit of business to conduct on the way? Lucy Metcalfe was sitting beside him in his van, there was a hamper in the back which smelled a lot better than most of the occupants he normally had in the rear, and Lucy had just told him that she'd cleared the whole afternoon so if he had time, she was free to spend it with him.

They'd opted to go to Skelbeck Foss at the far end of Bruncliffe, a spectacular waterfall which cascaded over a series of limestone ledges and was surrounded by gorgeous scenery. It was the perfect place to sit and while away an hour or two, even on a cloudy day. And it didn't have the negative connotations of the much more rugged and dramatic Thursgill Force, just up the hill behind Lucy's converted barn, a place which had featured so violently in events back in November. Events which had nearly taken

Lucy from them all and which had made Herriot realise just how much she meant to him.

Eight months on, he was finally doing something about those feelings. He'd never been called a quick mover but right now he didn't care if he was mocked for his dallying when it came to romance. He was on his first date with Lucy, and hopefully it would be the first of many.

Before that, though, he had something to do.

'So you're sure you don't mind if we drop in at the Dinsdales' place on our way past?' he asked again as he drove down Hillside Lane from Lucy's towards town. 'It's just I promised Kevin I'd have a look at that tup of his and the last thing Louise needs is the worry of a sick animal on top of everything else.'

Lucy nodded. 'I think it would be a very caring thing to do. Poor Louise must be going out of her mind with stress.'

'To say the least,' murmured Herriot, indicating for the turn to the Dinsdale farm.

They pulled up in the farmyard, and got out into a silence that felt devoid of life.

They started with the wedding videos. The entire team on either laptops, computers or mobiles, combing through footage to find something to prove Louise Dinsdale had been absent long enough from the reception to commit the crime they were about to accuse her of. It took them less than half an hour to find what they were looking for.

'I think I've got it!' Delilah announced, turning her screen around so everyone could see, Nathan and Nina on the couch, Samson next to her and Ida and Gareth on the other side of the desk.

They were looking at a frozen shot of the reception, taken about eleven thirty. The camera was focused on a group of lads from the rugby club, larking around on the dance floor, but in the background were two women, Louise Dinsdale and Sarah. Propped between them was Kevin as they helped him out of the room. The faces of the women were hidden from view but Delilah wasn't bothered about their expressions. Her finger was pointing at Louise's feet.

'Her shoes!' she declared.

'Oh my God,' muttered Nina, staring at the light-blue slingbacks peeking out beneath the flares of Louise's elegant green velvet trouser suit. 'How did I not see that?'

Samson looked at the pair of them and then at Nathan. 'What am I missing?'

His nephew shrugged. 'Search me.'

Ida too was looking perplexed. But Gareth was nodding.

'They're a different colour. In fact, a completely different style,' said the gamekeeper.

Samson looked again while Nina was frantically scrolling through footage.

'Here, see!' she said, twisting her laptop so it was next to Delilah's screen. 'This is from earlier on in the evening.'

She clicked play and there was Louise, sitting with one leg crossed over the other, displaying a pair of dark green satin shoes with a buckle strap and a block heel which perfectly matched her outfit. Samson looked at Delilah's footage and sure enough, those shoes had become blue slingbacks.

'Is this enough?' he asked. 'That she changed her shoes? Maybe her feet got tired?'

Delilah was shaking her head. 'Louise is super stylish.

Even if her feet were killing her, she wouldn't have put on a pair of blue shoes with green trousers.'

'Not unless she had no other choice,' said Nina.

'Seriously?' Samson looked at Nina and Delilah. 'You're willing to accuse a woman of murder simply because her shoes don't match her outfit?'

Delilah shrugged. 'We've got to start somewhere.'

'How about,' said Ida, arms folded across her chest, 'tha starts with the horse's mouth? Head up to the Dinsdales' and just ask her. Happen as if tha's right about Irwin and what he did, that lass has been to hell and back, and even more so since yesterday with Kevin taking the hit for her. She might appreciate a bit of straight talking.'

'Sounds like sensible advice,' said Gareth.

Delilah was already reaching for the keys to the Mini.

'Hello?' Herriot called out as he walked with Lucy towards the Dinsdales' farmhouse.

The curtains were closed on the front rooms, upstairs and down, and as they walked around to the side, the porch door had been left wide open, swinging gently on the breeze which was gusting up the dale.

Something wasn't right.

A sound from one of the barns at the back made them both turn. Another sound. Something almost feral.

'Louise?' called Herriot, changing direction now and heading around the rear of the house, Lucy behind him. Into another yard, two barns built off it. In the closest one a tractor had been left dismantled, bits strewn all over the ground. Bits which had been there a while judging by the wisps of straw covering some of them.

Herriot started walking towards it but a sharp keen of grief sliced the silence and made him pause. For this wasn't a good noise. It was a noise which made his spine rigid with fear.

'The other barn,' said Lucy, hurrying across the yard to the furthest one, face concerned.

'Wait for me,' he said, turning after her, a sixth sense he didn't even know he had screaming at him. Telling him there was danger. But Lucy had already reached the huge doors and entered the dark interior.

'Lucy! Wait!'

The blast of the shotgun cut through the morning air and sent a cluster of pheasants in the field beyond clattering and squawking into the sky.

31

For the second time in twenty-four hours, Delilah tore up Hillside Lane in the Mini, taking corners with the skill of a rally driver. And for the second time in twenty-four hours, Samson was an uncomplaining passenger. He'd just got off the phone from Danny and was digesting the news.

'They're about to release Kevin Dinsdale,' he said to Delilah. 'No charges brought.'

She glanced at him. 'How did they realise? The timings?'

Samson shook his head. 'He's right-handed. Danny spotted it. Apparently the full forensics report which came in yesterday afternoon makes mention that the wound to Irwin's right side – the one which caused him to fall and led to his death – was most likely made by a left-handed person.'

Delilah whistled. 'Benson missed that?'

'Seems so. But sharp-eyed Constable Bradley didn't. I told them where we've got to and our suspicions, and it seems they'd come to a similar conclusion but with less proof, so Sergeant Clayton, Danny and Benson are already on their way over here from Harrogate. They're about half an hour away.'

'I suppose that means we'll just have to deal with whatever we find ourselves until they get here,' said Delilah.

Samson nodded. 'Of course, there might be nothing to deal with at all. This could be a wild goose chase—'

A shotgun blast from up ahead carried through the open windows, a bevy of panicked pheasants flapping up into the air and crossing the road.

Delilah took the turn onto the Dinsdales' track at a speed which reflected her alarm. As she pulled into the yard, they saw Herriot's van already parked up.

'Lucy!' Herriot said as he raced into the gloom of the large barn, meagre light filtering down through the odd corroded hole in the corrugated roof above.

He blinked, eyes adjusting to the rapid change. Ahead of him he saw her, Lucy, standing stock still, hands lifted in a gesture of helplessness as she stared at something ahead of her.

'Thank goodness,' he said, hurrying to her. 'You're not hurt!'

'Stop where you are!' The voice came from behind a tower of hay bales. Female. Shaking. Louise Dinsdale stepped out into full view, a shotgun in her hands trained on Lucy. That was shaking too.

'Louise!' Herriot automatically started moving forward, a couple of long strides, the gun swinging his way.

'I said stop!' she shouted. Her eyes were wild, something in her demeanour suggesting she'd gone over the edge of sanity.

Herriot was alongside Lucy now. Inching his body forward, attempting to shield her.

'Louise,' he said again, voice low, calm. Trying to subdue the fear screaming through his veins, not for himself but for the woman he'd brought into this dangerous situation. 'It's me. Herriot. I called in about the tup.'

Louise nodded. Bit her lip. 'I can't let you see him just now.'

'That's fine,' said Herriot. Keeping his tone soft, making no sudden movements. Going into the mode he used with irate livestock. Only difference was, spooked cattle didn't carry guns. 'But what about you? How are you doing?'

The gun quivered, barrels pointing to the floor as Louise looked at him. Tears in her eyes.

'None of this was meant to happen,' she said.

'I know,' Herriot lied, not having a clue what was going on. He took a step forward, Lucy completely behind him now. 'I know, Louise. We all know.'

'He was a devil. He ruined my life. I couldn't see him do it to someone else . . . Elaine and Nina – he was grooming them. Like he did me—' She choked to a halt. Wiped her sleeve over her eyes, the shotgun dropping even further.

'You don't need to explain,' said Herriot. Stretching a hand out slowly, making it clear it was in comfort not in threat.

'But I didn't mean to kill him.' A raw sob broke from her. 'I just wanted to warn him I wouldn't let him get away with it again. But he went for me, just like last time, and I was so scared, I hit him with the binoculars.' Tears were flowing now, down both cheeks, her body shaking. 'I knew straight away he was dead and then . . . and then . . . I couldn't think straight. And now . . . Kevin's confessed and it's all my fault. So I came out here . . .'

Her glance fell to the gun. She stared at it as if seeing it afresh. As if remembering what had brought her out into the barn in the first place. She began to raise it, barrels towards herself. Her intention clear.

'No, Louise!' said Herriot, moving forward at a pace, grabbing for the gun. His hands on the metal. Someone behind him. Lucy. Grabbing Louise. And then an almighty roar, in his ears, thumping through his lungs, the breath knocked from him. He collapsed to the floor, stunned, not sure if the screams were his own or someone else's.

The second shot had them running. Across the front yard, down the side of the house, towards the barns.

'Which one?' shouted Samson as Delilah streaked ahead.

She pointed to the barn on the left and ran towards it. Towards the sound of screams. A woman. Other voices.

Samson followed, breath coming in fearful snatches. Into the dark of the big structure where three figures were on the ground, one cradling another, the third lying dazed.

'Lucy!' shouted Delilah, already there, already bending down to the two women. Louise Dinsdale in Lucy's arms, her screams fading to cries as Lucy held her and stroked her hair. 'Anyone hurt?'

'I think we're all okay,' murmured Herriot, still prone, shaking his head, his eyes not quite focused.

'What happened?' Samson was by them, crouching down, giving Herriot his hand and helping the vet sit up.

Herriot shook his head again. Took a deep breath. 'Louise was cleaning the shotgun and it went off,' he said, his eyes locking on Lucy's.

Lucy nodded. 'It was a total accident. Poor Louise.'

Date with Justice

While Louise Dinsdale just cried, the sound of bitter heartbreak and injustice one which would stay with Samson for ever.

32

The Dinsdale case cast a pall over Bruncliffe like no other. The lack of justice in the arrest of a young woman who had only sought to protect others. Whose only crime had been trying to prevent a man from inflicting the horrific abuse she had suffered on yet more women. And while there was some comfort in knowing Louise Dinsdale was going to be facing the lesser charge of involuntary manslaughter, it was scant consolation for the community. Or for her husband, whose attempt to spare her a punishment he felt she didn't deserve had failed. Kevin had returned to the farm and promptly put it up for sale, riven with guilt that his efforts to save it had wrecked the sanctuary Louise had managed to create for herself.

For Kevin had been oblivious to Ross Irwin's connection to his wife. While he'd known the reasons for her abrupt termination of her university studies, Louise had never named the man who had attacked her, wanting to leave it all in the past. Respecting her privacy, Kevin had never pressed for details. So when he'd had a recommendation from another farmer for an ecologist willing to provide the right survey results at a cost, Kevin had only seen a way to preserve their livelihood in a place they adored. Even if the means of preserving it were somewhat illicit.

He'd contacted Ross Irwin and thought nothing more of it. Not even when the charming, well-presented man turned up at the house. If he'd sensed that Louise was a bit quiet, Kevin had put it down to the fact that she wasn't convinced cheating the system was the way to go about securing the planning permission for the camping pods. And if she excused herself from every other meeting with the man, her husband had seen nothing in her behaviour to raise concern. As for when Irwin was killed, even though he hadn't wanted to believe it, like many in the town Kevin thought Will Metcalfe had lost his temper with fatal consequences.

But there had been little clues. The smell in the Shogun the morning after the reception. Hungover and of weak constitution, Kevin had gagged as he opened the car to head up onto the fells with the vet. A rank odour of dead sheep had assailed him so badly, he'd handed the keys to Herriot and asked him to drive.

Then there was the matter of his spare work boots and overalls – the set he left in the back of the Shogun for emergencies. They'd not been there. When he'd raised the matter over breakfast the Monday following Irwin's murder, Louise had claimed to have no knowledge of where they'd got to. Yet he'd found them out in one of the barns, the overalls balled up around the boots and stuffed in behind the seat of the John Deere he'd been in the process of fixing before the money had run out. What had been most perplexing was the blood covering them. And the pair of green satin shoes stuffed in there with them, also stained with crimson blotches. The shoes he'd last seen on Louise's feet at Harry and Sarah's wedding reception – an event his wife had been missing from for a substantial amount of time. Because Kevin had noticed her absence from the rugby club, despite his inebriated state. He'd even gone outside several times looking for her. But he'd seen no cause to doubt her assertion that she'd returned to the farm to check on their ailing tup, until he was faced with that ruined pair of shoes.

It had been enough to set him thinking. That and Louise's precious Zeiss binoculars going missing too. Although their absence from the windowsill had been explained away as an accident. She'd insisted on replacing them, albeit with a much inferior set, but that had been an alarm bell in itself because Louise had become incredibly frugal since times had turned hard, and while Kevin wouldn't have begrudged her anything, it had been a surprise that she'd spent money that way. The irony, of course, was that if the bloody things had been on the windowsill where they were supposed to be in the first place, Irwin might still be alive and perhaps he would have been the one facing prosecution. But Kevin had borrowed the binoculars while out rounding up sheep, using them to scan the fells for any errant ewes. As usual, he'd forgotten to put them back, leaving them on the dashboard of the car and thereby handing his wife the weapon which would be both her salvation and her undoing.

So while Kevin was no Samson O'Brien when it came to detective work, he'd managed to put two and two together. To notice his wife's withdrawal since Harry's wedding. Her nervousness, the way she jumped at the slightest sound. Not that he'd been Mr Calm himself. When Samson and Delilah had rocked up the morning Will was arrested, their questions had unnerved him, given what he'd been involved in with Irwin. It didn't need a genius to work out that ten grand in a backhander wouldn't be viewed in a good light by the authorities he was seeking planning permission from, let alone by the police investigating Irwin's death. He'd been sweating buckets, thinking his scam would be uncovered, unaware of the bigger threat looming which would tear his world apart.

The final pieces of the puzzle had fallen into place when Samson and Delilah had called in the second time. The way O'Brien had looked at the new binoculars and then asked about the old pair, Kevin had known right then that his suspicions were right. Louise had killed Irwin. He'd also known that Bruncliffe's bloodhound was hot on a scent and needed luring away. Taking the fall for Louise hadn't been planned. The idea had been handed to him on a plate, and with the finger of blame already pointing his way, all Kevin had to do was accept it.

Except for the fact he wasn't left-handed. Why hadn't he seen that? The difference between himself and Louise, that tiny technicality which ruled out his confession and ended any chance he had of saving her from the judgement society would demand.

But if Kevin was riven with guilt about introducing Ross Irwin back into his wife's life and the repercussions that caused, Louise was far more resolute. Delilah had been to see her at the farm – the criminal lawyer Matty Thistlethwaite had organised for Louise having secured bail, arguing that his client wasn't a flight risk given her circumstances – and had come away impressed at the woman's fortitude. The distress Delilah had witnessed that dreadful day in the barn had been replaced with a determination not to let Irwin have any more impact on her life. Or on her family. She'd received lots of support both from the townsfolk and from women's groups around the country as her case made the news, and was hopeful that, with the argument of self-defence, she would get a lenient sentence, if not a suspended one.

'I never set out to hurt Irwin,' she'd explained to Delilah as they sat in the kitchen a few days before the farm sale, Kevin working out in the yard with Will, preparing everything for the auction. 'I'd noticed him with Nina in the restaurant and then with Elaine at the reception, and I recognised his behaviour. The same kind of harmless flirting he'd done with me only . . . I knew what lay beneath that suave exterior. What that flirting could lead to.' She paused, Delilah reaching out to squeeze her hand. Louise shook her head, expression pained. 'I just couldn't take it any more. I mean, how could I stand by and allow him to get away with hurting another young woman when I have a daughter of my own? What kind of example would I be setting to Ava?' She shrugged. 'When I saw him leaving the rugby club with Elaine in his car, I followed them on impulse.'

'You suspected Irwin might try something on with her?'

'Yes.' The single word was terrifying in its certainty. 'I'd overheard them discussing going to Malham Cove so I took a guess that's where they'd gone. When I got to the car park at the tarn, the Land Cruiser was already there.

I changed into Kevin's boots and grabbed the binoculars, thinking I'd be able to keep an eye on Irwin from a distance, then I made my way down the bridleway. Just in time as it turned out.'

'So you saw what happened with Elaine?'

Louise gave a grim nod. 'It was like watching a replay of my past. One minute they were talking, then he lunged for her. Fair play to Elaine, though, she kneed him and sent him sprawling. When she grabbed his keys and took off, I was so furious – with myself in some ways for never standing up to him. For not making an official complaint when it happened. It was like I was nineteen all over again, but this time I wasn't afraid. So I went marching down towards him. He was getting to his feet, looking more livid than hurt. I think he knew from my face that I'd witnessed what he'd done. He started trying to laugh it off. But I didn't give him a chance, just told him straight up that I was going to the police about what he did to me back in Leeds.'

She took a deep breath, reaching for the mug of coffee in front of her, her hands shaking as she continued.

'He went for me. Shouting about how he'd see to it that I didn't tell anyone. About how he'd make sure his report would bankrupt us if I did. He had a hold of my neck, I could feel his fingers pressing on my windpipe, and I just panicked. I hit him with the binoculars. He fell again. But this time he didn't move. And that's when I saw the blood.'

There was a long silence before Louise told the rest of the story. About her decision to move the body, concerned that Elaine Bullock would get the blame if she didn't. About the overalls used to cover her wedding outfit.

About how the shoes she'd left in the boot got stained and necessitated a quick visit to the farmhouse for a replacement pair, not thinking that would be her downfall. And then the return to the reception, Irwin's corpse out in the car the entire time.

'I'm sorry for all of that,' Louise said to Delilah. 'I'm sorry for the pain it put other people through – Elaine, Sarah and most of all your brother. Will and Ali have always been fantastic neighbours. Even now, after everything . . .' She glanced out of the window to where Will was helping Kevin stack a load of sheep hurdles in a trailer. She smiled. 'He bought that bit of land, you know, Will did.'

Delilah nodded, aware that the controversial site for the camping pod was now part of the Metcalfe farm.

'What folk don't know,' continued Louise, 'is he insisted on paying Kevin over the odds for it. Despite all the trouble I caused—'

Her voice caught. Tears threatening.

'It was Irwin who caused the trouble,' muttered Delilah. 'Him and him alone. You shouldn't be feeling any guilt.'

'Aye, but I should have just admitted what had happened and taken the consequences. But as for Irwin being dead, I don't feel the slightest remorse.' A wry grin appeared on Louise's pale face. 'Although that hotshot lawyer Matty has conjured up for me says I shouldn't admit to that in court.'

When Delilah left her that morning, Louise Dinsdale was standing in the doorway of the home she was about to lose, a proud smile on her face as she watched her daughter doing her six-year-old best to help the men working in the yard.

Date with Justice

The farm auction a few days later saw a record turnout despite the short notice, Harry on his podium, bringing the contents of the Dinsdales' farming life under the hammer. Tractors, trailers, livestock, the house itself. And the farming community of Bruncliffe made sure that everything went for a decent price, deliberately bidding up items, not allowing offcumdens to get bargains and seeing to it that Kevin and Louise secured enough to start a new life. Even Samson, up from London for the day, got carried away by the occasion, ending up with a quad bike he had absolutely no need for rather than allow a farmer from a different dale to get it too cheaply.

The support from the community went even further. A property in town was made available to the family at an extremely reasonable rent and Kevin was approached by Ash Metcalfe, who far from being scarce of work, was now inundated. With two more commercial premises to fit out and a couple of kitchens already booked in, Ash was glad to have a man of Kevin's woodworking talents alongside him. Louise had also found work, Nancy Taylor having retained her as an accountant for the new business, promising there would be a position waiting for her, no matter the outcome of the court case. As Troy Murgatroyd, the curmudgeonly landlord of the Fleece, declared while walking away from what had been the Dinsdale farm with several bird boxes under his arm – which he'd been seen to pay a very high price for – it was Bruncliffe at its finest.

33

A mere ten days on from the Dinsdale auction, Samson found himself in Bruncliffe once more. Having returned to London almost immediately after the Irwin murder enquiry was concluded, his week-long break to recharge his batteries at an end, he'd been thrown straight into work. But all the while, he'd been aware of the date in his diary. A date Delilah had told him to miss at his peril.

17 September.

The sale of Twistleton Farm.

'I seriously don't know why you've insisted I come back for this,' he muttered, standing by the Mini outside the office building at an ungodly hour for a Saturday morning, masking his despondency with disgruntlement. Also masking his nervousness at what he'd done. At the monumental decision he'd made.

'I told you before,' said Delilah on a sigh as she unlocked the car and they both got in, 'it's not me who's insisted. It's your father. He probably wants you there for moral support. And Ida too – she's driven me half daft this week, nagging me to remind you.'

'But it doesn't even start for another hour! We're going to be kicking our heels waiting around.'

Delilah shrugged. 'Again, I suggest you take your complaints to Ida. She was adamant we had to be there by eight thirty or we wouldn't get in.'

Samson slouched down in the seat like a truculent teen and turned up the heat as they drove out of town. It was only mid-September but already the early hours had a winter bite to them. He watched the scenery go by, the stone walls, the slope of the fells and then the spectacular entrance to Thorpdale, the place he'd called home as a kid.

'I'm not sure I can do this,' he said as they approached the Capsticks' cottage, Twistleton Farm visible in the distance.

Delilah glanced at him. 'I know. I'm sorry to put you through it. But I think it means a lot to your father to have you there.'

Samson turned back to the window, the purple of the hills so familiar to him. He felt the pain swell in his heart. His hopes of living there about to be dashed for ever.

'It's the date,' he muttered. 'That's what's making it even harder for both of us.'

'What about the date?'

'It's Mum's anniversary.'

Delilah gasped, a hand going to her mouth. 'Oh God, I should have known. I'm so sorry.'

'Don't be,' said Samson. So many years gone by. So much his mother hadn't seen. But for once he was glad she wasn't around to witness what was about to happen.

The Capstick cottage flashed by, an unmistakable figure outside the barn, hitching a trailer to a vintage grey tractor.

'Has George got my quad bike?' asked Samson, focusing on his old neighbour in an attempt to keep the grief at bay.

'He has.' Delilah shot him a grin. 'And he's made a few adaptations. It now goes a bit faster than it's meant to.'

'Typical George,' said Samson, laughing despite himself at the thought of Ida's brother having fun tinkering with a new toy.

Twistleton Farm was just ahead now, the farmhouse tucked tidily into the curve of the hills, the barn to the right, just a burned-out shell after Rick Procter's attempt to torch the place. With a long row of cars already parked on the narrow track nose to tail, Delilah pulled up behind the last of them and Samson got out into the sunshine, Tolpuddle leaping out past him and turning circles of delight, nose up, sniffing. Samson smiled. Took his cue from the hound and inhaled a deep breath. Felt the air fill his lungs in a way it never did in London. Air tinged with the smell of heather and grass and the distinctive scent of home.

'Right, let's get this over with,' he muttered. 'And then we can all get on with our lives.'

With leaden legs and heavy spirits, he started making his way up the track to the house which held so many memories.

For a farm sale on a Saturday, the crowd wasn't massive. In front of the ruined barn, Harry Furness stood on his portable podium, gavel in hand, and surveyed the gathering.

While the Bruncliffe farming contingent was well represented with the likes of the Hardacres from the Horton Road, Jimmy and Gemma Thornton and their newborn baby from up on Bowland Knotts, Clive Knowles from Mire End Farm, Will and Ali Metcalfe and Will's parents, plus quite a few regulars from the auction mart, the turnout from the extended farming community wasn't what would normally be expected. However, that was more than made up for by the wide spectrum of other inhabitants from the town who'd come along. Troy Murgatroyd was there, along with half of his clientele from the Fleece, including Seth Thistlethwaite. Fellside Court had also got a good showing, Samson's father understandably present, along with his friends. Herriot the vet was standing next to Lucy Metcalfe, his beaming smile telling the world that he'd finally summoned up the courage to do what many in Troy's pub had been taking side bets on for a year, while Matty Thistlethwaite was impeccably dressed in suit and tie, even on the weekend, cutting a dapper figure next to the more dishevelled Gareth Towler, whose russet hair and beard were sticking out at all angles as he petted Bounty at his feet. Representing the commercial side of Bruncliffe were Barry Dawson from Plastic Fantastic, Barbara Hargreaves from the butchers and Kamal Hussain from Rice N Spice, Nina Hussain and Nathan Metcalfe standing towards the back, Nathan's two adopted lurchers on leads beside them.

But while all of those could be said to have a vested interest in the sale, either for personal or business reasons, there were a few folk in attendance whose presence had Harry scratching his head. Nancy Taylor, he supposed, was at least involved in property sales, but had no experience in selling agricultural premises. And as for the out-of-uniform Gavin Clayton, the sergeant had never expressed any curiosity when it came to auctions yet here he was, clutching a coffee and a bag of what looked like chocolate muffins, as though this was going to be his morning's entertainment. The unlikely couple who caught Harry's attention the most, however, were the two women standing to one side, both frowning. Ida Capstick felt his gaze and her scowl deepened. A neighbour to the farm about to be sold, Ida's attendance could be understood. But what was flooring Harry was the woman she was standing with – Mrs Pettiford. The two were hardly cut from the same cloth yet were definitely united in some way, surveying the crowd in much the same manner Harry was, with an eye to what the auction might bring.

If he didn't know better, he'd have thought they were there to do his job.

He glanced at his watch. Almost time. Where the hell was everyone else? Because a sale like this would normally draw folk in from a vast radius, particularly as this was a government auction, Twistleton Farm being sold under the Proceeds of Crime Act and so bound to go for a song. He was hoping to get it to the half a million mark, even though in different circumstances it would fetch far more, but to do that, he needed more people.

Giving it another few minutes, Harry kept an eye on the narrow track which was the only way into the dale, but there was no sign of traffic coming along it. In fact, now he thought of it, there hadn't been a single car come down the road in the last half an hour. Resigned to a meagre crowd – and possibly a lower sale price – he rapped the podium with his gavel, silencing the muted conversations.

'Right then,' he called out, as his watch hit the hour. 'Nine on the dot. Who'll get me rolling?'

Constable Danny Bradley had received the call from an irate motorist at about eight thirty.

He'd been expecting it so he'd known what to do.

He got straight in his car and drove up Fell Lane. Slowly. Really slowly. The kind of driving that would make locals furious, creeping round bends, slipping down into second for the slightest incline. As he crawled along, he hummed to himself. Enjoying the day. Enjoying the drama.

Fifteen minutes later – for a journey which should only take ten – he came round a corner and saw the end of the tailback. He parked, got out, positioned his helmet carefully on his head – checking it in the wing mirror for good measure – and ambled up along the vehicles towards the front.

'About bloody time! Get them to shift!' muttered one driver through an open window.

'Bloody ridiculous!' grumbled another.

Danny did his best Sergeant Clayton impression and made his way forwards with a cheerful smile, infuriating the waiting drivers further.

'Ain't no laughing matter!' snapped one. 'Auction's going to be bloody over by the time we get there!'

'Now then, no need to be uncivil,' said Danny, making his accent as broad as he could. Hands in his pockets he sauntered on. Past over thirty vehicles – a mixture of high-end 4x4s, expensive cars and a smattering of more utilitarian farm jalopies – all the way to the cause of the traffic jam.

A trailer with a puncture was slewed across the narrow road, a flock of pink sheep having spilled out the rear and meandered through the cars, bleating noisily and further blocking the route. And on the far side of the trailer, looking ready for a fight, was a scowling Carol Kirby, soon-to-be wife of Clive Knowles from Mire End Farm.

Arms folded in defiance across her chest, she was making no move to either fix the puncture or get her animals off the tarmac.

'I don't know if I can bear this,' muttered Samson as Harry got the auction underway.

A hand shot up, Oscar Hardacre making the first bid, and a slice of pain pierced Samson's soul. This was it. This was finally it. Twistleton Farm was about to disappear from his life for ever, his memories of his mother along with it.

He felt Delilah's hand slide into his, her fingers curling around his palm, support given without being asked. Across the throng of bodies, he saw his father turn his way. Saw him nod, smile. He looked . . . chipper was the only word which sprang to mind. Like he was out for a fun time, not about to see the home he'd made with his wife and son sold off to some offcumden. All on the anniversary of his wife's death.

As the thought struck Samson, so did another. He looked around, and then leaned over to Delilah.

'Notice anything odd?' he murmured, tipping his head in the direction of the crowd.

She frowned, glanced left and right, behind her, and then her eyes widened. 'There's no one from out of town here! How bizarre!'

Bizarre indeed. At the Dinsdales' farm sale the place had been swarming with vultures from all over the county, looking to capitalise on someone else's misfortune. Yet today, for an auction which had been much more widely advertised, there wasn't a single face Samson didn't recognise.

Several more hands had gone up at this point, the gavel

pointing back at Oscar Hardacre. A hundred and sixty thousand the latest bid. It was still within Samson's theoretical means but a long way off what was expected. Despite the house needing a lot of work, a property like Twistleton could go for half a million or even more, the prices in the area driven up by so many folk coming up from the south with money to burn; folk who would see the place as an idyllic holiday retreat rather than a working farm. Samson was praying it didn't sell to someone like that. Far better it be the likes of the Hardacres, adding land to their already substantial acreage. But Oscar was shaking his head, even at the relatively low amount being asked.

'One hundred and seventy, anyone, anyone?' Harry pleaded, looking puzzled at the lack of interest.

Matty Thistlethwaite gave the slightest of nods, a mobile to his ear, making the bid on behalf of a client. And Samson's heartache intensified. For whoever was on the other end of that call, it could only be the very kind of person Samson didn't want the old O'Brien home going to.

'One hundred and seventy I am bid,' confirmed Harry.

Samson tipped his head back and looked up at the clouds scurrying across the pale blue sky. And tried to remember to breathe.

George Capstick was getting ready. He'd hitched up a small trailer to the back of the Little Grey, loaded it with mangel-wurzels and closed the tailgate, without latching it. He looked at his watch.

'Liquid-cooled four-stroke single cylinder not just yet,' he murmured to himself, his latest statistics taken from the Honda Fourtrax quad bike he'd been fixing up for Samson.

A grin flashed across his face, the thought of the little ATV reducing the stress building in his chest at what he'd been tasked to do.

He crossed the yard and entered the kitchen, finding himself drawn to the large dresser. He reached out and opened the middle drawer. It was empty. He'd known it would be. But he was just checking. Just making sure that Ida had done it. That she'd finally taken all the money she'd been saving, the money she called 'the Devil's money'. Because today was the day that the Devil's money would be used to make things right again.

Nodding in contentment, he headed back out.

He got up onto the Little Grey, started her off and pulled out into the road. He didn't head right towards the throng of parked cars in the distance at Twistleton Farm. Instead he turned left.

He'd timed it to perfection. As he reached the designated spot he swung the tractor sharply to the side, almost jack-knifing the trailer and putting such a jolt through the unlatched tailgate that it flew open, spilling beets all over the road just as the first of the offcumden vehicles was approaching.

George climbed down off the tractor and did his level best to look helpless as the car came to a halt, the route blocked by a vintage tractor and a sea of mangelwurzels.

'Four-twenty cc dual hydraulic disc brakes job done.'

'Offers now at one eighty. That's one eighty, folks – a bargain at that price, you know it is.'

Harry's desperation was showing as the auction failed to ignite. He was staring at the crowd, trying to browbeat bids from them, and when Clive Knowles raised a laconic finger, Harry leaped on it.

'That's more like it! Come on now the rest of you, don't be shy,' he cajoled. 'One ninety, do I hear one ninety?'

'You can hear my bloody stomach rumbling,' shouted Troy, 'so get a move on and wrap it up so as I can get back and have my breakfast!'

There was a roar of laughter, Harry scowling at the landlord. Samson looked to his left and saw Ida, not laughing. Far from it. She was glaring at Matty Thistlethwaite with an expression which could have melted stone. And next to her was Mrs Pettiford, likewise looking thunderous. Meanwhile Matty was murmuring into his phone, one eye warily on the two women. What the hell was going on?

'One ninety!' exclaimed Harry, gavel pointing in Matty's direction as the solicitor tipped his head. 'But I'm not leaving it there folks. Who'll give me one nine five?'

Only a five grand increment, Harry really up against a tough crowd. He looked towards Clive Knowles, but the farmer from Mire End was shaking him off. Not interested. Ida too was now staring at Clive, eyes spitting fire. But the farmer had his arms folded, his chin tucked in, and wasn't budging.

'A prime location, decent land, a house which could really be something . . . don't sell me short of the double ton . . .' Harry was looking around, eyes flitting from one to another. But no one was moving. Not even blinking, as though they suspected the despairing auctioneer would knock the lot down to them at the merest flutter of an eyelash.

'One ninety it's at,' Harry raised his gavel, voice taking on a tone of resignation, 'one ninety, one last time . . . sold to the client of Matty Thistlethwaite!' The gavel crashed against the wooden podium.

In the background, from beyond the barn and out on the road, came the sound of traffic, a slew of vehicles pulling up, parking any old way, irate-looking people running towards the site of the auction.

But it was too late. Twistleton Farm had already been sold. And for the meagre sum of £190,000.

The place descended into pandemonium. Loud voices demanding a resale. Farmers who'd travelled long distances kicking off about obstructions on the road. Samson wasn't taking any of it in.

All he could think of was that price. One hundred and ninety thousand pounds. He turned away from the barn and sat down on the small wall which bordered the vegetable patch, his heart breaking.

He could have afforded it. He could have got a mortgage. He had a bit saved. Between that and his salary with the Met, it would have been enough. Only thing was, he didn't have a salary any more. Or rather, wouldn't in a month's time. In his back pocket, a copy of the letter he'd handed in two days ago. It was done. The decision made. He'd chosen Bruncliffe and Delilah.

But if he'd known? Would he have opted to keep his job and use it to buy Twistleton? Even though it would have meant remaining in London for the time being and only being an itinerant occupant? And Delilah? Would their relationship have survived?

'Penny for them.' The woman in question had sat down next to him, the cacophony in the background showing no sign of abating, Harry having a heated exchange with some bloke from Leeds who was declaring he was willing to pay half a million for the place and that the whole thing had been a fix. Something about pink sheep and mangelwurzels in there too, which made no sense to Samson.

He shrugged. Smiled. 'I was thinking I could have done it. If I'd known it would go for a song, I might have scraped that together.'

Delilah nodded. 'Me too. I could have sold the cottage and you could have had the farm back and repaid me over time.'

'But I'd have had to have stayed in London to pay the mortgage . . .'

She smiled. Slipped her hand into his and kissed his cheek. 'I know how much this place means to you. I'd have made that sacrifice.'

All at once the dark clouds of regret cleared, the melancholy which had engulfed him dispelled like mist in the morning sunshine. He'd done the right thing. Made the right choice. Delilah was where his future lay, and that meant coming back to Bruncliffe. Even if he couldn't come back to the place which had actually been his home.

'There's something I've been meaning to show you,' he began, reaching for the letter. 'I didn't say anything—'

'Samson!' Matty Thistlethwaite was walking towards him. Ida and Mrs Pettiford with him. Closely followed by pretty much the entire contingent which had made up the audience for the auction, Clive Knowles, the Hardacres, Nancy Taylor, his father and the Fellside Court crew, plus all the rest.

Samson stood, sensing this was something that merited

him being on his feet. The look on Matty's face was pure business.

'This is for you,' said Matty, holding out a piece of paper he'd pulled from his briefcase.

Samson took it with both hands. Glanced at it. A legal document, something about a trust fund, in his name . . .

'What is this?' he asked the solicitor.

'A document to attest that as of –' Matty checked his watch – 'twenty-six minutes past nine this morning, you are the rightful owner of the property known as Twistleton Farm.'

There was a long silence. Samson letting the words settle. Trying to make sense of them. The crowd of friends and neighbours were watching him, Delilah too, her mouth a perfect 'O' of surprise.

'I don't understand,' he finally managed. 'How can I be the owner?'

'We pulled in a few favours,' said Eric Bradley.

'And found funds in unlikely places,' added Arty Robinson, a wink aimed at Ida. 'To which we applied Bruncliffe's own Proceeds of Crime Act.'

'Not to mention passing the hat around.' Mrs Pettiford gestured at the crowd. 'Over ten grand raised in record time!'

'Happen we'd have paid more to be shot of him,' grunted Troy Murgatroyd, sparking laughter.

'Then it was just a matter of making sure the auction went our way.' Will Metcalfe was pointing back towards the road, and the irate people who'd arrived too late. 'A few improvised road blocks limited the buyers to a select group, so when the bidding started, we could control it.'

'We threw in the odd bid to make it seem genuine,' said

Clive Knowles, 'but that was just to get it to a realistic price.'

Ida glowered at the farmer. 'A price lower than we'd agreed. Two hundred it were supposed to be. Make it look more legitimate.'

'Nowt wrong with saving a few bob here and there,' he protested, triggering more laughter. 'Besides, reckon the Dinsdales could benefit from what's spare.'

'But . . . but . . . how can I own it?' stuttered Samson.

'Twistleton Farm was bought by an offshore entity called Phoenix Abroad,' explained Matty, his glance resting momentarily on Nancy Taylor, who simply smiled. 'But the deed was purchased in your name.'

'Don't worry,' said Nancy, seeing Samson's concern. 'It's all legal and above board.' Her tone turned wry. 'We simply utilised some of the financial knowledge we acquired over the last year, but this time to the town's advantage—'

'You bloody sods!' boomed a voice from the back, Harry Furness a picture of indignation at realising he'd been conducting a rigged auction. He strode through the throng to the front, wagging a finger at Matty. 'I should have known when you were supposedly on your mobile and yet I had bugger all signal! I should have sensed there and then summat were up. You could have bloody told me what was going on. Had me up there on the podium sweating cobs that I'd lost my bloody touch!'

'How could we tell you, Harry?' demanded Matty. 'You're legally bound to conduct a fair sale.'

'Reckon that's the first time he has done,' muttered Troy Murgatroyd, to more laughter.

Harry opened his mouth to reply. Stared over towards the

barn where Danny Bradley was ushering the latecomers away and back to their cars, an off-duty Sergeant Clayton watching on with amusement as he consumed his coffee and muffins. Then he turned back to Samson and held out his hand.

'Welcome home, O'Brien,' he said, with a firm handshake. 'Couldn't have sold this place to a better person.'

A roar of approval went up from the gathering, Ida nodding in agreement, Joseph dabbing at his eyes as Samson moved over and drew him into an embrace.

'We've got it back, Dad,' he murmured into his father's ear. 'We've got our home back.'

He felt his father's arms hold him tight, and he knew this was where he belonged. Where he'd always belonged.

'Your mother would be so proud of you,' said Joseph, leaning back to see his son's face.

'And of you too, Dad.'

Joseph nodded. Smiled. Tears on his cheeks. 'Three years sober today.'

Samson hugged him again.

'So when's the housewarming?' shouted Arty.

'A party!' said Clarissa. 'I can organise that!'

Edith shot Arty an amused glance while Joseph stepped back from Samson's embrace and surveyed the crowd.

'Now let's not all get ahead of ourselves,' he said, before turning a look full of love on his son. 'There's no rush to move back up here, Samson.'

Matty was nodding. 'The property will be looked after in your absence by George Capstick, his caretaking fees paid for by the trust until such times as you're able to return permanently, should you choose to do so.'

'Last thing we want, lad,' said Ida, 'is for thee to feel

hidebound to come back. But tha's got the option, should tha decide to.'

Samson turned to Delilah, who'd remained uncharacteristically silent throughout. She was pale. Shocked. As out of the loop as himself and Harry.

'What do you think?' he asked.

She shrugged. 'I think what Ida said is right. This,' she gestured at the farmhouse, 'is amazing. A dream come true. But it has to be your dream. You have to come back here because you want to, not because you're tied to the place. Don't let this make your mind up.'

And he knew then that he could never love her more. Her ability to put his dreams before hers. To encourage him to give his other life a fair crack of the whip when all she wanted was to have him here in Bruncliffe. Something he'd finally realised was all he wanted too.

He reached into his pocket for the letter. 'Here,' he said, passing it to her.

She opened it. Looked up at him. Shocked afresh.

'It's a copy of my notice – I handed it in yesterday. I'm leaving the force.' He turned to Matty. 'So as for the trust, I'm hereby informing it that I will be returning to Bruncliffe for good in exactly one month and if it's okay with everyone who helped chip in to buy this place, I'll be moving in straight away. And as for you, Ms Metcalfe,' he continued, focus back on her, seeing that smile, feeling his heart swell in a way only she could make it and filled with a sense of certainty about the impulse which had overcome him, 'I wonder . . .'

He paused. Took her hand in his and dropped to one knee.

'I wonder if you'd do me the honour of being my wife?'

He was aware of a collective gasp behind him. Of Delilah's smile dissolving into surprise, her free hand going to cover her mouth. Of a silence that seemed to last an age. Then she grinned.

'Yes! Yes! Yes!' she yelped, throwing herself at him, almost toppling him over while Tolpuddle started barking in delight.

Samson was oblivious to the rest apart from Delilah in his arms. Him lifting her and carrying her up the path towards the home which harboured so many of his memories, and would now help build his future.

As one of the thwarted prospective buyers would report back to his wife that night when he landed home in Clitheroe after a wasted journey, the place went mad. Cheering and clapping as some bloke proposed to a young woman before carrying her over the threshold of the rickety farmhouse, which had apparently gone for a song. And as for the pink sheep and the mad bloke with the vintage tractor and the shedload of mangelwurzels, it was true what they said . . . they were a right rum bunch of folk across the border in Yorkshire. A right rum bunch indeed.

Acknowledgements

In a book bearing the title *Justice*, it seems more important than ever that I pay tribute to the expert knowledge that has helped make the background of this novel as realistic as possible. And I cross my fingers that I have 'done justice' while reflecting that expertise on the page. If not, I apologise. In the meantime, a slice of Sarah and Harry's wedding cake and a glass of champagne is owed to the following wonderful people.

From the outset, it was the great crested newt which propelled me to write this tale. A chance overhearing of an article on the radio about the moves being made to protect these precious amphibians from the endless progression of developments in our green spaces, and suddenly I had a plot. This was four years ago!

The poor newt had to wait for its turn in the spotlight while I busied myself with the volumes that preceded it. All the while I tried to learn everything I could about the ins and outs of planning permission and the essential role ecologists play in that process. That I chose to make one of my ecologists a rotten apple in no way reflects on the remarkable work carried out by those in the profession, and there is no finer example of such professionals than the team at PBA Applied Ecology.

Paul Bradley welcomed me to the PBA offices and patiently answered my wide-ranging questions with a passion which made me want to train up and join his crew! Likewise, the lovely Elizabeth Judson went out of her way to help facilitate the meeting, and her joy for the work she's engaged in shone through as she showed me around and introduced me to her colleagues. I'm happy to report there wasn't a rogue among them. (Although Paul's new pup, Freyja, had a certain twinkle to her eye!) Thanks all.

Further assistance, this time of the avian variety, was provided by friend and birdwatcher, Jo Robinson. Over a coffee and delicious homemade cake (the best research setting!), I learned a lot about the peregrine falcons in Malham Cove, the wide variety of binoculars on the market, and the difference between a lens cap and a rainguard (Danny Bradley take note!). Similarly, David Dewhirst willingly supplied advice on the local flora. For the knowledge and the great company of both, I'm eternally grateful.

Of course, it wouldn't be a Dales Detective story without a bit of help from the farming community and, yet again, Rachael and Robin Booth were on hand to answer my naive questions. And, yet again, they didn't laugh when I posed them. Not to my face, at least!

Apart from the unique expertise each novel demands, there is always a bunch of folk in the background who assist with every publication with unfailing good grace and enthusiasm. Claire stepped up once more to be my first reader, despite juggling work and family. And my mum made sure I had space to write, literally and metaphorically, in what was a difficult time. An extra helping of cake is owed to both.

Date with Justice

At Pan Macmillan, editor Vicki was her usual brilliant self, offering encouragement above and beyond her normal amazing levels, and working tirelessly to get this book into shape when the timetable slipped. A heartfelt thanks goes to the team behind her as well, especially my editing posse of Charlotte, Melissa, Fraser and Nicole – all a joy to work with.

Likewise, the *équipe* at La Bête Noire performed miracles to turn a manuscript into a translated novel while on a very tight schedule. *Merci* to Camille, Dominique, Stéphanie and everyone behind the scenes for making sure that fans of *Les Détectives du Yorkshire* got their annual fix! Meanwhile, at Mission Control, Oli, Alexandra and the AM Heath gang continue to take the series to new territories overseas. More champagne for those good folk, please!

In a break with tradition – if you can have such a thing after nine books? – my rock and soulmate, Mark, is getting the penultimate mention this time around. He knows more than anyone how much support I needed while *Date with Justice* was being crafted, and he provided it with unstinting love, patience and cups of tea.

Finally, a personal note. The latter half of this novel was written as my dad was entering the last few weeks of his life. It was a privilege to be able to spend that time with him, to share the ongoing plot with him, and to see his smile the day I typed the final word. He was, and is, the fount of my ability. He was, and will remain, an inspiration, not just in creativity but in how to live.

This one is all yours, Dad.

THE DALES DETECTIVES
WILL RETURN IN
DATE WITH DESTINY

In Bruncliffe, Delilah is reeling. Elated about Samson's proposal and his resignation from the Met Police force, she can't help feeling nervous about their future. He is all she has ever wanted, but what if marriage isn't the answer?

Samson thought his future in Bruncliffe was settled, but he's unnerved by Delilah's cold feet. From death to malice, mystery to poison, deceit to betrayal and evil, they have weathered every storm sent their way, but a part of Samson can't deny that the black sheep he was in his past would never truly be welcomed home to Bruncliffe. And, if Delilah isn't sure about their future, then maybe it is time to leave.

Samson and Delilah should be starting a new chapter. Except it's never that simple, is it? Especially when Arty stands accused of murder and the theft of a valuable painting after the reappearance of an old flame of Edith's.

In a case that will bring so many of Bruncliffe's secrets out into the open and run the risk of confronting a criminal with nothing to lose, this final investigation for the Dales Detectives may be the one that breaks them for ever . . .

**The final novel in the Dales Detective series
coming spring 2025**

The complete
Dales Detective series

'A classic whodunit set in the spectacular
landscape of the Yorkshire Dales, written with
affection for the area and its people'

Cath Staincliffe